Leave a Light on for Me

Jean Swallow

Alyson Classics Library

LOS ANGELES
NEW YORK

MANUFACTURED IN THE UNITED STATES OF AMERICA.

THIS TRADE PAPERBACK ORIGINAL IS PUBLISHED BY
ALYSON PUBLICATIONS,
P.O. BOX 4371, LOS ANGELES, CALIFORNIA 90078-4371.
DISTRIBUTION IN THE UNITED KINGDOM BY
TURNAROUND PUBLISHER SERVICES LTD.,
UNIT 3 OLYMPIA TRADING ESTATE, COBURG ROAD, WOOD GREEN,
LONDON N22 6TZ ENGLAND.

FIRST PUBLISHED BY SPINSTERS/AUNT LUTE BOOK CO.: 1986
FIRST ALYSON EDITION: SEPTEMBER 1991
FIRST ALYSON CLASSICS LIBRARY EDITION: JULY 1999

99 00 01 02 03 🖋 10 9 8 7 6 5 4 3 2 1

ISBN 1-55583-513-9
(PREVIOUSLY PUBLISHED WITH ISBN 1-55583-133-8 BY ALYSON.)

LIBRARY OF CONGRESS CATALOGING-IN-PUBLICATION DATA
  SWALLOW, JEAN.
    LEAVE A LIGHT ON FOR ME / JEAN SWALLOW.
    ISBN 1-55583-513-9
    I. TITLE. II. SERIES.
  PS3569.W23L43 1999
  813'.54—DC21   99-25340 CIP

CREDITS
•OPENING EPIGRAPH IS FROM *OUR PASSION FOR JUSTICE: IMAGES OF POWER, SEXUALITY, AND LIBERATION* © 1984 BY CARTER HEYWARD, THE PILGRIM PRESS, NEW YORK, N.Y.
•COVER PHOTOGRAPH BY JUDITH MESKILL. TINTING BY KRISTEN THROOP.

Publisher's Note

Icould start off with the frayed, needle-pointed-to-death maxim "Home Sweet Home." Instead I'll ask two questions: Where the hell *is* home? And, even if you've found it, how can you possibly keep it sweet all the time? Is home the quiet of your own house? Your bed that soaks up the sun on Saturday mornings? Your parents' living room, adorned with childhood photos and dusty trophies? Your best friend's kitchen table where you've poured out secrets like hot coffee? The arms of your lover? Your own heart? These questions tug at all of the complex women in Jean Swallow's ambitious and now classic first novel, *Leave a Light on for Me.*

For each of the four main characters, home is an elusive creature. Sure, each woman lives in a home: a place to sleep, eat, make love, cook, clean, snarl, gripe, cry, and—*sigh*—be bored. For robust but shy Georgia, home should be a place filled with conversation, love, and *excitement.* "I come home and there's no home…What is life?" Georgia asks herself daily, if not hourly. She loves Morgan madly, but how can love feel so lonely? Like many of us, she yearns for routine, but finds it incredibly boring.

To Morgan, building a home means purging the phantoms that have haunted past homes, as she exorcises not only her own demons, but also Georgia's. In the process, she almost escapes the home she has counted on her whole life: herself.

For Elizabeth, home is finding someone who will understand her daily trials as a doctor, a friend who will smile when she discovers her nickname is Wolfie, a woman to love her—even if it means breaking up the home of Georgia and Morgan.

And then there's Bernice, our sincere and sassy sometime narrator who disappears and reappears throughout the book, but lingers sweet as pecan pie in the background. Bernice builds a home for everyone around her, but in a sense Bernice *is* home, not just to her best friend Georgia but home to the novel itself. As readers, we venture away from Bernice's porch, her TV room, her kitchen filled with the aromas of North Carolina eats: fried chicken, black-eyed peas, greens, yams, cobbler. But we return like hungry dogs time and again to the warmth of her stove, the warmth of her chatter. "This is one good story I got in mind," Bernice tells us at the start of the novel, and soon enough we're hooked.

Set in the mid 1980s during the height of the AIDS epidemic in San Francisco, the novel adeptly weaves four stories into one, with luxurious detail and rich dialogue, while questioning "home" and tackling many other issues: trust, friendship, homophobia, sexism, family, and desire. You'll find, I'm certain, that desire slips from the pages, invites you to come on over and sit for a spell in the comfort of a splendid read, and urges you to leave your own light on—your reading light, that is—for hours at a time.

Angela Brown
Los Angeles, Spring 1999

For Sherry Thomas
and
for The Three, Taz and Tamara

If I had only a single line today, it would be to plead with you to remain human—in spite of all temptations.

Carter Heyward
from *Our Passion for Justice*

Chapter One

How We Got Washed In The Blood Of The Lamb

Well, hey y'all! I *thought* I heard a car pull up. Come on in. Hey, Janie, good to see you. Roo, how you been? Hey, Deb. What, is everybody here? All at the same time? Did y'all come in one car? Shoot, it ain't that far out here.

Well, now Deb, least it ain't Bezerkeley. Those folks are still the farest out of everybody. Come over here, girl, let me give you a hug. You crazy fool.

Where's Nancy? Oh, that's right, yep, I remember now. That game over Sunnyside? Well, maybe she'll come when they finish up.

Who's playing, Janie? Well, I guess we won't be expecting her none too soon. That's an even match in the cellar, good Lord.

I agree, Roo. I don't expect they'll be done before noon tomorrow, myself. They have a right good time though, don't they? Sometimes I like those games the best, you know what I mean?

Well, just the four of us then. Come on in, y'all. Let's don't stand out here gabbing all night on the front stoop. Neighbors'll think I ain't got no manners. And besides, I got a special treat for y'all tonight. Go ahead, go right on down the hall.

Keep going, Deb. Go all the way back to the deck. See if we can sneak through the hall here without us bothering Annie. I'm not for sure she's working but she looks like she could be. Better for us to talk out there, least until it gets too cold to sit. I've been sitting out there myself, drying my hair while waiting for y'all.

Here. Make yourself at home. Get you a glass of tea, grab a chair, take a load off your feet.

Now, Deb, don't give me a hard time about my hair tonight. I know I look like something the cat drug in, but I ain't done yet and Lord knows, ain't no need to treat y'all like strangers, not after all this time.

Is it two years now? Can't hardly believe it, can you? Just keeps adding up, week after week, I reckon. I'm mighty glad we started meeting like this, mighty glad. And to think if it weren't for women's rec softball, we'd have never met. That and being the best umpires around. Yeah, I'll drink to the great breed of women umps, yeah! Everybody get tea? Well, put those glasses up here; let's toast. Mmhum.

Good, eh? Can't beat Carolina iced tea. It's the best. Long sight better than any old Yankee tea out of a jar. Why, anything not made like back home is Yankee, don't you know that, Roo? Don't matter if we are in California. It's still Yankee. Shoot, I almost forgot, hold on a sec; let me get the popcorn. I made it special for y'all tonight. After that, I got another treat. You'll see.

Here. That's good too, ain't it? New stuff. Well, new to me, Roo. Georgie just taught me. Brown stuff's tamari. Go ahead Janie, try it. Yellow stuff's brewer's yeast. I know it. Only in California. Go on, Janie. You'll like it, I swear. No? Well, suit yourself. Roo? Yeah, I knew you'd like it, you tree-hugger you.

No, I ain't going to tell you the other treat yet, Debi. Just hold your horses. I'm getting there. Hold on now. I'm just going to duck in the kitchen for a sec, get some cookies for Janie. Can't let the girl starve.

There, Janie, see if you don't like them better. Okay, y'all set? Now get comfortable, girls. Get ready for the main treat. I've been excited about this ever since I last saw y'all. Well, anyway since about the day *after* I last saw y'all.

What happened was, when I left off from y'all two weeks back, I was in a state. Couldn't get to sleep to save my soul. Thrashing about. Finally, Annie helped me work it through and I've been dying to tell y'all; I been like the tail on a happy mutt all week, just thinking about telling y'all.

Well, all right now. Y'all remember last week when we got to talking about how bad things were getting? I don't remember how we got started... Oh yeah, that's right, Janie. I came late; I had that early game over in San Pablo. I remember now. Well, when I come in, let's see, I think it was you, Deb, you were talking about some friends of yours who'd been together a couple of years and they were breaking up and it was ugly and hateful, and making you sad.

And then Janie said something about how she was feeling bad too, because the women's teams were getting fewer and fewer, and folks seemed to care less and less. Then we talked about how much we all hated ref'ing the men's games. And we talked for awhile about how things for women seemed to be getting worse, that before our very eyes, changes stopped happening and then things started going backwards and we didn't get all that far to begin with; y'all remember that part?

And then, let's see, Nancy said something about Reagan, and his warmongering and bombing and such, and we all agreed on that being about the worst, and then we got real glum and it got late and after awhile we all got quiet, you know, and hugged goodbye, and I went home feeling bluer than a dead baby, how about you?

All right, okay, Roo, I'm sorry. Just an expression.

But you know what I mean? Well, I got home and moped around like a sick cat and finally Annie—who'd been listening to my tale of woe and rubbing my back—finally she said, 'Now darling, it ain't all bad. It's bad, but it ain't *all* bad. Some things have a way of working out,' she said. 'Why, look at Georgia and Emmer,' she said. 'They're happy now and who would have thought it?'

And I thought about that for a minute and then realized, yeah, now that is true. I had worried myself sick about those two for months at a time. So I sat there after Annie said that and thought about how they were getting on, and I tell you, I did begin to feel better. Just felt a little happier. Pretty soon got a sort of a grin on my face.

And Annie said, 'See?' So then she said, 'You ought to tell your friends about George and Em. Cheer them up too.' And I said, 'Yeah, that's a good idea.' Bright girl, my Annie. That's why I married her. She's full of good ideas. It's a great story about those two. It'd cheer up a dead man.

Sorry, Roo. Anyway, I got to thinking about telling y'all and I thought to myself, why not? We used to tell each other stories like this all the time back home and those stories surely made the evenings bright.

Well, true, Deb, they weren't telling stories *exactly* like this story, I mean not, you know, lesbian stories, but I remember, it would be a hot night back home, too hot to move and we'd just be sitting there on the porch and somebody would start a story and we'd just sit there and fan and listen.

And I swear, I *swear*, it didn't seem so hot, you know; after awhile and after you stopped looking, you'd discover you felt just a little bit better. By the end of the evening, we'd all feel better. So I thought, you know, it ain't the heat we're trying to beat, but still. I thought, maybe I'd treat y'all to some down home, and see if it don't translate. This is one good story I got in mind. What do you say?

Oh I'm glad. Oo, I love this story. We'll fill in Nancy later, and I swear Deb, you'll be wishing we was just starting when it's long past time to go home. You just wait, you sitting there and saying well all right, but when have I steered you wrong, girl?

Thing is, we got to get some good old warm in our hearts. Can't go on without it. And, why not? God didn't make us to cry all the time. That's why She gave us such pretty things as teeth. Smile now; let's see yours.

Okay, all right. No more bad ones. I cross my heart and hope to die. Stick a needle in my eye. *All right* Roo. I can't help it. I know y'all don't talk like that where you're from, but I am *mild* compared to them back home. Don't be mad now. All right, I'll try. Swear. Zip my lips.

Okay? Oh but girls, girls. Let us do like the preacherman said: 'Do not be distracted from the matter at hand.' There's a story here what wants telling. Get comfy now. If y'all get cold, we can go inside. Y'all got enough tea? Popcorn? All set then?

I'm real sorry I don't got no prayer fans. Y'all just have to do without. I know it's a shame. I truly hope y'all can manage. See if you can't just set back, and enjoy.

I'm going to enjoy myself, I tell you what. It's one of those stories that's got a happy ending, plus, it's about one of my favorite people. Y'all heard me talk about my friend Georgia? Yeah, Janie, the one I moved out here with. Main woman in my life besides Annie. Well, this story's about Georgia. And Morgan, her girl, who we call Em or Emmer, on account of all her names start with "m."

Now, Deb, don't get started. I didn't name her. She's got some four names. Irish, Georgie says. Aw, Deb, cut it out. Didn't your mother ever tell you not to make fun of other folks' ways? Well, mine did. Okay, it's true; I agree with that. It is weird, but no weirder than some other folks' names. No, I *don't* mean the ones what call themselves Oakbranch or Moonbeam. I don't know about you, girl. How you're going to last in California, I swear I do not know.

But let me get back. Don't distract me girls. I distract myself enough. Em's name don't make no nevermind. It's just a nickname, yeah, like you, Roo. Anyway, the story's about Georgie and Em, and some other folks I knew, even though I wished I didn't, but we'll get to that.

Yes, we'll get to that. But we need to start at the beginning. And that's with Georgia. So let me tell y'all about Georgia. You're one lucky somebody if you got a woman like Georgia in your life. Many's the time I've felt blest since I been knowing her, even when she's acting like a little devil.

Yep, Janie, I'd call her family. Lord, yes. Can't live with her; can't live without her. Sure, we're just like family in that way. You know? I mean, we were only lovers for the first two years and I been knowing her now, oh, for about sixteen years. Is that right? My Lord, it can't be that long. But it is. Mmhum.

Well, and we have been through it, my Lord, we have *been through* some trouble times, been in some tight spots, lived in some strange places. But, you know, even with all the places we have been, some things are the same everywhere, even if they look different, you know what I mean? I mean, if you're lucky, some things can happen anywhere.

And me and Georgia, we have had some wild streak of that kind of luck, not that George would say so. But when you hear the story—well, let me start by explaining to y'all Yankees how me and Georgia got washed in the blood of the lamb in Berkeley, California, that first year we were out here, back in 1978. Maybe that'll help y'all start to get the picture. Seems like a long time ago now, but Carolina seems even further back.

We'd been out here about six months then, and we'd come to sort of seek our fortunes, you know, come to the Gay Mecca. That's what Georgia kept calling it, Mecca. Well, I can tell you the first six months after we got here, it sure didn't seem like no Mecca to her. For awhile there, she was talking about jumping off the Bay Bridge every two days, but she's finally given that up, thank you Jesus.

Not that she's given up brooding; she still does that every now and again. I think it's in her blood. Some folks are just like that, you know? But she was like a broody hen then, she was, sitting there and going broody and quietly, very quietly, going berserk.

And I was heartsick for the girl, for the longest time. I'm happy to report though, she's letting herself have a little peace these days, even if she did struggle through the blood of Shiloh to get there. But she did it. She did do it, my Georgie girl.

And you know, ever since Annie and me talked about this, I've been thinking about those Shiloh parts. In the bad times, we always say to each other, 'Oh now darling, things'll get better, you'll see.' And then we try not to notice anything until it's over. And we hurt ourselves with that not noticing; we do. What I mean to say is, if we just go about our business and don't pay no attention to what's coming and going, and all we do is say things going to get better, it ain't enough, you know what I mean? I mean, my Lord, you can't eat the future, you know?

Well, when we first got here, there was a lot of that trying to eat the future business, let me tell you. And things was about as clear as mud. But in those days, me and George stuck tight, like ticks on a dog, I mean it, both of us just wild with excitement and fear.

San Francisco. Lesbians everywhere. It was something.

Down there in the Castro where we had supper that first night we drove into town, why they was lots of us in the street, boys holding onto boys, girls hand-in-hand. I know I was wide-eyed as a goat. It sure was different from back home in North Carolina, where we'd just lost our lease when they found out we was queer, where boys from the mill went around beating up on folks like us, or worse.

'Need a man tonight, little lady?' they'd ask. Oh my Jesus, if I had a quarter for every time I been called little lady (and me big as I am) I'd be a rich woman today. Not that Carolina is so different from other places. No ma'am. It's just that it was our home. And it's been our name for pain too, that's for sure.

Anyway, for us, when we got here, it felt like we'd gotten on some special kind of underground train and gone to someplace real different from anywhere we'd ever been. And really, for us, for the first time in our lives, it was the right train, you know what I mean? But George used to say we'd changed our names and moved to another country.

We didn't, of course, she's still Georgia and I'm still me, but it was hard to make sense of how different it all felt, you know? I mean, it's not like folks don't get killed here, I mean, they *assassinate* queers here. Least look at what happened to Harvey Milk. They couldn't let the first queer city Supervisor live, no ma'am.

But I was proud of us after Harvey got killed. Lord, were you there at the candlelight march that night? Roo? Janie? You hadn't got here yet, had you, Deb? Well, let me tell you how it was.

A hundred thousand of us gathered in that few hours; y'all re-member how word went through the community like a grass fire on a hot August afternoon? I was grateful, you know, that it didn't get out of hand.

But when they passed sentence on Dan White, that sorry excuse for a human being, when they said he only had to stay in jail a couple of years, some of the boys got mad and went a little crazy, burning a few cop cars and such. I thought it was hard to blame them really. I mean, I'm not happy about the riots, but we did stand up for ourselves. I don't know. It's hard to know what's right when folks are beating on you, you know what I mean?

Of course, more folks than us been messed up in the head from getting beaten on. Look at St. John the Divine and his Revelations there. You know? Cut off from his heart, all that plague and pesti-lence just to get back, to rain troubles on them what caused him trouble and calling his fury the voice of God to boot; I mean, that boy got the Devil in him and got confused. Some folks still reveling in the old boy's confusion, pleased for the chance to do that harlot name-calling, you know what I mean?

Well, the name-calling's bad and calling an earthquake revenge is worse. But at least the God's revenge business becomes trouble-some when the earth gets parched in the preacher's own backyard. But the most dangerous, and what folks don't see so clear, is all this about getting cut off from your heart. That's the worst. All the other just jumps in once you can't find your heart.

And that's what happened to White, if you think about it. Now White's dead and by his own hand too. Well, that's what they say: what goes around, comes around. The Lord works in mysteri-ous ways, don't She? She just takes Her own sweet time, that's all. Course, even though White's dead, it wasn't never just him. They's lots of them what thinks they can preach like Paul. Danny was just one what got obvious, that's what I think.

There were a lot of them looking obvious that first summer we was here. Now, Roo, you thought I'd got off the story didn't you? You thought I was going around the barn the long way, didn't you, girl? Did I scare you, sounding like a preacher myself? Lord, you Yankees. Cute, but always in a hurry and fearful of any talk near to the Rapture. Well now, calm yourself. You just set back and sip your tea. Some of us from the South, we weave our stories, and like Shirley says, the truth is made of many strands, yes ma'am.

Well, the truth is, when we got here, it wasn't so easy. It wasn't Mecca then and it still ain't. In those days, Harvey had his office down to City Hall, but there was the Briggs Amendment mess too—folks trying to fire the gay teachers, and the way I figured it, when they go after the gay teachers, the rest of us ain't far behind. It had me worried some, but it wasn't no worse than what we'd left behind. And plus, they was so many of us here. I figured, Briggs and White and the rest, they couldn't really stop us. It *was* our time.

They could hurt us; it could be in the air, you know, but they couldn't really *stop* us, you know what I mean? Something happened when we all got together.

It's like at the ballgames, you know, how beautiful we look, out there playing in the sun. See, they couldn't say we was strange anymore. Too many of us to be strange. And too many of us for the lie that we were just a few. Too many of us for the lie that we wasn't beautiful, because we were and we are and you can see it plain as day when we are together.

And when we saw that, me and Georgie that first summer, it was almost as though our lives started then, almost like we'd just come up from one of the underground subway trains they got here and surfaced in the sunlight of one of those great Gay Day Parades.

Sweet Jesus, that first parade! I mean miles and miles of queers. All kind and make of us. And Georgia walking around in a daze. Kept saying, 'We're not alone, Bernice Sophia; we'll never be alone again.' I think she really believed that then.

First time after she said it, she held out her arms and danced around in a little circle in the middle of the Civic Center Square, her glasses slipping down on her nose, her pretty lips in a wide grin, her cute little face glowing, her curly brown hair like a halo, in the middle of all those other beautiful queers on that warm sunny Sunday.

I just hugged her; you know, sometimes she is so happy, she's small like a child and all you can do is hug her little self. And really, my own heart was swelled full that day, too. Because, truth to tell, things was so bad when we left home, I wasn't for sure either one of us'd ever smile again.

So when I saw her little face light up that day, even if I didn't believe in all she was saying, you know, really, it didn't make no nevermind. She was smiling, all tender, and I was about to burst to see her like that, to feel both of us, finally, able to breathe.

But I didn't say nothing. She hates it when you say stuff like that. I just smiled and draped my arms around her. You can't rightly tell her when you loving her because she's being beautiful. She likes to think of herself as tough, little as she is, and really, she is tough, more than she knows.

She's getting better about it, but she didn't know then how tough she was, really, because she'd always been kind of scared to know how she got through some of her life. When she looked back she saw only all that hard pain. And sometimes it was hard to find her softness, you know? I think what happened was her softness got froze somewhere along the way.

I mean, we all got memories we got to learn to live with, and it ain't ever easy for nobody. But some part of Georgia got froze and it hurt to see it, and burned to touch it. Of course, the onliest way to cure that is to get a hold of that frozen part and hold it until it warms in your hands and comes back to life. And the onliest one what can hold it is the one what's frozen.

But for Georgia and me, we know most of what each other's got to live with, even if some of it's froze and some ain't such a pretty picture. I tell you, after all this time, I figure most of it is just what it is. Somehow, it don't scare me no more. I reckon the time helps. I been knowing Georgia since 1969, which ain't such a long time, but I met most of the folks in her life from before that, just like she has with my folks. Ain't hardly anybody in my life knows me like Georgia does and I'm the same for her.

Especially out here. You come out here and leave all your people behind and you're like a leaf gone off a tree. That's when all God's creatures need a one-what-knows. And George is my one-what-knows. That ain't the only reason I still love her, no, we got more than that. But it sure gives us a cord you can't wish away.

My one-what-knows? Why, Roo, it's like, well, let me see if I can explain it for you Yankees. Well, you know how it is when you're queer, you lose some folks along the way. Some of them just toss you out, beating you before you can get out the way. Some of them act like they's something wrong with you, or try to shame you into being quiet (so least you don't sound queer and make them worried about they own selves). And some of them just disappear without a sound, like cottonmouths in dark river water, which is about all they are, you know what I mean?

But I think, if you can survive the fire in your heart when you turn around and most of the folks you loved are gone or worse—

and you ain't one of the too many of us what's got too much heartache piled on the fire already and find the lack of loving the final flame licking at your lips—if you can stand it, and can make yourself new, why, after awhile, you look up and some folks what love you are still there. If you're lucky, and God ain't forgotten you altogether, they'll be some folks still standing with you.

And those folks, well, they get to be your ones-what-know. And that happens for most queers, but it happens to other folks too, folks what had to leave they homes for some or other reason, folks cut off from the soil what grew them. Lucky folks got more than one, but some folks got nearly none. Me, I got George. You see, Roo? She's my one-what-knows. And even though we both messed up some, really, it don't make no nevermind. I know she's no angel. Neither am I. That ain't it.

She loves me like I *was* an angel, you know what I mean? She makes me feel I got the heart of an angel, and I help her remember that about herself too. That's what matters.

That's what makes it all worthwhile, you know? I'm telling you, it's one of the only ways to thread your way through the Shiloh battlefield. If you got folks around what love you like that, you can do anything. It's what it's all about. I know. I had my own time when the river run blood.

Oh, it's all right, Deb. You can make fun. I don't mind if you think I'm a simple, sentimental fool. I know we look like innocent babies but I'm as serious as a judge. And it's true, girl; I agree. They's other stuff what comes into play. But I tell you what, we come a long way, Georgia and me—and we come fighting and brawling and screaming at each other, falling over each other in the bloody mess of our lives. But here we are. You understand? Here we are, standing up, together. And it's that feeling that first brought us together—and I know it's what'll keep us close.

We was in college when we first met, that state school Georgia's always been a little ashamed of. I was glad to have gotten in and fearful of the money, you know. My old man had pretty much turned his back on me by then, wrote me a letter about how he didn't want to see me no more, about how I was a Communist and Lord knows what else.

I wasn't a Communist, you know, not then or even later, but he'd about had it with the boys at the mill making fun of his daughter, going on to school with those weirdos and all that up in Chapel Hill, instead of getting married or least getting a job. Sweet

Jesus, I'd had an easier time of it if I'd run off and gotten pregnant. I know Daddy was talking to the shift boss about a typing job for me in the front office at the mill. Hurt him bad when I went off. But I had to. You know? I had to.

I don't *know* what I'd have done without Shirley. Shirley stood by me then, though we both knew she couldn't say so to Daddy. Shirley's always been real good to me, even before Momma died but especially after Daddy went to work in the mill, and we moved off the farm, and I thought I'd died too. Shirley took up for me then and she did when I was in Chapel Hill too.

It wasn't all I wanted in those days, not near enough. I wanted a momma and even though Shirley was about as close as you could get, she wasn't close enough. I mean, once your momma's gone, she's gone. You have to learn to live with it. But Shirley did good by me, always, and when I was in school, she'd write and send me some money when she could. I know she saved it out of her tips from the shop, and part of me felt real bad about it, but I took it. You can't hardly imagine how much I wanted to be like the other girls in those days, pretty clothes and cars their daddies paid for, not having to work, you know. It fairly ate me up.

But then, in our second year, I met Georgia. We was working on the line in one of the dorm cafeterias, plopping down mounds of cardboard potatoes on the other kids' plates. Awful stuff. And them on the other side, why they never looked at us, never saw us. It wasn't that much of a shock for me, even though it always hurts, you know, but for Georgie, well, I believe she began to understand some things then.

Her folks, who did have the cold-hard, had thrown her out for real; we are talking here no money, and she couldn't get loans in those days and wasn't able to get a scholarship until later. And anyway, the girl never did study. She was one of those what could get by with no studying, no going to class, though she did do her papers. And some of mine too, bless her heart.

Well, I fell in love with her right away. Not that she'd notice, between the spuds and trying not to blush if one of the gorgeous girls on the other side took a plate from her and didn't see her, even if they'd been talking together before she'd come to work. Me, I'd of been satisfied if Georgia had blushed around me even the least little bit. But, we was just girls what worked together for the longest time. And every day I'd think to myself that it was more than I could bear, to watch her watching them.

Oh, I knew what I was doing. Sure I knew. I wasn't a Communist; I was the Lord-knows-what-else. I've been knowing what I was since I was just a little bitty thing. And I knew right away about Georgia too, long before she figured out why she was blushing. But by and by, she stopped waiting for them, and started talking to me. Well, one thing led to another and after awhile, I could see on her face, in the way she turned her head away and hid her hands, that she knew about herself, too. And that's when I started courting her.

I was as happy as a dog in dirt, I'll tell you. And her face, well, she started to glow like a ripe peach. The first time I made love to her, I thought I'd died and gone to heaven. But I knew I hadn't. Her skin under my hands was real and when I looked down and saw all of her, how round she was, how womanly she was, how beautiful she was, well, I near went out of my mind with happiness.

My Lord, that was a long time ago.

Brr. I'm cold. Is it getting too cold for y'all? Can I get any y'all a sweater? No? Okay. Let's see. Where was I?

Well, it was real fine for the first little while, I can tell you that. But when we started talking about living together off campus, I think it scared her off, you know? That and some other stuff. Sweet Jesus, it's been so long, and even now, it hurts to remember. Lord knows, I did love that child with all my heart. And still do, truth to tell, even though it's different now.

But that's how it is with the first woman you ever loved, don't you think, girls? Somehow, you just never quite stop loving them. I don't know, maybe we never stop loving anybody we love. Sometimes I think we just learn new ways to live with it, you know what I mean?

Well, anyway, when Georgia got so scared with us our last year, she took up with some uptown girls, drinking, dating boys and carrying on. And that hurt too, let me tell you. Oh, I don't care now, but then, well, it fairly broke my heart.

When I graduated, I took a job down east, took my sorrow and pain away and didn't come back. After a couple years, I got mixed up with a married lady; she picked me up in the grocery store over the frozen peas. I still can't believe I did that. My Lord, what a mess. Tears, begging, the whole sorry mess. I mean, if she'd just been able to say it was her own self in the sack, loving what we was doing, I might have been okay. But she was too afraid to know what she was doing in that bed, and ashamed of the joy she had in what she wasn't afraid of, and the combination sent her hunting. And blaming. And guess who was closest to the end of the gun.

True, true, Deb. I *was* real lonesome. She ended up saying *I* was sick, and that she'd help me find a man. Last thing I needed was a man with his old gun. But for awhile, I kept on. Thought she'd come to her senses. I even went to church to see her. I didn't know enough then. I didn't know about gay girls acting straight and lacking the guts to be honest with theyselves.

Am I being cruel, Roo? All right, maybe it ain't that she lacked guts, but that she had too much ache. I heard that idea before. But I'll tell you one thing, the ache of the fainthearted has caused a lot of trouble in this world. That kind of ache just multiplies on itself. I don't reckon it's her fault, or any of them what falls in love with us but can't brave the rest of the storm and won't look at theyselves. It may not be their fault, but it hurts the rest of us all the same. Sweet Jesus, don't make me go through that hell again!

Well, anyway, the thing is, after I come to my senses about that, I got myself back to the Hill. I thought I'd die if I didn't see at least a few queers, at least some what was proud of it, and knew it for their best feature, you know what I mean? Took me five long years to get myself back, but I did it, finally.

And all that time, even through my troubles with my Baptist married lady, I told myself Georgia didn't leave me because she didn't love me. But it took me that long to get it through my head that Georgia's leaving didn't have nothing to do with me and Georgia. It was more about her fear and her frozen parts and her drinking. Not that I was such a saint, myself.

No, I made my contribution, too much, actually. But I never been much of a drinker, knock on wood. Probably all those years of tent revivals and such, and after Momma died, Daddy never touched a drop, and Shirley never did nohow. Oh, it wasn't that I didn't try. I just couldn't bring myself to do it much. I mean, I tried at first, you know, to keep up, but it kept making me sick. Made Georgia sick too, but she didn't stop for the longest time. Had a hard time of it, that girl.

I still think maybe if it hadn't been for the drinking, she'd been able to hold her fear, but maybe we wouldn't have made it for long anyhow. Who can tell? Anyway, seemed like she couldn't leave the bottle alone, not when we were together, not when we were apart.

She was still drinking when we got to San Francisco. Lord, she drank the whole way out. She was a pain in the butt, I'll tell you what. Puking and carrying on and such as that. Made me scared to let her drive her own truck and when I get scared, I get pissed. But now I have a feeling she was scared to death herself, not having a job here, not knowing what she was doing. And some I think she was drinking to get that frozen part to defrost, you know? But it don't work that way, and took her awhile to learn that.

Anyway, truth to tell, I was pretty scared myself, but I figured I'd find something. They's always somewhere needing a good nurse. It's not that I love the work exactly, you know, but it's an honest job and it sure beats sitting around and talking and never getting around to paying your bills, like my girl Georgia has been known to do, once or twice.

I just fairly hate that, not carrying your own weight, you know what I mean? Got to work. And I don't mean just for the money, neither. It's like ref'ing. Lord knows, we don't do it for the money. But sometimes, I get crazy when I see folks not working when they can, and complaining about they don't know what to do with theyselves. Makes me think about Daddy working all those years in the mill; he's retired now, you know, just hangs around the garage and makes stuff and coughs and wheezes up that ol' white muck.

And sometimes I can't get Shirley out of my mind, thinking about her at the shop, all those years of washing those ladies' hair, them with the time to spend all afternoon, sitting there while Shirley combed them out, and her listening when they talked their dumb stuff, and not listening when they talked like she wasn't there. And finally getting a measly tip at the end, hardly enough to buy a Co-Cola with, mind you, and I think about her saying, 'You got to make do with what the good Lord gave you.'

I don't know about the good Lord part, and I wish it weren't true, but she's right about the other, you know. Folks got to work, some of that work for pay and then some work for free. Like setting up chairs for Wednesday evening prayer meeting. It ain't fun, but it's only fair. You get some; you give some.

That's easy to say, but it ain't always easy to do, especially if you think you ain't got any to give away. It's like with Georgia. From the first time I knew her, she never had a job that was right for her, you know, or one that even started to match what she could do. And when she got out here, she couldn't find a thing.

I think part of the trouble with her is she's never had no real idea what she *wanted* to do. Or maybe she never let herself know. I mean she's had jobs, you know, but it's more like she gets to the place where she just takes anything, and then hates it.

And then she'll leave. Sooner or later she'll get her lion on, that part what'll tear any living thing to shreds, and then, why sooner or later, she'll have to get another job. She can stand it for awhile, but then, something deep down starts to hurt and she gets more and more frozen until she gets the lion on and then, she's gone.

She's doing better now. I mean, I'll get to that. It's all part of the story. But before, well, my Lord, I don't believe she kept a job longer than a year. And you couldn't ask her about it, even to help her. She'd tell you nothing hurt no more. Course nobody was more shocked than her when the lion came on. I don't know. Sometimes when the lion'd come, it'd be as though she didn't know how to get mad her own self and was just doing what she saw somebody else do. Somebody somewhere, I ain't sure where. But she wasn't like herself.

And that wasn't the worst. The worst was she'd say, 'What's life?' Far as I'm concerned the onliest answer to that is *Life*'s a magazine. But she wasn't talking no joke. She'd have taken that lion and stuffed it down her throat, and all you could hear was muttering about 'what's life' and after awhile you couldn't hear a thing. She'd froze it. But the thing is, you can't really freeze that lion stuff. The heart of it beats away, burning in the dark like a devil fire.

Well, I tell y'all what. I didn't understand it myself for the longest time. I was only able to start to put the pieces together when I met her folks back in '78. Weren't the whole answer but it gave me a corner to start from. See, I believe it might have been from her daddy she learned lion ways. Her daddy, Cameron. Oh yes, I know of him, him and Almighty Martha, her mother, too. Martha's the one with the freezer bags. The last time we saw them it was on a "picnic" though Lord knows, I wouldn't have known it for a picnic, myself.

We sat there together, the four of us, right before me and Georgia took off for California. They never did know what to do with Georgia. Martha so regal and such, using cloth napkins on a picnic, can you imagine, and storebought picnic things, *pate* and such. No fried chicken in sight. No deviled eggs. No pie, no cake.

Wasn't much of a picnic if you ask me, not that anybody did, you understand.

And Cameron, laying around and hemming and hawing in those white pants he right away got grass stains on. Why, that man never done nothing in his life except ruin his clothes, dream, and haul his family around for all his dreaming. He's a ad man; you know, he writes the ads for TV and such. Or least he did. He drinks too much, you know what I mean? Can't hold on to a job. I mean, they never say that but I got eyes in my head.

He's still a handsome man, though. And can spin a tale like you wouldn't believe. It's plain why they all love him, a pretty man like that. But I can see why they all hate him too. It's a hard row Georgia's had to hoe. And she's like him, in more ways than one, I can tell you.

Like, when she's with me, she tells me stories all the time, just like him. I could listen to her telling those stories for hours and be happy to listen to more.

She's been telling some kind of stories ever since I been knowing her. She'll be quiet, and we'll be walking along and after awhile, she'll start. That's how we got here in the first place. Georgia spinning dreams. Wasn't nothing else to do in Carolina. If we was in Mecca, we'd have something to do in the morning, she'd say and laugh.

She always laughed about that. Some boy in high school had proposed to her, telling her being married would give them something to do in the morning. When she asked what, he said they could go out and buy some furniture for the trailer. I don't know if she knows he must have been pulling her leg; anybody could take one look at Georgia and know full well that boy would have something on his brain more exciting than furniture the morning after he'd been married, but the story makes her laugh and I never know if she's laughing about the sex or not.

Anyway, Georgia kept telling a story about California, how moving could really make a difference. And so we came on. I tell you, you can get into trouble listening to that girl. 'Something to do in the morning,' sweet Jesus. Thing was, for real, I was broken up with my new girl and couldn't bear to find another. And then that mess happened with that old mill house Georgia and me was renting. Boys breaking in and tearing up all the lesbian stuff, stealing underwear and rings, throwing our small secret things on the floor and walking on them, smashing them to bits.

Well, the robbery itself near broke our heart
enough, and we was scared, but we thought, you
be okay, it might be just that once. But then, it seer...
even walk down the street. I mean seriously, folks stopped talking
on their porches and stared when we walked down to the Seven-Ele-
ven. My Lord, it was too hard. And they didn't just stare. They
whispered. Loud whispers, you know? 'Boy bitches,' they called us.
'Dick finger dykes. Sinning perverts. Filthy. Disgusting.' I heard
them all.

And I can still remember shame starting up my neck and blaz-
ing through to the roots of my hair. Thought I was dying. But then
Georgia would get her lion on, and whisper soft in my ear, 'Smile
at them. Say hello, goddamnit. Don't let them think they got you.'
We walked on, smiles plastered to our lips like we was undertakers
until we walked in our own door.

And then, I'd cry. I'd start blubbering up the minute we turned
the kitchen light on and made sure no one was there. But not
Georgia. Never. I never once saw her cry over it. She'd just sit there,
open a beer and say that when folks at the hospital realized how
bad we was being treated, why, things would get better. We'd have
help. 'This is America in 1977,' she'd say. And then she'd say she'd
finish that beer and then get ready to go to bed. Of course she never
did have just that one beer.

Well, folks at the hospital found out how bad we was being
treated, all right. They knew before we did. And when we realized
that, we knew the game was over. Sweet Jesus, work was where it
all started anyway, some boys spreading the word about Georgia
being queer, trying to get folks to pay her no mind. We was working
in the same hospital then; she was a ward clerk in the emergency
room, and I was up with the premmies. But she was trying to
organize for the union. And she was doing a good job. And some
folks didn't like it.

She'd been made bold by a spirit crusher, when she had to quit
her school program after they told her she'd never get no good
appointment as professor because she was a girl. I thought it was
better that at least one of them came right out and said it. Better
than a silent snake in the grass. But not Georgia. She didn't think
it was no favor that she got told to her face.

First when they told her, she ranted and raved, but didn't do
no good. More men than one called Stonewall. After awhile, she
just ran herself down. Stopped raving. She took a look around then,

saw no other women there and her mouth got set real tight. And that's when she quit. Quit quiet. Outside, no noise, like always.

Then after that, there was this crusher hospital union business. I don't know. It was like I could see her freezing in front of my very eyes. Like her mouth got set in a deep-freeze line.

When we heard we was getting booted out of the house, and she was losing her job, and the union washed they hands of her, it was a hard time. She got to drinking whiskey and I couldn't bear to see it in her eyes. They'd get all vacant and hard at the same time, you know what I mean?

So when she said 'Let's go girl,' and I could see the vacant and hard getting dreamy and soft, like moving was going to make a difference, I just smiled and said, 'Sure.' I listened to her stories, like always. But I reckon I didn't quite believe them completely, like she did.

Oh, it's turned out all right. But it's a hard time when you ain't got no home to go to. I can tell you, it was touch-and-go there for awhile.

Believe I will get me a sweater at least. Anybody else want one now? Yeah, let's go in the kitchen. We can shut the door and sit at the table. I just don't want to bother Annie.

Here. Put the kettle on for some hot, if y'all like. Now where was I?

Oh yeah. Thanks, Janie. Well, when me and Georgia first got here, we found us a little place down in the Mission in the City, in the inner heart of the Mission, though we didn't know that then. We thought it'd be good because it was sunny and lively, and you know, cheap. But by the second week, we were both terrified, I can tell you that honest.

The thing is, folks here aren't poor the same way they are back home; they get mean here, mean and crazy, like they'd just as soon cut you as look at you. I finally decided it's because they don't know you. So many folks all crowded together and they don't know each other. The rich folks now, they got lots of space. But not us down in the Mission.

And all kind of different colors of folks. You've got to excuse me, Janie. Lord, I know it sounds stupid, but I thought they was just black and white folks in the world. Got out here and realized I didn't know jack-shit. I hardly knew where we were. And we was broke too, and no garden in the back, shoot, no green land for miles around this godforsaken city.

And on account of being so scared, I got work right away, being an aide, working temporary until I could pass my California boards. But Georgia, she kind of lost herself for awhile there. She'd call me at work, crying and carrying on, but there wasn't much I could do. And she was drinking all the time, I mean it, all the time. And that about pissed me off, you know, already being scared myself.

I'd gotten to the point of being mean about her drinking, but about two months after we got here, she decided to do something and she stopped. I mean completely. She never touched a drop from that day. You want that girl to do something halfway and you gonna have to do a gene transplant, you know what I mean? Still, it's like Shirley says: 'Your weakness is your strength; your strength is your weakness.' You know?

Anyway, it was hard on both of us, I'll tell you what. She did it by herself, but finally she got to talk to some folks what was doing the same as her and it was better then. But for the first few months she wasn't wrapped too tight, I can tell you. Teetering around, walking into walls, running a temp, one minute happy, the next jumping out of her skin. It got better, but I wished, you know, that there was something for real I could do for her, bless her heart, only all that ever seemed to help was rubbing her ears and listening to her, you know, trying to get her to talk.

Then one day I was talking to Shirley on the phone, not telling her everything, you know, but she can read my voice like a book and she said, 'Well, I don't know what all kind of trouble y'all girls got yourselves in now, but it couldn't hurt none to get you down to church and ask for some help from the good Lord.'

Right. Mmhum. Well, I wasn't on any better speaking terms with her Methodist Lord than I was with the Baptist one, you know, and the idea of trying to drag Georgia into some church was more than even I could hope to do, but I got to thinking about it you know, and finally I decided maybe there *was* something we could do. I mean, this was California. Maybe we could find some kind of something, and me, I'll try anything, once.

So I looked in the *Radical Rose*, and sure enough, you might recollect, they was all kind of religious groups for lesbians then, why even the Baptists had something. I couldn't hardly believe that, and I didn't really want to see what it could mean, but I knew then there had to be something for us.

Finally I settled on this weird sounding psychic workshop for women. I mean, psychic sounded weird, but still it sounded like the only thing close to us, you know? Georgia and me always knew when the other of us was in trouble, we could talk without talking and that was a kind of psychic thing, right? And Lord knows, we were in trouble then, so it sounded about right to me. I hauled Georgia off one Sunday afternoon, not taking no for an answer and we went on over to Berkeley, about four blocks from your house, Deb.

Well, we couldn't find the place for awhile. Then, after the third pass around, we finally realized it must be on the second floor of this big old building on Shattuck. We found the way up and there was about ten women inside sitting around waiting for the leader, who finally came in, looking like maybe she sold shoes down to Macy's, you know what I mean? Dressed nice, tidy, uptown. Like if she'd been wearing socks, they'd have matched, you know? She had sandals on, but you know what I mean?

When I remember that day, I can still feel that warm sunshine coming in the window, and I remember about those sandals, and how good Della, the leader looked, and how raggedy me and Georgia looked and how Della kind of shined from inside. I remember that because I was determined, you know, once I saw it out here, to get some of whatever that was for us.

And we did, we got some even that very day. We got into the circle with all the others and started doing some kind of imagining thing about cleaning our channels, which I didn't exactly understand, and letting the light of the universe come through us, which did make some sense. Then we was supposed to feel one with the world, and one with our sisters around us and lesbians everywhere, and one with the universe.

Well, my heart kind of swelled up and I felt myself crying and joyful all at the same time. It was real nice, like the cool breeze after a soft summer rain on a hot August night, I can tell you. I got pretty much wrapped up in it, thinking about home and such. And I cried and then after awhile, I just sat there and felt better.

It was like before Momma died and I was a real little kid and we went to the tent and the preacherman said, 'All of you who want to dedicate your life to Jesus, to be finally able to rest in the arms of sweet Jesus, come forward and get born again.' I always liked that part, watching people's faces, you know, and sometimes

Shirley would go and once I went on up, and it made me feel real good, real good.

Well, it was sort of like that. Georgia's face was so pretty that day. I mean, she got real scared afterward, but some of that frozen went out of her that afternoon, not all, but a chunk, for sure. Anyway, I know we both got helped that afternoon. I saw it. I could see it plain as day. I remember us sitting there together and holding hands and how she looked real good.

I liked that afternoon a lot. And I got hooked up with some other psychic kind of classes then, and then finally I realized what I needed was a garden and so I made me one. That's a kind of religion, all those green growing things; really, sometimes I think that's what God is, you know what I mean? The thing what makes things grow, you know?

Now I go to my garden and get my hands down in that old dirt and it feels good. It still looks kind of funny to me though; it's not sandy like back home nor even red clay like at the mill, but it grows things all right. Not things like back home; I can't get tomatoes to grow out here to save my soul. But rhodos and zukes grow just fine. I like to help those little creatures grow and it helps keep me sane, you know?

Usually, Georgia comes out and helps with the garden, which is good, because, like I said, for a long time I didn't see much of Georgia after that first year of us living here together. She fell all in love again and vanished. Just trotted off like she done in school. Hurt me bad.

Well, maybe that's a little worse than it was. Anyway, it's over now. Georgia more than made up for it when my California heartache walked out on me. Now, I don't want to tell you her real name—y'all might know her—but she left me for dead. The night she left, I thought my heart been stomped all over with those Castro boy boots she used to wear.

But Georgia got her lion on then and guarded over me like Shirley would have. She helped me make my first garden here in California. We went looking for a pot and found one, and made the snaps grow, just like back home, following the recipe in some poem Georgia found printed up in a magazine and written by Catherine somebody, some other Southern dyke. We are everywhere; it's true, Roo.

Anyway, the thing is about Georgia, some things she's done for me made up for a lot, and she introduced me to Annie and I'll love her forever for that. But I tell you what, what she done while falling in love with Morgan was not among her best moves. I keep trying to remember it didn't seem so bad until it was over. What I mean to say is, I don't guess it was so much different from what happens when anybody falls in love, and goes away for awhile, you know what I mean?

What happened was, I met this woman Morgan, the one we call Em. She was a computer teacher up at the hospital, teaching us to keep these special records on this new computer machine (of course if you ask me, a piece of paper's just as good, and a body can hug a whole lot better, but if I have to, I can do as I am told). Anyway, this was, well, it must about been about six years ago now, though I can't hardly believe it.

I had just started ref'ing over in the City and was just making some new friends and Georgia was coming along, cheering, some nights, when she didn't have no meeting to go to. We was having a good time. And I liked this Morgan from class.

Y'all might have seen her in some of the games. She's tall, well, not as tall as me, but she's good size. She's kind of too skinny, but you don't see it so much as that head of gorgeous red hair; she's a looker, I can tell you that! When I saw her playing on one of the softball teams, I knew she was okay. I liked her for real; she was a good player, fair and serious, playing hard, but playing for fun, you know?

Well, one thing led to another and Morgan, I called her that then, asked me and some others to come to a party they was having; they won the division that year I remember. I brought Georgia to the party with me; she was in the stands watching Em anyways, I found out later. Well, we went to this party at Em's girlfriend's deli and the two of them, Georgia and Em, I mean, practically fell in love on the spot. Oh, it was a mess.

Within a couple weeks they got all hooked up and the girlfriend got mad and the teammates got mad, because the girlfriend was the team sponsor—Good Lord, it was all over the place. And, like I said, I was hurt too. But they used to be times when Georgia just couldn't see what she was doing and you couldn't tell her a thing. One of those times was when she was letting herself be happy.

And she was so happy then. Her little face was just lit up like a candle in the window, warm and expecting, but not for me, you know. I'd be home, waiting for her for supper and she'd dash in to get a change of clothes. Sometimes, Em would come in, real cool, you know, but looking bashful and wild, all at once. Those two. Sweet Jesus. And I tried to be happy for them, but I was missing George and I was missing her bad.

Well, not very long after, Georgia and Em moved in together. It was how it always was for Georgia; when things started to get a little better, she just kind of got swept away. She's always lived that old country song, thinking something was going to make it easy from now on.

Anyway, they were in love and such and I just didn't see her. For about a year, we only saw each other about once a month, and on the holidays, you know. But time went on, and we'd talk, and the more we talked, the tighter we got. And it got better, but it wasn't the same.

My heart still ached when I saw her; I won't lie to y'all. But you know, part of that was me; it surely was. There was a part of me what didn't want to give her up to nobody. And I had to make peace with that part before we could get much further, you know?

It took about four years for us to make it right again, or at least for my heart not to have an ache like an early frost when I saw her. By then, she got a job working as a secretary downtown. It was a job Em helped her get, I think. She'd quit the ward job over at City Hospital that I'd been after her to quit for the longest time. Her eyes had got hard once more and I remembered, when we left Carolina, she swore to me she'd never be nobody's clerk again. But there she was. And so I urged her to git; get away, get some kind of job she could want.

But she didn't. She only got this other clerk job. Sure, it was more money than the hospital and sure, it had a better title, but it was the same. I couldn't hardly believe that Georgia could be civil enough to some of those folks to last for more than an hour, but she'd been there about ten months, usually her limit, when all this started for her.

When she started feeling it real bad, she started coming around more. First, she started talking about her helping me make the garden that summer. She didn't, but that's how it started. And it was right about then she first got word about her mom being sick.

And, I'll tell you. Even though I was sad she was having such a hard time, I was glad to see her. It's not easy to find a body to talk to about Carolina. Most folks out here, they just don't understand how the sun hitting green leaves after a four o'clock rain could make you cry. But Georgia does. And she'd come by and let her own self slip into a little back-home when she and I were alone together and I was glad about that, because for awhile there, it didn't seem like we had too much to say to each other.

When she first took up with Em, it was like she was trying to be shed of all her Southern stuff. Now I understand that. Folks make fun of you if they think you from back home. Course, folks make fun of you if they think you're queer, too. You just have to be who you are and let folks go they own way. But I surely missed Georgia when she went away, you know? I surely did miss her.

But you know, the thing about Georgia trying to lose her accent and all, well, it wasn't just the outside. She was trying to lose something inside too. And those days it was bad, what with her mom and all. She couldn't say it, but I'd seen her cry about Carolina even then. Crying without making a sound, when she didn't think I could see. It wasn't like she used to when she was drunk, but even now, I reckon we both cry sometimes. In those days, didn't seem like Georgia could find a place to light, and I knew part of it was just plain homesickness.

Oh, she wouldn't say so, but it seemed like she couldn't never be still, some part of her all froze up sure, but the other part wild or lionish, always going here and there, even when she came over to watch TV with us. Like she'd lost something and aimed to find it no matter what.

She and Emmer been together then about five years, and I reckon she thought she'd lost some of the romance, and she had. We all do by that time. Question is, can you change enough to get some new for that which you lost, you know what I mean? I mean, thing is, they's some folks what are made for each other, and some ain't, and some got to figure out they are and can't do nothing about it but learn to live with it.

It ain't ever an easy time, if that's your row to hoe. And poor Georgia and Em, before it was all through, things got real hard. Things at the beginning was bad enough, and for both of them. Em had her own problems. As for George, it ain't easy when you think your momma's dying, even if you ain't been close, and those two were closer than they'd thought. Because if you don't think you got a home already, you're in real trouble if your momma gets sick. You're cut off for sure then, and you know it. Nothing seems right then, nothing. Not your girl, not your job, not your life.

And then in walks the Mysterious Stranger, which I am sorry to have to say once again, yours truly provided the introduction for. Well, I didn't know any better. In she came, through the barn door that I, like a fool, left open. And she was tall, gorgeous, smart, rich and available. All the things Georgia thought she wasn't. Not that we knew any of this then. I tell you, I couldn't believe all that was starting to happen that spring, after we got the garden in.

And that's the part I'm going to tell y'all about next.

CHAPTER TWO

COME VISITING

When Georgia finally looked, the sunlight had already faded to where she couldn't see the numbers reflecting on the silver digital face of her watch. She had to turn the truck's cab light on. Eight o'clock. She snapped the light off, and pushed the plastic watchband up off her skin and towards her wrist. There was a red outline where the band had been and she rubbed the spot without looking. From the other side of the Bay, humming over the round railings that crested the steel-paneled half-walls of the bridge, Oakland's orange wharf lights spread in the twilight. Somewhere inside her she registered the warm, but it was very far away.

More clearly, she was thinking about the time. It seemed to her she'd last looked at her watch about two hours ago, but the watch said only half an hour.

How can that be, she thought, and glanced again at the melting twilight. Sometimes the hours just seem to slip away like water. But they weren't slipping away fast enough tonight. She changed lanes. It would be hours before Morgan came home. Maybe she should have gone to the game with her, she thought, watching the car on her right merge in front of her. If she'd gone to the game, she would have missed the whole thing. She sighed, braked the truck as the traffic slowed and looked again over the bridge railings at the soft light.

Daylight savings time had stretched the sun into summer, but the weather was late. Spring had finally come only that week, and Georgia's body had noticed, happily. She got up that morning and her body said, it's going to be a scorcher today—which wasn't right, because it was never a scorcher in San Francisco—but her body remembered other places, other times, and didn't understand that the morning temperature didn't mean the same thing. All it meant here was that the fog would burn off, eventually.

Georgia didn't listen to any of it anyway. Even now, as she pushed her glasses up on her nose, even as she felt a slight sheen of sticky sweat uncomfortably on her glasses, none of it mattered. She gave only passing thought that maybe she should have worn a shirt instead of her old sweatshirt, shapeless and hot. Traffic picked up and she shifted into third.

She did think of rolling down the truck window, but remembered the pall of pollution hanging over the bridge when she'd looked out from the freeway access, and the space between her eyes began to ache picturing dirty air hanging limp and heavy like a wet sheet.

She left the window up and felt the heat then, felt herself sweating. She pinched the bridge of her nose under her glasses and tried to wipe a little of the sweat away. It was May, after all. Hotter here than it will be at home, she thought. Her undershirt clung wetly under her arms. She thought, well, I'll stink by the time I get to Bernice's but who cares?

And then, hearing the radio, she thought, why do they play that wimpy shit? God, if you're that worried he's cheating, he probably is. Just leave the jerk.

She wished for a cigarette and suddenly leaned forward to push the radio button to change the channel. She didn't listen to the new station. She thought, well, Bernice wouldn't care if she didn't smell like a rose. Didn't matter to Bernice. She ran her free hand through her hair. God knows, she'd smelled worse, looked worse in front of Bernice. Back home, she'd looked a lot worse and a lot more times. She sighed and looked over her shoulder, checking for cars before she switched lanes as she passed under the I-580 sign.

She slipped into that place of driving, just driving. She drove and watched the traffic. She flipped radio stations. She rolled down the window. But she didn't think the rest of the way over. She was able to stop thinking. She just drove. When she drove into the driveway of Bernice and Annie's house, she turned the truck off, and sat there, her forehead resting on the steering wheel.

After a minute, she sat up and peered at the house. The house was dark in front, but around the back, she could see the deck lights were on. Then she looked back at the house, and saw the den lights on too. Probably Annie was working. Bernice must be waiting for her on the deck, she guessed, and so she climbed out, felt her face grimy from the road, felt her pants too tight.

She went around back, slipping through the hedge and the fence and called "Hey" when she rounded the corner.

"Hey yourself," Bernice called back from up on the deck.

She couldn't see her yet, but after hearing Bernice's voice, she smiled, and picked her way across the uneven and unlit ground, happy, her friend's voice calling her home. She looked up and saw Bernice waiting for her on the concrete step at the bottom. Georgia walked straight up to her then and leaned her body forward, almost falling into her, sagging a bit. When Bernice wrapped her arms back around her, Georgia didn't hug her for a moment; she just let herself melt into Bernice's big, strong body.

"Lord, it's good to see you again, girl," Bernice said as she rubbed her hands over Georgia's hair. Bernice kissed the top of her head then and turned, leaving one arm around Georgia's shoulder and started them walking up the steps.

"Good to see you too," Georgia said.

Bernice gave her a squeeze in answer and drew back as they walked up the stairs apart. Then she said, "Well, girl? You all right this evening?"

When Georgia didn't answer, she asked again. "You look lower than the belly of a snake in mud. Look like the police run over your dog. How are you doing, girl? You look like you made a bargain with the Devil and he's come for his part."

"Thanks a lot, Bernice," Georgia said, smiling but rubbing her hands through her hair to give it some order. She didn't look at the other woman.

"Always nice to get a compliment on my looks." She paused at the top of the stairs and turned to Bernice. "Do I look that bad?"

"You look bad, honey. You sounded bad on the phone. What's happening? Come on, sit down. You want some tea or something?"

Georgia shook her head and lowered herself on to the top step, rather than the seat Bernice offered. It was awhile before she said anything. She crossed her arms over her knees and looked out over the backyard and back towards San Francisco, watching the lights fade and glimmer as the night came on.

She felt Bernice watching her, but she didn't say anything. Silently Bernice sat down beside her on the same step, and Georgia felt her near and was glad. They didn't talk or look at each other. Georgia knew she ought to say something, but she couldn't figure out what, or where to start, and decided to just soak up the warm from being near her friend.

After a bit, she cracked her shoulders and then suddenly noticed a rectangle of ground spaded up in the backyard, and neat rows of mounded soil. Shadows from neighboring houses made it hard to see all of the rectangle, to know how big it was, or how far back it went. But it didn't matter. She knew what it was. She would have known what it was in her sleep.

"Did you already plant this year?" she asked, surprised, as she turned to look at Bernice. "Why didn't y'all call me?" she asked.

"Why honey, we did that last weekend. You were busy, working all that overtime, remember? I called, and talked to Em, and she said she'd tell you. Didn't she tell you?"

Georgia was quiet again.

"Yeah. I remember now," she said after awhile.

The twilight around them deepened. The yellow lights from the Oakland container ship wharves arched over the Bay and dimmed the city lights.

"I planted an extra row of carrots for you, just like always," Bernice volunteered.

Georgia didn't answer, but she stopped looking at the garden and laid her head down across her folded arms and closed her eyes.

"You didn't come all this way on a school night to talk about the garden, did you girl? What's wrong, baby? Everything okay at home?" Bernice asked, and Georgia noticed again how her accent got stronger, the quieter her voice got. But she didn't say anything. She couldn't. She couldn't figure out where to start.

After a bit, she moved over on the step so that their arms were touching. And finally, she said the only thing that seemed to make any sense.

"Bernice, what are we doing here? Why'd we come here?" she asked. She could feel her heart for the first time since she'd gotten off work and she heard her voice start to crack. It seemed then as if the whole of her would split open, starting between her breasts and splintering into shards.

Bernice wrapped her arm around Georgia's shoulder and said, "Well, for awhile, it gave us something to do in the morning, didn't it?"

"I don't think this is how I want to spend my mornings anymore," Georgia spat out, turning away. "Nor my evenings either."

Bernice raised her eyebrows in mild surprise at the abrupt movement and looked into the night as Georgia was doing.

But she didn't see what Georgia saw, didn't see each light as an individual house, didn't understand it meant warm and knowing there was a way home. Didn't know Georgia saw them as lights in a kitchen or lights in a bedroom, lights a father had left on for a child afraid of the dark. She didn't see the lights; she saw the city, crowded together and she thought then that if George was looking at that, she was surely going broody.

"When are you going to tell me what's going on?" she asked, her voice low and soft, worried.

"Daddy called when I got home from work tonight," Georgia said, dully, as though she were speculating a train being on time.

In the silence that followed, she heard Bernice suck in her breath. Georgia looked at her, but Bernice didn't look back. She just said, "Oh, what did old Cameron want this time? Drunk again? Crying again?"

Georgia turned back to the yard and noticed how all gardens look brand-new for a few weeks. She wondered how the earth would feel between her fingers but, instead, felt her hands aching as though they had been burned empty. The ache stabbed at her through her palms, and she thought she might cry. She set her mouth tight against it. She heard Bernice's voice echo down into her and knew she had spoken long ago. For a moment, all she could hear was Bernice's question over and over. Finally she answered it.

"My mom collapsed at the Kroger, Monday."

"Beg pardon?" Bernice said, startled.

Georgia turned away from the garden, clenched her arms to her ribs and looked Bernice full in the face. "She had a stroke. She's not conscious, still. Weird, isn't it? It wasn't even the emphysema. I thought that'd be enough," she said, only this time she wasn't sure she'd made her voice loud enough to be heard outside her head.

Bernice just stared at her. "Lord, Lord," she said finally. "*What* is going on, girl?"

"I just told you," Georgia whispered, her teeth clenched. "Didn't you hear me?"

"Well, gal, give me a little more info. Cameron did tell you a little more didn't he? Like where is she? Can she talk? How bad is it? What's the prognosis?" Bernice said slowly, too slowly it seemed to Georgia.

"Bernice, I don't know. He wants me to come home," Georgia bit off, propping her head on her hands once more. God, who knows the answers to that stuff? She should have gotten more answers, she thought.

Again, they were quiet for awhile. And Georgia looked past the garden to the lights again, watching the lights. It wouldn't be like this back home. The lights didn't glow up from the city. It would just be dark past the circle of light of your own house, if there were lights on at your house. If you had a house.

If you didn't, you could pick a street and walk down it. And you could see, all seasons; if you walked down the street, you could see other houses with other lights on, shining out past hedges or trees, sprayed out like sunshine on the porches, warm into the night.

If it was a night like this, if it was summer, in the kind of neighborhoods she and Bernice lived in, windows would be wide open, screens diffusing the light, and you could hear folks talking or radios, the light yellow and open as the windows in the night air. Beyond the circles and streams of light, the night was deep blue like the robe of a queen, and warm enough to wrap around you.

It wasn't like here. She could feel the clutch in her heart tighten, that clutching place where tears started and she began to chew on her lip, slowly, like she was rubbing a soft spot. It wasn't like here. The sky wasn't orange like here, not with that hum of light that never turned off. Not that it meant people weren't alone.

"How do you feel, Georgie? Are you sad?" Bernice said when Georgia sighed. Georgia started, shied away from the sound of her voice.

"Hell no, I am not. Bernice...," she said and started to feel the cracking again. "Oh God," she said, turning away, and reaching up under her glasses to stop the tears.

Nightime wasn't ever like that back home anyway, except when she and Bernice lived there together. It wasn't like that when she was growing up. It wasn't ever like that. Oh, there were lights. But in each room. Shut doors. Alone.

There was the air conditioning. So all the windows were kept shut. And you didn't walk after nightfall. And you didn't talk to each other, unless you were fighting. You went to your room and shut the door and hoped no one came to knock. And the entire house was silent. At least for awhile. At least from the street. Until you heard voices through the walls of your room. And even then, there were ways so you didn't have to hear, until they knocked on the door. Or until they just opened it and sprawled in. That's what it was really like. And still was.

Abruptly she said, "Bernice, you're probably the only one who'll believe this, but he and I had a fight. Ten minutes on the phone and we managed to have a fight. I did ask him how bad it was. I asked him if he was taking care of her good. I asked him how she was feeling. It took me twenty minutes to get out of him that she'd been in a coma since Monday. Bernice, this is Friday for God's sake. Finally, I realized he was drunk and wasn't calling about her at all. He wanted support for him. For *him*."

"You've had that fight once or twice before, girl," Bernice said softly.

"I know. Shit, I don't care, anymore. I mean, I could have, I would have been okay if I could have just hung up on him. But I think maybe this time she's really sick. And I don't know if I can hang up on him if she's really sick."

"Mmm. So what did you say to him, George?"

"I told him I'd call him in the morning, when he was sober. He wanted me to make reservations right then and call him back to let him know when I was coming."

"Good idea to call in the morning. Let's hope he doesn't drink all night again," Bernice said and reached over to pat her knee.

Georgia couldn't help crying when she felt Bernice's warm hand on her knee. The tears started slowly and fell slowly. Somehow, when Bernice was nice to her, it made her feel like all she could do was cry, even though she hadn't during the phone call, nor anytime after. She gasped, trying to stop.

"Bernice, don't you have any cigs?" she rasped out.

"You know I don't smoke during the season, girl. Come here."

This time, when Bernice put her arm around Georgia, Georgia leaned her head onto her shoulder and was still. "Breathe, baby girl," Bernice said, and when Georgia did, she could feel sobs beginning in her throat, sobs of wild cries, and she tried to choke them down, tried to get a handle on them. If they started, she knew if they started, she would scream and she couldn't do that, not in front of anybody. She pulled back and wiped her eyes furiously under her glasses. Finally she took the glasses off and wiped her eyes with the large hankerchief Bernice was holding out.

"What else did he say? What about little Cam? Does he know?"

"Who knows? Who cares? I don't even know if I care."

"It's okay, Georgie," Bernice said and hugged her closer.

Georgia knew again she should say something, but again, she couldn't figure out what. She shifted her legs and leaned forward. When she did, the crystal Bernice had given her thumped on its ribbon against the place between her breasts and it hurt. The ache hurt.

"We can talk about something else for awhile, and just set here together," Bernice said, her accent thick, Georgia thought. Was she really going to have to go back to see them after all this time? Was it real this time? Could she sit in a room with him and not tear his throat out? Not tear hers out? Not drink while he did? What was she supposed to say to him? What should she have said to him? And what about her mother? What about her mother? What about her mother?

The cracking started again and she forced herself to listen to Bernice. To listen to the sound of her voice.

"Well, girl, I'm sorry about Martha, but we'll think of something to do. Probably it ain't as bad as it looks. It never is. I got to say, it's real good to see you, no matter.

"How's the Emmer? How's things at work? How come you were working last weekend? We missed you," Bernice said, her voice too loud, it seemed to Georgia, but she let it rest.

Let it rest, she said to herself. Let it rest for a minute. She felt a sigh escaping and then she heard the rest of Bernice's words and felt as though a different spring was winding up and she suddenly felt her pants too tight to sit hunched down the way she was.

She got up and stood at the deck railing, her back to Bernice. "I was working because Williams didn't get his shit done on time again. So I *had* to come in. I didn't have a choice. He said I'd ducked the last two times he needed me for overtime, and besides, he needed my 'special skills' on this one."

Georgia stopped. She couldn't feel the crack opening anymore; instead it felt as though she couldn't breathe. She wished she hadn't come over, that she'd just stayed in the truck and driven on. She felt her keys in her pocket and then folded her arms across her breasts.

After a minute Bernice reached over and touched her leg. "Your special skills, meaning you'd write it for him, or fix it or whatever?"

Georgia moved away from the railing and went to sit in one of the deck chairs. "Yes. Well, it's part of my job, sort of. It's for just this kind of opportunity I should have gone on and finished my dissertation. I'm sure Williams would have found a way to use research on antebellum women's property rights. God knows, we haven't had the war that would make any difference in that yet. But I *am* a skilled worker, you know. Writing all those research papers has translated into the real estate investment marketplace.

"Oh yes. Even though I'm not paid for it. Even though I'm paid just to type. Everyone knows Williams would have gotten rid of me if he could've afforded to. He hates me, but he loves how I can make him look good. And me, I mean, I have a job. I'm grateful," she said and felt like her throat was closing up.

Bernice got up and sat in the other deck chair. "Grateful's not exactly what you mean, is it, girl?"

"Look, it's my job. I go in every morning and I type, type, type. And if it gets really horrible, if Williams is a complete and total asshole, then I go hide out up at Ricky's office. But usually, I can't. Usually I have to sit there and write his fucking proposals and cover for him while he's out screwing his lady love. And so I while away the hours, working my ass off, researching his projects, filing his fees, writing his reports, making his arguments.

"And at the end of the day I come home and I fix dinner for Morgan and me, and then I go read the paper or a novel, or I go to the games. Or I just wait for Morgan to come home from the games. Or maybe it's not her or the games. I don't know anymore. Sometimes I don't know what the hell I'm waiting for. I ought to be doing something you know? I ought to be doing something with my life. I swear, if I knew what it was, I'd do it."

She broke off for a moment and then began again, her voice twisting bitterly in her mouth. "But I'm not so different from everybody else, right? I mean, that's life, right?" She didn't wait for an answer.

"It's a great life. I love my job. I'm lucky to have one. Jesus, Bernice, who cares? That's life, right? What else is life?"

As soon as Bernice opened her mouth, Georgia said, "Don't answer that." And then there was silence in the night air and she heard her question echo again and again, sounding in the night like an ocean foghorn.

She rubbed her hands over her face and wished they'd talk about something else. It was true about her job. What else was there to say? Or do? She wished that she could just get up from the deck and go home. It wasn't any better here than it was at home.

Bernice got up, rubbing her arms. "I'm cold. I've got to get me a sweater. You want one?" she asked, walking back into the house.

Georgia didn't answer, and Bernice didn't cut the deck lights on when she went in so Georgia was left alone in the deepening coolness. She sat very still, the tightness between her shoulders streaking down her arms and searing her hands where she gripped the deck chair. She tried to relax her grip. What's life, she repeated, looking at the outline of the garden in the dark, but a job, a home, a routine? So what's the point of getting angry about any of this; what's the point?

But as she looked out over the garden, the rows, the overturned fresh and clean earth, she began to remember and began to really see, see the new rows, the way she did every time she saw a new garden in twilight. She began to see again how their first garden had looked just after they had planted it when they had come out to see it one more time before they went to bed.

They were sunburned and her skin was fiery but the night air was cool, and soft, and their bare feet got wet in the early dew. They stood there and looked, just as she was looking now.

And she remembered how bright the sun burned that day, how they had laughed, the smell of the red moist soil and their skin after they had sweated all day. They had argued about how many rows of carrots and Bernice had chased her around the periphery of the plot when she insisted on three rows. 'All right,' Bernice had screeched, chasing her, 'but you'll eat every blessed last one of them in the third row!'

And she did. Carrot juice and carrot salad. Carrots for breakfast with her eggs. Carrots at lunch with her tomato sandwich. Carrots with the stalks still on, the root washed clean with the garden hose. She had loved every last one of them. And when they had pulled them up from the ground, almost every one, perfect or not, was bright orange, sweet and crunchy. So. She still had her own row. She smiled.

When she heard Bernice coming back, heard the sliding door roll on its track, she turned and saw her friend, big and familiar, and she loved her in her old giant purple sweater with the saggy pockets.

"Keep talking girl. I just got cold. It gets cold out here fast, don't you think? Aren't you cold girl?"

Then Georgia could feel a rush of cold come sliding back with the air creeping down around her neck where her sweatshirt was loose and old, and she thought, Jesus, where did I just go? What is going on? I can't keep doing this. I've got to stop and think about this. What am I going to tell him? Send me plane fare? What'll I tell Williams? Hi, my mom's dying and my dad's too drunk to take care of her, so I have to go home like a good little girl?

And then she said to herself, I will not go back. I won't go back into that place. I don't care if she is dying.

"So what'd y'all do last weekend, besides work?" Bernice said as she sat in her chair with a sigh.

Georgia stared at her for a moment and then jerked herself back. She rubbed her hands together and said, "Mostly, I just came home and collapsed. Em was coaching her team Saturday morning, like she does now, and when I got home, she was in her room, with the computer. I came in to see her and she came out and sat with me while I ate, and then, we went to sleep.

"Sunday, I went in again, and I think she had a game. She's coaching one team and playing on another this year. Keeps her busy, what with her having more work to do because of Elliott and Joe. She's at a game now, actually."

Georgia rubbed up her arms too. It *was* cold. But Morgan would be there when she got home. And maybe she'd be able to tell her. Maybe tonight they'd have a chance to talk.

"So, she doesn't know yet?"

"No. But I'm sure we'll be able to talk tonight, before I have to talk to him in the morning."

Bernice nodded. "That's good. Good to have a girl like Em. She's a good one, all right."

Georgia agreed silently. Morgan would know what to do. There would be time tonight. And what if Morgan was tired after the game? And what if she had to go early to coach tomorrow?

Well, so what? They'd stayed up many times when they'd both been exhausted. And anyway, really, this wasn't such a big thing anyway. It wasn't like her mother was dead already or anything. And who knew? Maybe he was making it all up, exaggerating like he did when he was drunk. He did that all the time. All the time.

She'd call back in the morning and it would be nothing. Maybe not even enough to keep them up and awake. And Em got so tired these days, what with running a lot more of the business by herself. And the teams.

But, she thought, how do I know what they'll do? It could be anything. It could be nothing, or she could be dead in the morning.

Goddamnit, she needed Morgan's help with this. Where was she? Why wasn't she here, helping? Georgia sat there still as the night. Every part of her wanted to get up and to get down in the garden and scream into the earth, just scream, no words, no explanations, just the noise, not even really hers.

Bernice cut in, her voice low, "Are you cold, girl?"

"No." Georgia shook her head.

"Mmhum, yeah, I can see maybe that raggedy old sweatshirt's keeping you warm. Did you eat supper?"

Georgia just shook her head again. "Not hungry."

"When did you eat last?"

"I don't know. I'm not hungry, Bernice," she snapped.

"All right girl, all right, no need to raise your voice at me."

Georgia looked back at her. "I'm sorry, Bernice. I don't mean to be mean. I just... I just feel bad, you know? God, Bernice, I don't know what I'd have done if you hadn't been here tonight. I'm sorry."

Bernice reached over and patted her on the knee. Georgia reached for her hand and held it tight.

"Well, I'd feel mighty bad if I was you, Georgie my girl," Bernice said. "I'd feel mighty bad. Why don't we go on in and see if Annie put supper away yet. We had some nice greens and yams and chicken. Come on in here with me, girl. You can't kill the son of a bitch from here."

Bernice hoisted herself up, leaning on Georgia's shoulder, and shook her a little as she did. Georgia just sat there for a moment, and thought, what difference does it make? What difference did she ever make, whatever they did? If her mother had to die to get away from him, well, that was her choice. Who could ever guess what those lunatics would do? And what was the point of her trying to figure it out, anyway? She got up to follow Bernice into the kitchen.

From the dark of the porch, the kitchen lights were bright when they went in, and the room still smelled like roast chicken. The smell made her slightly nauseated, but when Bernice put the plate of cold chicken and sesamed greens down in front of her and she took her first bite, she realized she was starving.

She ate without looking up and was almost done when she stopped to drink her milk, and then she saw Bernice sitting opposite, watching her and smiling.

"Maybe I was a little hungry," she said, wiping her mouth off and offering a half smile.

"I reckon," Bernice said back. Georgia smiled full then and finished up the little left on her plate. They sat in silence until Georgia got up to take her plate to the sink.

"So how are you?" she asked. "I've been sitting here, jawing, hogging all the space. How's Annie? She working again? She works as much as Morgan, I swear."

Bernice kept her seat at the table and didn't answer until Georgia had rinsed off her plate and came back and sat down at the table.

"I think she's in there working. But she'd have left us alone tonight anyway, give us a little time to see each other. I know she'd love to see you. You want me to call her?"

"Sure," Georgia said, and got up with Bernice and followed her into the den. There, Annie was working with the television on, papers all spread out around her.

"Darling, are you working still?" Bernice said as she cracked the door open.

"I'm here, working away. How are you two? Did you get a chance to talk? How are you Georgia? Nice to see you. It's been too long," Annie said, looking up at them from her place on the floor. Bernice didn't move all the way into the room, so Georgia peered around her.

"I'm doing okay, Annie. Work's awful, as usual. I was just telling Bernice. I don't know what I'd do if last fall they hadn't hired this wonderful new woman. I met her in the elevator about four months ago. She works on a different floor, but I meet her for lunch and stuff. Saved my life."

Bernice hooted and turned around to look at Georgia. "That so? Girl, are you picking them up in the elevator these days?"

Georgia smiled and shook her head. "I swear Bernice, around Annie you got a one-track mind. You honeymooners. It was just that I saw Ricky for the first time in the elevator, and she was juggling some stuff and I helped her. Turned out she was the new company librarian. I get all the old charts and maps and records of all Williams' mistakes from her. When things are really awful, I hide out there. I told you, Bernice. She's my safety-valve. She's been really helpful. And smart. And interesting. I think she's interesting."

"But she's a dyke, right?"

"Well, sure she's a dyke, Bernice. What you think?"

Bernice poked her in the ribs and then turned back to Annie and grinned.

Georgia shook her head and said to Annie, "How are you?"

Annie smiled at both of them, lingered on Bernice and then · looked back at Georgia.

"I'm fine. But if I'd known how much they were going to work me when I got this promotion, I would have turned it down."

Annie and Bernice laughed together. Georgia thought about Morgan briefly and then, hearing the television, wondered how Annie could work with so much noise and distraction.

"What're you watching?" she asked.

"Falcon Crest. It's so trashy. I just love trash shows, don't you?"

"Never touch the stuff, myself, but you know me. I wouldn't know a television unless it bit my stereo."

They all laughed then.

"Well, I bet the Emmer knows all the angles on this show," Bernice said, talking back over her shoulder to Georgia.

"Morgan's been working a lot lately," Georgia said, rolling her eyes at Annie.

Bernice interrupted her. "Hey girl, you know, I made a referral for her the other day. Wonder did she get that job? Doctor Liz Bathory. Pediatric oncologist. Come poking around, wants to know how I learned the machine. Kind of a high and mighty, but she's a M.D., rich girl. Tell your girl I want some commission money if she does call, okay?"

"God, don't give her any more work, Bernice. I'll never see her. She's as bad as your girl."

Bernice laughed and turned back to Annie and said, "If we leave you alone now, darling, will you be coming to bed before midnight?"

Annie looked up at her and grinned. "Depends on who's in the bed when midnight rolls around."

"Better not be anybody in that bed besides me anytime, girl," Bernice said and walked over for a kiss.

Annie turned her face up and Georgia watched them kiss, watched them tease with their eyes for a minute and then, embarrassed, said as she backed out the door, "I got to go home, y'all. Take care Annie. Don't work too hard."

She turned to go and heard from the hallway Annie calling out, "Nice to see you again, Georgia. Hope to see you and Em real soon."

Georgia walked back to the kitchen and pulled out the drawer where they kept the phone books, found the yellow pages and had pulled out the A-L section before Bernice got back.

Bernice sat down without a sound and they sat together at the table in silence. Georgia turned to the "Airline" section. She looked up and saw Bernice watching her, but she didn't say anything. Finally, Bernice cleared her throat and said, "Are you going?"

Georgia kept her head down. "I don't think I have a lot of choice, as usual, with them."

"You need some help?"

"I guess I can dial the phone," Georgia said dryly. She kept looking through the yellow pages.

"I reckon you can," Bernice said. "But where you going to go? You going to stay with him? Have you thought about getting a room somewhere near the hospital instead? You going to call little Cam?" She paused.

"Or do you have to do every blessed thing by yourself, as usual?"

Bernice's voice was sharp then, but when Georgia didn't stop turning the pages, Bernice spoke very softly. "It don't have to be the way it was when you left, you know, girl. You ain't the same. It won't be either. Set down and think about this for a minute before you get all tangled up in doing things how you used to."

Georgia stopped turning the pages. "What do you mean?"

"Why're you going?"

"To help out. To see her. What if she dies? I don't know."

"You might want to figure that out before you spend any money, girl. Thought you were going to talk to Morgan first."

"I will. I will. Who's being snippy now?" She glanced down at her watch and, surprised, looked at Bernice.

"How'd it get to be so late?" she asked.

"Time flies when you having fun," Bernice said without smiling.

"I got to get home. It's almost eleven," Georgia said and got up and walked around to hug Bernice. Bernice stood and Georgia slipped her arms around the taller woman's back, resting her head just under Bernice's chin.

Bernice said, "You going to take care yourself? You going to call me? I love you, girl. Don't forget. It ain't going to be easy. You call me, you hear?"

Georgia felt her breath catch in her throat again. "I love you too, Bernice," she said. "I don't know what I'd do without you."

Bernice pushed her away and grinned. "Why you'd just find another fool to plant your carrots," she said and laughed.

"Go on home now, Georgie. Talk it over with your girl, and call me. Let me know what y'all decide."

"I will," Georgia said, nodding and starting to walk out to the front door. Bernice followed and pulled Georgia's sweatshirt hood up from behind.

"And don't forget your lion."

Georgia turned at the door and kissed her. "Can't find that lion when you need her," she said.

"Well, you keep a watch on for her. Can't be that far away," Bernice said as she closed the screen door.

"I'll call," Georgia said and got in the truck. She slipped into reverse and blinked her lights as she left.

Eleven. It would take at least half an hour to get home. Surely Morgan would be home by then. Georgia felt the ache between her breasts turn hard and panicky. Well, it would be okay. Morgan would be there.

She checked the side mirror as she merged on to the 80 and turned the radio on. She smiled in recognition at the song that filled the car. That song had been popular when she and Em were courting. Five years ago, when they were courting. Sounded like it was ancient history, but really, it wasn't all that long ago. There had been a time when they, like Annie and Bernice, were warm, electric, hot.

She remembered, could see them so clearly, coming home— from softball team parties where they'd listened to that song—running up the stairs and into their bedroom, couldn't wait, breathless together, not even just at the beginning, but later, six months, a year, two years into it, when they knew they'd found each other and that there had been no mistake. That they had passion, but something else too, so that when Morgan pulled her onto the bed, losing her balance and falling on top of her, they'd laughed.

And then kissed, laughing. And then kissed slowly. And then stripped, so slowly, by the light of the street. And made love, slowly, talking in whispers, here, slower, fuller, make me full, fill me up, I do love you, I do.

And the streetlight bathed their bodies in harsh light and it was so clear, Morgan's body was so bright, hard angles, shoulder, hands, firm round breasts folding into her own full body, the very softness of their lips and whispers, and the softness of their skin against each other, sliding soft, and her hands full of Emmie's hair, auburn even in the streetlight.

How long ago was that? How long was five years?

On the road, she looked at the yellow light at the toll plaza, braked in, watching as always to see if the toll person was a dyke. One look, a woman, but no. Not with those fingernails. She paid without speaking, accelerated, and merged the truck into traffic again.

She'd be home in a moment. Well, it was true things weren't the same as they had been in the first few months. But they never were. Everybody knew that sex came and went. It would come back. It wasn't a problem with them, after all, the love was still there. And what with Morgan's work stuff, well, it was okay, she could wait. It would be better. They just had to take some time.

The important thing was Morgan'd be there now, like always, and she would know. She would know what to do. When she pulled onto their street, she passed Morgan's old Jeep parked illegally and she smiled. She could see the light on the upstairs landing was on, but their bedroom was dark. Well, maybe Morgan was waiting for her in the kitchen.

The second time around the block, she cursed and parked her car illegally too. For sure she'd be up early in the morning anyway and could move it. Price you pay for living in the queerest city on earth, she thought with a grimace. She pulled the handbrake as hard as she could, locked the door and walked quickly to the low fence at the apartment courtyard, checking behind her as she stopped to unhook the fence gate.

She slipped in and walked up to the second story, fumbling with her keys as she walked. In the light on the landing, she finally got the right key, unlocked the door, and with one last glance behind her, shut the door and walked in.

She had opened the door without trying to be quiet, thinking that Morgan would of course be up, and even if she wasn't, not minding if she woke her. But when the door swung open, the house was too quiet for anyone to be awake.

The kitchen light was on and she walked, still not quiet, down to the bedroom, towards the kitchen. The bedroom door was ajar, but the room dark. In the light from the hall, she could see Morgan asleep, her face looking pinched. For a moment, Georgia stood in the doorway and tried to decide whether or not to wake her. Then she turned and crept down the hall, going to the kitchen to see if Morgan had left her a note.

On the kitchen table, on the bottom of a market list, were Morgan's block letters, penciled in. "Couldn't wait up any longer. Game got over early. Hope all is okay. Wake me up if you need to. Love."

She sat there and shook her head, knowing she wouldn't wake her up; there had been too many nights lately she hadn't slept through. Georgia rubbed her eyes. Well, it would keep until the morning. Probably wasn't anything, anyway. Probably was just her father. It would wait.

She got up and checked the refrigerator and saw that Morgan hadn't made their lunches. She leaned over, holding onto the open door handle on the refrigerator and cracking her shoulders.

And then she remembered. It was Friday. But she, at least, would be at work tomorrow. She had another project and Morgan was probably coaching. Well, her mother probably wouldn't die overnight if she'd been in a coma since Monday, if she was in a coma at all. And she and Morgan could talk after work; maybe she could finish up early. Or anyway, they could at least talk Sunday morning. Morgan couldn't have a game Sunday morning.

She saw the food in the refrigerator then. Might as well. She made her lunch from last night's leftovers, washed up, wiped off the counter and cut off the light.

Quietly she went back down the hall, cut off the hall light and stripped in the hall, gathered up her clothes and slipped into their room. Morgan tossed restlessly when she opened the closet to get her nightshirt.

She folded her clothes on the chair and went to the bed. As she lifted the covers slowly and slid into bed, Morgan pulled her close, lay alongside her and mumbled, without opening her eyes, "Don't wake me up now, I'm asleep. I'm glad you're home. I love you baby."

Georgia kissed her and then rolled over. She crossed her arms over her heart and closed her eyes, her mind still moving. American. Maybe Piedmont. Probably Delta had the cheapest fare. She'd call tomorrow.

When Morgan reached over and wrapped around her, spoon-like, her small breasts pressed against Georgia's back, Georgia sighed and tried to let her body go, and hoped her mind would let go, too. Bernice was right. Wasn't anything she could do from here. She watched the streetlight for a long time, going over in her mind the report Williams had left for her at four that afternoon. Longhand. He needed it by Monday morning. Organized into sections, polished, filled in.

She went over it and over it, how soon could she get it done. She didn't think about her mother. Or about back home. Or Morgan.

By one, she'd organized the report seven times and was stuck on the third section and realized she couldn't figure it out from there. She got up, got a drink of water and threw some covers off the bed. Morgan rolled over and pulled a pillow over her head. Georgia got back in, the sheets cool to her now. The trouble before was that it was too hot. She could never sleep when it was too hot.

CHAPTER THREE

THE COVENANT

Morgan stood in front of the bathroom mirror, carefully closed her left eye and applied a light line of kohl. As she drew the wet brush across her eyelid, she thought how odd it was she did this now, and that it did look good.

Her hair, calmed with the mousse foam into a shape acceptable to the men downtown, still curled wildly around the crown of her head. Golden-red waves held themselves in disheveled place and she paused before painting her right eye to dip her fingers into the slowly dripping tap water and wet a few wisps she had pulled out over her forehead. Quickly then, she did her other eye.

She glanced at the kitchen clock as she hurriedly left the bathroom. Quarter of six. Time to get a cup of tea and sit for a second before walking the three blocks to the streetcar just before it went underground at Carl and Cole. She had to get in early for her ritual Monday morning meeting with Elliott before class. Elliott would tell her about Joe, and about what she would need to do at the company that week. Some of it would be a part of his work she had never done before, and she would do it because he would need to be with Joe.

After the meeting, she would teach her class, and after five, she would do whatever other work needed to be done. Forty hours of teaching, another ten or twenty for Elliott. Well, maybe only ten this week. And Christ on the cross, maybe this week's class wouldn't be like last week's.

Sitting at the table, carefully folding a worn linen napkin over her navy gabardine skirt just back from the cleaners, she sipped her tea, gingerly and quietly. Even now, she could hear her father slurping milky tea from his saucer, grunting his morning noises.

She sipped slowly, not moving the cup back to the saucer, scarcely moving it away from her lips. Georgie slept restlessly in their bedroom down the hall. The fog hung morning-heavy over the Haight and she knew the office would be cold too, wind from the ocean screaming between the too-tall buildings that blocked the sun from warming the tunnels of downtown.

Cold in May and a new class again this week. Last week she'd had a class of doctors, the type that butted up against class schedules and times, and muttered when they made a mistake that they didn't need to learn any of this stuff; they had secretaries after all. Did she think they needed to know how to do it, like some kind of clerical? Their lips always seemed to curl when they said this, and Morgan usually had the impulse to say something about "dumb women" but she never did.

Last week though, she'd lost control of the class, and she knew the moment she did it. Acid formed in her mouth remembering when Dr. John Wilson told her she should keep her words to a minimum and keep it simple and in English. Wilson was gaunt and dark haired, probably been in America forever, would have been obnoxious even if he hadn't been a surgeon.

"You mean speak in a kind of English you can understand," she said back too fast, with her smile coming too slowly. In the silence after, she could hear a collective sucked-in breath and then someone said, "That's telling him." For a moment, then, they were all silent.

After that, of course, he'd fought her, turning the class upside down, trying to show she didn't know what she was talking about. She was glad when Friday came. Good thing he was a surgeon and worked with his hands; if he'd had half a brain, he'd have been a lot more trouble to deal with, Elliott said.

She'd talked to Elliott when it was over, Friday afternoon at their weekend check back meeting, while they shared a bottle of his ever-present soda. He chuckled and sympathized and said he'd have told Wilson if he didn't want to learn what she had to teach, why maybe he should just come back another time.

She smiled at Elliott, and smiled with him. Of course, she'd never do that, and on the class evaluations, she noted the two women in class had written about how hard she'd tried to accommodate the wishes of the class. The men had written the course needed to be restructured. Jesus Christ.

She put down her tea and took a bite of buttered toast. Chewing slowly, she thought of how things used to be different. She used to love teaching; there was a time she found the doctors' manipulations funny. And she loved watching the women realize they could do it, could run the machines. When the computer became one less thing to be afraid of, they began to smile. When they understood they could actually make it work for them, to do as they wished, the tightness in their faces slipped away and as they went on, pushing keys, some became gleeful, and she loved that most of all.

But these days, such moments seemed few and far between. It seemed most of the women didn't want to know and most of the men thought they already did. She felt tired all the time.

She wiped her fingers off on her napkin and took a sip of tea. But probably her tiredness was from working so much. Or maybe it was all the coaching. Maybe her schedule was too full. Maybe, she thought, you aren't sleeping.

That was true. But it was her schedule that was the main problem. Well, she thought, maybe she could find another coach, let her take over. But then, what would she do Saturday mornings? To fill Saturdays, even now, so that she didn't think about the kids, even now, a year later? What would she do? Sit here alone, remembering, like she had those first months, instead of going down to the shelter and rounding up the kids? Holding them, teaching them, playing with them?

What would she do? She wondered again what Rebecca and Carol had done when she didn't show up that Saturday a year ago. She wondered again what words their mothers had used to tell them. That she too had disappeared? Where? Where had she disappeared to, and what would she do Saturday mornings?

She got up abruptly, throwing her napkin on the table, and took her cup and plate to the sink. She glanced at her watch and tip-toed down the hall to the bedroom. Georgia slept soundly even though the morning fog was as light as dawn. Morgan looked down at Georgia, smiled a little, her anger softening and turned to go. As she did, Georgia lifted up from between her two pillows, unfocused but hearing, and called to her.

Swiftly, Morgan went to the bed and kissed her. "I'm off, baby. I'm sorry I woke you. You okay? It's about time for you to get up."

The sleeping woman reached her arms around Morgan's neck and pulled her down to her cheek and held her there for a moment, as though they were still sleeping together.

"Oh, Em, do you have to go so soon?" Georgia asked, her voice a whisper.

"Georgie, I'm late already."

Georgia let her go and fell back on the pillows and opened her eyes a little.

"Okay. Are you okay? Will you be home tonight?" she asked.

Morgan leaned forward, touched as always by Georgia's ability to love her in her sleep, but anxious too. She had taken too long to eat her breakfast and she really was late. She shook her head at Georgia.

"I have a game tonight baby, remember?"

"Oh, right. Well, call me if you can. I love you Em. Hope Elliott's okay. I love you. Call me."

Morgan kissed her goodbye, rushed to the kitchen and in one hand gathered up her shoulder bag and the canvas sack in which she kept her softball things. With her other hand, she began to shrug her way into her suit jacket. She thought for a moment about making sure Georgia got up, but decided against it. Let the kid have a few minutes more of sleep. She'd be up soon enough.

Jacket on, she got her keys out to lock the deadbolt behind her. It was going to be a long day. Another day, another dollar, please God, let there be a lesbian in class this week. Just one. She didn't care who, and ran out the door to catch the streetcar downtown.

By the time she'd gotten on the car, she realized why she was worrying about Georgia. She seemed so small again this morning. As though she were shrinking in front of her very eyes. Well, she thought, the best she could do now was call at lunch. Wee little thing. Georgia had been out of her mind about her mother the last few weeks, couldn't get any real information from her father, the bastard. And the weeks just seemed to stretch on with no change, in either her mother's condition or Georgie's.

Neither one of them got better. God, she wished it would be over soon, and that either Georgie would stay and let it go and make her peace, or that her mother would get worse and Georgie would go home and make her peace. Or in any event, that her father would leave them alone. Leave them alone and let them make their own peace, Mother of God.

Families. No damn good to anyone. She shook her head to clear it and checked the impulse to go on, turning instead to the streetcar window. She watched the houses march by. Well, it was hard not to think that way when you haven't been able to sleep for the last six months, she thought, as the car slowed. Hard to work, hard to do anything. She shifted her bags. But it can't be helped.

Can't control, well, anything these days. God only knew where she'd be working this week, or how it would go.

She smoothed her hands over her skirt. At least there was money in this not knowing. She and Elliott were certainly making enough these days. Their clients paid through the nose for them now. And if they got that new hospital-wide contract, they'd be set for quite awhile, no matter what happened with Elliott, or how much he needed to be gone.

If Nanna only knew how well they were doing, despite everything. They probably would get that contract; their training requests were up and their evaluations good. They'd almost made it. If only Nanna were still alive, she'd send her money and have her visit; they'd have a great time, now. She thought about that, her face blank as the streetcar roared along underground, careening precariously on the sunken rails that led downtown.

When the car lurched into the Civic Center station, she thought again, well, Nanna would be proud, but what about the women on the farm? Things *had* changed. She looked out the window, blackened to sheer reflection in the tunnels underneath the City. The women on the farm. Here she was, in a skirt, with makeup on her face, and behind her ears, for Georgia to discover later, Chanel No. 19.

She smiled ruefully. Not bad for a Navy brat who came to San Francisco after a losing wrestling match with college and a several year residence at a collectivized lesbian farm in Oregon, where she'd had lessons in how to be a good '70s dyke instead of a good Catholic girl. Somewhat similar, she reflected with a grimace. Not enough sex and too many discussions about whether you got more points in Heaven for letting the wafer melt as opposed to chewing it.

So many debates. So much anger. And now, dear God, they'd roast her. They'd eat her alive. Sold out. Capitalist pig. Yes, indeed, she was a capitalist pig and she paid the rent on the lovely old Gold Rush flat she and Georgia had in the Haight and they could all go to hell in a handcar. Them and the bitches at the shelter.

She let out a long sigh and then surreptitiously glanced around at the others on the train. The usual assortment, nobody looking at each other. She examined her hands, held tightly in her lap. No calluses now. This was 1985, she thought grimly. When are you going to stop caring what those women think? When are you going to stop caring what happened to Rebecca or Carol or the rest of the children at the shelter? Or how about the women there? Or sucky Stockton saying she couldn't teach kids.

Well, by God, she could teach adults. She had a class to think about, and how the computers would be set up and who would be afraid and how could she, in fact, speak an English they could understand. She let her mind go back into the classroom, her face as sheer as the train window, listening above the deep pool where she'd drifted only for the driver to call the stop that was hers. Montgomery Street. Downtown. At least half the train left with her at the call, rushing up to the cold street corners.

"So, how's it going?" Elliott asked as she checked her mailbox for messages and mail. That's what he always said. Morgan turned, smiled, glad to see him.

"So, fine," she said, reaching up to pat his shoulder. There was a certain feeling she'd never figured out what to do with around him, even though she'd had six years to figure it out. She looked up at him and wondered again if she should give him a hug. She'd hugged him on occasion, but not much, not because she didn't love him, not because she was afraid of him, but because he was a man and she didn't quite know how to hug a man and have it fit okay. It always felt funny when she hugged him. Sometimes it felt even more awkward when she didn't, but mostly it felt too personal, too strange, too different from the code they had worked out for their daily closeness.

"Well, it's Monday. A new week, new clients, the world goes round. How was your weekend?" she asked him, smiling, touching his arm.

"I got your roster for you," he said, handing her the printout. "You got ten this week. I don't envy you."

She took the list and scanned it for women's names. Well, at least three. Maybe one would be interesting. She held her hands up, limp, and shrugged her shoulders in imitation of Elliott.

"*Nu*, where's the excitement, where's the party? Why don't we fly to Hawaii for the week, old man?"

He laughed, shook his head, not a single gray hair moving from its blowdried place. "*Nu*, why don't we give up eating, little one?"

She smiled at him, her heart open at this Monday morning ritual.

"Class starts at eight in the ninth floor training room down at City," he pointed out on her roster assignment.

"Meaning, we only have a little time to talk before I go, right?" she said, walking back into the roomy office they shared and pouring herself hot water for a cup of tea. Dunking the tea ball with one hand, she walked carefully to her desk and he followed, taking the seat next to the desk. She rummaged for the things she might need, a training disk, the foils for an overhead projector, dry-erase pens for the example board. He handed her another printout.

"Probably you'll need this," he said and she took the password listing for temporary access to the mainframe for the trainees. She noticed his hand shook.

She stopped looking through her desk and really looked at him.

"Thanks, Elliott. What time did you get in anyway?" She looked at his eyes for the signs of sleeplessness so often there now.

"Early. Joe had a hard time, up all night, dry mouth, diarrhea, you know."

"Oh God, Elliott, no sleep for you either? I'm sorry. I'm so sorry." She sighed and reached over to take his hand. "How is he?"

"He's okay. It's hard for him. The pills and everything. He's good about it, though. And you know, this Friday he came to temple with me. I'm not sure why, but it helps even though I don't think either one of us believes it at all. So different now. I've been away from any kind of services for years, and Joe, God, Joe was raised Catholic. Funny isn't it, how everything falls away."

She pulled her hand back and sat in silence looking at him. He looked at her and then at the floor. And her thoughts steamed again: how angry she was that her father couldn't have the disease and let God take Joe's away. It wasn't fair; the son of a bitch, it wasn't fair. What kind of God was this, giving AIDS to men like Joe, men who had made a decent life, but letting men like her father live?

Or how about Georgia's father? Maybe they could trade his life for her mother's. What kind of God could there be? Fucker. She shuddered and mentally made a cross before she could stop the image in her mind. At least she didn't do it in front of Elliott. But her mind didn't stop flashing. Shouldn't curse God, Nanna would shake her head. Nothing can be that bad.

But it was. She could remember so clearly how Joe looked when she first met him, six years ago when he came up to the office to pick up Elliott for a softball game. He was younger then, of course, but about forty pounds heavier, and his skin glowed, his body was trim. He worked out four nights a week with Elliott, the two of them side-by-side, so different-looking. Joe so small, a blond Italian. Came up to tall, dark Elliott's shoulder.

They had been together fifteen years now. She'd really gotten to know Joe when the three of them played softball on the San Francisco team in the co-ed division of the Gay Games, three years ago. God, what a game that had been! They'd creamed the Boston team. She smiled, remembering, and she looked up at Elliott, still so strong and big, but hollow-eyed now and wasted. She could feel her heart begin to ache as she turned from him and struggled to keep it out of her voice.

"Elliott, so where are you this week? Close enough for lunch?"

"Mm, Morgan, I thought maybe I wouldn't teach this week. I thought I'd try to do that office research on the classes, the surveys that we need for the new contract. We need to do it. We need to make that push and get secure there. Get something secure around here. And I need to be pretty free this week anyway. Joe may need to go back in again, the doctors were saying on Saturday."

He took a deep breath and Morgan watched him turn away. But then, when he turned back, his voice was strong again.

"Anyway, missy, I can't go out on the new call. The client requests a woman and I just don't think my swish will convince this one." He put his hand on his hip, made a face and they chuckled together.

"So is she a dyke, Elliott?" Morgan asked, trying to laugh, but hopeful too.

"A dyke doctor no less. Researcher. Cancer doctor that works with kids. She wants you to teach her and her staff."

"Well, what's her name?"

"Mm, Bather, Backer, something. Elizabeth. You know her?"

"No. I don't think so. How do you know she's a dyke?"

"Well, dear, I don't think a faggot would request a woman, now, do you?" He went over to refill his tea cup and wagged his finger at her.

"Maybe not," she said, rummaging through her desk again. "Anyway, I can always hope," she said and grinned at him.

"Well, I couldn't possibly go, even if she asked for me by name, which she certainly did not. I think the surveys are crucial to get done, don't you?" he asked and she knew he was trying to talk himself into doing them.

They *were* crucial, and he did need to get them done so they could start writing the proposal. But as usual lately, business wasn't what he was thinking of when he said crucial. She watched him, worried.

He lowered his eyes, but then, coming back to the chair by her desk, slouching and draping himself into it, he asked in his Tallulah voice, "Did I hear a lunch invitation? Sure, I can meet you down there for lunch. Nobody's clocking me on this project." He grinned and laughed one of his old strong raucous laughs.

She grinned back. "Noon then? At the deli?"

"I'll just come down around noon," he nodded, "and wait for you on the benches near the side lawn."

"Don't forget your cap," she said and he nodded again, pulling out his old blue Dodger's cap and showing her the new pins he'd gotten over the weekend from some friend of Joe's. He had almost all the National League pins now. They agreed, still, the Giants' pin was the best. And then, it was twenty of eight, time to go.

Outside, she stood on the corner, waiting for the bus. She shifted the straps of the two bags on her shoulder and set down her briefcase of materials for the course so she could sip the rest of her tea before the bus came. She tried to distract herself, knowing she would cry about Elliott and Joe again if she didn't.

Twenty minutes later, she was standing in front of the classroom where she'd been so often in the years she and Elliott had been working together. She tried to breathe deeply before she went in. It would be okay. It would. They'd write the proposal and he could slack off. They wouldn't always have to be scrounging for new clients, which meant new programs and new training modules. She could carry the load for awhile and just keep teaching the old programs they'd already set up. And they both could rest a little. He could do whatever he needed to do.

She walked in and began to set out the training materials. As she did, the new students came in to the training room in pairs or alone. But they called to each other and her heart sank a little. It's always harder to teach friends. And then, the man she would come to know that week as Connor came in. So goddamn many Irish in this town. And they all look alike. And he, of course, asking who in her family was from the old sod. Give me a break, she thought.

She tried to remind herself that the class was only a week. She looked around the room, checking for supportive faces when she closed the door at nine. Wait, there in the back, two of them, she looked at their name cards. Amelia and Jackson. If Jackson wasn't a faggot, she would eat her hat. And the woman Amelia, too early

to tell for sure, but a possible. On the thin side, and nervous-look-
ing, but there was something about her, like she might be one of
those who call themselves "gay" because they couldn't quite say
the word lesbian. Or maybe she was just closeting. It was getting
harder and harder to tell these days.

She dragged her eyes back to the rest of the room. Four more
men. Then the two other women, obviously clericals. She smiled at
them. And then someone named Roy. And then that Connor. Goddamn. Was it necessary, she thought, looking at the ceiling, was it
necessary to send me somebody who looks just like my goddamn
father?

She stood up in front of the class, fingertips of her long thin
hands resting lightly on her lecture notes, waiting for the conversa-
tions to die down. Presently, she began to speak over the last of the
voices (Connor's was the loud one in the back that wouldn't stop,
of course), winding into her introductory talk.

"My name is Morgan McCormack. I'm here to teach you how
to keep your inventory and patient records on this wonderful
machine they call a computer. I'll also be teaching you how to do
reports and print documents as you may need.

"I've had six years experience using this system, starting as
many of you have," and here she nodded at the two women sitting
next to each other, "in a clerical pool. There isn't much about these
software programs I don't know, and what I don't know, I can find
out for you. We'll be talking about the programs and the computer
in a minute, and the difference between the two, but first, I want
to tell you about the way I teach and what you can expect."

The class, as usual, was quiet to this point. A few slurps of
coffee drinkers, but most eyes were on her. The dykely looking one
in the back was exchanging glances with the faggot. Well, we'll see
about that, she thought and smiled.

"The way I teach is that we are all adults. I'm here to give you
as much information as I can, and you are here to learn as much
as you can. I expect you to be on time and to take notes. If you
have to miss time in class due to your patient load or other respon-
sibilities, it's up to you to get notes from someone else."

As usual, the men shuffled and shifted in their seats as she said
this. The one called Jackson in the back was grinning. He raised
his hand and she called on him by name.

"What time's lunch?" he asked and the women chuckled. Ah,
the clown and maybe a little bit of a resister she said to herself, but

also caught herself smiling. It was the kind of question she herself would ask. Thank God for queers, she thought.

"Lunch is from 11:45 to 1 p.m. I expect you back on time. Now, let me run down a few more things."

She smiled as she said this and turned her eyes to Jackson who smiled and then looked at Amelia, the possible. Amelia smiled a wide grin back. The men, including Connor, mostly turned their heads towards the terminals in front of them. Well, to hell with him.

Abruptly, she turned to the board and started writing. Might as well get it over with, she thought and began outlining the course, making standard jokes, judging the mettle and tone of the class from who laughed at which jokes and trying to get a feel for what was to come. Every time she looked at Connor and caught his eye, he looked straight back, unsmiling. Shit, she thought.

The first day wasn't too bad. She mostly got caught up with Jackson and Amelia, appreciating it when they laughed at even her most sly jokes. Maybe she played to them too much, she thought and wondered if her grip over the others was slipping. Connor was certainly getting harder and harder to reach, paying less and less attention, his keyboard keeping up a steady beep as he played with the computer instead of listening. She couldn't tell what he was up to. The rest were fine; the women appreciative, thank God; the men having trouble taking notes and blaming her for talking too fast, as usual. The women, as usual, smiled at this. She smiled back.

By the third day, she felt Jackson and Amelia were saviors in the corner; Jackson especially had a wonderful knack for bringing laughter into the room just when a pall came over it. She had lunch with Elliott on Monday, managing to get him to sit in the sun for at least part of the time, and the last two days she'd worked through lunch, because she'd had to coach, or play, right after work.

And okay, it was a tight schedule, but if it wasn't for the softball, she might go crazy, she thought. Got her away for awhile. Because it wasn't just Elliott and Joe she thought about on the way home or on the way to a game after work. It was him and Joe, and the men with purple lesions on their face that rode the bus to the hospital with her. It was work. It was Georgia, so hurt and upset in that place inside she'd never been able to touch. It was being asked to leave the shelter by the very woman who knew why she should be there. It was being asked to be quiet about who she was, when who she was made her one of the best teachers around. It was, it always was, the memory of her father.

She would try to think about some strategy for the next softball game to blank them all out and then she would get on the bus and see another man, painfully thin, with an earring and a faint smile for her, and she would think again about Joe and what would certainly happen in at least six months, maybe less. And if Joe, then what about Elliott? Dear God, what about Elliott?

She couldn't bear to bring it up with him now; it seemed like asking him to plan his own funeral. But what would she do if he got it? He wrote the programs; he taught her how to teach them. Whenever he called their business a dog and pony show, she knew he was the steady pony and she was just the dancing dog.

What would she do if something happened to him? It wasn't as if she could go back to what she was doing before she met him. Jesus God, he'd pulled her out of that cesspool at the dental clinic where she thought she was going to commit ax murder before the year was over. He'd come to train her and they had walked out together, with her hired as his second. He taught her to teach. To read the programs. To make the patches when necessary. And faggot that he was, he helped her learn how to dress like she'd been born into it. Bought her the first suit she ever owned. And was gentle about it. Like she imagined a brother might have been. Like a father should have been.

Even in the old days, when they were working night and day to get the business off the ground, he'd shared everything. Even when he ordered out for their late dinners, as soon as she'd gotten used to eating sushi and milkshakes, he was generous to a fault, ordering much more than the two of them could possibly eat, just to make sure she got enough. He'd drawn up incorporation papers after they'd worked together three years and given her a third of the stock, saying she'd earned it, and that the only stipulation was that she wouldn't sell it out from under him, that she had to be the trainer for Samuels and McCormack until one of them croaked. That was a joke. That one of them would croak from too much sushi or milkshake or some combination of the two. It was a joke then, Jesus Christ.

And now? If they didn't get that hospitalwide contract, the business would be as dependent on him as it had always been. She couldn't do it without him. God, they needed that new contract.

What would she do without him? She heard the words tear in her ears at the oddest hours. And it wasn't just the business, she knew that. She'd just put it there. Because she was terrified for him.

Because even if nothing happened to him, losing Joe was enough. He was so different now, so hurt. And she had been with him and Joe when those asshole boys in the Avenues shouted at them, tormenting until Elliott threatened to hit one of them. Jesus, didn't it even end when they got sick? When they were dying? When they were dead?

When did it stop? She thought about him even when she thought she wasn't. But she didn't know how to say any of it, to him or anyone. He wasn't, after all, her husband. He wasn't even her best friend, being a man. He was just a faggot she knew. She was a dyke. They ran a business together. Had some good times. What was the name for what they were to each other?

She just didn't know how to say any of it. And she wished that she could, at least to Georgia, but even without words for it, or for the uncertainty about Georgia's mom, it was a comfort to Morgan that they continued as it seemed they always had.

If she didn't have work to do or a game and Georgia wasn't working overtime either, she went home and they had dinner. It was true that she missed Georgia terribly at the games, felt sometimes if she didn't see her there, she would never see her. But Georgia was right when she said she needed to stop coming so much. She did need to go her own way, not just cheer Morgan on hers. She was happier. It was the right thing to do.

And she understood it, but she missed her. At home, at least, they had finally figured out how to let her watch some television and let Georgia read, both of them in separate rooms but able to see each other, together in the house. When they would get ready for bed, they would be together and then would fall asleep in each others arms, exhausted.

At least Morgan was exhausted. And even when they didn't talk, she was comforted in their peaceful togetherness. She loved it when she came home and Georgia was there; even more so now, since with the extra workload from Elliott, she wasn't home so much. But Georgia had been gone herself lately, working overtime, or just away, in her room with the door shut, far away. But things change; Morgan knew that. It was a hard time for Georgia too. She had to keep trying to remember that.

After all, they'd been together a long time. Five years was a long time. And she still hoped they'd stay together for a longer time. Sometimes she just looked at Georgia and smiled, maybe over a dinner out or through the doorway with Georgia peering over her book in the next room, and she thought to herself how glad she was to have Georgia, pretty Georgia, and to be married. She didn't say so to Georgia, but she still loved to look at her, those full lips, kind eyes behind her glasses, her curly cowlicked hair, her full luscious body and breasts. True, they didn't make love so much as they used to, but how could they in this exhaustion?

Well, there were other things too. Sometimes now, there were times when she looked over and Georgia's book had dropped in her hands and the woman was staring, away, not there. And it scared her. Sometimes it wasn't just that Georgia was gone; it was that she couldn't find her anymore.

But mostly, she felt in relief, it was the same between them. Many mornings when she lay in bed, thinking about Elliott and Joe, waiting for the alarm to go off so she could get up and get ready for work, or in the middle of the night when she woke with her father's face in her eyes, Georgia lay sleeping beside her and she would pull the sleeping woman to her. She would press herself against Georgia's back, and feel comforted, and she hoped her arms reached into Georgia's heart too.

But often, there was pain when they talked and it seemed she never knew how to say things right. The thing with Elliott and Joe had been there for six awful months, and when Georgia found out about her mother a month ago, Morgan began to feel crushed, helpless, immobile. The two together were too much. She felt unable to speak or give Georgia peace with her words and so she tried with her hands and her body, as they slept.

And sometimes, in those times, she could stop her heart, and just breathe deep from Georgia's sleepy skin and the stillness. She could just float. Some mornings Georgia would turn, turn them both, pull her arms tight around Morgan and hold her hands in the heart spot between Morgan's breasts. Morgan wouldn't stir, Georgia's hands warming her heart. It seemed then she could stay there all day safe. And often, she'd go back to sleep, too, but lately, even in the comfort, she couldn't sleep and she'd get up, kiss Georgia on her way out, and get to work.

That was the morning. In the evening, she'd come home and Georgia usually had dinner ready. They'd exchange news of the day, Georgia telling stories on the folks she worked with or some new utter stupidness of her boss. But Morgan hardly ever talked about the company. Her job seemed mostly the same, week after week, with only a variation in names. And a variation in how much of Elliott's job she could do. And a variation in Joe's health. How much could you talk about that?

Georgia didn't exactly understand. It seemed to her, she'd told Morgan, at least they knew what was happening with Joe. It made Morgan think Georgia didn't understand what was happening at all. And anyway, Georgia cared about Elliott, but didn't see him often, didn't see Joe's daily wasting away, didn't really understand why Morgan cared about Elliott so much. They had never socialized together anyway, the four of them, except sometimes at the ball park or an occasional spaghetti dinner Joe would cook for her, with her favorite sweet Italian sausage Elliott got special for the occasion. No, they weren't friends as couples, and Morgan didn't know how to explain Elliott, even to herself.

But anyway, it didn't matter, because more and more Georgia had been wanting to talk about her work, and how much she hated it. It was awful to hear what she had to do for those pigs. Morgan didn't understand why Georgia didn't just leave. But month after month, Georgia related one outrage after another. Morgan knew part of her didn't want to hear even as she listened. She didn't know what to say in reply. God, clericals. Like fucking battered women, going back each day to take more. But now, since Georgia had heard about her mother, Georgia just sat there and didn't say anything.

After dinner, Georgia would go into her room and shut the door. When Morgan knocked, she would be on the floor with old pictures, or old letters, and she wouldn't be in tears, but she looked like she should have been. And what could she say to her then? How could she love her with the door closed? And what could she say after she said I love you?

At least the mornings were soft and real. Even if they'd fought about Morgan's being gone so much or Georgia being so silent, even if they hadn't resolved the fight, Georgia's body would forget in the night and welcome her in the morning.

Georgia's body made her feel strong, ready to face anything, even Elliott's tired smile. It made her feel like she and Georgia would weather even this.

But on the fourth day of that week, she wasn't quite strong enough for Connor. As soon as it happened, she told herself she should have been ready, but she wasn't.

About ten in the morning, Connor interrupted her to ask a really complicated question about using the graphics program to develop a three-part form, using an extremely theoretical example. She tried to answer him three times, realizing all the while that what he was asking had nothing to do with the content of the course. It was aimed at her, covered by a seemingly real question.

He wouldn't let go. He kept twisting the question around, like a dog on a hunt, catching the whiff of blood. The class became quiet. Jackson turned in his seat and said, "Listen man, she said she had to research the answer, let up." Amelia had her head down in her notes. The other women also turned away. Then Roy and the other men, silent at first, began to echo Connor's question after his third try.

Finally, she said, "Connor, I'm sure what you are asking is extremely important to you." She saw Jackson bend his head over his notes and she began to feel sick, but she went on. "So what I'm going to do is see if I can get someone down here to answer this for you. I'll see if we can get Elliott Samuels here after lunch. He practically invented the system. And now, if you can wait, I'd like to be able to get on with what the rest of the class needs to know right now."

She waited pointedly for a reply, staring at him. He sat sullenly in the back, his arms crossed over his chest, and said he'd wait. She wouldn't look at him then. Goddamn bastard. Thank God she was seeing Elliott at lunch. Let him handle this asshole. Just like them, just like those fuckers. They ask you a question but they know the answer already. They want to watch you twist in a decision you can't make. They hold you up and make those you love watch you get torn apart. The voices in her head stopped suddenly. But she knew they were alive in the silence and she knew they were only resting. She called for the morning break.

She grabbed her jacket, felt in the coat pocket for a piece of gum and turned her back on the class as they filed out. She called Elliott from the troubleshooting extension phone by her main terminal. They were gone, except for Amelia and Jackson, when he answered. She explained the situation, keeping her voice formal, and asking only for his help.

"Sure, I'll come after lunch," he boomed into the phone in his old loud voice. "You all right, *shayna maydele*? Don't let them get you down," he said, not waiting for an answer. She only murmured 'Thanks,' and walked out to the green around the hospital. She began to walk across the lawn in front of the cancer wing, chewing the gum as though it was a lifesaving rope. She wasn't there at all.

Goddamn assholes. She saw, instead of Connor, instead of the green of the lawn, the living room in her parents' house, and her father sprawled on the couch, his Navy uniform askew, one arm hanging over her younger sister's shoulder, brushing the child's budding breasts. 'Well,' he'd said, as Morgan prepared to leave on her prom night, 'well, with your mother working, and you going out and all, why all I have to keep me company here at home is little Kelly.'

She'd come to show him her dress, the one she and her mother had worked on silently, those months he'd been at sea. Those months she'd been free of him and his night visits to her room. Those days she'd been able to find her voice when Jerry had asked her out. But still, she wanted her daddy to see, to know how pretty her dress was, really, how happy she was. He'd always said he loved her. Wanted her to be happy.

She'd looked at him that night, remembering always how the can of beer he had by his side beaded with moisture and dripped slowly down in the heat of that southern California night. She looked at him and couldn't look at Kelly. She wanted to scream. She wanted to get out, prayed for Jerry to come any moment, prayed that God would strike her father dead on the spot.

When Jerry did come that night, her father had been rude, grilling him, poor terrified gay Jerry. And Kelly sat on the couch and didn't move. God, none of them moved. That night she and Jerry went to the senior prom and later, instead of making out, they plotted how to run away, how to get both of them off the base and how to get away to San Francisco. It would be easier for Jerry, they figured; if her dad tried to stop her, Jerry said, use a knife and call; he'd come right over. He took her home then, and promised to come by in an hour or two for her.

She opened the back door to find her father, drunk and waiting. When he came at her, she grabbed the bread knife lying on the counter and sliced his palm open. It seemed so easy, so easy and slow, like opening a can of beer and watching the foam bubble out the top. Like slow motion, watching the foam arch, watching the blood spurt from his hand.

She laid the knife on the counter and knew as she put it down that she could have killed him. He had wrapped his hand in a dish towel and was watching her in astonishment and pain. She spoke the words she had rehearsed for years, warned him not to ever touch her or Kelly again. She walked out then, into the warm night, to wait for Jerry, at the corner, like they'd said.

She waited up all night for Jerry, but he never came. The next day in school he acted surprised when she asked him where the hell he'd been. Well, Jesus, he said, she didn't mean she thought they were really going to do it, did she? What was she talking about? Maybe someday, he said wistfully, well, they would get out of there soon. It wasn't that bad at her house, was it?

She never said another word to him. She finished the school term alone, dating no one, waiting for her father to go away on his next six month cruise. She watched him every night. When she had come home finally late that Sunday morning, he claimed he accidentally cut his hand himself, claimed it even to her. He watched her, but he never touched her again.

She got a job putting greasy hamburgers in a bag at a drive-in, working first shift, and then she walked over to the drugstore and worked late. She worked all the hours no one else wanted. By midsummer, she was able to leave, first by visiting her mother's sister in Portland, and then by going early to freshman orientation.

She didn't come back. Oh, she'd kept in touch, given them her address, and called because she'd promised Nanna that she would look after her mother. Though little her mother had looked after *her*, for God's sake. No, when she left, that was the beginning. And the end.

She looked up abruptly and glanced at her watch, startled at how far she'd walked. So many years since then. And here she was, in San Francisco, teaching computers, with just some asshole in her class. That's all it was.

She stretched her arms out, turned around and straightened her collar and the gold necklace in the shape of a bird in flight that Georgia had given her on their first anniversary. She walked back then quickly, fingering the necklace, muttering to herself that Connor was not her father, thank God. And wishing, as always, that Nanna was still alive, that she hadn't died so soon.

It was when Nanna died that her father had started. If only Nanna was still alive. Oh God, how could she still miss her so much, after all this time? Goddamn Connor. What was she going to do about him? And break was almost over. She began to hurry. Well, fuck Connor. She could do anything she set her mind to. Hadn't Nanna always told her that? And hadn't she? Hadn't she?

And anyway, Elliott would come. And she was a good teacher. Fuck this Connor. Goddamn Irish. She slowed, tossed her gum away and walked in to class.

Amelia and Jackson smiled apologetically. Well, where had they been during Connor's attack? Solidarity, like hell. She didn't look back at them. She didn't look at Connor. She just kept on teaching until it was time for lunch.

Elliott was wonderful at lunch, reassuring her, telling awful Irish jokes and then winking at her as they went into class. She introduced him and he swung into action, just like in the old days when he was teaching her to teach. Shut that asshole right up. Ran right over him. Got into the machine code and began to switch back and forth between the code and the program. Made his examples more and more complex. Made Connor back off without humiliating him, even when it was clear he hadn't a clue to the difference between the code and the program.

And finally, he emphasized Connor needed to get through this class first, before he could even begin to know how to ask the kinds of questions he was wanting an answer to. Even though she was sitting behind Connor, Morgan held a hand over her grin, because Amelia and Jackson periodically turned to look at her.

By the end of class, she was relieved and grateful. But by then, Elliott had to leave, and she could see the color washed from his face, making him seem even more exhausted than usual. Again, she touched his arm, kind of clapping him, like men do sometimes to each other, when they don't know what to do to say thanks.

She stayed after in the classroom, straightening up, replaying the scene in her mind, what she could have done differently, what she would really like to say to Connor. Then she realized Amelia had come back into the room and was standing there, looking at her as though she thought something was wrong.

"Why, Amelia, did you leave something?" she asked, putting her teacher face back on. Amelia stood there for another moment. Then, not looking at her, she began to speak and Morgan was dismayed, understanding finally what was coming. Usually it was a man who came to her after class.

But this time, it was shy Amelia, asking her if she'd have lunch with her the next week. It was lovely, but it wasn't something she did. Elliott and she had agreed long ago that the disruption to the class, not to mention business, was too great.

She looked at Amelia and tried to explain it to her, trying to let her know she shouldn't take it personally. But Amelia stumbled away, nodding in agreement and shame, and left quickly. Well, it couldn't be helped, Morgan sighed. She picked up the last of her things and moved slowly towards the bus stop and was grateful the class had run late so she'd have a seat, which she never would have had at rush hour.

She was tired. Elliott had been great though. And nobody had made any cracks yet about him. They might these days, the way people were treating gay men now. But even Connor seemed to crumple under his charm and expertise. Still, what would they do if he couldn't teach anymore? Jesus. Jesus God, she wished there was somebody she could talk to who would understand.

She rested, her eyes closed, her head against the back of the seat. Well, maybe when she got home, she and Georgia could talk, maybe she would get another coach to take over the team, or at least think about ways to cut her schedule down, ways to be home more. Maybe they could talk about how far away Georgia seemed. About how she missed her. About how fucking hard it was to do this work almost alone.

And maybe this time, Georgia would understand. Maybe she could help her figure out why she was so exhausted. Maybe they could talk. Maybe she would just be there for a little while and listen. Maybe it would be more like it used to be.

But when she got home, it was too quiet; Georgia was waiting at the door. There'd been another phone call. From her father. Her mother had taken a bad turn and the doctors were saying she'd had another stroke in the night. Her father said she was really dying now. And that he wanted her to come home directly. Just as he had last month. And Georgia didn't know what she should do. She needed to talk.

But when Morgan suggested she wait, like last time, Georgia seemed to turn away. Too late, she realized she'd said the wrong thing again. When she suggested Georgia should go ahead and go, Georgia said no, no, Morgan was probably right. And then it was as though Georgia just vanished in the air.

They ate in silence. After dinner Georgia suggested a walk and they went out into the coolness and fog of a night in the Haight. They didn't talk. And in the silver mist, Morgan got angry again.

How could she do her job effectively under this kind of pressure? Every day, it was something new. She never said the right thing at home; Georgia wasn't there anyway, and she couldn't sleep. No wonder Connor came after her today. Goddamn it, why didn't Georgia just do what she wanted? Go home; stay; but decide. She said nothing though, and they walked quietly home and silently got ready for bed.

Sometime in the night as they slept, Georgia twisted away from Morgan's outstretched arm. Morgan woke huddled against the cold and remembered she had been dreaming about hunting animals and tearing meat off bones cooked on an open fire, as though there were no more civilization; a war had swept it away. She had cracked a bone open and sucked out the marrow before she realized it was her own thigh bone.

She had been looking down at the bloody stump when she woke. Georgia woke with her, and tried to gather her into her arms, but Morgan had moved away, over to the edge of her side of the bed, and lay there without sleeping, until the alarm went off for the last day of that week's class.

She walked in that morning feeling haggard but little else, trying to concentrate on the lesson, on the round-robin, spelling-bee type of review she always did on the last day of class. She taught without jokes that day and without pleasure. Connor was subdued anyway, and the class chastised from Elliott's lecture. Amelia wouldn't look at her. Jackson's cracks fell short. Morgan felt cold and lonely. And all she could say was that she was so glad the week was over. God. Another day, another dollar.

CHAPTER FOUR

THE FIRST FEW WEEKS

Elizabeth Bathory, deciding one last time against the gray in favor of the blue, changed her suit again. With an impatient pull at her slip, she sat in front of the mirror of her grandmother's mahogany dressing table. She fanned both sides of her floppy bow tie, gave her soft permed brown hair one more pass with a steel bristle brush and then, holding back the long wave that always fell over her forehead, misted her hair slightly with spray.

And then she looked intently in the mirror. Setting the spray bottle back down on the glass top without looking, she clasped her hands in her lap, sat up straight, tried to see herself as if for the first time. She smiled her reassuring-a-patient smile.

"Okay? You look fine. Look, it's only a training session." She glanced up at her hair again. Try as she might, it was never right. Honestly. She looked away and shook her head as if to shake off her frown, forgetting her hair for the moment, but remembered it anxiously as she felt it moving. She glanced back at the mirror, and saw, surprise, her hair had held, still looked like it grew that way.

"See, Wolfie?" she said out loud. "Your hair isn't so bad. And after all these years of training, you should be able to do well in a class. You look good enough. Stop worrying."

"Okay?" She leaned over and unplugged the curling iron, then sat up straight again. The frown returned to her image.

Keep it up, Shorty, you'll have wrinkles by forty, Bebe's old tease echoed in her mind. She sat still as a mannequin, covered in the cobweb of memory. She heard Bebe's voice again saying, you look fine, Wolfie, and with the sound in the silence, she was able to move.

She put on a touch of lipstick, put the tube back in its place and stuck her tongue out at herself.

Then she really smiled, stood up and pushed the dressing table bench away. She said out loud, "You idiot. You *would* think this was a big deal. Just get going. You really don't have time to think about this." She arched her eyebrows in the mirror one more time and humming, stepped into her blue spectators.

She hurried to the bathroom, her heels beating out her haste on the hardwood floors and clicking on the tile of the bathroom. At the far end, she leaned over and opened the bathroom window for Minx to come and go as he pleased. She turned and nearly fell over him as he raced through her legs. He watched her warily from his post in the open window over the top of the toilet.

"Trying for orphanhood, young man?" she growled at him as she caught her balance on the side of the shower. "Don't break the leg that feeds you. Otherwise, go for any other human you see. Guard the house like a good boy today," she said as she hurried back to the kitchen. She pulled her briefcase off the table on her way out the back door, and clattered down the three flights of stairs to the garage.

After she slid into her onyx Saab, she checked her hair one more time in the car mirror before driving off to the hospital. *Why wouldn't it look right? Why had she been cursed forever with thin, wimpy, useless hair?*

And that wasn't all, she thought, backing on to Connecticut Street. Her face looked a little puffy too. But maybe it only looked that way to her. Or maybe it was puffy because it was so early. Imagine teaching at this hour! She shook her head in distaste and then, at the first stop sign, checked one last time in the mirror.

All right. Maybe her hair was going to look okay today. That, at least, was a relief. And for once, her skin was clear. Anyway, it would all have to do. Honestly. This was more time than she'd spent in years on how she looked. She looked fine. It was all nonsense.

She drove the short but hilly mile in edgy, early morning traffic, and it took her only ten minutes, garage to garage. She nearly sideswiped a car as she drove in. Swinging into a parking place, she thought, this really is too early. Can't drive this early. Terror on the road. Or at least the garage. Smiling, she shook her head and locked up the car, humming the rest of the sax line from Kenny Loggins' new love song.

She walked over to the hospital, stopped for a croissant-and-coffee-to-go at the hospital cafeteria and then waited impatiently with the thundering hordes of students and patients for the weary elevator. They packed themselves in like cattle, and she held her briefcase in front of her for protection.

When she finally pushed through the crowd to get off on the tenth floor, she was momentarily surprised to find her door closed and locked. Then she remembered she'd given John the week off. Cursing under her breath, she fumbled with her briefcase, croissant, coffee and keys, before putting the briefcase down in front of her door and trying to get the key in the lock. Her coffee dripped out from under its lid onto her shoes. Damn. She put the cup down on the floor next to her briefcase, balanced the croissant, and bent to the lock.

Elizabeth E. Bathory, M.D., was spelled out in blue letters on white plastic just above her bent head. And then, on a separate plaque below hers, in smaller letters, John St. Pierre. She relaxed slightly as the key turned in the lock, and she looked up.

Just the sight of the lettering gave her satisfaction, even after a year, even though the door with the nameplates led into the smallest office and lab in the entire department. She pushed the door open with her fingertips and took her key out. The department chair, Richardson, had done everything he could to deny her lab space for the last three years. In the end, she'd only gotten it after James had created a stir about the department having no women chief investigators, not even one old ugly married one, during the last year's annual meeting with the Associate Dean.

She stooped to gather up her coffee and the rest of her things. It wasn't that James cared about the advancement of women, she knew. Or about her advancement. Hardly. But his ploy worked as he wanted. Two days after that meeting, Richardson had come to her corner in James' lab with a lot of fanfair. And given her this closet. It was a closet, really. She knew it and they all knew it. But she didn't care.

She didn't care what any of them said. James had come out of his office that day and watched the whole thing with a smile on his thin lips. After everyone had left, while she sat at her desk and pretended she had charts to finish, he'd said, "Congratulations on your new closet." She glared at him, but he just smiled. It was so like him. To make the cut when no one was around, so she would know he could do it at any time, so she would know he was in control.

She remembered him smiling. He was happy; with her moving, he had more space in his lab for more graduate students. And it also meant she owed him. Well, let him think what he wanted. He owed her plenty too. It was her work he was floating on. She pushed the door in with her hip, her hands full. Here was all the proof she needed; no matter what Richardson or James said, she'd won round one.

And there was always next year. Then more funding. More staff. Eventually, a secretary. And eventually, Richardson would have to give her more space. Eventually, he'd be gone. But she would be here. As long as this children's cancer clinic was the best in the city, she'd stay, doing all she could.

The sun streamed in over the glassware and spotless equipment and she felt it move through her, reassuring as a touch, as she walked back to her tiny office. She set down her things and turned back towards the lab.

This was *her* lab. And she kept it, or rather had finally trained John to keep it, the way labs should be kept. So different from a lab run by men. It was a wonder they discovered anything at all. Even with as much time as they usually wasted. She walked over to the windows and adjusted the blinds.

She turned, judged the light better, and looked over the familiar arrangements. Her eyes focused on the new and hideously expensive little computer system. At John's urging, she'd finally written the funding for it into the grant, and the money had come through.

Well, they did need it, she thought grudgingly. There was no way they could assess the new test protocols without it, but she grimaced as she looked at it. She hated computers. She finally got the lid off her coffee without spilling it and stood in the doorway between her office and the lab. As she took her first sips, she looked at the new machine. God, they overcharged for scientific equipment. They'd never get away with it on the open market.

She blew over the surface of her coffee. But if the machine freed her up from the endless equations, well, maybe it would be worth the cost. And it couldn't be that hard to learn. After her residency, nothing could be hard to learn. And John didn't seem to have much trouble last week. Of course, that might have been the teacher. Well, she thought, we'll see this week, won't we?

She walked back to her desk, sat down and looked out towards the ocean. The city seemed to drop away; the streets ran right into the blue-gray waves, and she could feel the water against her skin still, the first drop into cool blue, the same crashing motion, rubbed helpless against the sand.

She stretched against her chair and wondered once again, as she had for much of the weekend, about the computer teacher, Morgan McCormack.

If she had to deal with computers this week, at least she'd have something nice to look at. Oh stop, she thought immediately. She was acting just like a man; that's exactly the kind of thing Richardson would say. She shook her head ruefully. But was she supposed to have no reactions? Not only was she supposed to provoke no man to sex, but she was to have no feelings herself?

Well, McCormack *was* gorgeous. And there wasn't anything she could do about that. A fool could see it. But was that—well, what about it? She sat up in her chair and pulled herself towards the desk.

Certainly that wasn't what was causing her to act like a dog in heat, hanging around, asking stupid questions? She unfolded two napkins, one for her lap, the other to cover the desk. Caused her to arrange this private series of lessons? Honestly. She could hear her mother. Honestly, hasn't this gone far enough? What about thinking about the woman all weekend? This was craziness.

Elizabeth unwrapped her croissant and began to separate it into small, bite-size torn pieces. It may be craziness, she thought, slowly tearing the croissant. It may be craziness but it was delicious.

You don't know a thing about her, she argued back.

Not true, she answered. She knew some.

She knew Morgan taught computers, owned her own company and had developed all the training programs. She was probably, but not obviously, gay. She was tall, lean and well-dressed. Good clothes and not from this year's pick of the clothing catalogues. That said something.

And you *could* tell some things about a person just from their looks. Morgan carried herself well. She was so sure, so smooth. She was like the woman in a brilliant ice-blue silk moire gown Elizabeth had seen once as a child, when she watched her parents leaving for the evening with another couple. She stared from the balcony, watching the dress and the woman and vowing, determined, some day she too would have such a dress.

Or, she thought as she popped a piece of croissant in her mouth, maybe even then she was vowing to have the woman, not the dress.

Stop it, she thought, shaking her head and laughing a little. You *are* being awful this morning. That may be fine for the weekend, but not for the office. Get back here, and stop acting like a schoolgirl. She took a sip of coffee. For a moment, she was able to line up her thoughts and go down the list as if she were reading a patient's chart.

Start at the beginning, not at the body, she told herself sternly. All right. Here's another thing: Morgan was kind. She was kind to John, especially when he didn't quite get it, which seemed frequent, she thought. But Morgan had been kind to her too, or maybe not kind; they hadn't had an occasion where Morgan needed to be kind to her. They had talked easily, about John, about the computer, about the training program. But it wasn't what they'd talked about, she realized. It was how Morgan had talked to her. She had talked freely. Was that the right word? Or maybe openly? She tapped her fingers on the napkin. Maybe.

She took another bite of croissant. Yes. Openly. Without wanting something. Morgan seemed to be interested in her as a person, not as a doctor, not as a meal ticket. And not as something to fuck. Or fuck over. The ugliness of the word felt sharp in her mouth. Crude word.

Crude business. Much cruder than she'd ever dreamed the business of being a doctor could be. If she had to deal only with her patients, the children who came to her, innocent, hoping she would make them feel better; if doctoring little ones was all she did, things would be different.

But they weren't her only work. To be able to get to them, to help them, to do anything for them besides hold them as they died, she had to do this other work, trying to find some way, some slow research piece, some weapon against the cells that went wild in their little bodies.

And if research had meant only the meticulous lab work that had always calmed her, the slow titration of science, that would have been fine too. But research didn't mean just that. It meant departments. And chairmen. And funding grants and applications. Supplications.

It meant meetings. And talking. Bartering. Selling. Commerce, not science or medicine. How long had it been since anyone in this wing of the hospital talked to her like a person? She tore the croissant pieces smaller. But now, this Morgan, well. It was different. They seemed to be able to talk.

To talk. Like people. She sat then with her hands in her lap and sighed, her voice catching in her throat, aware there was no one else in the lab, that the door was closed and she was sitting there, alone.

Alone, late nights. Alone, early mornings. Alone, working. Alone, except during the day when John came. Most of the time, he was a good worker and she was glad to have him for the cover too. But it was hard to have a conversation with John: everything was a joke or about sex. His next favorite topic was acquiring a new gadget for the lab.

He never seemed to understand she had to raise the money for everything. That she was alone. That it wasn't the same for her as it was for the male scientists he'd worked for. That it wasn't easy. That things didn't just come according to some schedule. That just because she had an M.D., she didn't have the world in her hands.

John didn't understand that. He didn't understand a lot of things. But after all, he was just staff. With James, who *did* understand but didn't care, there were other reasons to stay away from any closeness. With James, she did the work; he signed the papers. It worked out well; it was sometimes friendly, more often truced. But even with him, she worked alone.

She took another sip of coffee, and an old ache stabbed her and spread through her body, bubbling under her skin like hot plastic stretching thin from the fire underneath. With it, the old questions came, as smooth and mean as a lawyer's cross examination. Was this what all of her work and pain had been for? All these years of trying to work around stupid idiots who had graduated from some European medical school and hadn't thought since? Who knew each other from their yacht clubs because they spent more time there than at the hospital? Who talked on the golf course, or over their whores at their out-of-town conventions?

Is this why she'd smiled and dodged all these years? So that she could sit in her office with no one to talk with?

There were the kids, at least, she thought, trying to stave off the flood of feeling. There were the kids. And by God, she'd do something yet. She would. Frankie Boyd's black and blue eyes floated up in front of her one more time. She could and she would. And that's what mattered. She knew it. She knew it.

But to be treated as a person, she thought again. As a whole woman. To talk, just to talk. She was starving to talk to someone. Starving. It felt like she hadn't talked to anyone in years.

Years? She heard herself suddenly and would have stared, coldly, at whoever said that. The cold anger almost encircled her pain.

She took a bite of croissant, trying to swallow the lump in her throat. But it didn't quite go down.

Well, yes. Years. Who did she have to talk to? Who understood any of this? Not John. Not James. Certainly not her department chair, to whom she should have been able to turn if she couldn't talk to James. Theoretically.

But Richardson was infinitely worse than James. He had made two ugly passes at the very first faculty dinner. Finally, and only because of James' string of innuendos, Richardson had stopped bothering her because he thought she and James were sleeping together. Which was disgusting. But better that than the truth. Better for James too, since he *was* sleeping with Richardson's wife. But regardless, Richardson had backed off and gone after someone else. Now, finding her useless, he was just waiting for her to fail, to get the office back for his little underlings. Much less helping or listening, he was now actively working against her.

Well, despite him, she'd gotten this second grant. So what if Richardson had made fun of the money because it was an Affirmative Action grant? Money was money. Even if it was "lady" money as he scornfully called it. Call it what he would, it was still money. Her lady money spent just as well as his boy money. He thought he'd get her out by reducing her department funding? He'd need to think again. She'd worked her butt off for that grant. And finally publicly, politically, gone against him.

Eight months ago, James had introduced her to Agnes Johnson at Wesleyan Hospital after a seminar they'd given there. They discussed her research project, and right away Johnson suggested the two of them collaborate on a new project combining Elizabeth's project and Johnson's latest findings. Agnes' immediate suggestion was that they go after an Affirmative Action grant from City for Elizabeth, since she was young and hadn't gotten any grants before. Elizabeth had been embarrassed at first, but not very when she'd seen the money show up in her department accounts. Johnson had been right all along.

Johnson was only a Ph.D., but she was older, had been around, knew the tricks. Elizabeth could tell by what Johnson *didn't* say. When they had met to discuss the grant application, and she'd asked certain questions, the other woman would smile slightly and change the subject. But very shortly there would be a smart comment, just skirting open scorn towards Richardson's research, and the others in her department. And then, after a tight smile at

Elizabeth's laughter, Johnson would get them both back at work on the application.

Johnson was shrewd, cold, and unapproachable. But for all her distance, she was precise and reliable, Elizabeth had discovered. They'd put together a good, solid application package. And they'd gotten funding. As they should have. It was a solid proposal with an innovative protocol. And a good chance for significant findings.

And Johnson had a name in her circles. Maybe circles Elizabeth should be moving into. If it weren't for the kids, she'd be gone already, rid of Richardson and his hassles. Her smile faded. She looked down and saw the croissant gone and the paper napkin crumpled in her fist. She shifted in her seat to pick up her nearly empty coffee cup and grimaced. Actually, she hadn't worked her butt off. It was still uncomfortably there. This morning, she had weighed three extra pounds for all the eating she'd done Saturday night and that chocolate torte she brought home after getting a couple of videos for the evening. Probably all that went directly on her butt. That's where it always went.

She looked at the flakes remaining from her croissant. Well, that's all she would eat today. At least it tasted good. And here it was Monday. A great day to start getting some of the extra off. Yes. Here it was Monday. Monday of the computer, ugh.

Originally, Elizabeth had hoped to teach herself how to operate the computer by using the manuals that came with it, but when she'd tried late Tuesday night, she was furious to find they weren't even written in English. It looked like English, but it made no sense. By Wednesday afternoon, she knew then that listening through the door while John was taught, and while she was trying to get caught up on her paperwork after doing rounds last week, wasn't going to work either.

Unfortunately, having Morgan teach her meant another week lost. And more money spent. The woman wasn't cheap but she did seem to know what she was doing. And at least if the material was boring, Elizabeth thought as she finished off her coffee, what wouldn't be boring was the teacher. The mysterious Morgan.

There *was* something very mysterious about her, Elizabeth thought, tapping her empty coffee container against her desk. She was gorgeous, but there was this compelling something else too, something in her eyes or maybe... She drifted off, staring at the Sierra Club calendar on the opposite wall. Maybe it was the way she held her hands. Sometimes, it looked like she was hugging herself. Or maybe it was just that she needed hugging. Elizabeth smiled at the picture of Yosemite in springtime.

Maybe *that* was just her imagination. Then again, maybe Morgan had lost her first lover tragically and was now trapped in a hideous marriage, or who knew what? The possibilities for saving her were endless. She grinned then and turned her attention back to her desk, throwing the coffee cup away, straightening things up.

Saving damsels in distress, her favorite fantasy. Well, that was enough of that. You'd have thought she'd given that up after Terry. Let them save themselves, she thought and frowned. And anyway. She didn't even know if Morgan was gay. She'd heard her mention a woman's name to John. But she didn't know if she was a "roommate" or what.

Anyway, so what? So Morgan was easy to talk to. So big deal. Maybe they could talk. Maybe they would have lunch sometimes. Maybe they would get to know each other. Maybe, maybe… well, anything would be better than Saturday night.

When she'd been watching the videos on Saturday night, she stood up and walked away from the middle of a very boring feature film about a woman poet. Some English actress she knew she was supposed to recognize in a ninety minute monologue, barely moving her head. About ten minutes would have been enough. God, save her from artsy-fartsy movies. Enough! What *had* John seen in it? And why didn't they make movies about women who were really interesting?

She'd gotten up in disgust and had gone to look out the window. She stood there for a moment before she realized—looking out over the city, seeing the lights vibrant in the night, the view very romantic—that she was all alone on a Saturday night. Again.

Oh, it wasn't that she hadn't had an invitation. She'd had several. A dance, dinner, movies. But she just didn't care to. She didn't care to. That's exactly what her mother would have said and it was exactly what she meant.

She'd taped on to her bathroom mirror the fortune cookie message that said "Better to be alone than in bad company." She'd put it up right after she'd broken off with Terry. But with Terry gone, a lot of extra time had flooded in. Face it, she said to herself Saturday night, you are as bored with your life as you are with this movie. And she had wanted to cry.

But not this morning. Things certainly *were* clearer in the daylight, she thought. She unfolded her arms, set her mouth in a straight line and turned to put on her white clinician's coat. Certainly she didn't want another lover, not after the debacle with Terry. Talk about cold as ice; even now, three months later, she didn't want to think about Terry. It was always a disaster to date someone who was in a position to affect your professional performance. She'd never date another doctor in this hospital, no matter what ward they were on. Never.

She began to brush her hair. But it was so hard to meet new women. It wasn't as though she could risk being seen in a women's bar. Or hardly anywhere. Except private parties. Where she saw all the same closed faces.

Clones. That's what the gay men called each other and that's what these women were, just as surely as the boys down on Castro. Gay women had their own version of clones. These women, this circle of professional women, they acted like clones, with nothing interesting to say, except who they'd heard was sleeping with who, who was cheating on who and what successes *they* were.

They even dressed alike, with the same clothes and the same expression on their faces, that hard dressed-up-and-watching-women tightness, as if they had some valuable secret; always watching, cold, with the latest expensive clothes, and the barest hint of smoldering sexuality which wasn't on fire or even smoldering after a week. Then it became status and she, the lady doctor, was frequently but not always the prize. She imagined them talking to each other in the women's restrooms. Comparing. But not telling whatever the secret was.

She shuddered. It was hideous. It was enough to make a person go back to men. Well, not quite. But those women, she shook her head. It wasn't really clear to her. Why were they like that? Even Terry had seemed that way at first. Of course, after they'd started to talk, Terry's face warmed.

Right, she said to herself. For about two months, her face and her body warmed. And then, ice again. What was it? If you could, or wanted to get past the ice and their endless inside jokes, a lot of those women must be interesting. Whatever their secrets were. Or maybe, she shrugged, maybe they had no secrets. Maybe they were just hard to get. And empty once you got there. And boring. And she would find she'd rather have been alone. The story of her life.

She turned abruptly when she heard the outer door shut. She was glad then she'd granted John's request for the week off so he could go up to the Russian River and watch the spring. Really, if he wanted to see spring, he should have gone to the desert, but knowing John, he was probably more interested in fauna than flora. Whatever his reasons, it was good for him to be off. After all, he couldn't proceed with the testing if Elizabeth was using the computer, could he? She dropped her brush into her briefcase, fluffed her hair one more time and went out to see who had come in.

She was caught a little off balance when Morgan turned around from looking at the framed posters she'd bought to decorate the lab. She hadn't quite remembered how those eyes looked, light grey and blue, like the ocean after a hard rain.

When Morgan smiled and extended her hand, Elizabeth was taken aback, Morgan's smile was so friendly and open. Well, she thought when she had recovered and gripped the other woman's hand. Well. She *was* as lovely as she'd remembered over the weekend. Maybe more so.

"Elizabeth," Morgan said, as she took her hand, "It's so nice to see you again. I'm awfully glad to be coming back here this week."

Elizabeth smiled in return and let go of her hand, instantly sorry to have done so. She laced her fingers together and thought how very nice it was to shake hands with a woman who actually shook, not crimped.

Morgan was still talking. "John was a very quick learner and was interested in the equipment, which is a big plus. And, as you said to me last week, you're eager to learn too, so I'm looking forward to our week together. It's very pleasant for me to be working with another woman and I'm sure we'll do very well this week. Did you have a chance to think about the application questions I asked you about last Thursday?"

She is gorgeous, Elizabeth thought. Right down to her long fingers. And that hair. She doubted Morgan's hair was permed, and she couldn't quite stop herself from thinking about what it would feel like if she wove her fingers through it. She brought her eyes back to Morgan's and saw no hardness there, only an open searching. Then she realized Morgan had asked her a question.

"Certainly," she said, scrambling for the old interns' trick of answering while asleep after being on duty for thirty-six hours. "Why don't we just hang up your coat and get started?" She extended her hand for Morgan's coat and watched as she slipped it off. Breasts the size of her fist, just the right size, and firm. A chemise showing through the opened top of her blouse and a tanned neck.

Elizabeth mentally shook herself. She was relieved when Morgan began talking about the computer and said to herself silently but no less sharply, this will never do. They did have to work together. And after all, she was paying this woman. She wondered briefly just how much she would cost for everything, before she took herself firmly in hand and started talking computers.

Monday seemed to fly by. As did Tuesday morning. It seemed like a dream, with Morgan's low voice just behind her shoulder, helping her understand, guiding her in and out, laughing softly with her.

When Morgan went out alone for lunch both days, it wasn't because Elizabeth hadn't tried to persuade her to eat with her. But Morgan had been firm and professional, as she had been all last week. She had things to do. Well. So did Elizabeth. She sat at her desk, sipping from a can of diet soda and looking out the window at the edge of the city and the ocean beyond.

Wednesday would be the last full day they had together. And then, it would be just mornings. These two days had gone by so quickly. But not as easily as she'd hoped; there had been a tremendous amount of material. And Morgan wasn't all that great a teacher. At least, Elizabeth thought, Morgan hadn't explained the main program very well yet. Of course, she didn't really have to know all the details anyway; John would do most of it. All she needed was to get the gist of it and she was sure she'd get that by the end of the week.

But in all honesty, she knew neither the computer program nor the teacher was the problem. Morgan was having much more of an effect on her than she'd bargained for. She felt shaken by the woman and was having trouble concentrating. Fantasy was one thing. This was something else altogether. And she couldn't remember feeling like this in such a long time.

She ran her finger around the top of the soda can. Such a long time. She realized with a shock that she had awakened early that morning, eager to get to work. And then she realized that for the last two days she'd been having fun. Forget the computer. The woman was funny. They laughed together most of the time. And she was bright; Elizabeth didn't have to explain much to her. She was interested in everything.

And, one more thing. Maybe the most dangerous of all, she thought, drawing her finger down the side of the can. Morgan was tender with her, even when she couldn't quite get the answer, even though it wasn't her fault.

Maybe that's what was happening. It was unnerving. There had to be some explanation for it, for what was happening to her. Just before lunch, when she had looked down at the keyboard as Morgan was demonstrating, the keys began disassembling in front of her very eyes. Instead, she saw Morgan's hands, tanned, tapered and strong, gently lying on her grandmother's white laced sheets. The ones she kept for special. It had been such a long time since she'd felt like this. She didn't know, maybe, had she ever felt like this?

She shook herself and picked up her soda. These were just fantasies too. God, you'd think she was a child and Bebe was just in the other room, ironing. She needed to stop it now before it got out of hand.

She had a lot of work to do. And not working these last two days had really backed her up. At least she didn't have rounds this week, but there were still her own patients to see. And she was exhausted, needing to spend time with them, but having to see to them after she finished with Morgan each day.

And so she didn't have time for this lack of concentration; she just didn't. Agnes Johnson was expecting preliminaries by the first of next month. That was only two weeks away. She had a lot to do, including taking the first sample for testing on Wednesday night.

Her mind drifted to Jimmy Page for a moment. Another bone marrow test. As if he had a chance. As if they could do a thing for him. And she'd had such trouble getting the needle in his gaunt little back last time. She suddenly felt nauseated. Oh God, why couldn't they help him? How much longer could he hold out?

Her stomach folded in on her and she sat there, still for a moment. And then, finally focusing on the soda in her hand, she took a sip. Look, the fact was, she didn't need this business with Morgan. She was not going to get involved with this woman. Well, maybe as friends. She sipped her drink. All well and good, Bebe said in her ear, but you have to come home on time, before your parents return.

She finished the soda and stood, watching the ocean. Well, maybe she should take a walk, as Morgan had suggested; maybe a walk would be good. She stood, took off her coat, and slipped into her suit jacket. She realized she'd been sweating slightly. She had felt liquid all morning, languorous in her chair, supple and malleable. She wondered if it showed. She wondered if her sweat was from the strain of not letting it show. She shook her head and went out to wait for the elevator. When she got down to the street, she saw a taller woman, red-blonde hair tossed on the top of her head, strong sleek legs covered with sheer hose, black heels, a black Chanel skirt. When she turned the corner, she saw a woman in a navy suit, or a crimson jacket, grey gabardines or any of the other clothes Morgan had worn to train John last week. But, of course, none of them was Morgan.

Elizabeth walked slowly down the hill, then down the next. She felt the sun on the back of her neck like a warm hand, and she wondered what it would be like to have Morgan's hand there, pulling her forward into a kiss. But after awhile, she tried not to. Why waste her lunch hour? It wasn't as though she couldn't think about anything else. She decided not think about Morgan at all.

She began to wonder how long it had been since she'd been out walking at lunch. Maybe a month ago, when she'd met Sylvie downtown for lunch. She remembered feeling that afternoon like walking down to the edge of town, to the ocean, as though time meant nothing and she could just walk in the sun to her heart's content. She felt let loose, then and now. She should call Sylvie next week. It was her turn to call, after all. Good old Sylvie. What would she say about this?

Sharply, she told herself to stop it again. She walked faster, stretching her long legs out, hands tucked in the small pockets of her suit. She didn't think about computers, as Morgan had suggested she try not to. Nor did she keep looking for the other woman.

She thought about Jimmy Page and how she knew she was going to lose him like she had Frank Boyd. She thought about Agnes Johnson and the testing schedule and whether or not it was even possible to keep the schedule. And she thought about how much she needed to do, not for Jimmy or Frankie. But for the others.

For the others she would hold in her arms and sing to before she laid them down on their stomachs, so small on the gurneys. Then she could take a huge needle, and stick it in their small backs, hoping she could find the right place on the first try to draw out some of their bone marrow for testing. Those little ones. She forced herself to think about the protocol, to go over it again, the columns of numbers and equations gradually replacing the children's faces and the ache in her stomach, and she was able to let go some in the stretch of her mind.

When she came back promptly at one, Morgan was waiting outside her office, leaning one slim hip against the wall, a paperback book in her hand, and a smile on her face. Elizabeth felt as though she had been hit from behind and wondered if she had staggered. She stared at Morgan, her heart suddenly alive, her blood racing.

"So, you did go out," Morgan called to her. "Good. You'll be able to concentrate better this afternoon." She looked pleased.

Elizabeth caught her breath at the smile and allowed herself only a slight nod in return. She dipped her head, went up to the door and turned her back to Morgan. But as she put the key in the lock, she could feel the turning, turning in the mechanism, tightening her own body, her legs tightening against one another.

The afternoon passed without a word of distraction. She thought she was beginning to get the program and she felt vastly relieved at the end of the day, as though she had been holding herself tight all afternoon and had finally relaxed.

But, still, she was startled when she heard herself saying as they were leaving, "You know, you're making it awfully hard for me to get to know you. I understand that you have a professional approach to your work and I respect that. But I wondered if you'd join me for lunch tomorrow?"

She felt the words come tumbling out and, embarrassed, quickly turned away, acted as though she were looking at her notes. But when she heard Morgan agree, she looked up and saw the other woman blushing. Her slow smile then felt uncontrollable and she was humming when she finally was able to look in on her patients that night.

During Wednesday's morning lesson, she was circumspect and tried to pay attention, only it was so boring. Push this button, then that. At first when she missed a question completely, she felt like crying, but then she found herself getting irritated. How could she be expected to devour so much information in so little time?

In the middle of Morgan's review of the question, she had to reach over to get the phone, and she was suddenly shy after her right breast brushed Morgan's shoulder. Well, she couldn't help it. She didn't do it on purpose. But she wished she had. Only Morgan didn't do anything except talk about the stupid computer.

Finally, though, at last it was lunchtime. At the stroke of noon, Elizabeth took her down to the Vic, a dark, expensive South of Market grill. Finally, out of the lab! And in this light, Morgan looked less like a stern teacher and more like a woman. A very beautiful woman. Elizabeth looked at her over the white linen and the crystal glasses and felt her legs twist again, like the key in the lock. Morgan looked back and Elizabeth lost her place, became flustered and again said the first thing that came into her head.

"So, tell me now, what do you do when you aren't at work?" she began, tentatively, twisting the stem of her goblet. God, what a stupid thing to say, she thought. And nothing stronger in her goblet to help her tongue than Perrier.

She would have ordered white wine; in fact, had been looking forward to ordering a split for the two of them, but when Morgan had ordered the French water, she'd ordered as Morgan had. She hoped Morgan wasn't the type not to drink, or had a problem with it, but who knew these days? It seemed to be the current rage not to drink. It was a Puritan fad she hoped would pass soon. She was relieved when the other woman didn't bring it up.

"I have a very dull life for someone you think is so fascinating," Morgan began, watching her closely, her face momentarily guarded, but then slowly beginning to smile. Elizabeth felt her irritation slipping away and then, for the next hour, she was aware of nothing past their table.

Over Dover sole and saffron rice for Morgan and a Caesar salad for Elizabeth, they talked. Mostly, Elizabeth asked questions and Morgan answered. She played softball. She coached softball. She had taught children for awhile down at some battered women's shelter. She and Georgia had been together for five years.

So. Finally. Elizabeth nodded but didn't say a word. Morgan continued. She was from Chicago, well, her mother's family was from Chicago. Her father was a Navy man. CPO or something. Whatever that was. Not an officer, but you couldn't help who your parents were.

But she'd certainly made something of herself. This business she'd made. And without too much compromise, apparently. Elizabeth was startled the first time Morgan said the word "lesbian" and was glad they were at a booth at the Vic, where no one could hear them. She looked around anyway, but there was no one she knew there. Morgan was certainly free with her language, she thought with a slight grimace, picking the anchovies out of her salad, and then, surprised, realized what the word was for Morgan.

Unafraid. That's what it was, that confidence. She was free in some way. Elizabeth looked up from her salad and stared at her. It wasn't just saying what she liked; it was more than that. There was no hardness in her face, that's what was missing, that's why she looked so different. She stared at the woman and only turned away when she realized Morgan was blushing.

"I'm sorry, Morgan," she said more softly than she meant to, and was surprised when the rest of the words came out. "It's just that I've never met anyone quite like you."

"Oh, sure you have," Morgan said and laughed, full-throated. "Tell me about your life. What are you researching up there? Do you have a practice, too?"

Later, Elizabeth thought, I should have answered her then, probably. But in that moment, she was taken aback and had fallen into her old fencing. She knew she was doing it and that she was frightened; she just didn't know why. So she fenced. She wagged her finger at Morgan and said, laughing, she never talked about her patients, but anyway, she'd played softball in college and hadn't been able to talk to anyone about it in years. Had Morgan ever heard about the Montgomery Rays? She'd seen them? Her, too. They laughed together. She explained how she used to go to all their games when she was an undergraduate. Weren't they unbelievable? Unbeatable, too. What a team. Amazons.

They smiled at each other, maybe too long, and Elizabeth watched Morgan blush again as she wouldn't look away.

Morgan's heightened color only made her more beautiful and Elizabeth could barely take her eyes off her. And she thought she'd hardly ever seen such a beautiful woman. She watched as Morgan blushed and in embarrassment, looked away and began to comb her hair off her face with her long fingers, those gorgeous long fingers.

It was the first time Elizabeth had seen her undone. She wanted to reach over, calm her hands, tell her not to be afraid. She wanted to pull her chin up with her hands. But she did none of that. Not trusting her hands, she pushed her salad away, leaned forward and said as gently as she could, "Tell me about your softball teams. Really. I'm interested," and hoped Morgan would understand all she wanted to do with those words.

Morgan cleared her throat, looked up, smiled unsteadily and began to talk. Elizabeth cupped her chin in her hand, stopped eating and listened. She didn't know what Morgan was saying. And she didn't really care.

By the end of that lunch together, Elizabeth realized she was visualizing involuntarily. Most often she was feeling Morgan's hands tracing down her body, starting at the palm of her hand, drawing down under her arms, her ribs, her long waist. Each time, Elizabeth would momentarily lose herself, and shudder, the familiar wrenching grasping her again and racing through her body.

Later that evening, much later, after taking Jimmy's bone marrow sample and getting it stabilized for testing on Monday, much later as she stood by the window in the great room of her apartment with a glass of wine, later she said to herself, why not indulge herself? Morgan would be gone soon—and so what did her little mind games matter?

She leaned her head against the cool window for a moment. They weren't going to do anything. Morgan was married. And even if she wasn't, they had nothing in common, nothing Morgan understood about the day-to-day grind of the testing, slow as the dye dripping through a packed test column. She didn't know the anxiety of writing the grants, the wheedling for department support. Nor did she know what it was like to be on rotation and do one more bone marrow on a seven-year-old child, thin, pale, looking seventy, who would be dead before the year was out.

She didn't know what it was like to sing to him while she danced him down to the operating room. She didn't know what it was like to hold him up so he could see the sunset and to have to answer his unanswerable questions, with his trusting hand in hers, with his soft head where she would kiss him goodbye, bald from the drugs she gave him to try to save his life.

Morgan didn't know what it was like to go looking for some of the parents who always seemed to be busy during working hours, to try to get them on the telephone, to get them to take some interest in their own dying children. Or what it was like to lose another one, brittle and fever hot in her arms. Or the race, the hellish race to see if the new protocols would work, if they'd calculated the dosages right. Or to look in the eyes of children made sick by the drugs, and tell them she had to increase the dosage; to meet the eyes of the parents who did stay and say to them, 'It's all we can do.'

She leaned her back against the wall weakly then, rolling away from the window, and thought about those sets of eyes and then thought again about Morgan. Morgan didn't know those things. And she wouldn't. Ever. She wasn't a doctor and she wouldn't ever understand. How it hurt. How it made her frantic. How important it was. How much she loved the children. How they kept her up in the middle of the night. How hard she had to work, how much she had to hold inside, just to keep even.

Morgan couldn't know those things. And so, they wouldn't ever, well, probably after this week, they wouldn't ever see each other anyway. And she would be alone again. There was nothing she could say to Morgan that would make her understand. Even if she could take her to see Jimmy, it wouldn't matter. Because Morgan would be gone in a week or two. Gone. The word vibrated in her head like a drumbeat, and finally she willed herself to let the sound go. She poured herself more wine and stood at the window a long time.

She succeeded that night in turning her face away from Morgan. The rest of the week wore on slowly and too quickly. As the time went on, Elizabeth told herself again and again to get a grip on herself; she told herself not to behave like a fifteen year old. Not to move her chair closer. Not to say she couldn't concentrate. Not to mention how she had begun to think of her away from the office, nor to mention what she had been thinking.

She kept thinking that getting Morgan to talk would help her get that grip. But she found herself agreeing to come to a softball game and wondered briefly Thursday night how that could be. Her at a women's softball game? Now? At this point in her life? She shook her head when she realized that's exactly what she was going to do.

They had gone to lunch together again on Thursday. That day, Morgan talked about her business, talked and talked, almost as though a dam were breaking inside her. It was terrible about her partner, what was his name? She mentioned her worries about John. Morgan didn't answer. They were silent for a moment. Sometimes she thought it was their own fault, the way the men had sex; sometimes she thought John had acted just like an animal. But it wouldn't do to mention it. Men and women were just different that way. Always had been. And in any event, knowing that didn't change anything. The men were dying, no matter what. To talk about it now wouldn't make it any easier for Morgan. How hard it must be for her, having so much invested in the business.

And it was sad really, how she'd talked. As if she hadn't anyone else to talk to about it. And she realized as she thought about it, late Thursday night, Morgan had hardly mentioned this Georgia person. Oh, she mentioned her like a wife, but not like a lover. And she had brushed aside her questions about Georgia. Well, Elizabeth thought, that doesn't mean anything.

But there were other slight, clear signs that Elizabeth found herself treasuring, going over and over in her mind, watching Morgan again and again as she had watched her as she taught. She hadn't seen them before Wednesday afternoon, but she was certain she had seen them after.

She watched the other woman not move away when their knees touched, nor draw back when their hands brushed. And she felt the current returning, in different ways: sometimes from Morgan's body, more often from her eyes. It was as though electricity streamed into a mirror, reflected in a mirror, and the current went wild and gathered strength in the reflection.

It felt beyond fantasy then, but still, Thursday night she cautioned herself, as she lay in bed alone, looking out over the city lights, no. Not even if Morgan acted interested, nothing was going to happen. And she promised herself she would not say a word to Morgan or make a move, one way or another. After all, Elizabeth repeated to herself, it never works out like this. You have nothing in common. This is worse than Terry.

And she was married, just like Terry. Time to stop. Stop. I've called you twice now, Bebe said. Don't make me call three times.

It can't work. And besides, she thought, as she felt her throat swell with loneliness, as she cast about to quash the little scream in her throat that said why can't it ever work, she shouted over that cry, besides, she wasn't a homewrecker. She was a doctor, and a damn good one, and she had work to do.

But the memory of Wednesday after class stuck with her and she saw that memory, instead of the night lights flickering across the city. Morgan had gone to change in the restroom across the hall for a game right after work, apologizing as she left the office. When she came out of the restroom with her makeup off, heels traded for sneakers, an oversized blue jean jacket covering a soft short-sleeved T-shirt and a clean pair of jeans, Elizabeth found herself meeting her in the hall, while they waited for the elevator. Elizabeth wondered if that was how she would look on a Saturday morning.

As Morgan began to zip up her jacket, Elizabeth just barely caught herself before she reached over, and slipped her arm around, in between the jacket and the light T-shirt and drew her close, lacing her other hand into the wildness of that glowing red hair and pulling Morgan's mouth on hers.

She abruptly turned her face to the window and managed not to make a move towards Morgan. She shifted her briefcase from hand to hand and thought she might have to lean against the wall for support. She was glad when the elevator finally came.

Friday morning she woke with the woman's name on her lips and soaking wet. Well, Bebe said, you've done it now, young lady. And she knew it had to stop. It had to stop before she fell in love. Before she made another move, she tried to make a diagnosis. Well, if it wasn't any different from the other ones, and she was sure it wasn't, she knew, if she really got to know Morgan, she wouldn't like her. It always happened that way.

So this time, she would save herself some heartache. She couldn't sleep with her. And she wouldn't. She would get to know her, sure, that was okay, find out more about her. And maybe they would be friends and maybe they wouldn't. But this time, she'd do it right and it wouldn't hurt so much. That's what she would do. It would be okay.

She told herself that over and over. But she hadn't been her usual controlled self when she'd invited Morgan to dinner the last thing on Friday morning as they were wrapping up, and she'd been surprised when Morgan had responded. When she asked, Morgan smiled slightly, as though she'd been expecting Elizabeth to do so, turned her head away and said, 'Sure, when.' And then she ran her hands through her hair, and Elizabeth got distracted and couldn't answer right away.

Morgan looked at her when Elizabeth didn't answer, and said, "Well, how about Wednesday?"

"Sure," Elizabeth managed to say. She closed her eyes, trying to stop the electricity pouring from those gray eyes into her. When she opened her eyes a second later, Morgan had gotten up to get one of the computer manuals and Elizabeth, relieved, wrote down directions to her house and her phone number. Morgan said thanks and grinned at her but hadn't called.

Just as well, Elizabeth thought. Just as well.

CHAPTER FIVE

OAKLAND LIGHTS

Hey girls! Good morning, good morning. Well, I see y'all found your way. Hey, Nancy! Good to see you again! Stand up here and give me a hug. How's every little thing? We surely did miss you last week. Wait until you hear.

Oh, she told you already? Too good to keep it to herself, I expect. Well, I got more in store this week. And we ain't even got to the sex part yet. You'll like that part. Oh sure. I know all about you girls from Moline.

Nance! Why, listen to you, girl! You must be meaning somebody else. I don't have a slutty bone in my body. I swear. Not a one. You go ask Annie; she'll tell you. I'm as upright as a deacon.

Girls! Please! Ain't y'all got no manners? Y'all are hurting my feelings now. I am truly, truly shocked at y'all's behavior. I just don't have those kind of thoughts, myself. And anyway, there are no sluts where I come from. Only belles and honest, God-fearing married women. And the belles don't live where I live. No, ma'am. I've hardly met a belle, myself, though if she looked good, I might look back.

Me? Why I'm married, Roo, you know that. Look out now, here's Bruce and we ain't even looked at the menus.

Bruce, these women are after me. I can't keep up lest you let me have some coffee. Y'all want coffee? Make it three, please, sir.

Now, I admit to y'all, there was a time when I was younger that I may have been corrupted some by you Yankees. I'll allow as how that might be the case. You outside agitators! I know all about you and your fallen ways. I hardly know why I associate myself with such trash.

Maybe because we all sink into the same gutter every so often. Lord, it's good to see you girls.

I know it. But is it all that early? I'm sorry, Roo. I don't know what gets into me. I'm always like this in the morning. Never too early for me. Drives Annie wild. Why, ain't y'all awake yet? Shoot, it's almost nine. The day's half over.

Look, here's Deb. Hey, girl! Come on over here. Sit right down. Good thing you got here; we were about to give your seat away. See, it's this one, the one what's got your name written on it. Here, let me clean it off, brush that egg away. Steady, girl. Whoops, Roo, save me, she's swinging again.

Don't hit now, Deb. Don't hit. I bruise easy. Give me a kiss instead. Look out, look out for the glasses! Don't be knocking everything over, girl! My Lord, a person just can't take y'all out in public, can she?

Thank you, Roo, yes, get her in her seat, will you? I swan I don't know what I'd do without you. You settled down Deb? Can we start now?

On the word of Lady Deb, I call this meeting to order. No, we ain't said hardly a word. I just got here myself and Janie called just before I left the house; said her game had been switched to this afternoon and she had promised to take the kids to the park to skate. So it's just us.

No, Deb, nobody had trouble getting here, did you girls? Got lost on the way over? You got your specs with you, hon? That why you almost set on the egg? Now, girl, you know this place ain't all that much out of the way. And besides. They're the only place in town what's got decent grits and the biscuits are to die for. Well, I know it's not exactly near any of the fields we're on today. But I had to, girls. I mean, I had to put y'all in the mood. For the story I mean.

Cut it out now, Deb. My Lord, you sure come to the right table. Everybody's got it on the brain today. This what happens when you get a pack of women umpires together? Wild, y'all are *wild*. Where's the moon today? In sex?

Okay. Okay. Yeah, they know me here, but we best settle down anyway. We can get Bruce to come around when y'all ready to eat. I know it's right early for eating; I can't myself until coffee gets recirculating with my blood. Transfusion time, girls.

In the meantime, that's right Roo, in the meantime, back to the story. Aren't y'all dying to know what happened? I knew it! I knew you'd get hooked, Deb, you little trout you.

Here's the coffee. Good. It is good, ain't it? Somebody remind me where I left off, will you? Oh, right, Debi. Mmhum. Now I want every one of you look me in the eye and tell me you don't know this story!

Here we got two smart girls, married to each other, but with problems elsewhere, and even though they love each other, and they not looking for any trouble, in comes the Mysterious Stranger. Now girls, where have you heard this before? Hell, probably more than one of us lived through it. Every five years or thereabouts, we all get up and change partners, right? So what do you think happened?

Not so quick, not so quick, Deb. We don't get to the end until we get to the end. For sure, at the time, I didn't know how things were going to turn out. I mean, I had my suspicions. But like I said, it's only clear at the end, when you can see the scoreboard, so to speak.

I swan, Deb, you got your mind in the street this morning. I was thinking softball, not sex. But girls, for a fact, you can't score a life like you can a softball game. You know? It's more like an ocean than a home run, you know what I mean?

And there were plenty of swells out on that ocean during this time I been telling y'all about; Sweet Jesus, Georgia looked like all-alone Hatteras in the middle of winter, naked in the wind, waded out thigh-deep in that cold gray January ocean, with the rain driving ice sideways into her heart and her with her eyes locked on the shore, not watching on the waves rising up behind her, ready to drag her under.

And sure, I could see all that. I just didn't know the names of all the waves, nor when they was fixing to hit, you know. I mean, I knew one was her work. And one was Morgan being gone all the time. And the worst was waves from an ice storm and those were about her home and her momma. I knew that much. I knew enough to know it was going to be a hard time. Didn't have to watch rings around the moon for that.

But you know, one thing I finally learned about Georgia and me, back when she was giving up drinking, was that I couldn't fight her battles for her. Not that I wouldn't like to. Not that I don't try from time to time. When she gets the way she was when we were waiting to hear about her momma, there ain't much more I'd like to do than pick her up, put her in bed and keep guard at the door until the weather clears.

But it don't work like that. And so, I knew this time, before I made some of the messes I'd made before, I knew all I could do was be there with her, you know? Just be with her, and if the waves came on, duck as best I could so I'd be there for her when they was gone.

I'll tell you, the water was getting considerable more choppy on account of old Cameron. After that first phone call, George called him back the next day, and he sure enough had changed his tune. Didn't need her right then. Only in a day or two, a week maybe, he'd call back and say, okay, now, come now. It was like that. Come and go.

The thing was, her ma was in one of those in-between states, getting better some, but they didn't know how bad all the damage was, and couldn't say if she'd get back what she'd lost. And then even the parts what she'd got back, they had to teach her to do all over again, like teaching her to talk, like that.

And so, me being a nurse, I understood some of what was happening, and I'd try to explain how it went to Georgia, and sometimes she listened and sometimes she couldn't. Sometimes, she'd call me up when I was working and say, now Bernice, I know you said so and so, but I can't remember. So, you know, it was like that. She was pretty whacked out about the whole thing. Not to mention the rest, which was all she'd talk about some days, you know; she had a regular route worked out between daddy Cameron and bossman Williams and Em.

Well, I took to calling her every other day or so for the month or two after she first found out about her momma. During those months, the days did stretch out. And I think the time business was part of what it was all about for George. You know, that everything don't happen in thirty minutes like it do on TV.

Anyway, I tried to help her hold on. I'd call and say some fool thing, like, hey, have you manifested a gift from the universe of a hit man for the men in your life? Put them out of their misery? Least so you got less to worry about? Like had she typed up notes for to put in their travel kits from old Mohamar about terrorist plans so they'll get stopped at the airport and properly disposed of? Tampered with Williams' Tylenol, that kind of thing?

Now, Roo, come on, they weren't all that bad. Georgia used to laugh at my jokes, really. I didn't mean anything by it; they was just jokes. Revenge jokes. Or gay girl jokes. I'd try to have one of those for her every day. Oh good Lord, yes. Lesbian jokes. Like one of George's favorites was, how do you tell the difference between a bowling ball and a penis?

What, you haven't heard that one, Nance? Oh, it's an old one. You can tell the difference, because, if you really have to, you can eat a bowling ball.

Well, my word. Look at that, even Roo laughed at that one. I know it's a bad joke. It's terrible. That's why it's so funny. See, the thing is, girls, me and Georgie always used to tell each other bad jokes. Now, y'all may not appreciate the finer points of humor, but me and Georgia, well, we used to howl at each other.

It was one of those things a girl could count on, you know. But during that time, not no more. She started sounding real far away when I called her on the phone. She sounded like she was in Alaska, you know what I mean? And it wasn't no problem with the phone.

When I heard that, I decided I'd better go see for myself. So one Wednesday afternoon, I got off early and headed over just before five. I had a bye that night, but nobody at the hospital knew that, so I got gone a little early, at least enough to beat the traffic.

I was glad to get out, too, and not just for Georgia. Patient of mine had died that morning, just a boy really, small gay boy named Willie. He was a good boy and I liked him. Tore me up harder than most. Sometimes I fairly hate being a nurse. This AIDS business going to get worse before it gets better and I hate it, you know?

Anyways, when I got over to Georgia's that night, what do I find but her draped over the couch in her room, looking like she might be dead too, playing old Don Williams on her little tape box. Face all flush, from a bath or maybe from crying, I couldn't tell which, and she was lying there in her ratty bathrobe, just crooning away.

Now, it wasn't like I'd never seen her there, listening to music by herself. More and more, since she'd stopped going to every single game Em ever looked at, when I'd call or come by, George would be in her room, playing her tapes, just listening, or sometimes, listening and reading at the same time. And at first, I didn't think it was such a bad idea, her getting back to her own life. But when I heard old Don that night, it scared me bad.

See, the only time that girl played Don Williams or Patsy Cline of her own accord is when she was getting ready to completely lose it. I mean, she does it when she's getting ready to fall over the edge, like something awful's about to happen and she can't get out of the way fast enough, so she tries not to look and huddles up instead, you know what I mean?

I saw it once when we was in school, when she was fixing to leave me the first time and I seen it a couple of times since. So when I saw her this time, I got chilled. There she was, with Good Old Boy Don, the two of them singing away, done lost they lovers, everything's ruint, might's well die.

Well now, George has made a career of making a fool of herself for love. Not that she's alone on that account. But for George, it's any kind of love. No matter, who. Family, folks, girl friends. I'd seen it before and I thought I was seeing it again.

Naturally, I thought it was about her momma. I thought maybe she'd had another phone call and things was worse. Shoot, I said to myself, two deaths in one day, this is going to be hard.

But no. I asked her, 'Did she hear from Cameron?' 'Nope,' she says. 'Not since last night,' she says.

'Well,' I says?

'Same-old, same-old,' she says, nodding her head in time to the music.

Old know-nothing Georgia. Well, I knew when she got to that place, conversation wasn't going to go anywhere fast, so I just sat myself down on the couch next to her and we listened to the old songs until I could let go Willie some and get my bearings. After awhile, I begun to think to myself, well, things could be worse. She could be still making a fool out of herself over whiskey. Some things were getting better. I mean, at least she wasn't off the planet in that way, you know what I mean?

So I thought about that. And then I looked around at her setting there, eyes closed, nodding with the music and I could see as plain as the nose on my face that she was still off the planet; no matter how she was getting away, she sure wasn't there in that room with me at that very moment. Good Lord, you could practically put your hand through her, she was so gone.

I sat there and listened to Don with her and thought, well, you don't ask somebody if they can see they're about to be hit by a hurricane. You don't ask if it's all right with them, or argue, you know, about the weather. You just get them up and out. Then you can ask them all the questions you want. Anyway, that's what I thought at the time.

Maybe I should have minded my own business, but I mean, at that point, I didn't care if she knew what she was doing when she sat around like that, listening to those folks on the tapes. I knew.

And so I said to myself, get this child out of here. Go some place. Anywhere. But get gone. Get out. Right now.

I looked around, trying to figure how to get her out, and said the first thing what came into my head, which naturally had to do with food, seeing as how it was my dinnertime. And since I was with Georgia, naturally I asked, "Hey, girl, when was the last time you ate?"

She just shook her head, didn't even look up, didn't treat it like a serious question, kept singing softly. Well, I was fit to shake her then, I'll tell you.

"Girl, I did not come over to watch you listening to records. Come on, darling, let's go see what's for supper," I said and grabbed on to her arm, hauled her off to the kitchen, turning the player off as I went.

She pulled her arm free but came along behind me anyhow. We got to the kitchen and I opened the fridge. She sat down at the table and laid her head in her arms. I turned around and saw her like that and let the food go. I came and sat with her. In a minute, she looked up at me sideways. I tried to smile.

"What's the trouble, baby?" I asked, rubbing my hand on the top of her head where she likes it.

She let me rub for a minute and then she shook me off, stood up and went to the refrigerator. As she opened it, she said, with her back to me, "Bernice, I just can't stand this."

I turned around in my seat to watch her. "What? What is 'this,' girl?"

"This is the fourth night in a row she's not home for supper."

"She playing ball tonight?"

"All the goddamn time she's doing something. Old friends, new friends, softball. I tell you, I'm getting sick of it."

My ears perked up then, what with the mention of new friends. Oh my Lord, is that what's happening, I said to myself? I got up and went over to the refrigerator and stood with her. She shut the door.

"Nothing here to eat, Bernice."

"Hold on, girl," I said, opening the door back up. "I seen some squash in there, some tomatoes. Want to fry up some chicken?"

"Don't want to eat," she said, back at the table, her head back in her hands.

"Okay. How about some of these black-eyed peas?" I asked, standing with the refrigerator door wide open.

She didn't look up. "You cooking?" she asked finally.

"No. You cooking for me," I said.

She didn't move, didn't even open her eyes. I tried again.

"I want some peas. You make them for me?"

She got up slowly and nodded, came around and leaned into me. I just hugged her and rested my head back on the fridge. Sweet Jesus, I thought, I have got to get her to talk.

"Get me some music, won't you Bernice?" she asked as she let go of me to get the peas. "I can't cook without music, you know that."

"All right," I said finally and walked back to her room to get the player. All right, I said to myself, but if you think I'm bringing Patsy and Don back up here, you got another thing coming. I squatted down by the tapes. All in order, and just like her to do that.

I looked through. The country was all in the back. Looked like she hadn't played it for awhile. She had all this other stuff in front, jazzy stuff, classical stuff. Must have been what she listen to, since Em. And the stuff I wanted was behind the country stuff. But Em didn't dance, so why should it be in front? Pretty soon, I found what I was looking for and put a couple of them in my sweater pocket and got the tape player.

By the time I got back out to the kitchen, she looked a little better. She was standing at the sink, holding up some peaches.

"You want cobbler?" she asked, kind of wistful-like.

"Is the sky Carolina blue?" I asked. "Make me happier than a pig in mud, girl." I set up the player on the table and pretty soon, fiddle music filled the air.

She stopped frying up the squash for a minute and turned to look at me with a grin on her face.

"That Marie Rhines? God, I haven't heard her in ages."

I grinned, too. Well, they's lots of ways to fight the weather.

"So tell me what's happening in your life, girl," I said, sitting at the table, pretty pleased with myself after clogging around the kitchen table to "Mr. Rick's Rag," dodging her when she put the biscuits in the oven.

But she didn't answer me. She stood with her back towards me, facing the stove. Then she turned everything down, sighed and went over to roll out the dough for cobbler.

"How's work?" I asked.

She didn't turn around, just kept rolling out the dough, fitting it in the pan. Finally, she said, "God, Bernice, let's not get into that.

Tell me how you are. Talk to me about your job. It's got to be better than mine."

Just then, the tape went off. Short-sided. And the kitchen got real quiet. So quiet, I lost my place. And all I could think to do was to get up and put another tape on; get that silence gone, you know. So I got up and for some reason, the first tape that got into my hand was early Marvin Gaye. I put the tape in without watching and he started on.

I turned back to the table, my eyes down, still trying to figure what to say, when she intercepted me and started to dance with me.

Well, you know, when me and George used to date, we really cut a number. I mean, we were *good* together, doing that old shag and bop. We had routines and all like that. So when she caught me around the waist and took my hand, I just started grinning like a fool and dancing with her.

We danced through "If I Could Build My Whole World Around You," "That's The Way Love Is," right through some numbers with Tammi to when he was starting in on "I Heard It Through The Grapevine."

Then she stopped. In the middle of the song. I hadn't been listening, you know, not to the words, up until then. I mean, I was listening to the bass and the beat and kind of singing the words, but I wasn't listening. Until I saw her face.

And then I knew. She turned away from me, finished up the pie and put it in the oven. The tape played on. I didn't know whether or not to turn it off. Finally, she went over and turned it off herself, still, without a word. I just watched her. Wondering how to say what I knew. I watched her shoulders under her sweatshirt as she stood at the hutch, getting the dishes. Watched for a shrug or a hold, watched for the chance to work on some small little toehole, to force the wave to break. But I didn't speak.

"How's Annie?" she asked finally when she started to set the table.

"Annie's just fine. We're doing well. She's working tonight. I'm going to see her after supper. More to the point, girl, how's Em?" I said, deciding to just head into the wave.

She laid the cutlery out nice and orderly. Took her time.

"Oh, Em's fine, I guess. Well, you heard, before. I'm a little mad at her. What with Elliott being gone so much and her coaching and playing both this season, it seems like I hardly see her."

She went back to the hutch and pulled out the glasses. I didn't say a word.

"I guess I'm pissed because I miss her. But you know, Bernice," she said and she turned to the table and her voice got louder. "You know what really gripes my ass?"

I shook my head and took the glass she handed to me.

"I tried to get off for lunch today, to meet her for lunch, you know? And Williams gave me something at 11:30 that he said he needed by 1:00. I told him I had a lunch date. And you know what he said?"

I shook my head and watched her. She was moving faster now, pulling food off the stove and putting it in the table bowls, her face pale, her voice brittle like ice.

"He said, 'Break it. I need this now. I have no interest in your private life.'"

She thumped the frying pan back on the stove.

She mimicked him. "'Break it.' I'll break his butt. I swear he's really pushing it. I've just about had it."

Well, I said to myself, as I put some peas and rice on my plate, well, it wouldn't be the worst thing in the world if you mouthed off to that one and got it over with. Got yourself a decent job. But I didn't say that.

I started to butter a biscuit. "What about that new friend of yours, that one—what's her name—Ricky? Don't she make it no better? Is it getting worse, George?" I asked, still trying to get her to come out with it. "Or are you just feeling it worse?"

"Ricky does make it better. She's the only one I can talk to about this, except for you. I'd have committed murder-suicide without her by now," she said and got herself a biscuit too.

"I don't know if it's just getting worse. Maybe it's just me. Hard to tell. But he gave me a special extra assignment last week, and it was a mess. It was the worst mess. Scrawled, handwritten shit. And no order, no organization. No charts, no research. Just some ideas he'd heard at a lunch. Not thought out. Not applied to the specific situation he'd outlined in about three sentences. Basically, there wasn't anything there. Except a lot of work for me.

"And it really pissed me off. Maybe more than usual, because I knew what it was. It's not like it was a routine assignment. Not like I didn't have enough to do. No, it was one of those special assignments they make them do when they're up for promotion, you know, to see if they can do it. Well, I said to myself, I'll be damned if I'll do his promotion papers too. So I typed it up just the way he wrote it—and why not? He doesn't think I can think, never mind write, so why should I treat him any different?"

She had put food on her plate but she wasn't eating. I watched her as I ate, but she was pointing with her fork, not eating with it.

"I mean, forget my degree. Forget my dissertation. Forget I have a brain." She pointed her fork right at me, prongs out. I just kept eating, and soon, she let the fork down on her plate.

"I'm just his secretary. So let me be just a secretary. Well, that's what I thought then, but now, you know what? Now I know no matter what I do, he'll raise the stakes. And he can, because he owns me. I need that job. And he knows it. If I didn't, I would have quit today; I could have said, here, get somebody else to pick up your socks. I'm not doing it anymore.

"But I didn't. I didn't say anything. I went out and had a cigarette and came back and started on it. And I finished on time for him. And I'll be working on that special assignment this weekend too. Another weekend. And it's pushing back his regular projects. How would I go home even if I wanted to?"

I got up for the honey to drizzle on my biscuit and was back at the table before I heard all what she had said. When I heard it, it made me nervous. So I asked her, "You smoking again? Think that's going to help what ails you?"

I guess maybe I sounded a little more mean than I meant to because she turned away and propped her head up with her hands. Finally, she turned back around to me.

"No, I am not smoking again," she said and her voice was so quiet I knew she was really mad. She rubbed her hands together. "No, I am not smoking. You're right about it, I know. I had one—one—and it tasted like ashes in my mouth. That's what I get from listening to you and your lung cancer talk. You made it sound like a bloody stump. You and Em, who hates it, you know.

"But it doesn't matter about Em, now does it? Frankly I don't even know if she's coming home tonight. She hates me to smoke, hates the smell, says she's going to stop kissing me when I smoke. Says it's bad for me. Well, maybe it is. But who cares? How the hell would she know if I was smoking or not? I should have kept doing it, you know, like a dirt test. Will she or won't she be home long enough to tell?"

I groaned inside. She was pulling out all the stops. There was a bloody stump here all right, and George was beating herself over the head with it. I watched her cry that way she does, with no noise. Poor thing. Finally, I asked "Georgie, honey, you think this talk will punish her? Or you?" and I was trying to make a joke out of it. But it didn't work.

"Shit, who cares?" she asked, wiping her tears off her face with the back of her hand. "Goddamnit, Bernice, I can't do anything anymore, can't smoke, can't drink, can't eat. Only do as I am told. And don't you start in on me. Don't give me any orders. I'm so sick of people giving me orders. I just can't stand it anymore. And I'm really sick of Williams. I don't know who the hell he thinks he is. But if he keeps at it, he *will* be in hell, I can promise you that."

Well, I knew when to keep my mouth shut. I had some more peas. Finally, she started back up.

"I don't know if he's ordering me around because he can't do the work himself or if he just won't," she said. "Some days, I think he's a simple idiot and can't get dressed in the dark. Other days, I think he just can't be bothered. And why should he when he can buy somebody like me? Why should he?"

And then I knew. I could hear it in her voice, like the bass line. It wasn't in her words. It was the way she bit them off, like they was poison. Well, they were. I knew what she was doing. She was hating herself for him. She was hating herself for several of them. And it tore me up to see it. And I knew, I knew if we sat through too much more of this, there'd be no lion. Only a poor whipped girl, standing at the edge of the ocean.

But she went on before I could think what to say.

"Bernice, I don't know what to say to him when he gives me that kind of stuff and says he needs it by Monday and then walks out. I can't think of a word to say. It is such a shock to me that people could treat each other like that.

"I mean, I just don't get it. I wouldn't treat a dog the way he treats me. And I'm always so surprised by it. You'd think I'd get used to it by now. But no. I go back for more. And I can't ever think of the right words to get him off me, you know? To let him understand what he's really doing. So, like today, I just look at him. And he just stands there, almost out the door with his head down; he knows when he's doing wrong. He knows. But like today, he just goes on out, and I just sit there. And take it. But what was I going to do? What the hell am I going to do?"

Well, I said to myself, she's asking me. She's asking me. I might's well say it.

"You could quit. You know that? You could quit and get you a job where they treat you right. Why don't you ever just tell the fool off? Give him the *correct* time of day? Why do you wait on him, girl? Where's your lion, honey? Where?"

There was silence then. I put my knife and fork down like Shirley taught me and they hit the plate together and clattered in the silence. Well, I knew I'd messed up bad. And sure enough, the ice came rolling in like a winter hurricane.

"What kind of a job that treats me right? Doing what? You think it's better anywhere else? Do you? It was exactly like this at the hospitals, at every clerical job I've ever had, and at the History Department when I was a grad student. You know that as well as I do. You have a better idea? Maybe got a job for me?

"Sure, I have a job where they treat me bad. I did it. It's my fault," she said, her voice deadly cold. "I did it again. I been doing this kind of thing for these assholes all my life and I don't know how much longer I'm going to be able to keep doing it.

"I just can't believe this is worth it. What am I doing with my life? I ought to be doing something besides running after some idiot who can't tie his shoes. Damnit, Bernice. I am wasting my life. Wasting it. I don't get wasted myself anymore, but what the hell is the point of all this?"

She took a ragged, deep breath. I was getting ready to say something, when she said, real low, "Em says she thinks it might be part of my recovery program to keep this job and okay, I'll buy that. I never, in my whole life, had a job that lasted this long. My *father* never had a job that lasted this long. But am I supposed to die for it? Jesus, this can't be right."

I thought maybe then I'd been mistaken about the ice and I took her hand and rubbed some and she held on back and looked at me and tried to smile, but I could tell she was having trouble. She tried again, wiping her eyes and her nose with the back of her other hand.

"Oh hell, Bernice. It's not just work. It's everything, you know?"

I held on to her hand tight.

"Tell me what you got on your mind, George," I said, quiet as I could.

She took another deep breath. "Well, it's my mom, you know," she started, her voice low. I nodded. Then her voice got stronger.

"And, then, I'm really disgusted with myself, but I've been doubting Em. Just because she's not home. She's not really doing anything. Not fooling around, I mean. And I know that. I know she loves me. And I know she's feeling sad too, what with Elliott and all. And you know, I don't think she ever got over the shelter, I don't. I think that's why she's doing so much softball."

I nodded and held on. I thought so too, to tell you the truth. But I didn't want to stop her by saying so.

"I know she's got troubles, and I try not to think about how much she's not home. At first, I thought I was just being paranoid. But then—then, after awhile, I don't know. I don't know. It seems like I don't know what's happening with Em anymore. We. used to talk about everything. Now all we talk about is what our schedules are. We used to be together; we used to be in each other's pockets all the time."

She turned away, started chewing her lip and then said, "And now, now I think she's together with somebody else; I think she's talking to somebody else. I think she's talking to this woman named Elizabeth. I know they have lunches together. I know Elizabeth has been to at least one of Em's softball games. Maybe more. I don't know. I stopped going to the games."

Her voice had gotten lower and lower. She'd not been able to look at me. And then she turned, and I could see she was crying and she looked me straight in the eye and said, "Bernice Sophia, if it's true, I just can't sit by and do nothing," and turned to the tape player like it was another person at the table.

I sat there and thought, Sweet Jesus, we are in it now. But she might make it this time, I thought and I started to say 'Keep talking baby,' when she took her hand back, wiped her eyes and lifted up her hands and said, "Goddamnit, what's the use? This is stupid. I don't know why I'm saying all this. What is the point?"

All of a sudden she got up from the table and said, real quick-like, "Bernice, it was nice of you come over here, really. And I did enjoy making you some food, but now it's late. Annie's probably waiting for you to come home. Go on home now. Least you got a home to go to."

Well, I saw her being sad, and I was sorry about it, but, I swanee, sometimes I just want to knock some sense into her. Maybe I was just mad because I thought we'd almost made it through, but ever since I been knowing her, they's times she gets to thinking she ain't ever going to get what she needs, so she just closes her eyes.

I can't stand it when she does that. And I forgot I was feeling bad for her then and just let fly. I mean, I probably shouldn't have, but I did.

"What do you call this, girl?" I asked, gesturing to the table and maybe talking louder than I meant. "Just what do you call this place you are in?"

"Well, it ain't home, you know that Bernice. God, I just want to go home. I mean, not home home. But I want a place to go home to, don't you know, Bernice?" she asked, turning her head away so I wouldn't see she was starting to cry again.

Well that just about did it for me. I mean, what was I? What had we just been doing if it wasn't making home? I watched her, with her head turned away and her hand over her face and I was mad, I mean it. But then, I suddenly realized, maybe she didn't have no idea what we had just done. They probably didn't do it like that where she was from. Not from what she'd said about her folks; I doubted it.

So, when I spoke again, I tried to be soft. "Georgie girl," I said, real slow, hoping I could explain it to her, "You got a home here. You just made me a fine meal, just fine. Smell how it smells here. It smells like home to me, don't it to you? I mean, if you want a home, you just got to make this your home. You got to put some of that love you got into it, don't you know that? Start treating it like a home and it might start acting like one," I said, soft as I could.

Well, she couldn't see it. She just stood there by the table, crying, shaking her head. Now, you understand that I love the girl. I didn't want to watch anybody beating on her, even if it was her own self. I decided to take matters in hand. Couldn't make much more of a mess than was already there.

Shoot, I knew what was going on. Sure, I knew. Same thing as I had done when my momma took sick. Never mind what Em was or wasn't doing. What Williams was or wasn't doing. It was George I was worried about. And it was different details, but the same story as when my momma died.

Now you know that puts a woman through some changes. I mean, I don't care how a mother and daughter feel about each other, that's one of the ones God gives you to see how you coming along. Well, she was supposed to get a little crazy about then. I mean, ask me. Lord knows, I ain't forgot how it felt for me.

Some, if you ain't been through it, you can't imagine how it breaks your heart, tears it in shreds, bit by bit, night by night. Sweet

Jesus, it's like you still a little child, screaming and sobbing at the top of your lungs from seeing the Devil and his wickedness all night long and nobody never hears you, nor comes to comfort you. And it goes on, not just one night, but for a long long time. And every night, it's the same. I'd of been dead if it hadn't been for Shirley and Daddy too, I swear to God.

You beginning to get the picture? All right, now wait, they's more. You remember me telling you the part about how everything jumps in? Well, all kind of things happen, and you get confused, and pretty soon it begins to look like your whole life is falling apart, which it is, believe me. If one of your folks is dying, your life, as you known it, is falling apart. And some of us make what's happening on our outside match what's happening on our inside, so we can see what's happening inside. It's a mite easier if you don't do that. But I did. And so was George doing it.

And I know she didn't think she had a choice. If you don't think you have a choice, you don't have it, you know? And then it gets to be this kind of sink-or-swim method of living. It ain't a great way to go, but if you don't know no other way, you just got to go ahead and do it. And if you got to swim, and you ain't had lessons, you had best pay attention. I mean it. Paying attention's the only way to make it, if that's where you are. And I knew that's what I had to help George to understand. You can't sit there and let things just beat you to death.

Not that we don't let ourselves get beat until we're bloody. A whole lot of us. A whole lot of the time. And me too, sometimes. Lord, I do believe we been trained that way. George's favorite, like a whole lot of women I know, was to say things was just fine. Like everything's just fine when the witch from Oz comes and stands there with you, only you can't see her moving her arms around in a circle and cackling to beat the band and saying 'Poppies, poppies.'

I'm telling you it ain't fine. And that business like what George was doing, that old this-is-how-life-is business, ain't fine. That's a crock. I'd believe that lie if I couldn't see, before my very eyes, that it ain't life, it's sleepwalking. It ain't fine to be asleep in the middle of the road and can't move because you're asleep, and they's a chicken truck bearing down on you going sixty miles an hour, and you setting there asleep and in the middle of the road, you know what I mean? It ain't fine. And it ain't life. It ain't no kind of joke. It's just a way to teach yourself how to die.

Well, I tell you, I'd had about enough of that. If Em wasn't going to come home, if Williams was going to act like a fool, if her daddy was going to give her no help, George was going to have to learn it all at once, by herself. And I aimed just then to make sure she got half a chance.

Thing was, Georgia couldn't wait no more for someone else to love her and save her. She could well die waiting for them. Or die for sure trying to get Em to do it and kill what the two of them had in the meantime. Especially since it sounded like Em had her own hard stuff on her plate. You understand what I mean?

We usually get our girlfriends to take care of us when we can't swim, but it's a mistake. You just got to fill your own self up instead of always filling up somebody else and waiting for your turn, you know? Because the thing is, if you're born shaped like a girl, somebody somewheres always going to need it more than you.

It wasn't about Em, don't you see? Or the rest of them. It was about Georgia. What I'm getting at is that George had to make her home in her heart, mother or no, Em or no. She kept moaning about Carolina. Well shoot, I miss Carolina too, you know? But that ain't the point. She wasn't there and she couldn't be there. Not to live. No way.

And it wasn't nice, and it was sad, but it was what was. I mean, if she wanted a home—and she was going to need one after all this—she had to make a home, that's all. She had to learn to make it herself. And not just a place to live, but a place to be. A place in her heart she felt proud of and work she was happy to do. I mean, she had a job, came home with a paycheck, but with a sad bitter heartache too.

And I seen that before; all my life I seen Daddy come home with that kind of heartache, and I'll tell you, I couldn't hardly stand to see it in Georgia. I couldn't bear to watch them beat her down. It ain't that her job was that bad, not hard labor nor the dust, you know, what's making it so Daddy'll die from his lungs filling up on him, drownt on his own fluids, and him never able to swim, much as he loved the ocean, never went in for fear of drowning and now this. I tell you it ain't right.

But they's lots of ways to kill a person. And shame is deadly as dust. Georgia's job was humiliating her. And Lord, you can kill a person that way, not the same as with the dust, but just as deadly all the same, you know what I mean? I mean, I don't know which is worse. I seen them both. And I said to myself that night that I would not watch it again.

I sat there at the table, my plate pushed away, my eyes on her crying face and I said to myself, it's time for swimming lessons. I can't fight her battles, but I can give her half a chance. I can try to get her half a chance while I'm swimming alongside her.

"Georgie," I started, reaching out to catch hold of her hand again. "George, honey. I reckon you know most of this is about your mother."

She shook me off right away. Snatched her hand back like I was fire.

"Bernice, this has nothing to do with my mother. Is that all you can hear? That it's about my mother? Em doesn't have a thing to do with my mother. Wanting to go back home isn't about my mother. My shitty job isn't about my mother. My life isn't about my mother."

I watched another of my fine ideas explode in my face. I tell you, I was batting zero that night. But I had to go through with it. George was screaming again.

"Get off it, will you? Is this because you're a nurse that all you can talk about is my mother? That's all you've talked about for the last three weeks. Get off it."

"Tell me this. Are you going home or not?" I asked, like a mule, not backing down.

"I don't know," she shouted. "I can't get it right in my mind. That's what I've been trying to talk with you about all night, don't you see?"

The words hung in the air and then fell, like a bird shot out of the sky.

"I do see," I said, soft. "George. I do see. And I'm sorry it hurts so much and that we ain't talking real good tonight. Only one thing you got to remember, honey. I do love you girl."

She turned to face me. "I know it, Bernice. I do. I just don't know what's going on."

"You don't have to, you know," I said, getting up from the table and bringing her my dishes.

"But I do, don't you see? I do," she shouted.

She started to wash the dishes, part by furious part. I stood against the counter and looked out the window and knew there wasn't nothing else I could do. I had tried. And I knew I should go back to setting with her, before I got us into a real fight. I told myself that when she was ready to talk, she would. But it was a sad consolation when I went home that night. Sometimes, it's hard to have faith. I swear to God.

The only thing I was really able to do for her that night was to draw her a bath, after she'd finished the dishes. Scrubbed out the tub and got the water real hot. And I told her about this new book by a Southern dyke name of Bode, which I had brought as a special treat for her that night. I gave her the book, and I told her to not look at any clocks, but to just have a quiet and peaceful time as she could. And go to bed when she wanted, not waiting for anybody else. And to call me, any time, or just come by. There was always a place for her with us. If she needed, she should just call, or come on. I said it more than once.

I left her before she got in the tub, not at all sure she heard a word I said. When I kissed her goodbye, she kissed like her lips were dry leaves.

And my heart hurt. You know, how your heart can hurt for one you love who's getting the devil beat out of them and you can't lift a finger to help them? It hurts bad, sort of an ache, for a long time. And for a week after that night, it was the same. I was getting ready to go crazy myself for the girl, and if it hadn't been for Annie, telling me to just hold on, I believe I would have made a bad mess, trying to help where I wasn't wanted.

But eight days after, George called me at home. At night. And I can't tell you how happy I was to hear from her. I can't tell you.

It started out same as usual. She said, 'Hey' and asked me what was I doing.

"Watching TV," I said without thinking. I do that sometimes. Folks ask me a question and if I'm thinking about something else, I'll tell them the truth—it's just a natural thing for me. I have to concentrate hard to tell lies. But I wished as soon as I said it that I'd phrased it a little nicer, you know. Because I could tell from her voice she didn't want me watching television; she wanted my complete-and-total, and I didn't blame her.

"Good show?" she asked.

"Not so good," I said, glad for the chance to let her know I did want to talk with her.

"You got time to talk?" she said.

"Hey!" I said. "What are friends for? Let me get on the other phone. Lord, I'm glad to hear from you girl," I said and I meant it.

"So, Georgie girl, what's up?" I said soon as I got to the other phone.

"Bernice, I'm a mess," she said, the words coming out so softly I could barely hear her.

"Talk up girl," I said. "I'm here. You okay?"

"Bernice, I think," she started but didn't finish. She started again, "I'm a mess, Bernice."

"What's going on?" I asked again. And then, I finally thought to say, "Will you turn off Patsy in the background there? I can't hear you."

She did. And then, somehow, the phone felt cold and clear like a winter night after an ice storm.

"Bernice," she said, "You have to keep me off the phone."

"Why? Somebody need to call you? We can get off the phone right now, for as long as you need, child, if that's what you're worried about."

But it wasn't.

"Bernice. Bernice." It was all she could get out. It almost sounded like she was gasping for air. I tried again.

"Slow down baby girl. Keep breathing. Take your time."

Nothing on the line. Then I could hear her crying. I mean, not sobbing. She doesn't do that. But her breath was raggedy like she couldn't breathe and I knew she was crying. I was glad at least for that. Now, maybe she would talk. And presently, she did. Choking it out. All I could do was wait for each piece.

"Bernice.

"I think Em's...

"I think Em's having...

"Damnit. I think Em's having an affair.

"With that Elizabeth person."

I waited, wondering was there more. But she didn't say anything for a minute, so I pressed on. I felt heartless, but I knew we had to try to get it out, like buckshot; sometimes getting the poison out involves probing around. I tried to be as gentle as I could.

"That so?" I asked. I waited for an answer. When she didn't say nothing, I asked again. "What makes you think so, honey?"

She told me again much what she had said before. Except this time she wasn't asleep about it. She was feeling it this time. And she told me how it felt like it had happened all of a sudden, but it couldn't have.

I just kept saying "Um-hum" or some stupid thing through it all. She was going real slow still. I wondered when the anger'd show, if the lion was here at all. After what had happened before, I wasn't really sharp on pressing too much, so I just waited. And then, at the end, after seemed like most of the hurt came out, I just had to try one more time.

"So is something particular bad happening now, honey, or you just scared and wanted to talk?"

And there that lion was. I was kind of glad I wasn't near.

"Shit, yes," she growled. "I just watched my hand pick up the phone and dial Elizabeth's number. Em gave it to me one night when she went over there for dinner and she thought Elliott might call. I kept that piece of paper and as I was dialing, I thought, well, maybe it's as scary for them as it is for me.

"I just said that to get me over, you know. Then I thought, maybe I'll just call and act like I'm selling magazines and ask Elizabeth if she has time to talk. I thought, maybe I'll just call and hang up. And then, before I knew it, the phone was being answered.

"And then I thought, what the hell are you doing? Put that down. Put that thing down before you make a fool of yourself.

"And I did, but Bernice, I couldn't quite figure out what to do next, and then I knew I was some place beyond panic, in that place where it felt like I had been drinking, but I hadn't been."

Her voice was back to normal and she sniffed a little. "Well," I said, "Go on girl. I'm listening."

"But do you know what I mean? It was like those times when you know you promised yourself you wouldn't have more than two drinks and then the waitress comes around and you hear yourself ordering another. It's not like when you are already drinking the third; it's like you hear yourself ordering a third and you remember you said you wouldn't and you can't make your voice stop."

Well, this is it, I said to myself. This is it. And I swore to myself that I would not blow it this time. I would not fight with her, I would not. None of this telling her what was going on. If I was to help, the best I could do was let her feel it herself. Shoot, I knew that. I had learned it before. I hated it, made me feel like I was putting her through it, but I knew it was the best I could do. The other way sure didn't work.

So I said, "What are you doing now?"

"Calling you," she said soft, the old joke hanging between us. She did sound a little more hopeful. It was a good sign she'd put the phone down before, and I was trying to figure a way to say that to her, but before I could, she said in her old voice from home, "What are you doing? I'm sorry to be interrupting like this. I just needed you for a minute."

"It's okay, Georgia honey. I'm glad you called. And you know, I believe you. I do. I mean, I believe the part about you being a mess. You sure are. I don't know about the other two, and I'll tell the truth; I don't care. But you, I care about. So we going to do something for you. You understand?"

"Bernice," she started, but I pushed on.

"I want you to tell me how you feel," I said, as slow and distinct as I could, like I would have if I'd been talking to someone on the ward I didn't know. I wanted her to hear me. I wanted to make sure she heard me.

"What are you talking about," she asked, fast, her words coming out like steam from a kettle. "What do you mean? I just told you. What are you doing to me?"

"George, now wait, honey. I'm not doing this to hurt you. Try to tell me how you *feel* about what you just told me."

"I feel awful. How the hell do you think I feel?" she growled again.

"What else?" I tried to keep my voice light, but I'll tell you. I was scared. I was scared she'd hang up on me and I'd have blown it again.

"What the hell do you mean? How am I supposed to feel? What are you talking about, Bernice? Am I supposed to like it? Goddamnit, you tell me to call, I'm calling, and what are you doing? Practicing therapy on me?"

"George. Honey. Come on. You remember this. You remember this part from before. You know, if you don't talk about how it feels, it'll cut you to ribbons. I'm not doing it to hurt you. Remember from when you quit drinking? The only way through is through. Come on, darling. Try it again."

There was silence on the phone. I tried again, rushing to fill in words. "You're my best friend in the entire world," I said. "And I'm trying to be your friend, girl. But you got to help. Feeling awful ain't exactly a description. You tell all those stories. Tell me one now. You describe it to me. I know it feels awful. Tell me about it."

"George," I interrupted her when she started to shout. "Georgie, please try. As a favor to me. Do you feel madder than a cat in water? Do you feel hurting and breaking? Do you feel stabbed in the back? Tell me the names of them. Tell me how you call what you're feeling."

There was more quiet on the end of the phone. And then she rasped out, "You bet I'm mad. I'm mad at you too. I'm mad at all of you idiots. Treat me like a piece of shit. What's happening to my life? I thought I was doing okay. What are you all doing to me?"

"Tell me, girl," I said, real soft, trying not to blow it. "What are we doing to you?" For a minute, there was no sound on the line. I felt my hands getting sweaty, but waited.

"I can't," she whispered finally and I could hear her breathing ragged again.

"George, honey, don't stop now. Let's see," I said quick, racking my brain for ideas. "Fifty questions, girl. You remember this. Do me fifty feeling questions like we used to."

She didn't answer. I hurried on.

"You're for sure mad. You said that. That was good. Okay. Now, how about sad? You sad?"

I heard her breathing. But that was all.

"Okay. Crying is sad, right? Come on, George. Talk to me." I couldn't do it all myself.

"Right," she croaked out finally.

"And do you feel ripped off? Like you loved her and she ain't around for you?"

I waited again.

Then she started talking and her voice was stronger.

"Well, some, but Bernice, you know, I feel, mostly, well, it's not ripped off."

I could see her searching the sky for just the right words, the way she used to when she was first not drinking, when it seemed like she was having to dig out words strong enough to hold her meaning.

"It's that I feel alone in this house, Bernice. I'm married. I ought not to feel alone. But she might come home or she might not. And I feel alone at my job. I feel alone in the world, do you know? I can't tell what's coming or going. I can't get a grip. I can't put my foot down. Even in my own house. Don't you think I ought to be able to feel safe in my own house?

"I feel alone, Bernice. Do you know what I mean? I mean, if I open the door to my room, Bernice, what's there? What's here? What's here in the room with me?"

"George. Honey, you sound real little to me. Where are you? I mean, any other house besides where you are? Can you tell me how long you been feeling this feeling? How long you been alone in this house? Which house are you in, George? Tell me."

She didn't answer. And I could see her there, wild around the eyes, like she used to get when she was drinking and I knew she wasn't going to answer.

"George," I shouted, suddenly remembering the rest. "George. Get up. Get up and turn on every blessed light in that room. Shut the door and check and see everything. Make sure there's nothing behind you. Check and see what's there. Get up, Georgie. Get up."

And then she really started to sob. I heard her put down the phone and sob. And all I could do was wait. Except I started tearing up a little myself, and I wished to God I'd been there with her. But there wasn't a thing in the world I could do.

Finally, I couldn't hear her anymore and I wondered then, did she go off? Did she just decide to stop talking and go off? And I was about to shout into the phone or hang up when I heard her again, real small and quiet.

"There's nothing here but me, Bernice. And I'm alone. And I've been feeling this for a long, long time," she said, her voice still small. She took a deep breath.

"Bernice. I think this isn't right. I think I should be able to be in my own home by myself and not be afraid. You know, I'm not going to get much more grown than I am. I think maybe I need to go home and take care of some of this, whether or not Cameron needs me. I think I need to talk to him. And to my mom. To see them. To see it. To see what's going on. I guess."

She stopped, her voice ripping a little and then she said, "I guess I ought to go ahead and go. Get it over with. I need to. See them. Feel it. Figure out what's what. What *was* what, you know?"

She was quiet then and took gulps of breath that I could hear and I knew she was crying but that she was going on. I started to cry then. I always cry when things are over, you know? When the worst is over and I can breathe? She's brave, my George. She's brave and smart, and I love her with all my heart.

And then she said, her voice still small, "Is that right, Bernice? Is that right?"

I wanted to answer her right away but I couldn't. Finally, I swallowed and said, "Honey, I don't know. I can't know. But it sounds right and I'm here with you, girl. I am right here."

"I love you, Bernice," she said in a minute and I could just see her wiping her eyes.

"I know it," I said. And then, because I couldn't think of anything else to say, I said, "Now you listen to the one who loves *you*. You ate yet?"

She said 'Yes,' and I didn't believe her, but there wasn't much I could do from where I was. So I said, "One more thing—no, two more things. For this, I think you get to add one more record to the juke box."

She didn't make a sound, but I could just see her smiling.

"Only one?" she asked, finally.

"You bandit," I shouted.

"Let me think," she said. I knew it was important. See, ever since we was first knowing each other, we had this thing where we'd let each other pick one record for the great juke box we're going to have some day. Money's no never mind. Whether you can get the record ain't important neither, nor is whether the other person likes your choice. But it's an important sort of something and we only do it sometimes, because we both know we only have about thirty slots apiece. And we want each of the thirty to be right, you know.

"Time's up, girl," I said after awhile. "Name your choice, darling."

"You'll hate it."

"Okay. So I hate it. You hated it when I put Streisand on. You hated it when I demanded the Delfonics when you was in your separatist time. So, now, it's your time, lady, you pick."

"I pick that train song Meg Christian sings."

"Why'd I hate it? I don't even know it."

"I don't know. I just thought you would."

"I mean, in this juke box you get to put what makes you happy, you know that. Does it make you happy?"

"Yes," she said and her voice was small again. "It makes me think I can do anything."

"Well, you can, you know. My Lord, George, you can do anything you set you mind to. I seen you. I'm glad Meg Christian knows it, too. When did she start singing songs just for you, girl? I didn't know she knew you. You holding out gossip on me?" I said.

"Oh Bernice, you old fool," she said.

"All right now," I said, wiping my eyes off and taking a deep breath. "Now. Here's the last thing. If you need a ride to the airport, you call. If you need anything, you call anytime. Day or night. You understand me?"

The last thing she said to me that night, the last thing she said to me until she got back, was that she'd call. And I did believe her.

I did.

CHAPTER SIX

CAROLINA IN THE MORNING

It was Dallas. It was an hour and a half layover. It was three in the morning.

Georgia had gotten a seat as far away from the ashtray as she could, but the smell of smoke still waded through the motionless, machine-made air surrounding her, pressing against her like people standing on a rush hour streetcar. The smell nauseated her. She looked up from her book and turned to the direction of the communal ashtray. There were three men standing and one woman seated next to it, all smoking languidly, like they do in airports, killing time.

As she looked around, she realized she'd been lucky; even if she hadn't been able to get away from the smoke, at least she had claimed a seat. Many of the travellers lay sprawled on the floor or walked around the confines of the boarding gate. She puzzled at the difference in the crowd, so different from the San Francisco airport.

She surveyed her fellow travellers again. Folks looked rumpled but in new clothes. They looked tired but not chronically. They looked a little like they were on a camping trip. Like they had placed themselves in discomfort for a reason and could control it. Middle class. And white. Almost all white. Middle class white folks going somewhere. Trying to save fifty, maybe seventy bucks. Just like her, she thought ruefully.

So why did she feel more comfortable in the airport back in San Francisco, if these folks were just like her, she wondered. And then, turning back around, confining her gaze to the carpet beneath her feet, she knew why. The others were mostly young families, couples, college boys. She was one of the few of either sex traveling alone. As a matter of public behavior, she refused to return anyone's glance, feigning boredom while she tried to keep her safety sense about her. Most looked at her only once anyway, and then turned away. Unaccompanied women were not seen, not valued, and no longer protected. She knew it, and though she was exhausted and alone, that knife edge of separateness robbed her stomach and mind of balance. She wished again she could sleep.

Instead, she tried to read. But her attention drifted away from the page. Her eyes examined the pattern on the carpeted floor. She wondered briefly whether her father or little Cam would meet her six a.m. arrival. She thought for a moment about how her mother would look, and whether or not she'd be able to talk with her. She saw Morgan's face when she had said what she was going to do while Georgia was away.

But the voices faded and mostly, she thought about a bed. She wished for a narrow single bed in a quiet gray bedroom of her own, with a couplet of roses on a mahogany dresser. She thought about the still safety of that room, tried to make the feeling and the room bigger, enough to hold her; but then, because she couldn't imagine where such a place might be, her images slipped quietly, almost effortlessly, into a replay of what had happened at work that day.

Before she could stop herself, she saw Williams' young face, red, furious, his blond hair falling over his forehead, and she looked down at the airport carpet and saw, just as she had then, the heels of his loafers and knew she would never again tell him he needed to get them reheeled.

She thought about that, shocked. Why had she ever told him that anyway? Was it because she'd been there for so long? Was it because she couldn't stand to see a nice pair of shoes ruined? Was it because he seemed like a kind of young Cameron, who needed to be told about his shoes? Who just didn't know what he would do without her?

Is that why she had told him what to wear? Ties? Shirts? What had she been doing all that time? She had never intended to end up dressing a young real estate banker. A banker. What the hell had she been doing?

And did it take this to wake her up? She sat tight and small against the chair as though she were still being yelled at, her head down, her hands clenched on her book, to ward off the sound. Well, he had screamed long enough at her today. It wasn't the first time, and it might not be the last time, but she knew as she sat there, that it would be the last time she would listen.

Or maybe, she thought, maybe this was the first time she had listened. She rubbed her eyes with her free hand. She had listened and heard him, and suddenly, like a knife held to the east, flashing in the light, she looked at him and things had become very simple. Reduced to most understandable terms. Impossible to misunderstand, this time. Impossible to be convinced of his side, this time.

Because this time, it was about her mother. And it was important that she go. He knew that. Anyone would know that. How could he not know that? She would only be gone the weekend and a day. She had told him three weeks ago she was going, no four, because that's when she'd had to make the thirty-day reservations. She had finally decided she would go when she wanted, not when Cameron wanted, and she had bought her ticket with her own money, and she had made her own plans.

And Williams had known. She had explained it to him. He had said okay. He had said, okay, and signed her one-day vacation permission form. He had signed.

And this time, there could be no question that *she* was being selfish, like he said, like he always said. She had to go. It was her mother. Surely he had a mother. Surely he knew that when he took time off to go to Napa to visit friends for four days last week, surely he knew that would throw his report schedule off. Surely he didn't expect her to stay to finish this report. Not on this weekend. Not now. It wasn't like she was being obstinate, like he said. It wasn't like she was being unthinking, inconsiderate of him, like he had said, like he was hurt. Like she would understand.

Because she heard him this time. And she did understand. And then, as he continued to try to get her agreement, and she pulled away from him, away from his vantage point, separating as though drawing back from the edge of a cliff he still exhorted her to look over, why, she coldly realized, it wasn't her; it was him. The problem was with him. It had always been with him.

She frowned at the floor and slipped her fingers out from between the pages of the book where she had held them, keeping her place. She squinted, trying to see him again. When she had said no, flatly, she had expected him to pull back, as though he could see she wasn't looking down into the pit anymore.

Didn't he know that? Wasn't he listening? He wasn't going to carry this out was he? Was he? Wouldn't he stop if she really made him understand it was important to her? He was the one always talking about team spirit, wasn't he?

Well, they weren't ever a team. How could he keep saying that? God, she hadn't really believed him, had she? Come on! Hadn't she just *wanted* to believe it? Was it that clear? Was he really doing this? This demanding? This forcing without threat?

She thought about his mottled red face, like a looming movie closeup seen from the second row. When he said there was no one else who could help him if she didn't stay to get the report out, and after all, it meant a big part of his future, she turned from his face to his loafers, knowing that she would never tell him to get them reheeled and wondering if she should say the word "fired" or if he would.

Of course, neither of them had said it and she thought then, as she recrossed her legs, stiff from the airport chair, neither of them ever would. He had started out of the office as though it had all been settled, and she looked at him, said, 'Well, let's try to get as much done as we can.' She watched him, his face red, his mouth hard, and she saw even then how it hurt him, his inside, to be forcing her this way.

And she was sorry for that, but as she saw his anger coming, waving like the glinting barrel of a gesturing shotgun, she set her mouth tight, swallowed all she had to say and turned away, back to her machine. Because she knew he was going to keep doing it, backing her into the wall with the shotgun, not needing to fire it.

She said then, 'Let me go to the library to check the sources for the redevelopment plans.' And behind her back, she heard him sigh in relief, and she knew he thought the confrontation was over. When he left, she got up and went to talk to Ricky.

She waited for the elevator only a minute, willing the hall to stay empty, racing her mind, saying over and over to herself that she had the permission slip. And that Ricky would know what to do. Georgia waited as the elevator lifted her two stories up, waited as her mind raced forward. This time, she had him.

The elevator door opened and she went into the cool library. The hall and the library were quiet; it was already two in the afternoon. The sun was coming in the tinted windows and no one but Ricky was there. The long tables were surrounded by cool shelves of books. In the still, warm air, she took a deep breath as she sat at the table nearest Ricky, and her shoulders lost some urgency.

Ricky looked up and over the stack of reports waiting to be catalogued on her desk and said, "Hey, girlfriend. What's happening down in the armpit today?"

And Georgia exploded, saying as she had so often, "Ricky, I hate this job. He has been unbelievable today. He doesn't want me to go this weekend. Needs me to stay. Said forget the permission slip. Can you believe it?"

Ricky looked at her, not moving. Georgia went on, in a rush, "Ricky, I can beat him on this, can't I? Can't I stop him this time? What do you think the rules are for him if I have his signed permission? What's your advice here? Can you believe this shit?" she asked again, with venom as usual, but also with wonder.

Ricky put her pencil down then and Georgia thought, watching her smile, that Ricky was welcoming her, and starting to say, as she always did, 'Now girl, take a load off your feet. Sit down and tell me what he done now.'

But instead, Ricky only said, "Now, Georgia," and Georgia, startled in the silence of her pause, not able to slide into the safety of their old pattern, listened.

Ricky leaned over her desk and looked at Georgia full in the face. Waiting, Georgia saw again the smooth soft brown skin of her friend and smiled, uncertain, reassuring herself by looking at the fuchsia red flower Ricky had on her desk and thinking how like her friend it was, how beautiful the flower, and Ricky, both were.

Finally, Ricky said, "You know, I have been meaning to say something to you about this. You want my advice? Okay. You been coming in here for the last half a year and telling me you hate this man. We go to lunch and you tell me you hate this man. We talk on the phone and you tell me you hate this man. And you work weekends for him and you cover his ass and you listen to his sorry love life and pick out his clothes. You say you like him sometimes, or feel bad for him, or some such shit."

Georgia sat up and watched Ricky's red fingernails pick up her pencil and point it at her. She got very cold inside, crossed her arms and looked away. Ricky kept talking.

"And now you saying you hate him again. And all this time, you let him treat you like dirt. You let him, you understand that? Comes a time, you can't let folks treat you like that. If you don't go this weekend, it's going to hurt you more than him, you know that's true, don't you?"

She paused and then said, "Georgia, now you know I'm telling you this because I like you. If I didn't, I wouldn't waste my time. I just don't like watching this, you understand what I'm saying here? I think you got plenty of sense. But I tell you what. I think you'd better start using the sense God gave you and get your ass out of this place where you are at.

"I tell you, from where I sit, it looks like time to walk to me. Just walk on out of here. Nobody's forcing you to stay. I don't see no chains around your ankles. Quit this thing. It ain't good for you girl. Get your papers and walk."

Ricky's voice echoed in the nearly empty room. Georgia, stunned, finally said, "Ricky. It's not that easy. You know that. Where would I go?"

Ricky, her red-lipped mouth tight, said, "Child, I do not know. But you'll find something if you look. You got a lot more chances to find work than lots of folks."

Georgia heard her and her face froze. She sat there, looked out the window and thought to herself, what made her think she had the right to talk to her like that? A couple of lunch dates? Some talks? She didn't even let Bernice talk to her like that, she thought, fury cold and cracking.

Ricky interrupted, tapping her pencil on the desk. "You know, my friend Clarissa has an opening for a library helper over at American. She told me last night she'd been interviewing college grads for three weeks. Children who didn't know shit from shinola. Well, in most cases, you appear to. And because of that, I kept figuring that one of these days, you'd tell me why you let Williams treat you like this, but I'm telling you, sometimes it don't pay to wait for the reasons. Sometimes, you just have to act and let the reasons catch up with you later. If you want, I can ask Clarissa if she'd be interested in somebody like you."

She paused. Georgia watched her own hands tighten in her lap and then hid them under the table, and felt panic roll over her like a wave beating her into the sand. Her anger rolled into her then, mixing with the panic, unsteady. Leave Williams? It wasn't that bad, well, it wasn't any different, it wasn't...well. She looked quickly at Ricky. The other woman was watching her and so she turned her head away. What the hell was happening here? This woman was supposed to be her friend, to be close to her, to understand. Why wasn't she helping? Why was she leaving her stranded like this?

"Only thing about Clarissa," Ricky said, a small smile on her face, "you've got to make up your mind fast. Clarissa won't wait. You two will get along great in that area."

Ricky chuckled then and Georgia watched her, astonished. "She does not wait. Not that girl." She tapped her pencil one more time and picked up her papers.

"And probably, you're going to have to interview by next week. Won't bring much money. Not what you're getting now. And you'd have to work weekends, I bet, and some nights. But it'd be a sight better than what you got now. No way Clarissa could be as bad as Williams."

Georgia looked at her, her mouth half-open and Ricky shrugged back. "You think about it. I think you could do it. You sure can't stay where you at. Don't take it personal, girl. God knows, you can't go on like this. I know you're pissed at me right now, but I'm telling you this as a friend."

She stopped for a moment. Georgia looked at the floor. Finally Ricky said, "You *are* going back to Durham, aren't you?"

Georgia nodded mutely. Ricky said once more, "Well, you think about it. And have a good weekend. I got more work than I know what to do with myself or I'd talk longer, girl. Come by when you get back; let me know how it goes. And don't get all bent out of shape at me for saying this. You'll be glad I did by Monday."

Georgia didn't say a word. She just got up and went back down to her office, sat at the terminal and began to work.

At four, Williams ducked his head in and said he was leaving for the afternoon, that he'd see her tomorrow. She kept on working. And when it was five and the report wasn't finished, she took the pieces into Williams' office, and laid them on his desk with a note that said, "I have your signature for pre-approved vacation. I must go home. I hope you'll be able to get one of the pool operators to finish this up. I guess we'll discuss it when I get back on Monday."

And she walked out, her anger like ice forced down her throat, coated smooth in the blood of her confusion. She turned Ricky's conversation over in her mind, as she had all afternoon. No way she could take a job that would keep her away from home more than now. That was the main problem as it was. She never saw Em. Ricky knew all that. They'd talked about it. What was she thinking of?

And why now? Why tell her now, this weekend? Why was it all happening now? She didn't need a new job now. She just needed to go home, that's all. She needed a new mother, a fixed-up mother. A new father wouldn't hurt either. But a new job? Now? Goddamn-it, why did her friends do her like that? When she needed them?

And as she thought about it, sitting there in the airport in Dallas, she felt Ricky was just the icing on the cake. Williams was the goddamn cake. She didn't understand how he could have done what he did. How had she worked herself into a position where he thought he could do that? Was he forcing her to quit?

Well, forget quitting. He could probably fire her now. Walking out was, after all, a pretty cut and dried cause for dismissal. She stroked the back of her hand and then looked around. No one paid any attention to her but still she fought not to cry. She tried to go through it again, tried to calm it down. Well, she'd done it. And all she knew then was what she knew now, even sitting at three in the morning in a strange airport, that after all this time, she *had* to go home.

She thought about how she'd looked around the office, cut off the lights and walked out, went home as though nothing had changed, and she was just doing as she would have normally. She fixed supper, packed, and when Morgan came home from the practice she'd been coaching, rode with her to the airport. She didn't say anything to Morgan about it. It didn't seem like the right time. Not that she knew when would be a good time.

She thought about Williams' face and shuddered. She saw Ricky's face again, her brows brought together, her pencil pointing at Georgia. She heard Ricky's voice, heard the rough warm of it. Well, maybe Ricky was right about some of it. She wasn't trying to hurt her. She could hear that, at least, in her voice. So if she wasn't trying to hurt, or to get rid of her, well, maybe she was on the right track. Oh God, as soon as Ricky said it Georgia knew she was right. But it was a hell of a way to say it, the last of her anger muttered silently.

But what about that job Ricky mentioned, she thought, anxiously. What was she going to do? Quit? How could she do that? What was she supposed to do, just jump in and swim?

When the spine cracked on her book, she realized she had opened it and was creasing the pages so far she was in danger of breaking the binding. She looked down, closed the book and looked at her watch. Well, she'd come. Couldn't stop now. She took a deep breath and tried to let go of the panic, the sight of their faces, the sounds of their words in her ears and the awful tight hardness in her throat. And then she heard a loud Southern voice announce her flight.

When she got on, she tried to sleep. But instead, she listened to Morgan, seeing her face again, her mouth talking, watching the words come out of her mouth. Morgan had said she was going over to have dinner at her new friend Elizabeth's house on Saturday, but otherwise she'd be home or at work. Georgia watched her mouth, believed her, but also believed she had something else to say. She strained to hear it. But she couldn't hear the words.

By five, as the sun was coming up, she gave up sleep and opened the window shade. Wearily, she watched the clouds, but even then, her mind tried to focus, tried to make sense. She noticed for the first time the clouds were different on the East Coast. The sun was different; the color of the sky was different, and it all looked familiar somehow, but slightly askew, as if from the wrong perspective, which, of course, it was.

She watched the clouds, watched the sun coming up. And then, suddenly, she saw below her, saw the ground, saw the green.

Even from the airplane window, even through the double panes of acrylic, crosshatched like the background of a metal etching, even through the air miles in between, Georgia was stunned at the green.

The plane was circling over the Raleigh-Durham airport, over the green, over the towns, the farms, and the small red-brown lines of farmers' roads that intersected with the two-lane blacktop, looping together like tangled fishing line through the green.

She hadn't been home in seven years. She hadn't said she wanted to come back even once. In fact, she'd denied it, denied all of it, had shaken her curly head at the rabid, diseased politics and turned away at the mention of it.

But there was a memory in her cells, stronger than her mind, stronger than her mental recognition of danger, stronger than desire or control. She could banish the memory, but she couldn't kill it. And that morning, maybe because she was exhausted, or maybe because she had used up her allotment of fight, or maybe just because she saw the green, memory of that land swept over her and she wept.

She wanted to be home then, and all uttered denials were canceled, swept away. She wanted to lie down and have morning glory vines wrap around her heart, grow from her heart in that green, in that heat and in the moist air that had held her like the embrace of an old friend. She wanted to lie down in that moist air, buoyant like a salted sea, as though she could float all day in that sunshine, in that air, moist like an ocean, and never have to move, but to just be there, and float, washed and gentle, just to be there, be loved by that sun, that water, that air.

She cupped her hand around her eyes, turned toward the window and wept as the plane descended. And she knew, as she wept, that this feeling—the memory of this feeling—had ridden around in her hip pocket, day in and day out, for the last seven years, like the face of the old friend, one she had loved beyond this life and whom she'd lost, lost and unable to talk with again, even though she'd seen that woman's face in every crowd, or heard her voice on the radio, through the tires, up from the street corners, and knew all the while that her own voice made no sound, even as she called her in return.

And she knew why she didn't, hadn't, wouldn't talk about it. It was useless after all. It wasn't that she couldn't explain it. She could. It was that it made no sense. She knew the words, but what sense did they make? Sentimental, that's all. Sentimental to try to go where you aren't wanted. Sentimental and stupid. That's all she was.

She knew very well it was people who made a place what it is. And the people back home wanted people like her dead. She knew that. That had been made perfectly clear. It didn't make a lot of sense, but it was clear.

She didn't know how, couldn't believe even then, that she'd actually gotten out. And she didn't know, if she went back, if she could ever get back out again. She hadn't thought once of coming back without having fear stab her, a clutching fear so strong she couldn't find its name.

But that morning, as she gripped the side of her seat, as the flight attendant requested preparation for landing, as her aching muscles and cramped heart pressed forward, she could see nothing but the green. And in turn, the green reached up to her through the plane, in the early morning brightness, through the interminable Carolina blue sky and called to her, lie down in us.

It was as if that green was a hypnotic trigger in her heart: all the California shades of dusty gold meadow and soft blue sky were swept away as though they had nothing to do with her, as though the seven years she had painstakingly spent consciously, willfully building a new life, a new self, why, that must have happened to someone else.

Because she was here. Of course she lived here. She had always been here. This is where she belonged. And this was where she would never, ever leave. It was that simple. The other had happened to someone else. Had she been in a dream? Had she ever been away? She got ready to leave the plane as though she had been away for only a day or two.

She gathered her things and felt tired, so tired, and knew if she could just get home, she'd sleep for days, she'd sleep and wake up and it would all be in place again, would make sense again, and she would know what to do.

But when she walked out of the plane, stepped out on to the open-air stairs, the early morning May heat hit her like a slap in the face and she began to wake up. She staggered from the blow and then, clutching the railing, was grateful, because she began to remember, in the heat, what Carolina was all about.

She moved haltingly down the stairs, walked over the tarmac and into the waiting room, not wanting to look, but forcing herself to take quick scans, for brief moments.

She heard him first, his voice still young, even though his face had hardened into a man's face five years ago, during the first six months the Navy had him.

"Yo. Hey, little sister," he called, his private joke, immediately staking his claim, but her heart warmed, even as she heard him and understood; she was, in that moment, glad to be claimed by him.

"Hey, Bud," she answered, walking up to him. He wrapped his arms around her, kissed the top of her head and took her bags.

"Hey. What's happening, little sister?" he asked, grinning like a monkey.

"You will stop this little sister business," she said tartly, but grinning back at him. "I will be nine years older than you until the day you die. And you will always be little Cam; there is not a thing in the world you can do about it."

"Good to see you, little sister," he said and kept grinning. They walked out to the car. The airport seemed unbelievably small to her and he seemed even more like a man than when she'd last seen him, three years ago. Still, he was her Bud. And she'd missed him.

When they got in the car, she asked him not to cut the air conditioner on and he said, 'Sure thing' and they rode to the house, windows down, air blowing in, in the steamy heat. She saw the tobacco waist-high, nearly time to top. She saw the red, red clay.

She saw how one of his eyes drooped at the corner and saw his hands shake.

"You up late last night?" she asked as he pulled out a cigarette, poked it in the corner of his mouth and lit it like James Dean. Good Lord, she thought, he's not even old enough to know who James Dean was.

In a moment he answered, as he exhaled.

"Yeah. I was up, kind of keeping Dad company."

She didn't answer, just kept looking out the window.

"I don't do it often, you know. I don't drink that much," he said after awhile.

"You don't have to answer to me, Bud," she said although she was pleased he had. "I guess you know the percentages as well as I do. I've told you often enough."

She looked at him, but he kept his eyes on the road. They were silent. The road snaked forward, wandering. He'd cut over, going the back way, probably as much for his benefit as hers, but she was glad for it.

"How is the son of a bitch?" she asked, looking out her window, trying to keep her voice light.

"Come on, George," he said. "He's having a hard time too, you know," he said, his voice almost pleading.

"Don't I know? Don't I hear it on the phone? Don't you?"

"No," he said, glum. "He only calls me to borrow money."

She turned to look at him. "Are you lending him money?" she asked, incredulous.

"Some," he said, keeping his eyes on the road. "Not a lot. Listen, anyway, I have it right now. He's having a hard time, George. Point of honor, really. And he's our father, you know," he finished.

She looked at him. Blond hair, shorn close to his head, blue-eyed Navy man. Officer. Leader of men. Sense of honor. God knows, she'd tried to instill a sense of honor in him. Honor and compassion. Justice for all people. Fight for right, not might. She'd taken him with her to the demos. And look what had happened. Not much of a parent she'd turned out to be.

Very softly she said, "If you're lending him money, more fool you."

She saw him flex his fingers on the steering wheel three times.

"You know, you're going to have to make an effort here. It's not being easy for any of us. Wait until you see her."

There. It was out in the open.

"Well, how is she?" Georgia asked, not willing to discuss the coded 'make an effort' with him.

He looked at her and she thought he was going to cry. "She looks like someone you won't even know," he said, whispering.

Georgia reached over and combed his hair with her fingers and he was silent, trying not to cry.

"Okay, Bud. It's okay. It will be okay," she said. He didn't answer, but sniffled a few great snorts, like a man again. The tender spot between his head hair and his beard had hardened some time in the last seven years into pale blond spikes. He must shave every day now, she thought with a jolt.

He drove into the driveway, and they sat there together in silence for a moment. It was not a house she had ever visited but it wasn't unfamiliar. There were only a few basic designs, with only slight variations, for newly-built, middle-class houses in the New South. This one was a standard split level, though why they needed one now, she couldn't answer.

Painted white frame with the split-level in brick. Shutters that didn't work, just for show. No porch, just a brick front stoop. Concrete driveway. Green yard, fresh mowed. Two young trees tethered to the front yard. A few dry azaleas up along the front of the house. Red clay staining the brick at the foundation.

"You mow the yard?" she asked him.

He nodded.

"Looks nice."

He nodded again.

"Buddy," she started, and he turned to her, "Bud, what do you say? Solidarity forever?"

He grinned at their old code, but his grin was sad. He quickly opened the door and said, "Let me get your bags," as though she were a grown-up lady he didn't know. Or didn't want to know. Or couldn't know.

She held her head in her hands for a moment and then got out too.

Cam was walking towards the house and she followed him.

"Dad's still asleep. You want to sleep some? Are you hungry or what?"

"They teach you how to make coffee in that Navy?" she answered.

"Yeah," he said, opening the door and grinning again. "I can make coffee that'll put hair on your chest." In the silence that followed, he turned to her and saw how she must have heard what he said. His mouth fell slightly open, aghast.

She laughed as he blushed. "George, I didn't mean you needed any hair, I'm sorry..."

She interrupted him. "Let it go. I think it's funny. It's like that time Mom sent that basket of fruits and nuts to Morgan and me because she couldn't figure out what else to send us for Christmas. Remember the fruit and nuts to the fruits and nuts?"

They were both laughing then, leaning against the walls of the entry room, shushing each other, helpless, hands over their mouths. They laughed until they cried and then, still snickering and choking, she followed him up the stairs and down the hall past their parent's room to the spare bedroom.

He walked her in, lifted her suitcase onto the bed and went to close the door.

"Jesus, I hope we didn't wake the son of a bitch up. He's a bear in the morning. I had forgotten about 'Martha's famous every occasion San Francisco present.' Wasn't that what Morgan called it?"

She nodded, wiping her eyes.

"How is Morgan?" he asked.

"Oh, I think she's fine. She's working too much, as usual," Georgia said.

He smiled. "She always does."

"I know it. Now where's that coffee? You think you could make it a little weaker for one of the weaker sex?" she asked.

"Maybe. But you haven't convinced me of that yet," he said and smiled. "Kitchen's on the other side of the front door. Come out when you get set," he said and walked out, closing the door behind him.

She went over to the window and looked out. Concrete driveways. Asphalt streets. Rectangle yards of putting green. She suddenly felt the air conditioning, set too low like her father liked it, and she was cold. Really cold. She shivered and rubbed her arms and turned back into the room. She unzipped her suitcase, looked at her rumpled clothes, and then wondered if her bathroom was separate from her father's and went to inspect.

She poked her head into the bathroom. Yep, three doors. One from her room, one from the hall and one from his. Damnit. She went in and then saw the latch on the door leading into her father's room and also one on her side. Well, maybe, she decided, maybe she'd chance a shower after coffee. She went back into her room.

As she walked in this time, she realized the room was full of all her childhood furniture. Her books. Her bed. Her pictures on the wall. She shuddered and fled to the kitchen.

Little Cam was in there, making coffee, and breakfast, it smelled like. Frying sausage. She went into the room without saying a word. Was he making biscuits? When did he learn to cook?

"Bud, what are you doing?" she asked him, walking up to the counter.

He grinned, and gestured to the coffee. "Making breakfast for my little sister," he said and went on beating the biscuits.

"When'd you learn to cook?" she asked, following his hand.

"Lot of stuff you learn in the Navy," he said, still grinning.

"You did not learn this in the Navy. You making grits too?"

He nodded. "No, really, I learned it from Elinor." He laid the biscuits on a cookie sheet that looked new.

"Still hurt?" she asked.

"Yeah. But I think she might come back to me. I think about her all the time. I bet she does, too. I don't know. I miss her." He was silent as he put the biscuits in the oven. The grits perked in the pan and the sausage popped.

"How about some coffee?" he asked too loud.

"You know what they say, Bud. You can't hurry love. You'll find somebody," she said, her hand on his arm. He just nodded and poured her coffee.

They both heard Cameron start the shower at the same moment.

"Oh God," little Cam moaned. "We woke him."

"Don't despair," she said and grinned. She took a sip of coffee and spat it out. "Give him some of this," she said, gasping. "He'll never talk again."

They snickered together. "What can I do to help?" she asked, and they finished making breakfast and were eating by the time Cameron came down.

She was shocked to see him. He'd lost weight, his arms boney, his belt worn and tightened to the last notch. His pale blond hair, what was left of it, lay slicked back on his gaunt head. He looked like a ghost, except for his eyes, red and watery and darting.

"Well, you two could wake the dead. You younguns got any consideration at all for your elders?" he said sternly, as he went to get a cup of coffee.

"Hi, Dad," she said, unable to help herself. After all, seven years wasn't such a long time. No need for a kiss or a hello for such a short time.

"We *are* considerate of your esteemed venerableness. We considerately saved you some coffee on purpose; Cam made it just for you. Remember me, your daughter? Have some coffee and maybe you'll remember."

Cam cut his eyes around at her. Cameron poured his coffee and didn't respond.

Finally, his hands shaking, he came and sat with them. "You always had a mouth on you, didn't you sister? Glad you could make it, finally." He didn't look at her as he spat the words out.

Little Cam said, "Dad, you said you'd be nice. She's here now. Let it go."

Cameron rolled his hand around his face and over his eyes. Finally he said, "All right, Junior. How was your flight, sister?"

"Great. Great flight. Slept the whole way."

Cam kicked her under the table.

She buttered her biscuit. "How are you?" she asked pointedly.

"Fine. Your mother's coming home today, you might recall. Things will be just fine when she gets here." He sipped his coffee.

She turned in astonishment to Cam. He just shook his head and mixed his egg yolk in his grits.

She turned back to her father. He was watching her.

"Good," she said, trying to cover her face. "What time do we go?"

"Well, I have to go to the office for a bit. I thought we'd get her about one. They said anytime after noon. Can you make that?" he asked, mean at the end.

She looked at him unsteadily. "Daddy, I came home, didn't I?"

He finally nodded. He got up, weaving it seemed to her, and took his cup to the sink. "I'll just get ready to go to work and leave the place to you two. Then you can make all the noise you want."

When he left the room, Cam shook his head. "That wasn't so bad as yesterday."

She stared at him. He buttered another biscuit and then put a sausage patty on it and started to eat.

"Hey, how about some barbeque for dinner? They've got a great new place down by the river," he said. "That's what Mom said she especially wanted when she got home."

"Bud, when did y'all find out she was coming home today? I didn't know that."

He continued eating and shook his head. "He just told me yesterday. I didn't know. But it's nice, ain't it? Now, what about the barbeque?"

She rubbed her eyes. Finally she said, "Whatever you think is best. Some things never change, I swear to God," she said, shaking her head, resigned. They heard Cameron go out the front door with a slam. She sighed and felt all the energy in her body go out of her. She wasn't sure that she could sit at the table another minute.

"I think I'll take a shower and lie down for a bit," she said. "Thanks for getting me. Thanks for breakfast. I love you a lot, you know," she said, carrying her plate to the sink.

"No prob," he said. And then he looked at her. "You didn't sleep a bit on the plane, did you?"

She shook her head. "Now, don't scald me in the shower, will you? Hold off on the dishes until I'm done."

He grinned and took another biscuit.

"Good thing the Navy runs those things off of you," she said.

"I get to eat more because I'm a man," he said, and she flipped him the finger as she left, but she was smiling when she did it. Before she went upstairs to her room, she poked her head into the living room. There, Cam had clearly been sleeping on the sofa-bed, but he must have cleaned up and put his things away before he came to get her. His stuff was tidy, tight, military.

She showered, put on a long flannel nightgown, went to her room, pulled down the shades and got into bed. She tried not to look around her as she drifted off to sleep.

Three hours later, she heard Cam's sharp rap through the door and then, as he peered around the open door, she realized she had slept.

"George, you'd better get up. Cameron's on his way home to get us."

She shook her head and was awake immediately. "Okay. Get out of here and let me get ready. How much time do I have?"

"Less than ten minutes," he said and closed the door.

She hurried, and was aware she was glad she didn't have time to think.

She felt the panic rise up when she was with them in the car, and then when they were walking into the hospital. She felt sick, and wasn't sure she wouldn't vomit breakfast all over the front hall as she had in first grade. When Cameron went up to the front desk, little Cam touched her hand for a moment and mouthed 'You all right?' She shook her head and he led them over to the visitors' seats.

"Just keep breathing," he said, sounding like an officer, which, she supposed he was. She did as she was told.

It seemed like Cameron spent a long time at the desk, but then he came and sat with them, lit a cigarette, and said, "It won't be long now."

In a moment, little Cam lit up too, and shook her out one, extending the pack towards her. She put her hand up, saying no and turned away, away from the smoke and finally walked over to the window. She just happened to turn around as her mother was wheeled off the elevator, pushed by a skinny orderly.

At first she thought, hey, the orderly guy is gay. What a relief to see another queer. And then she thought, oh my God. Is that my mother? Oh my God.

Martha was slumped in a wheelchair, her hair gone half-white and pulled back with a barrette. She was dressed in a blue sweatsuit, with white tennis shoes attached to her feet. Her clothes looked draped on her. She'd lost even more weight than Georgia could imagine. And, Georgia realized with a shock, she wasn't able to move her face, hold herself up or move her arms. Georgia watched her, rooted at the spot where she first saw her, and then she felt herself walking towards her, tears streaming down her face, her arms open. She reached the woman without a sound and hugged her as best she could, stooping and clumsy around the wheelchair.

Her mother was moving her mouth and making sounds. Georgia tried to understand, turning her ear towards her, but volume wasn't the problem. She couldn't get it. Finally she heard Cam behind her saying softly, "She says, 'Hi honey. What's new?'"

The three of them laughed then and Georgia said through her tears, "This is a lunatic family," and watched her mother's mouth as she tried to laugh. When she looked up, her father was behind the wheelchair, clearing his throat.

He said, "Let's go, get this lady home where she belongs."

Martha tried to twist her neck back around to look at him, though she couldn't, and her mouth couldn't quite make the shape of a smile, but Georgia could see she was trying.

This was her mother? The woman she had last seen leaning on her elbow, lying on the quilt they'd spread over the grass in the Quad, laughing at her father while they all drank white wine and devoured the special food Georgia had gotten just for her. The picnic just before she and Bernice came to California. They'd had *pate* and linen napkins, and her mother was surprised, but pleased. They'd had a great time that day, and Martha had been at her best, regal and tender all at once, like a rose.

And now? This was her mother? She couldn't even hold her head up. Georgia looked at Cam, wild, and he smiled sadly, took her by the arm to help her up and said, "Let's take her home, George." Then he looked away as his father started pushing the chair and the four of them set off.

It was a long trip home, with stops here and there to get a rented hospital bed delivered immediately, pick up a rented wheel-chair and put it in the Marquis' trunk, buy a special toilet seat, get guardrails for the tub. Martha sat propped up in the front, near the air conditioner blowers and Georgia sat in the back, trying to help with purchases, more furious by the moment that Cameron hadn't taken care of the special equipment beforehand.

When they finally got Martha settled, in her room with the bed set up and her in it, with little Cam in the bathroom installing the railings, Martha looked like she needed nothing more than to sleep. Cameron went back to the office and promised to bring the barbeque home for supper.

Before he left, he asked Georgia 'Did she want chopped or sliced?' She wondered again how the man who had raised her could act like he'd never seen her before and was about to scream when little Cam said, "Oh I bet she still only eats chopped, just like always, Dad. Too bad she has no chance in wacky California to expand her taste in barbeque."

Cameron looked for a moment like he was his old self and he grinned. "Chopped. Okay. Lose all the flavor of the meat. But I know that's what you like. Just seeing if you'd changed."

She knew then he didn't remember for real and forced herself to smile at him as he left. Then she joined little Cam in putting the railings on.

"How much is he forgetting?" she asked in a whisper, worried they'd wake her mother.

"Oh, not much," he said. "Here, hold this end."

"How much," she whispered, putting one end in place so he could measure.

"It seems like a lot. He's in trouble at work, he told me last night. But he'll be fine," he whispered back. "We can't drill while she's sleeping. We'll have to wait until she's awake, later."

Georgia nodded. "What makes you think he'll be fine?"

"He always is, the son of a bitch," he whispered. "Look, I'm going to go shoot some hoops down at the corner. You want to come?"

She shook her head.

"Okay," he said. "I'll be back in a couple of hours. You okay?"

She nodded but couldn't look at him. He went out and she went back downstairs, read the *Morning Herald*, in detail, every line of every story, and then stretched out on the sofa. She could smell little Cam's smell in the pillows. And she saw her mother's face again, twisted up like melted plastic on the right side, her beautiful mother with the precision smile. How could it be? She felt like the earth had slipped in the twist of that face and she clung to the couch pillow. She felt cold and pulled Cam's extra sleeping blanket over her.

She tried very hard not to think, not to see her mother's head flopping forward. When she felt the panic start, she concentrated on the way the air felt in her nostrils, like Bernice had taught her. She felt it go in, felt it go out. She tried to shut out all other thoughts. And presently, in her exhaustion, in Cam's extra blanket, in her concentration on breathing, she fell asleep.

Cameron woke her when he came in at six with the dinner.

"Where's your brother?" he asked as he took the barbeque into the kitchen, the smell of it already wafting through the house. "Isn't anyone up with your mother? What the hell is wrong with you kids?"

"I think she's asleep, Dad. I've been listening for her."

"You were asleep," he said, disgusted and she could already smell the bourbon on his breath.

He went upstairs, and she heard him quietly open the door to their bedroom and then just as quietly shut it.

She started to put the barbeque in the oven, to keep it warm. Little Cam came in, loud, and said, "Boy, it smells great in here. When's supper?"

Cameron came downstairs and walked into the kitchen before he said, "Don't you think you can keep your voice quiet for once, you big jackass?"

Cam looked like someone had slammed a door on his hand. Then they all heard her calling.

"Time she got up, Dad," Cam said, bounding up the stairs, his shirt and shorts wet with sweat. "Time for some delicious barbeque."

Both Cameron and Georgia looked after him in amazement. A moment later he reappeared on the stairs, carrying Martha in his arms.

"She wants to eat at the dining room table," he crowed and Martha made her mouth close to a smile again. Cameron and Georgia looked at each other for the first time, smiled and shook their heads.

"Well, bring her on. I'll get her chair set up," Cameron said, resigned, and Georgia began to transfer the dinners from paper cartons and styrofoam cups, greasy bags and tinfoil, onto the china. She looked in the refrigerator, found a carton of eggs, half a roll of sausage, a six-pack of beer, a stick of butter, a can of coffee and some cream. There was almost nothing else besides an old opened can of tomato juice and a pitcher of iced tea. She wondered if Cam had done just enough shopping for their breakfast. That would be like a boy, to shop for just one meal.

Then she wondered if Cameron ever ate at home. Or ate at all. There was the tomato juice, but she knew what that was for. His breakfast. His morning toner mixed with vodka. And probably Cam had made the pitcher of tea like he had made the breakfast. She wished for a plate of sliced tomatoes but shook her head and let it go.

She pulled out the tea and shut the door. She didn't want to ask what they wanted to drink; if they wanted to drink alcohol, they would have to get it themselves. She decided to pour the tea and put the glasses on the table. If they got something else then, it would be conspicuous at least. Maybe that would slow it down.

By the time she'd poured the tea, Cam came to help her and they carried supper out to the table. There, Cameron had strapped

Martha into the wheelchair and was pinning a white linen napkin around her neck. Georgia turned to look at Cam, but he grinned and said, "This is a lunatic family, don't you love it," and patted her arm before they turned back to the kitchen to get the rest.

They sat down together finally. Cameron got up almost immediately to get beer, came back and said the blessing. Cam rolled his eyes at her. And then, the smell of the barbeque, the sight of the china and their place settings made her forget almost everything, and she smiled around the table. Her mother looked almost normal, if you ignored certain things.

"Dig in, kids," her father said and edged his chair over to her mother. He talked directly to her, asking her, "Marty, what do you want to start with? Brunswick stew? I got you some nice Brunswick stew."

"Or maybe a hush puppy," he said, as she made a noise. "Yes, Cam, I think she wants a hush puppy. Pass us one, will you please?" He said it without looking and Georgia heard Cam choke, and she passed the hush puppies to her father. She turned to look at Cam, his eyes big and afraid and full of tears, and she reached her hand across for his. He grasped her like he was falling out a window and held tight for a moment and then let go.

Then, suddenly, as he let go, in an almost normal voice, he said, "George, how about you? Slaw? Stew? Or you going straight for the chopped stuff?"

"I'm not going straight for anything," she whispered to him and her father turned around and stared disapprovingly at both of them.

"You'll not talk like that, Georgia Thompson. Not in front of your mother, not at this table, not while I'm still here, young lady," he said, continuing to feed her mother.

She watched him and her comment stopped at her lips. She watched him tear the hush puppy apart and feed it to her mother. And she saw him again, as she stood by his side when she was a child, as he fed little Cam when her mother was sick or couldn't come down from her room. She would stand at his elbow, watching him feed little Cam, singing songs to him, teaching her to feed him, to love him. Gentle, clumsy, full of the love he couldn't, wouldn't, didn't say out loud. No party laughter those mornings, no scary stories, no him at the center of attention. Just his shaking hands and his love coming clean.

And now, he was doing the same with her mother, and it was as it had always been, his hands and her shining eyes. Her love still able to return after all this time, after all this pain. Sure, these were her parents. She'd know them anywhere. This is how they were. This astonishing love and—as he took a sip of beer and tried to feed her at the same time, so that the hush puppy piece fell out of her mouth—this too. It was all of it. They were all those things. It was all true.

She almost wept and when Cam passed her the hush puppies, she met his eye, and he turned away, his eyes wet. Because she couldn't bear to watch anymore, she asked her father about his business. He answered her as though talking to her mother, as though her mother had asked the question. And then, when she asked Cam about his next sea assignment, he did the same thing. When the Brunswick stew began to dribble out of her mother's mouth, she stopped the sob in her throat, got up, pulled one of the spare chairs over next to her mother and took the bowl and spoon from her father.

"Let me do it, Daddy. You get some supper for yourself," she said, looking at her mother and trying to smile. He winked at her mother and took a long swig of beer.

"Old Tom Sawyer trick," he said to her mother and winked again. But she didn't watch him. She fed her mother. And she thought her heart would break. But she was very careful. She didn't let any spill. And her mother seemed pleased, rasping out something close to 'Thank you dear' when they put her to bed.

As Georgia turned to go, Cameron laid Martha down in the sheets and pulled the covers up over her. Georgia looked at them both, wondered if they should say bedside prayers as they had when she was little and going to bed and Martha was pulling the covers up over her. But little Cam stumbled out and she did too, leaving them alone.

After, Georgia cleaned up the kitchen. Maybe she could go shopping tomorrow. It would be good to get some fresh tomatoes. And peaches. It must be time for peaches. She started to make a list and was almost done when her father came back downstairs.

He watched her. And then, he got a glass, walked around her to put ice in it and reached up over the refrigerator to open the liquor cabinet. She saw the half-gallon bottles and bit her lip.

Her mouth in a thin line, she put down the pencil she'd been writing with and pushed her glasses up, turned to wipe the counter

down one more time before leaving. He cleared his throat as Cam
came in the room, looking as though he'd been in the bathroom,
washing his face.

"Will you have one with me tonight, brother?" her father
asked, his back to both of them. Little Cam looked at her, stuffed
his hands in his pockets and said, "No sir. But I believe I'll have a
little more tea. Is there any more tea, George?"

She let out her breath, and realized she'd been holding it.

"Sure," she said to him. "I can make you some more too, if
you want."

"Only if you want. There's enough for both of us here," he
said, waving the pitcher, sloshing the tea up its sides.

"Get your brother a glass," her father said.

"Daddy, I guess he's got two good hands of his own if he wants
a glass," she answered him.

Cam walked over and got two glasses. "You going to join us,
George?" he asked, holding up the second glass.

She looked at him then, and at her father who was watching
both of them. "I don't know that I'm invited," she said. "Aren't
you two going to have man talk or some other thing so Daddy can
get drunk?"

Cam put the glasses down while he put ice in them. "Why do
you want to be so hard on him, George? Daddy, don't you want
to sit with me and Georgia for awhile, let the night rest?"

Georgia and her father glared at each other. Finally her father
said, "Sure, let's sit together." He didn't smile or take his eyes off
Georgia. "Let's go out in the back. I think it's cooled off enough
to stand it." He stalked out the back door.

She looked then at Cam. "Was that an invitation?" she asked.

"It's the best you're going to get. Come on, George. Can't we
be a family again—just this once?"

She took the glass of tea he was offering and ducked under his
arm. "I don't know we ever were a family, Bud," she said, walking
out the door. Cam didn't respond.

They stepped out to a night warm in summer softness. Georgia
felt it slip around her, touch her soreness, her ache, her memories,
and she felt herself slip. She sat away from them on the brick stoop
and watched them in the twilight, watched the fireflies in the tree
across the way and watched the night sky turn royal blue. She
sipped her tea, apart from them. Cam talked on without her, let
her just sit for awhile.

In the dark, you could almost see how her father looked as a young man. You couldn't see how his pants didn't fit anymore, couldn't see his slight paunch or how his chin drooped.

You could imagine bright blond hair and fair skin, long fingers wrapped around a drink, looking like the Arrow shirt man, thin, supple, elegant, telling stories at a party, folks all around him, listening, laughing. His face pale in the night, but his eyes shiny and bright. You could almost see him laughing in the light, gesturing to her mother with his drink, the two of them laughing, his drink held high.

His drink, his drink. She didn't realize how much a highball glass full of straight whiskey was, or what it meant, when she used to watch them from her bedroom window, when she used to creep out of bed and watch their parties from her darkened bedroom— how she watched him and loved him and her mother, how they shone so brightly. How beautiful they were. How the ice clinked in their glasses. How their laughter sounded. What a party it was.

She shook her head. She didn't know what a party it was. She didn't know until later, when they would come in and kiss her goodnight. She didn't know until later, when they came in and screamed at her to get back into bed. She didn't know until later when she sobbed, alone, terrified, and knew she couldn't call to them because they were at a party. She didn't know until later, when she made parties herself, sobbing at the end, and terrified, and not being able to call to anyone.

She looked at him and saw how she couldn't call to him even now, even across the yard. She couldn't say to him, Daddy, I'm terrified. Mom is really sick. She can't come down this morning. And no one can help her. Daddy. Fix it. Can't you fix it? Daddy? Daddy, where are you? Where are you? Can't you hear me? Where are you?

She looked at him then, her throat full of words, full of years of words and finally heard little Cam calling to her to come over, sit with them.

She swallowed hard, got up, and brushed the seat of her pants off. As she started down the stairs, Cam went to the garage for another chair for her to sit in. She stood awkwardly, not speaking, beside her father. Cam brought the chair back. She heard the ice in her father's glass and she sat with them.

"Nice tonight, isn't it?" Cam said to neither one of them in particular.

"Um," her father said.

"Do you think we can hear her if she needs us?" Georgia asked.

"She was asleep almost as soon as her head touched the pillow," her father said, his voice kind again. "I cut the AC off. We can hear her. She'll be all right."

In her mind, she heard the way he had yelled at her about sleeping and not being available to hear her mother when he came home that afternoon, and it made her angry. She said, "Dad, why didn't you get all that stuff taken care of before you brought her home this afternoon?"

Her father started to say, "I've been working, young lady," but Cam cut him off before he could go any further.

"He just told me. He got her out early because you were coming home. That's why it took us so long at the hospital. They didn't want her to go yet. But he wanted us all to be together, like a family."

His voice was triumphant and he smiled when he looked at her.

"See? He ain't all bad, George."

She stared at little Cam in the growing darkness. She could still see his face, but she couldn't see his eyes very well. But she could see he was grinning. She turned to her father, surprised. He looked away and took another drink.

"Is that right, Daddy?" she asked. "Is she all right? You didn't have to do that."

"Cam's exaggerating as usual," he said dryly, still not looking at either one of them. "I only got her out a couple of days early. She's fine. It was just they wanted to do some physical therapy, but she told me she wanted to be home."

He took another drink. She looked at Cam. She could just see him winking. She took a sip of tea and looked out over the yard again.

"So, sister," her father said, and she jumped, surprised. "What are you up to these days?"

Cam chimed in, "Yeah, George, what are you planning to do with your life?"

Before she could stop herself, she said, "Well, I'm quitting my job when I go back."

The sentence shot out, wavering like a firefly between them, but clearly present. She wondered if she really had said it.

Then Cam said, "That secretary job? Good. You were too good for that. What are you going to do? Something with your degree?"

She looked at him. "Bud, an M.A. in history and two quarters will get you a cup of coffee."

"So what are you going to do, sister?" her father asked, looking at her directly over his raised drink. She noticed he'd almost drained it. "I agree with Cam. You were too good for that job. They were lucky to have you. What are you dreaming to do?"

His face was young then, and his eyes alert. She looked at him, astonished.

"Well, I'm not quite sure," she heard herself say.

"You ought to try to figure it out. You'll know inside, if you listen. I think it's always good to do what you dream of. I never did and look at me now. I wanted to be a farmer. I really did."

His voice trailed off but then grew stronger. "You'll never know if you don't try. You ought to try for what you really want, Georgia. Don't end up like me."

No one spoke. The night shifted around them. She wished she knew what to say to him, but then he cleared his throat and looked away and got up. "Believe I'll fix myself another and check in on your mother. Don't stay out here too long," he said and walked away.

Georgia and Cam watched him go without a word. She turned to Cam, her mouth open.

"A farmer?" she echoed. "You ever heard that before?"

"Yeah. Sometimes, when he gets in his cups, he sits and waxes poetic about the land. Haven't you ever heard him? He goes on and on about how beautiful the soil is. You remember those ads for that fertilizer you made so much fun of when you were first in San Francisco? He won an award for them. They were awesome. First time I saw those ads, I choked up."

They were both quiet. The sounds of the night—dogs barking, crickets, a slight wind, children chasing tag or fireflies—filled her ears.

"Oh Cam," she whispered. "I just don't understand him. Did you see how he was feeding Mom tonight? Not like he was doing a good job, or anything, but he was, well, you can tell he still loves her. After all this time."

"And she loves him," Cam added.

"Like a fool," she said.

"Like you do too," he said.

She didn't answer, but stood up and picked up her empty glass, turned to the door. "If there was anything I could do about that, I would," she said.

"You don't mean it, George."

"I do, I swear I do. You look at him one moment and he's a raging idiot. The next, he's the kindest thing. I don't understand him.

"And I'll tell you one other thing. I don't understand how she's lived with him all this time. All his jobs. All his stories. All his moving us around. And now look at her."

She broke off. "I don't understand any of it."

He got up too. "Neither do I. But at least we got each other."

She accepted his arm around her shoulder. "Yeah. At least we got that," she said wearily. They went in together. She put her glass in the sink and started up the stairs. Cam called out, 'Sleep well.' She said, 'You too,' and she went upstairs, into her room and shut the door. She got ready for bed, lay down, and read her book until she fell asleep.

She slept long and hard. The room was light when she finally woke up, in a panic and sweat-drenched. In that moment of waking, she couldn't remember where she was. She had dreamed she was down at Ocean Isle with little Cam and they had been lying out in the sun so long she was sweating. She shifted in the bed to find a cooler patch of sheets. Once she was awake, she lay motionless in the bed, her eyes open, one arm behind her head, listening to the house, watching the room, waiting for something, though she wasn't sure what.

And then, she heard her father gagging in the bathroom, like he had most mornings in her childhood, and she remembered. Before she could stop herself, she began to cry, crying without moving her head or making a sound; she cried, the tears rolling into her hair, her ears, her heart. There was no one here to fix anything. There never had been. For a long gasping moment she didn't know if she could breathe.

Finally, she heard Bernice in her ear, saying, 'Breathe baby girl,' and she did, but she was glad he was showering, because she knew he would hear her when sobs escaped with her breath. But after the struggle between breathing and silence, finally, trying not to gasp, she slowed down and her heart stopped pounding, replaced by a feverish ache, so hot, so deep, it was as though she hadn't a heart. As though someone had taken a shotgun to her at close range, as though her body were riddled with buckshot, her blood draining out of her. She lay there, immobile. And then she heard her father turn off the shower water, and there was silence until she heard him unlatch her side and go out his side.

She watched the light slipping under the closed shade for a very long time. Then, she heard Bernice again and she took a deep breath, jagged through the ache. She took another and swung her legs over the side of the bed and got up. She went to the bathroom, brushed her teeth, then put on her summer jeans and went, as always, to make her bed.

She bent to straighten the sheets, to fold her nightgown and something caught in her throat and she felt the pain come back, hot as whiskey. How could she not have known there was no one to fix things for her, after all this time? She sat down heavily on the side of the half-made bed and put her head in her hands and felt the tears escaping and as she did, something let go. She cried silently for a long time.

But she stopped crying as suddenly as she had started. She got up and went to the window, taking deep breaths. She opened the shade and looked out at the hot morning air. She wiped her eyes, turned to face the room, and realized she would have to ask Cam why they had kept all her things in this room and where his stuff was. Had he taken it? What were all her things doing here? She ought to take it home, get it out of here. Didn't belong here.

She walked out to the hall and listened for a moment at her mother's closed door, but there was no sound, and she thought maybe her mother was still sleeping.

She started down the steps to the kitchen, listening. Still silence. Maybe Cam had gone out too, with her father. She stopped on the stairs, angry. So what was she supposed to do now? Wait for them? In fury, she took the last steps two at a time and went to the front door. No cars in the driveway. Damn them. She turned back to the kitchen, steaming and thought to herself, well, if they weren't there, she'd make some coffee and sit with a day-old biscuit, and figure out what *she* wanted to do. She'd start with that.

She began to look for the coffee. Maybe later she'd be able to get to the market and get some real food for breakfast. Milk. Fruit. Cheese. Bread. Left to himself, Cameron would starve. But not her, she thought, running the water for her coffee. No. She would get some real food, at least for while she was here.

And until she could get the car, and get the food, she'd make herself some decent coffee. She slammed the pot down on the stove. At least she could do that. Maybe sit on the back stoop with her cup, if there was any shade. She began to smile at that. Like she used to watch her mother do, to get some time to herself. Her special mother-alone-time.

She thought as she poured water over the grounds, well, it will be my special time too. She smiled a little more then. She could do that. And let the idiots know when they got home not to leave her here with no car and no word ever again. She poured some fresh coffee into her cup, swirled cream through it and went to the back door.

The stoop was still slightly shaded, and so she went out and sat there, with the door open so she could hear her mother. She knew Cameron would yell at her if he saw it, because of the air conditioning, but, she thought smiling, after all, he wasn't there. She drank her coffee, and the hot liquid slipped down and soothed her inside, and she thought to herself as the ache in her heart slipped away with the warm, well, it's good coffee, it is. She heard a car come up. Probably Cam, she thought, not moving. Well, he could just find her. She had a lot to say, but not until she had finished her coffee. She took another sip, looked out at the yard and began to think about what she would like to do that day. After all, she wasn't going to be there that long.

CHAPTER SEVEN

INCIDENT AT GETHSEMANE

Morgan watched Lisa step into the batter's box. She smiled when the small woman used the bat to knock imaginary dirt off her imaginary cleats, and then stuck her butt way out and wagged the bat wildly behind her right ear.

"You clown," Morgan called out, "this is batting practice, not comedy night at Diana's Uptown. Settle down."

Lisa shot her a grin, but took a more modified position, and wiffed the next two easy pitches. She missed them by a breath. Same as in last week's game. Morgan watched her closely from outside the first base line. On the next pitch, Lisa pop-fouled. Morgan saw real frustration in her face, even as she pounded the plate and acted up and everybody in the infield laughed.

Morgan called out to Ann to hold the ball as she walked up to Lisa.

"You can't hit it if you close your eyes, babe," she said.

"Am I closing my eyes?" Lisa looked surprised.

"A second after you start your swing. Doesn't give you much chance if the pitch doesn't do what you think it will."

"I'm closing my eyes," Lisa said, disgusted, kicking dirt over the plate.

"Take it easy. We all do it sometimes. Sometimes we think we can concentrate better; sometimes we're afraid of getting hit by the ball; sometimes we think we can hit harder."

Lisa stood, dejected, with her head down. Morgan reached over and pulled Lisa's cap down over her eyes. Lisa shoved it back up and squinted at her.

Morgan grinned. "Let me give you a tip. Don't think of it as Stockton's head. You're trying to smash her head. I know you. But you're not built that way, friend. You don't have it in you. You may think you want to, but at the critical moment, you can't. It's like you always say, you're a lover, not a fighter."

Lisa just nodded, her eyes down, her right foot kicking at the plate again.

"So listen. Don't think of it as anybody's head. Think of it as a softball. Just a softball. Sure, it's hard if it hits you. But if you keep your eyes on it, it won't hit you. Other than that, it's just something made of string and leather. Little-bitty thing. You just need to get a piece of it to get it out of here. You don't have to kill it. Just hit it. Keep your eyes open and swing. Just the clean joy of hitting a softball. Try that."

Lisa looked up and grinned. "Right. I'm a lover, not a fighter. Okay, I'll kiss that ball, Coach," she said.

Morgan smiled, folded her arms over her chest and walked back behind the first base line. Lisa stepped back into the box. Ann pitched a nice slow one, and Lisa swung clean, easy and strong, her swing powered down her arms and legs from somewhere in the center of her back. Ball and bat connected with a loud dull thud and the ball arched and soared nicely over the centerfielder's head. Lisa stood at home plate and jumped up and down, squealing.

The centerfielder chased the ball down. Morgan looked at Lisa and said, "You going to run this out or you going to celebrate?"

Lisa gave another little scream and tore towards first base. She wasn't halfway there when the first basewoman waved the ball at her. She slowed and peeled off, grinning at Morgan.

As she started past her, she said, "I really wasn't thinking about Stockton just then, but you're right about part of it. I'd love to get the chance to blow her out of this ballpark."

Morgan smiled. Lisa stopped then and stood next to her, and they watched the next woman come up to the plate.

"So would I," Morgan said, her eyes on the batter. "All year, she's been my favorite imaginary target for line drives," she said.

This one was off balance when she hit, that's what was happening. Most of her hits were foul. Morgan called out, "Try putting your weight on your right foot to start off, Jackie." Jackie realigned herself.

"Has it been a whole year? Seems like a long time ago. How come we haven't forgotten?" asked Lisa.

"We have impaired development. Or maybe it's because we haven't gone to confession and learned forgiveness. You been in church lately? I haven't.

"Jackie, take your weight off your left foot. Lift it up a little if that helps.

"Anyway, speaking of ballparks and Stockton, I heard she's coaching out here. Can you believe it? Some team with mostly straights. I heard they were terrible, bottom of their division.

"Way to go, Jackie. Run it out. Run it out."

Jackie got on base and Anita came up. As Morgan checked them off her roster sheet, she realized Lisa was watching her. She looked back at her briefly before turning again to watch the pitch.

"So what are you doing these days instead of working at the shelter?" she asked, as casually as she could.

"I got involved with this thing at the library," Lisa answered, her voice eager. "And you know, hey, Morgan, you know, I think you might like it. Let me tell you about it... "

They both clapped when Anita hit a nice Texas Leaguer.

"Sure. I'd like that. But not now. Maybe we can get together later in the week for supper or something," she said, watching the next batter.

"Tuesday?" Lisa asked.

"Sure. Great." Morgan kept her eyes on the pitch.

Lisa said she'd call, and touched Morgan's arm for a moment before she walked back to the bench.

Morgan checked her clipboard. That batter was the last in the lineup. She called for the next woman to bunt, and then started the whole line going through the bunting practice. *Had* it been a year? She couldn't believe it, either. It felt like yesterday. She sucked her breath in. Well, one of these days, the past would be a memory. It would be clean, enough time passed.

She shook her head. Had she never had them lay down bunts before? They were awful. So Lisa still wanted to hurt Stockton, too. But she seemed to let go of it easier, like it was mostly gone. And it sounded like she was okay about it. Maybe she needed to get involved like Lisa had. To get involved with something new. Forget the shelter.

Getting involved with someone new always helped when your lover left you. Why shouldn't it work with other things you cared about? It should work. Maybe it was time to admit softball wasn't going to take the shelter's place. No maybe about it, she thought, watching the next batter and trying not to shake her head. Softball was good, but it wasn't the shelter. And it wasn't going to be. Maybe she needed something more along the lines of what Lisa was doing.

She kept making checks in the 'needs work' column on her roster. Lisa had been as hurt as her, maybe more. When they'd had supper once to talk about the purge, she learned more about Lisa than she had the whole time they worked at the shelter together. Lisa had worked as lay counselor down there for three years. And Morgan knew from her work with the kids that Lisa had been one of the best. But they let her go too.

Well, at least one of them, Anita, could bunt. She watched her lithe brown body streak towards first. She held the clipboard under her arm and clapped. The bench cheered too and Anita high-fived back. The next batter was miserable. Morgan went back to marking the roster.

'Nothing personal against them,' she imitated the sound of Stockton's voice in her head as the next batter came up. No, she didn't have to take being fired personally. The purging had gone on all over the country, she thought with a sour smile. Oh, lesbians were good enough to build the damn shelters; good enough to keep them running even when men came after them, literally, with guns; good enough to provide money and to work when no one else would, to build the safe houses, sometimes with their own hands. Who the hell did people think did all that work? Or would continue to do it? A board of directors? Professionals?

Lisa laid down a nice bunt and ran off grinning. But Morgan's angry scowl didn't change. Who the hell did they think cared about women enough to do all that work? Somebody who was paid to do it? The government funding agencies? They'd shut the shelters down sooner than men with guns would, she thought, kicking up a weed clump and scattering it in the grass.

Nothing personal is right, she thought; it was all political. Her mouth twisted into a smirk and she shook her head and then glanced at her watch. Noon. Well, this practice was over. Time to get across the Bay and check out that Oakland team she'd promised to scout for her own team. They'd probably meet the Oakland team in the finals next month.

Another month. God, the time flew. A year already. Well, the shelter, and Stockton, would get what they deserved. They would. That's what Elliott always said. He was probably right. She sighed, her hands sweaty and cramped. God, enough of this. She took her cap off and wiped her forehead with the back of her forearm.

"Okay kids. Wednesday, six p.m. practice, seven o'clock game. You don't come to practice, you don't play. Have a nice weekend, ladies." She watched as they began to pick up their things. They were good kids. Maybe the batting practice would help some. Jesus, almost anything would help, would be an improvement over last week's skunk. But they were good kids.

Lisa walked off and called out, "Good luck, Coach. See you on Tuesday."

Morgan waved and started collecting the bats and stuffing them in the sack. She was tired already. She had just enough time to hurry over to Oakland, get back home to shower, and check the phone machine to see if Georgia had called, before she went to the office to finish up a last bit of the contract proposal that was due Monday.

Too goddamn much work to do. She squinted at the sky. What ever happened to Saturdays when you could just sit in the sun? Read a book? Actually watch a ball game on TV? Morgan kicked a soda can off the field and towards the orange trash can.

She took a deep breath. Not that Georgia would like it if she was watching ball games on television on Saturday afternoon. Georgia wouldn't like it. But if she didn't have to work this afternoon, she could have watched. Because George had finally gone home. Finally, she'd gone home. Poor kid.

Oh, the trip was good for *them*, and probably good for Georgia. But she couldn't imagine it was going to be easy. She couldn't imagine seeing her own mother with her face paralyzed. Even after she'd seen everything else. Seen the silence, the lies, the hitting, the bruises, the blood on her face. But her own mother had mended. At least the parts you could see.

She hoisted the bat sack on her shoulder and took it to the Jeep. Then she went back to get the catcher's gear. Her mother. She squinted into the sun at home plate and stood there for a moment.

Jesus, why didn't she leave the fucker before she got paralyzed too? She started to walk towards the Jeep, shaking her head. For the last twenty years, she'd asked herself that. And she never had an answer.

And for five years, every Saturday morning when she went to the shelter and saw the kids, she'd asked herself. She looked at the women with the kids, the ones with the scars and the ones with the bruises, and she wanted to ask them. Was that the best they could do? To stay? Was that what they thought they deserved? Jesus Christ, didn't the kids at least deserve any better?

To the women that came back twice, three times, she wanted to ask, for Chrissake, what are you doing going back there? What about your kids? Don't you care what they see? Why go back? You can't think he loves you. Or the kids. You can't be still believing that this is love.

But she never asked the women at the shelter. Because she knew she couldn't say the words. She'd said them once to her mother. Once was enough. She didn't know how Lisa did it. It seemed to her better to work with the kids. Better to do something for them. Before they grew up so hurt they only expected more. Before they grew up knowing how to hit, or how it was to be hit; before they grew up wanting to get away so bad they'd run all their lives.

Well, she knew what those kids needed and how badly they needed someone to work with them. She threw the gear in the back of the Jeep. She didn't care who Stockton had hired to replace her or how many degrees she had. Whoever they got, she didn't know half what Morgan knew.

The familiar litany filled her head. She clenched her hands into fists as she started back towards the plate and only relaxed them when she scooped up the ball bag. Angrily, she began stuffing in the dozen or so balls lying behind the plate where her players had brought them.

Women on the team using the field next began arriving and Morgan was conscious of them, limbering up, laughing, light-hearted, but no familiar voices. When she picked up the last ball, she slapped the bag to get the dust out and then headed for the Jeep, her public smile on, her eyes registering only women in softball uniforms, not women with faces.

Turning the corner around the left bench, she almost ran into Alice Stockton. She saw her uniform first, said a quick apology and made a sidestep, before she actually saw the face above the uniform. She stopped still, off-balance and astonished.

"Hello, Morgan," Stockton said pleasantly.

Morgan just looked at her and took a step back. She didn't want to say anything to her. She didn't want to see her. She couldn't believe Alice Stockton was standing a foot away.

"I thought I might run into you one of these days," Alice said in the same friendly conversational tone. "How are you?"

What the fuck is this, Morgan thought furiously. Is she going to make chitchat?

But before she could reply, she heard another voice, a male voice shouting near both of them. In unison, they turned to look in the direction of the noise.

A tall gangling man, his uniform hanging loosely off his lean body and his cap pushed halfway back on his receding forehead, was standing near home plate, shouting, "Who's in charge of this outfit?"

All practice on the field stopped. Everyone looked at the man, who was waving what seemed to be a schedule book and shouting, his mouth working his droopy mustache into a frenzy. He looked to Morgan like an old adolescent, a domesticated hippie who discovered construction work made him a man in 1968 and never changed. He stood at the plate and shouted again.

"I'm the coach of this team," Stockton answered, her voice loud enough to carry, but controlled, not shouting. Morgan watched her. It was almost her normal voice, she realized, but not quite. It was her formal business speech voice. The memory of it chilled Morgan, and she stood rooted, watching as Stockton walked over to the man.

In that same quiet, imperious voice, Stockton called to him as she walked, "May I help you with something?"

The man, too, seemed struck by her tone, but then he roared, "You sure can, lady. Get these girls off the field. You're in the wrong place. We've got the field now," he shouted, heedless of the fact that Stockton was as close to him then as two people on a sofa.

"Let me get my schedule book," she said. "Perhaps there has been a scheduling problem."

"No scheduling problem," he retorted. "You're just in the wrong place."

She didn't answer him, but said, "Stay where you are, ladies," to her players in the field. Nobody moved, but everyone watched: her team, Morgan, and the gathering crowd of his team and their wives.

Morgan had to give Stockton credit. The bitch did as well against men as she had against her: head held up, somehow conveying the impression the creep was wrong, that *she* couldn't possibly be in the wrong. Soon, Stockton came back from her car, holding a schedule book open and smiling pleasantly, as though a bank teller had made a simple error. Morgan watched the man spit a stream of tobacco juice at the spot where Stockton had stood. He turned away to talk to some of his players, told them loudly to start spreading out the bats and warming up.

"I don't think that will be necessary," Stockton said as she walked back, jerking his head around with her voice. "As you can plainly see, *we* have the field during this time period." She extended her book to him, opened to the page.

He pulled his cap down, took the scheduling book, and as he did, she demanded, "I'd like to see yours, also. Perhaps you had trouble with the time, or reading the name." She said it as though the man couldn't read, but not insolently enough that he could say anything back. Morgan whistled soundlessly, watching the gall.

When Stockton took the man's book, almost before he could orient himself to reading hers, she quickly pointed to a schedule line, using the bright red nail on her long, slender index finger.

"I believe this says you are to play on Atherton Field, not Aviation Field, which is where you are." Her voice curled as she spoke, somewhat like an elementary school teacher, disciplining a child. Morgan remembered that tone and, anger rising in her like heat waves off summer city streets, she turned to go. She had heard Stockton use that tone one too many times.

But Stockton called to her before she'd taken a step. "Atherton's about twenty minutes from here, isn't it, Morgan?"

Morgan stopped, turned and nodded numbly to her. Stockton turned back to the man, her voice loud enough for everyone on the field to hear, but her question was directed to Morgan.

"Since you probably have more experience than anyone on this field, Morgan, perhaps you can tell our friend here: if he hurries, can he possibly get his team to Atherton before he has to forfeit as a no-show?"

She had to smile then. She knew exactly what Stockton was doing and many was the time she had wished to do something similar, up against such a man, but she had never had such a perfect chance.

Watching him spit again, she found herself speaking with relish. "Not if he has a 12:30 game. It's 12:15 now. No way. Does he even know where Atherton is? Maybe you should give him directions. Maybe you should read his schedule for him again, too. Maybe the game isn't at 12:30 either. Then, at least, he has a chance."

The women on the field laughed out loud, the sound scattered but lingering for a long moment. The man jerked his schedule out of Stockton's hands and stalked off, surrounded by his team and their questions. He sneaked a spiteful look at Stockton and Morgan as he walked off.

Morgan stood chuckling, watching him, and then realized that as he had walked away, Stockton had walked towards her. She saw that Stockton had her hand up for a high-five and Morgan gave it to her, feeling strange, but still laughing.

"Thanks for doing the second part of a two-part punch, Morgan," Stockton said, her voice back to normal. Morgan stepped back and looked at her, trying to decide what to do.

Almost involuntarily, she said, "You're welcome. Glad to help. Nice of you to give me the punch line," she said and then stopped, surprised at herself.

"You're looking good these days, Morgan," Stockton said. "I hope everything is going well."

Morgan looked away and then towards the players on the field.

"I'm fine," she bit off. What was this? They were friends now, comrades- in-arms? Some fucking ally, she thought, trying to decide what to say before walking off.

"Listen, Morgan," Stockton said, and turned her back to the field, "I've been sorry for a long time about our little altercation when we last saw each other. I've always wanted to tell you I thought you did a good job, even though you seemed to think we were asking you to leave because you hadn't."

Silence stretched between them. Stockton finally looked away from her. When Morgan felt her move, she looked at her face again. As she did, all the anger she had felt for the last year floated up her throat, flooding into her mouth. And she knew she shouldn't speak it, not here, not now, not to this woman who could wither a pig like that, and who had certainly whipped her ass a year earlier.

Suddenly Stockton turned to look back at her and caught her with her eyes. "I hope you worked it out for yourself," she said. "As you can see," she said, gesturing towards the field behind them, "I took your advice and fielded a staff team. We do get to work out some of our stress."

She barked a laugh and then looked at Morgan again. "You contributed a great deal to the shelter, Morgan. I hope you don't still think of us as enemies. I think," she said, gesturing at the plate, "we have some of the same struggles. I'm sorry we all had to part on such bad terms. We do miss you."

Morgan took a step back as though she had been slapped. God Almighty. The woman hadn't changed a bit. Not even after twelve months.

"I just bet you do," she said finally. "I think your staff probably needs your direction now," she bit out. "And I have work to do." She began to walk away.

Stockton called after her, "See you around then."

Morgan didn't answer, only walked as fast as she could without running to the Jeep and jumped in. Once inside, she hurriedly started the engine, eased the sticky clutch out as fast as she dared, and shot out of the parking lot.

As she drove, the roar in her head got louder. What the hell had just happened? How could Stockton have acted exactly the same except for a few brief moments when they seemed to be fighting on the same side? She shook her head. And she'd just been thinking about her that morning. Jesus Christ. Speak of the Devil and in she walks. Christ on the cross. Stockton.

She stopped for the light. Jesus. She drummed her fingers on the wheel. It wasn't like she didn't have enough to do today without getting all wrapped up in Stockton and the shelter again. Shit. She didn't even have enough time to think about it. She only had an hour at most, not including travel time to get to the Oakland game and back. And then, a hot shower. Real hot. Then work. And after work, there was dinner at Elizabeth's.

Dinner at Elizabeth's. Well, at least something was going to be right about this day. At least something. She slipped into the right lane, to turn off up to the freeway entrance. She turned on the radio, trying to catch the A's game, trying to leave Stockton far, far behind.

She merged easily onto the freeway, pulling into the center lane and shifting into fourth. And then, around the last curve and under the overpass, approaching the bridge, she saw it. Traffic stalled. Lines of cars crawling. She hit the steering wheel and cried out. Just what the fuck she needed. And no way to get off the damn bridge now. She hit the steering wheel again and again.

She braked to a standstill, hung her arm out the window, and blew out all the breath in her lungs. What was jamming traffic on this goddamn bridge now? It wasn't as if she didn't have enough to do. She wondered if she hadn't gotten involved with Stockton at the field, taken up that time, would she be caught in this mess now? She took her foot off the clutch.

Goddamn her luck! This whole day was turning out to be a waste. Just like Stockton. Well, that at least was one thing. Stockton did look wasted. She looked like hell. Skin gray, like she hadn't been out of her office in months. Dry and blotchy too. Rings under her eyes. Served her right.

Morgan fingered her bird necklace, lying heavy on her breastbone. It didn't matter that Stockton had made pig meat out of some jerk today. Or that she'd shared her easy kill. Because Morgan remembered, as though it were only yesterday, she remembered Stockton's kill voice only too well.

And she heard it again, for the thousandth time, the cold business killing in Stockton's voice when she had opened the door to her office that afternoon a year ago, and said, "Come in, Morgan. I've finished up now. Let's talk."

She had followed Stockton into her office and wondered immediately what was happening, what was tripping her screaming danger siren. But she couldn't place it right then, idiot that she had been. She couldn't place the tone in that office.

They'd been meeting on Saturday afternoons for about a year by then, ever since Stockton had been hired. Morgan would stop by on her way out of the building Saturday afternoons. The first time, she had been surprised to see Stockton there, and pleased that even though she was a paid professional, she seemed to be working around the clock like the longtime volunteers.

And all year, Stockton had encouraged Morgan to come in and talk. About the shelter. About how it had been before she was hired, how the shelter had gotten started. The troubles. The personalities. Who helped; who didn't.

And about Morgan. Her childhood. Her life now. Georgia. They had weaved around Georgia's name, but finally, Stockton had said something about going to the Parade. And then a little about her friend she owned a house with.

Once they'd made that exchange, Morgan relaxed some, relaxed a lot. The information was slight, but at the time, Morgan thought, well, she can't speak. It's too bad, but she doesn't think she can. At least she'd found some way to let Morgan know. That was enough.

So mostly then, they talked about the shelter. What funding Stockton was trying to get. How to make the programs better. What to do for the kids. Stockton didn't know the first thing about sports, but she was interested, and they had talked, Morgan guiding her through it, helping, laughing, hoping. Hoping for the kids. For herself. For some sense that things would get better at the shelter, taken care of, in good hands, if not expert. She had relaxed and enjoyed their talks.

But when she followed Stockton into her office that last day, she thought, something's different today, something different in Stockton's voice. Cold. Not friendly. Her heart sank. When Stockton began to speak again, it became quite clear.

"How can I help you, Morgan?" she asked, and Morgan stared at her, knowing she'd been trapped, knowing there was no other explanation for that tone of voice. Knowing she was being lied to, even now.

And then she felt the fury streak through her, like a forest fire, racing through her blood down to every part of her. So Stockton was going to play it like this. Like Stockton didn't know her. Like Stockton didn't care to know her. Like they had nothing in common.

What a fool she had been to think that she could talk to her about being asked to leave! To think that Stockton maybe hadn't known and could change things. To think that Stockton wasn't using her to shield herself. To think that she could trust her. Oh Jesus, she thought then. Mother of God. What an idiot you have been.

When she didn't answer, Stockton's smile moved a little and then froze again. The woman's eyes were wary and cold as steel. Morgan could barely drag her eyes away from the smile. It look like it could cut glass.

Finally she forced herself to answer. She didn't say what she wanted to say; she just stumbled on, in her fury sliding into the little speech she and Elliott had concocted to help her keep her job. But the words turned in her mouth and what she had meant to be a request for help came out bitter, angry and accusing.

"I wanted to ask you how the decision had been reached on asking me to leave, and whether or not I can change anyone's mind enough to reconsider the decision."

But Stockton didn't seem to hear the anger in her voice, didn't even seem to be listening. As soon as Morgan stopped talking, Stockton cut back in, cold as a razor.

"You have no professional training in either recreation or therapy with children, do you, Morgan?"

And when she heard the voice again, she began to wonder why she was staying in the room. She felt Stockton's game in the hot nervous palms of her fists, in the restless ache in her legs. Saw what she had been doing all year. And she hated it. Hated how she'd been lied to, how she'd thought of Stockton as a friend, hated what a fool she had been.

And she thought to herself, what did her work matter now? She'd never get her place back. There was nowhere to turn around, nowhere to go, the fucking bitch had pinned her to the wall. And she struck at her then, wildly, as hard as she could.

"Alice," she said, slowly, trying to make her point carry, "I would like to point out that, to my knowledge, every lesbian who has volunteered, or who worked at the shelter in a paid capacity, has been asked to leave over the last two years, with the exception of you. I would be interested in hearing how that has happened."

Stockton leaned forward, her eyes glittering, but her voice controlled like a judge. "We do not ask a person's sexual preference when they come to us for work, or as volunteers. I am quite certain what you are describing is not going on. I have no knowledge of it."

And then Stockton's smile came back but her voice was the same sharp, precise knife. Without missing a beat, she said, "There is nothing personal in our asking you to leave. We are only upgrading our staff. But I think perhaps you are taking this personally, and you might want to think about what in your childhood is causing you to react so strongly."

Morgan sat there staring at her, stunned at the slippery shock into her private pain. She hadn't expected this stiletto. She hadn't expected any of this. She should have known better, goddamnit; she should have never said a word to this bitch. But she had. And Stockton had answered her. And now, she thought, her anger roaring in her ears, now, get this bitch.

"It seems to me, Alice," she said very slowly, "that if there is a purge going on, having your name mentioned in a lesbian context would be very dangerous to you. Wouldn't it? It seems to me that if there is a purge going on, the board ought to know about it. At least the board. And if I don't get satisfaction there, possibly the papers."

Stockton stood and went to the door and spoke so quietly Morgan could almost not hear her. "That will not help the children here, will it?"

Morgan felt sick then and stood too. Stockton put her hand on the door knob but didn't open it.

"Be very careful what you say about me, without any proof. I will not be intimidated, nor will I allow you to try to use vicious unproven rumors as blatant extortion for your own gain. Is that quite clear?"

They were both very silent when Alice's voice faded away. They only looked at each other, hard, tight, angry. There was no movement in the room for several moments, even the air hung still between them, their fury and fear stilling any noise, any passage.

Abruptly, Stockton made the first move to break the silence.

"And let me make one more thing very clear," she said. "If you came here to get me to help you get your position back, you have made a grave mistake. After this afternoon, I would recommend you for dismissal under any circumstances. This kind of behavior, your stress on sexual preference and your aggressive attitude are not what we want for the children at this shelter, I can assure you."

She opened the door then and Morgan stared at her, unable to believe that she could walk past her without slapping her. But she did. She turned and walked, keeping her back ramrod stiff. And as she went out, she heard Stockton slam the door behind her.

She could still hear that slam. She had heard it slam every day for the past year. She could hear it clearly over the hum of the traffic jam. And it made her as furious now as it did then.

She slipped the Jeep ahead a little. Goddamn traffic jam. She hit the steering wheel again. And what had she done? What had she done?

Nothing. There was nothing she could have done, she told herself again. What would it get her to expose Stockton anyway? Nothing. Stockton was right. It wouldn't have helped the shelter. It was a step she couldn't take, and she knew it, even as she nursed the fantasy like the last log on a fire. She couldn't expose another lesbian, even if she was a lying bitch. And anyway, she tried to tell herself, it wouldn't get her job back.

There was nothing she could have done, she said to herself, hitting the steering wheel over and over.

Except rot with it. Jesus. She had to get through this mess. The Jeep loved to overheat in these situations. She looked wildly around at the traffic and then realized she was almost across. Suddenly, she was off the bridge, looking at the miles of backed-up traffic stretching before her on I-580, right where she needed to go.

She threw up her hands and screamed. She looked at her watch. Goddamnit, she'd been on the bridge for an hour! A fucking ten minute drive had taken her an hour. She looked again at the line for 580, checked her rearview mirror and stuck her arm out the window to hand-signal a left turn. She got into the far left lane and looped off the highway, then back onto the same road, going in the other direction.

No traffic this way, she hissed to herself as she went through the toll. No, she'd probably make it home in twenty minutes. But she'd missed the fucking game she wanted to scout. And now, it would be two o'clock before she got home. Well, if she hurried, she still might be able to get some work done. Goddamn Stockton. This never would have happened if she hadn't stopped to talk with her. She whipped the Jeep along the upper deck of the bridge, speeding and weaving.

She sailed through the yellow lights when she got off the highway, and hurried down Turk, alternately cursing and blessing the timed lights. Home. She jammed the Jeep onto the sidewalk in front of her house, parked it and vaulted up the stairs.

She was breathless, her fury jumping through her skin. She stripped, threw her clothes on the floor, and hurried into the shower, yelling in the empty house, stopping only as the shower water blasted full on her face.

She reached for the washcloth and wiped her face, stood with her back to the water and braced herself on the shower wall. How dare Stockton say those things to her! Filthy lies. And today. Acting like nothing had happened. Goddamn fucking liar.

She kicked the water in the bottom of the shower. How could she have used her like that? Lied to her like that? All year! And then using those old tricks. As though the kids mattered to Stockton. As though what she was doing was for them. And as though she and Stockton had no relationship. Implying she had a personal problem. Even today. As though it were her fault. God, she'd heard that often enough from men when she had worked in an office. It was an old, old trick. Stockton probably thought she invented it. Thought she was being smart.

Well, fuck her. Had Stockton helped the kids by forcing her out? Was she so smart to think about that? What about their personal reaction to her being gone? Her own personal reaction had nothing to do with it. And they both knew it. It wasn't her personal reaction to the situation. It was her personal reaction for the kids. It was her fucking personal reaction to Stockton herself.

She'd had the same reaction today.

She stopped for a moment when she thought that, water streaming over her, her heart louder than the spray. And then, suddenly, she began to sob. And in the water, she saw her mother's face, calm, slicing potatoes for soup. She was twelve then, the oldest. She was trying to tell her mother, she was trying to say, she was saying her stomach hurt. That her legs hurt. That when her mother went to work, that her father...

Her mother kept slicing the potatoes. She said something like: your father what? She slid the potatoes in the pot. Just what was she saying about her father, just what kind of trouble was she causing now? She stirred the soup. Little troublemaker. Always into something. Always would be. Now that he's finally home from his trip for Uncle Sam. Be nice for once, her mother said.

Morgan shifted on her feet, almost unable to stand still. She remembered following the motion of the knife her mother had used to slice the potatoes and then stir them. She remembered trying to say, 'Listen Mom. Listen. He tells me... you don't know. Do you know who he says Uncle Sam is? He makes me touch Uncle Sam. Mom, this isn't a game. I know what he's doing. Please Mom, I just don't want to be here alone with him. Please. Can't we leave? Mom, I know he hits you too. Can't we leave Mom?'

Her mother turned from the stove, her eyes glistening, her arms wrapped around her ribs, her hair loose from its twist and falling on the sides of her face. She looked at Morgan like she was going to hit her. Morgan said again, hopping from one foot to the other as though the floor were burning underneath her, 'Mom, listen to me. Listen to me. I didn't ask for it. He's lying when he says I'm a whore. I'm not doing it with the boys from school. I swear to God, I'm not lying. He forces me. It hurts. He makes me bleed. Mom. Listen to me. Please take us away from here. Mom? Mom?'

Her mother leapt forward and slammed the knife down on the counter and screamed, 'Don't lie to me you little bitch.'

'Don't lie to me you little bitch.' The water streamed down her face. 'There is nothing wrong here but you, you little bitch. Can't you find something to do, besides telling me these lies? Go take care of your little sister. And get your father a beer.'

'But don't ever, ever, young lady, don't you ever repeat these filthy lies to anyone, do you understand me? I'll whip you until you can't sit down if I hear one more peep about this, I mean it.'

The water streamed down Morgan's face and she sobbed. She turned her face into the hard, stinging stream and she didn't turn away until she began to choke and then she stopped, turned off the water, turned off her mother's face, turned off her heart. She stood in the shower until her knees gave way. Then she sat on the side of the tub until she became very cold, the sizzle of fury in her heart her only warmth.

She began to towel off then. That was then. This is now. And it doesn't have anything to do with the shelter. It was just fucking Stockton, selling them all out for her career. Forget it. God knew, there was enough for her to do other places. And she really hadn't been able to do much for those kids, anyway. A couple hours a week didn't make much difference. It couldn't.

It was just seeing the bitch again today that did it, that set the fury going again. Well, anyway, it was over. She got dressed, put on a clean pair of old jeans and a T-shirt, hoping Elizabeth meant it when she said it was informal. And then, remembering Elizabeth, she remembered Georgia.

She walked over to the answering machine, turned it on and Georgia's voice filled the room.

"Hi, it's me. Oh Em, I wish you were home. I wanted to talk so much. I hope you're okay. It's hard. I'm having a hard time and I miss you, Em. I miss you so much. These people are lunatics. And my Mom, oh my God, Morgan, I, well, it's awful. I'll be so glad to get home. I'm sorry to have missed you. Dad's coming home soon, so it's not safe to call. Just get me at the airport tomorrow. God, it'll be great to see you. Take care, darling. I love you."

Take care. Take care. She mimicked Georgia's voice. And where the hell were you when I needed *you*? Where are you, Georgia? Why aren't you here with me, taking care of me, for a change?

Her anger splashed up over her. And what about Elliott? Where the hell was he? Lot of help he'd been lately, not at work and completely fucked about the contract. He'd been days late with his part of the proposal. If he'd gotten his work done on time, she'd never be in this mess. And now she was supposed to have it done. She'd have to go to work on Sunday, too. Well, fuck him. She just couldn't carry it anymore. She couldn't.

She smoothed her hands down over her jeans. But she would. And they both knew it. Oh hell, it wasn't his fault. She sat on the couch and laced up her dress sneakers. Well, she could get some work done, and then it would be time to see Elizabeth. At least there was that, at the end of this miserable day.

She sighed. Had it only been three weeks since that first dinner? It must have been, because the season started six weeks ago, and it was two days after that first dinner that Elizabeth had come to their first home game, but hadn't stayed to talk. Morgan, watching her leave, had raced straight home herself—and called her.

Well, and what of it? She just wanted to make sure Elizabeth was okay, because she'd left so fast. They'd only talked briefly. And then, two days after that Elizabeth had called to see if she was free for lunch. And then there were a few more lunches, just a few, and at them the small gifts Elizabeth had given her: a new tea cup and saucer for her to use at work, a vase for her desk, an elegant mechanical pencil. Morgan kept them at work, ran her fingers over them, smiled when she saw them. They made her feel good, as though for once she had things to make her look like who she was. Or anyway, who she wanted to be.

At their lunches, Elizabeth was her lovely, considerate self, so gracious. And she was always so well-dressed; Morgan wondered if she was dressing for her and she wanted it to be true. It made her feel terrific. Elizabeth always took her to someplace special, some hidden out-of-the-way place, with some kind of food she'd never heard of. There was the goat cheese and beet vinaigrette salad which sounded awful but tasted delicious and she loved it, just as Elizabeth said she would. It had been her favorite and she had asked Elizabeth to take her back to the Ironwood, but Elizabeth had only smiled and said, "Just wait. The next one will be better."

And she was thrilled, not just by the words, but also by the look Elizabeth had let slip between them. Morgan knew she had undressed her there on the sidewalk, right there at the corner of Carl and Cole and she was delighted, warmed, and then flamed.

God, how long had it been since she had felt this way? When she promised to stay with Georgia forever, it didn't mean she was giving up this *feeling* forever. It was bad, and she knew, and it thrilled her that it was bad. But as long as she looked and didn't touch, it was a safe kind of bad and she relished it.

She grinned and leaned back on the couch. There she was, old Morgan Mary Margaret McCormack, the bad girl. Her grin widened into a smile and she put her hand over her mouth. She chuckled and shook her head as she lifted her face back up, but the grin faded then, as Georgia's face floated up on the living room wall across from the couch.

Well, not really bad, not mean-bad. All she and Elizabeth had done was to meet for lunch and make a few phone calls. And that time in Elizabeth's kitchen was before they knew what was going on, so it didn't really count. It was a little like playing with fire, but they weren't actually doing anything. It was only a game. And so what? They had said they were not going to actually do anything, and they wouldn't. Elizabeth knew she was staying with Georgia. Morgan didn't want to leave, and she'd made that clear.

She shifted her legs, recrossing one over the other, one hand pushing down on the couch. But being with Elizabeth was so different from being with Georgia. God knows, being with Georgia wasn't so easy anymore. It was complicated. And Georgia asked questions that hurt, right as they were about to get down to it. Jesus, it wasn't so easy anymore, anywhere. Her whole fucking life was a complication.

Sometimes she wondered if she'd missed something, if something had passed her by and she was an adult now and this was all she was going to get. This was it? And now she couldn't stand to be here? Goddamn.

Well, she wasn't going anywhere. It was just a hard time right now. But with Elizabeth, at least for a little while, things were easy. It felt like...well, it felt like being off the ground for a moment, breathless and coursing, a little like she might fly out of her skin. A little like the electricity in the air was running straight through her and as though the voltage was exactly what she could stand before she would pass out.

And that was the best part, having that feeling. She didn't actually want to do anything about it. Because if she did, she knew the feeling would become something else. Something not so much fun, not so breathless, something more here. Something to deal with, Jesus, another complication she didn't want.

Really, she thought, sobering, looking out the living room window, at the soft late afternoon sunlight, really, the best part was that under all this, they had a friendship. And *that* wasn't complicated. Elizabeth cared how she was. She always asked how she was. She even asked how Georgia was.

And she had been so nice when she invited her to supper tonight, offering to cook for her, since George was gone and she knew Morgan would probably eat out of a can, otherwise. Well, it was true, she thought, tucking her legs up under her. And it felt great that Elizabeth would not only offer to cook her supper, but would also not make her feel like an idiot or a lazy no-good about not cooking.

She took care of her that way and it felt good. Imagine Georgia doing something like that now. More likely she'd be too upset about work, or her family or something. Morgan probably wouldn't even be able to talk to her for weeks after she got home.

Well, it was a hard time for both of them. And things would be better, after awhile. No need to mess up anything. She did want to be old with Georgia; she did. She couldn't quite imagine not being with her.

She stiffened again, Georgia's face insistent in the window glass. And she couldn't fight off the memory of how Georgia had sat, silent and anxiously twisting her fork around her lettuce at dinner before Morgan took her to the airport Thursday night. It was just after Morgan had said she was going to Elizabeth's for dinner Saturday night. Georgia had quietly asked if she were going to be home the rest of the weekend, which struck her then as a silly question and she said so.

"Why?" she asked. "Where the hell do you think I'm going to be?"

"Home, I guess," Georgia said.

"Where else would I be?" she replied, her voice fiery for a moment.

"I don't know. Ignore me. I'm just being stupid," Georgia said, her piece of lettuce mottled and bruised with marks from her fork.

Morgan sighed, folded her napkin and laid it beside her plate.

"George, honey, Elizabeth is just a friend, that's all. It's not a big deal. I'll tell you what you should worry about with me, is the contract proposal. And trying to coach my team out of the cellar. God, there's so much to do."

"I guess I was mostly thinking about when I could call. I'll miss you so much when I'm there." Georgia trailed off and Morgan thought she looked miserable.

Well, she shouldn't, Morgan thought irritably. She shouldn't. She and Elizabeth hadn't done anything. Just because *Georgia's* family was falling apart, it didn't mean the two of them were in trouble. They both had a lot of stress right now, that's all. Morgan watched Georgia watching her plate. And suddenly Morgan was irritated. She was more than irritated; she was furious. Why the hell didn't Georgia ever fight back? Instead of this manipulative victim shit? Eat your goddamn salad and say what you really think, she wanted to shout. But she didn't. She just sat there with her anger and it steamed out of her, across the table, and Georgia began to cringe as though she had been slapped. Morgan saw it, but couldn't stop. She got up abruptly and took her dishes to the sink. As she washed them, she tried to tell herself she wasn't being fair to Georgia.

She heard the words 'not being fair' echo as she sat on the couch. She reached over and began to play with the key ring she had put by the telephone when she came in. And she knew as she ruffled the keys that her anger at Georgia didn't just start that night at the table. She knew then she'd been angry for awhile.

She jangled the keys angrily, up off the table. She just wanted Georgia to stand up for herself and take control, for God's sake. For once. Morgan knew then she'd been having a hard time shaking that anger. When Georgia had tried to hold her as they slept the night before, Morgan knew she should have been there for her, but it was one of those nights when she couldn't bear to be touched, and she rolled away. Georgia's touch just made her furious. It was the night before Georgia left and she knew she should have been closer. But she just couldn't bear it. Sometimes she just couldn't stand to be touched, even if it wasn't about sex.

Well, maybe it was because she had been anxious about the damn proposal. The proposal! She checked her watch. Already five o'clock. Mother of God. She jumped up and then stopped, standing in the middle of the living room.

Goddamn it. Where the hell had the afternoon gone? By the time she got to the office, it would be five-thirty. And she was due at Elizabeth's at six. Damnit. She'd have to wait until tomorrow. Get up early, go in and do it all then. Jesus Christ. She sank back on the couch.

Well, another wasted day. Just what she needed. Damn. Well, there was always Sunday. She hated working on Sunday, although maybe Elliott would be in to help her tomorrow. Anyway, somehow, she'd get it done. And even that would be over soon. Then they'd know more about what to do about the company. And

Georgia would be home in a day. Things would come together. Even about Elliott. And Joe. And all the rest.

She leaned back against the couch, and closed her eyes. Her heart lurched again, aching. Yes. Things would settle out sooner or later. It was just so fucking much all at once. It seemed like it was crunching all at once. If she could just get a break. For a day. For a minute, Christ.

She shook her head and opened her eyes. And looked at the wall, bitterly. She should have been having a break today. Christ on a cross, she'd wasted the day, worried about Georgia and spending her day on Stockton when there wasn't a thing in the world she could do about either one. She should have been worried about the contract.

Too late now. She looked at her watch. All right. She'd go for a latte and calm down before she went to Elizabeth's, take the time to get herself together. She shrugged into her jean jacket, picked up her keys, hopped in the Jeep and went up to the Scoop Cafe near Elizabeth's place. For twenty minutes, she sat and read the paper, sipped on her latte. Well, really, today was just more proof that Stockton was a fucking liar. God, she was awful.

She used her spoon to get the rest of the latte foam out of the tall glass. But it was her own fault about today. She'd lost the day because she'd gotten angry, because she let Stockton make her angry. And she hadn't stuck to her schedule. She'd let it get away from her. Well, she just needed to get her life back in order. Things were really out of control. She had to slow things down. It would be okay. She turned to the sports page. When she had finished both the paper and her latte, she got up and went to Elizabeth's.

As she drove, as she walked into Elizabeth's building, as she walked up the stairs, she said to herself that the angry bad girl had been out enough today and that it would be good for her to cool this thing off, too. Be good for her and her hot head to cool off. Good for the friendship. Good for her relationship. God, enough was enough.

Chapter Eight

Safe At Home

The effortlessly full, late afternoon sun came through the corner west window in Elizabeth's great room, making the wide streak of plant hanging there bright and translucent. The plant, a luscious Swedish ivy, was hung halfway up the twelve-foot brick wall, between the corner and the last window of the seven window row. Its shiny-green, twisting stems fell almost five feet towards the ground. By midafternoon, it became completely luminous. Elizabeth loved the plant's fecund greenness, and to herself she called the plant, Bebe's Girl.

Bebe's Girl made her feel at home, as though the place were finally hers. She'd spent all last year and too much money restoring her studio and the rest of the old brick building. From the outside, it didn't look like much besides an old cigar factory, which was what it had been, but on the inside, she'd been able to do as she wished. And the outside was fine. She liked it looking hidden.

Not a great neighborhood, and not great looking, but it was hers. Partly because the bank had foreclosed on the property, and she'd been able to buy the building for much less than she had originally thought, and partly because she decided to go ahead and use the money from her mother, she was able to do exactly as she pleased. For once.

Addison, the family banker, had tried to block her as soon as she had asked if it were possible to liquidate some of the principle of her mother's estate, but who was he? Stuck somewhere in an untraceable time zone in Boston, even if he'd managed to drag his carcass out to California, he'd never see what she saw in the building. Or understand, if she could explain to him, how she wanted to make something so far away from Yarmouth and her parents' sprawling Victorian that the place might actually be hers.

So she'd dipped into the principle of the estate money, against Addison's vociferous objections and over his strangled, New England apoplexy. She'd restored the building, rented the other five units, and moved into the north side of the top floor. She'd taken care to make the loft exactly as she dreamed.

It was all hers and she'd made it all by herself. Well, her and Richmond. Without Richmond Villiers, the place would have been very different. Bebe's girl, for example, would have never been there. She wouldn't have dreamed of doing that. But Richmond did.

Richmond was a tall, swishy Texan. He was also obnoxious, she'd found out too late in the process. But she had to admit, he did have good taste. Not that the ivy was so well-regarded these days, she knew, but this one was so green and full and overgrown that it was special and made the bare corner of the studio bluntly, singularly spectacular in the way all Richmond's work looked. Funny, she thought, how such a flamer could make such quietly strong statements.

Even now as she surveyed the place, stepping out of her heels on the old Oriental rugs scattered over the battered hardwood floor, she thought again, between the two of them, they'd done a good job. Except maybe the stereo. He might have been right about the stereo. Not that she would say so to him.

That was their one fight, when she wanted to put the stereo in the loft. He came close to ridiculing her, mimicking her climb up and down the wide loft stairs to change the tape. At first she laughed and accused him of being better able to walk in heels than her, but then she heard the snicker in his voice and when he archly suggested she buy two stereos, she snapped that maybe he should find another employer.

Honestly. Faggots. They couldn't quite get it through their thick skulls that women did not have the same kind of money men had. When it was all over, she'd spent two hundred thousand restoring the other units alone, and she had counted every last penny. It was all she could afford. All she could ever have in a lump like that, certainly. And Richmond, like John, never understood that.

But never mind. It was hers now. And it was a lot bigger than a closet, she thought with delight, spreading her hands wide in the sense of its stark hugeness, remembering what Sylvie had said when she first saw it finished. Sylvie. How she managed to play such a mean game of racquetball this morning was a mystery, Elizabeth reflected with a grimace as her arm muscle gave off a small scream when she leaned forward to balance her wine glass on the window-sill. She hadn't played that well in college.

"Getting better with age," Sylvie had teased as she had walked off the court. Elizabeth felt as if she'd done permanent damage to her legs as she hobbled to brunch at the club. When eggs Benedict arrived for Sylvie and a salad Nicoise came for her, she wondered how it was that Sylvie thought she'd aged well. Sylvie had spread out, let herself go after having Melanie two years ago. And now she looked like she had in college: unkempt, the way small over-weight women looked, like all her clothes were just a bit too tight. Which they weren't exactly, but still.

Well, Sylvie was Sylvie. She had never cared a thing about clothes. Her looks weren't her strong point anyway. Her heart was, Elizabeth reflected, and then frowned. But at least she used to diet, which she certainly wasn't doing now. It was too bad.

She remembered watching Sylvie put a dripping bite of eggs and hollandaise into her mouth. Elizabeth had poked at the spinach in her salad. Where in God's name Sylvie got the energy to run around the court was beyond her. Weren't mothers supposed to be exhausted all the time?

She looked closer at Sylvie as she was happily draining her orange juice. No wrinkles either. Elizabeth sighed and popped a piece of calamari into her mouth. Well, maybe Sylvie had less stress in her life. Pretty easy life, actually, working personnel at some big corporate place downtown. She could never remember what com-pany. But Sylvie's job was salaried. Cushy. Dependable. Not like her own job.

Or maybe, she thought, as she sipped her wine by the window that afternoon, maybe it was because Sylvie was straight. Maybe she didn't worry about her job because of Greg. Good old depend-able Republican Greg. Thought Reagan was the greatest thing since sliced bread. And Sylvie thought Greg was the greatest thing since the breadbox. And now they were going to have another baby. How nice. How boring. Frankly, she expected more from wild, do-anything Sylvie.

She stood at the window and sighed. The ivy next to her seemed to sigh, too. She fingered one of the leaves on the ivy ab-sently, out of habit. The supple grooved leaves comforted her. She liked to stand by the ivy and look out the window at the neighbor-hood when she first came home from work. If it were winter, the setting sun would light up Bebe's Girl, and she would stand there with her arms folded across her chest, a glass of white wine near, thinking about the day before entering the evening.

This afternoon, though, Elizabeth was waiting until it was time to fix dinner. She was having a very special guest for dinner and she wanted everything to be just right. She took another sip of wine. And not too much of this, she thought, twisting the stem of her wine glass as she balanced it on the windowsill. She'd come straight home from brunch, cleaned the place like a fiend and now was resting, just for a moment, before she started making dinner.

Now, the sun was shining through the empty brewery building to the west and illuminating a wide swatch of hardwood floor in the great room. Elizabeth stood quietly for the first time in weeks, leaning against the arching varnished sill and looking out over downtown. So big, so small. San Francisco. In front of her were the skyscrapers and pedestals of the banking capital of the West, and behind were the still-working wharves of China Basin and Hunter's Point. All around and below were other old factories, mostly empty, and further near the square were the designer show-rooms, and other renovated factories where Richmond worked and where you could wander for hours without becoming bored with the textures, the subtle silky colors. She sighed slowly, trying to make her ritual work.

With one hand entwined into the ivy, Elizabeth stood there, still, watching the sunlight float in the air over the city. Slowly, she turned to the east, and stood looking at the Oakland side of the Bay. Tonight, if she came back to this window, she knew the lights from the wharves would shine yellow and warm into the night. Past them, the lights of Oakland itself, of the houses and families, would shine white. But now, at the height of afternoon, Oakland just looked green and remote.

It looked real. Not at all what it would look like this evening. Not at all entrancing. Or close. Not like at night, when you could almost reach your hand out to touch the lights, or like when the fog swirled in from the ocean, like a great hand that covered every-thing, and under which you could wander until you found... She shook her head abruptly.

Found what? She wasn't looking for anything. She'd found what she needed right here. She walked back to the couch, sat and sipped her wine, still looking out the window.

But she remembered that fog. Remembered it from very long ago. It was a little like New England in November. She remembered, suddenly, though she hadn't thought of it in a long time, once, when she'd lived in New Haven with Edith, before she'd moved here; she remembered one fall evening taking a long walk up around Cheshire, walking past the houses, just looking. Edith hadn't really understood, and she herself had only the barest recognition of what she was doing but it had seemed so compelling she couldn't stop, even when she couldn't explain it, even when they'd ended up in a fight.

It had been twilight that night, twilight in November, which made it very like here when the fog rolled in. And that morning, they'd driven to Boston together, Edith to see her fiance who was doing his residency there, and her, to see her father. It had been when her father was sick, after her mother had died. She had spent the day with him at the hospital where he used to have surgical privileges. He wasn't able to talk, just followed her with his eyes. She'd had to make conversation for both of them and she thought then that if Edith was a second late to pick her up, she would have to be carried out of his room in a straitjacket.

But Edith had come early and she was sorry to go then. They had driven towards home in silence, but she had finally asked Edith to stop at the Friendly's in Cheshire so she could get some food. She hadn't eaten all day. Edith stopped and sat with her while she ate. After she'd finished, all she could think of was how badly she wanted to walk, just walk around the neighborhood there.

And Edith had been nice enough to do that, and so they had, for a very long time, and she'd watched the lights come on, watched the houses warm up. At some point, Edith asked her what she was doing, and she answered without thinking, "Watching people come home."

She looked at Edith and Edith looked back, clearly not understanding. She tried to elaborate. It seemed as though everyone had a house to go to, she said. Edith remarked dryly that they did too and why didn't they just go on home?

She raised her hand to her forehead and unconsciously began to rub her frown away. Here she was in her own house, in broad daylight. Where had this come from? This was no time for memories. She tried to smile. But her throat closed up against the tears, and she remembered that night, wanting to have Edith hold her, but Edith wasn't exactly the type for that. It wasn't just that she was straight; Sylvie had held her once and it hadn't felt strange. It was more that Edith wasn't like that for anyone. She was more like Elizabeth's mother in that way. She remembered shoving the tears back then, and she gulped now, too.

Funny she would think of her father dying today. It had been ten years since he died—and eleven for her mother. And she missed them. Missed going home for holidays. Missed calling, missed her mother's late night calls. For all their faults, they had been wonderful parents, had given her so much. Until her mother got sick, things had been perfect, and even with her mother's illness, sad as it was, she had grown closer to her father, meeting him at the club for dinner sometimes, going to see his patients with him. Oh, they'd had the usual generation gap troubles when she was an adolescent, but what family didn't? When she got older, she'd been able to rely on them, to talk to them about almost anything.

Maybe that's what she missed today, being able to talk to her father about her work, physician to physician. She'd known, had grieved even as he lay dying, how much she would miss being able to talk. Even that day in the fog. And even now.

She saw the fog rolling in over downtown and realized with a start how late it was getting. She looked around. Minx was sprawled on the floor behind her, in the patch of light, licking his paw and watching her from time to time. When she moved, he came over and purred around her legs for food.

Right. Food. Well, no matter. She took a final swallow of wine. She had a dinner to prepare. She tried to smile again. Probably, this was all from not being able to talk at brunch. How was it that she and Sylvie had stayed friends for so long, with so little in common? Honestly. And so easily able to get on each other's nerves?

She went into the kitchen and to the refrigerator for the vegetables and more wine. She was making Bebe's curry tonight, which involved hours of chopping vegetables. Might as well get started.

As she took out the carrots, celery, eggplant, green beans, broccoli and cauliflower, she went over the brunch conversation in her head. It wasn't like Sylvie to be aggressive. Maybe it was the game, she thought, taking the vegetables to the sink. Maybe it was Sylvie winning the game.

True, she hated losing to Sylvie. She hated it. She'd hated it in college when, on the rare occasions Sylvie had gotten a better date than her and when they'd swapped stories in the ladies room, she realized she was with the wrong man. She hated it when she learned Sylvie was making more money than she was. And she especially hated it when Sylvie lectured her about her affairs.

So she was married. So big deal. She was also straight. It made things a lot different, though Sylvie would never understand how much different, even if she'd been trained to say it was. She hated that about her.

Today, she'd said in that surprised voice of hers, "So have you heard about these Gay Games? Jeffrey at work was talking about them. They have Olympic-style competitions all their own. Is there discrimination against them in sports, too? That's terrible."

I should have, Elizabeth thought, scrubbing the carrots so hard water was spraying the counter. I should have emptied the wine in her lap. No, Sylvie. Life's a bed of roses for gays. They have a great time.

She threw the carrot in the sink. For a moment, she watched the water run over it. Then she sighed and picked it up.

Well, of course she hadn't said that. She'd only said she didn't know that much about it, but apparently she wouldn't make the racquetball team. And they'd both laughed.

That wasn't the part that made her mad. She trimmed the clean carrot and started to wash another. Well, it had made her a little mad.

But, to be fair, Sylvie had been very supportive of her latest struggles with Richardson, his new reduction of her departmental funding support and his demand that she take on a larger patient load and a heavier teaching load. Bastard. She was never home as it was. And he knew she was carrying more than her share already. She had no graduate students to slough off on, no residents, no post-docs. And he knew it. Because he hadn't assigned her any.

Sylvie had been very sympathetic about all of that, partly, Elizabeth suspected, because she hadn't always had backup in her job. She'd said something about being undercut between one of her assistant managers and her boss. Seemed they exercised at the same health club and were trying to catch her out about something, about anything.

Well, she thought, starting on the green beans, washing and snapping them, men are the same all over. When they were in college, Sylvie knew that well enough. At least she did before she met Greg. But that was another thing they never talked about. There was lots they didn't talk about now.

Now, the safest subject was work. And today Sylvie had been excited for her about her research project with Agnes Johnson, which was shaping up very nicely. She and Agnes had conferred several times in the last month and Agnes had been pleased about the first of the preliminaries. And they'd had lunch twice. The second time, Agnes discussed several other researchers at Wesleyan that Elizabeth could be introduced to if things went well with the new protocols.

As it seemed to be going. The test results were very promising; so far, so good. John had settled down after his week off and they had gotten a lot done. Then last week, Agnes had suggested collaborating on a bigger NSF grant application, using their preliminaries as a basis for expanded work.

Fine with her. Great, actually. She began to separate the cauliflower stalks. Not that she knew much about Agnes. But their collaboration so far was a pleasure, really. No innuendo. No hand on her knee. No dumping work on her. No assignment of all the writing or the literature searches on her. Just smooth, fair, equal partnership. What an incredible relief.

It was the first time she'd done research with another woman. She'd always thought it would look bad. Or that it would get too sticky. But Agnes was a professional, thank God. Agnes hadn't told her a thing about her life. Which was a clue in itself, she thought. No husband's name thrown in. No pictures of kids on her desk. But no interest either. No other clues. Well, it didn't matter. For whatever reason, she was helping Elizabeth. And Elizabeth was grateful.

The most recent results seemed like a whole new opening, a whole new direction. The clinic work—she shook her head and took a sip of wine. The clinic work was getting to be too much. It always had been. And when Jimmy Page had died last week, it had been just about the last straw.

She took another sip, putting down her knife and stopping for a minute. Well, it had happened plenty of times before and would happen again. There wasn't a thing she could do about it, as a physician. But as a researcher, well. Now. If she focused on research, she wouldn't, she pressed her hand to her temple, rubbing slightly, she wouldn't have to watch their eyes anymore. The kids' eyes. Jimmy's eyes, his swollen belly, his hands reaching for hers.

She shook her head and turned the water off. She picked up the vegetable parts she'd cut off and stuffed them into the garbage disposal and turned the water back on, flipped the switch for the machine.

In the silence after she shut the machine off, she took another sip of wine. But, really, the research was going great. Just great. And when she'd told Sylvie at brunch, she'd been excited for her. And it was wonderful to share it with her.

No, the trouble wasn't then. Things had been feeling good, like old times, and she knew why she still was having brunches with this woman almost eighteen years later. It wasn't then. She started to wash the separated cauliflower.

Wait. She knew. She should have known at the time. Because she stopped eating. Not that the food was that good, but, she realized now, she hadn't eaten a thing after that. It was when when Sylvie had said, "So how's your love life?" That's when the trouble started.

She said right away she wasn't having a love life.

And Sylvie said, "Oh right. Who've you got your eye on?" And laughed.

Now what was that supposed to mean? Actually, she had been looking forward to telling Sylvie about her struggle to not get involved with Morgan, looking forward to Sylvie's wise head and her detached view. And the complete safety of telling Sylvie.

Why had Sylvie laughed like that? It was like, well, it had made everything dirty. And even when she'd told her about the dinner, Sylvie had said, "C'mon now, Elizabeth," and laughed again.

Good Lord, it wasn't like she was some kind of tramp, running around getting involved with any available woman; not, she wanted to say, like Sylvie had been before Greg, but she didn't.

Maybe she should have. She turned the water off and sat down at the table and unconsciously began to run her fingers over the placemat, following the circular pattern of the weave. It wasn't like that. It wasn't like what Sylvie had said.

And then, as she saw what her hands were doing, she stopped, frozen, and remembered how that first dinner with Morgan had really been, that dinner three weeks ago, their first and only dinner, except for tonight.

She'd been very nervous. She should have been. She wasn't quite prepared. It had been only a week after their computer lessons. And she was pretty out of control then, hadn't really gotten a handle on her feelings. When Morgan came, she hadn't finished making the sauce and so she seated the other woman at the kitchen table and was herself at the stove, stirring capers into the cream sauce she'd made for the trout.

She stood there at the stove, stirring, trying to start a conversation. She was just beginning to ask Morgan how her day had been when she heard her walking softly across the hardwood floor behind her. When she looked sideways she saw that Morgan was leaning against the counter, and running her fingers through her hair. She suddenly looked up and smiled at Elizabeth.

Elizabeth quickly turned back to the sauce. Without warning, she imagined those fingers on her own head and she panicked for a minute, feeling the twist answer between her legs. As soon as she could, she said something; made some stupid conversation, though she couldn't remember what it was. Probably something about Morgan's work. And it was sometime during that conversation that she had turned around and seen Morgan, who had finally walked back to the table and was drawing circles with her fingers on the place mat.

She remembered leaning against the warm stove and feeling her legs buckle. She felt the motion of Morgan's hands encircling her breast. She closed her eyes. And turned the burner off. And then she heard Morgan say in a low voice, "And then sometimes, if I'm really lucky, I get to teach women. And if I'm really, really lucky, there's someone special there, someone bright, interested and funny. Somebody who laughs at my jokes. Somebody lesbian. Somebody like you."

Morgan paused and Elizabeth wouldn't let herself turn around. In a minute, Morgan continued, "Of course, Elliott and I have strict rules about not fraternizing with our clients. It was one of the first rules he made me learn and I have stuck to it sincerely ever since. He'd kill me if he knew I was here."

Elizabeth gripped her hands around a potholder and took her time turning around. When she did, Morgan was grinning. Elizabeth smiled back slowly.

"Of course I'll never say a word. My lips are sealed. But I'm delighted you are here tonight," she said, her eyes following Morgan's hands and then, briefly, looking into her eyes.

"Oh, I'm not here," she said. "I just look like I am temporarily. Actually, I've never done this before, this having supper with a client. But my time with you last week was an exception to most of my rules."

She paused again and this time looked directly at Elizabeth. And then she stopped smiling and said, "And Georgia's working overtime again, so I'm really glad you asked me over. It sure is nice to have someone ask me how my day was."

She looked down and started to draw on the place mat again, her fingers spread and each lightly circling.

Elizabeth slipped her hands behind her and looked over Morgan's head, out over the night lights of the city. That's when she knew. Morgan did really like her. It wasn't just a job for her either.

And as she leaned against the counter, she suddenly realized she was needing that support to keep standing. Almost from the first, she thought to herself, you knew almost from the first you were falling in love with her. And then, because she couldn't stop herself from saying something, because she didn't know how to stop what was going on without saying something, and she knew she had to stop it, she finally did speak, and she said what she had told herself that past two weeks she never would say.

"I've enjoyed getting to know you these past two weeks, do you know that?" she asked softly, moving over to sit across the table corner from Morgan.

"And, you know, if you were single, I'd have been in bed with you in a minute. Do you know that? But I know you're with Georgia and that you've been together a long time now. And I respect that relationship. So I'm really glad we're becoming friends. I'm glad we can at least have that."

She smiled. But then, looking at Morgan's stricken face, she thought, well, what is this? What is the point of being good to her if she's just going to look like that? I should just take her in my arms.

Don't do it, she silenced herself. Don't move. It can't work.

Morgan sat at the table, stunned, not looking up. She didn't answer. Finally, she said she was glad Elizabeth had been so responsible and that she liked her even more for being upfront about her feelings. But she looked miserable when she said it. She was trying to smile. They were both trying to smile. Elizabeth kept trying. She knew it was better this way. She knew it. Regardless of what Morgan's face looked like.

She had tried to get up to put the trout on, but just as she did, Morgan said, "Anyway, what would I ever say to Elliott? And what would we do in the morning?" Elizabeth had stopped still, looked at Morgan and Morgan was silent too. It seemed to Elizabeth that she was looking straight into her heart.

After a moment, she heard herself say, "Well, I guess I'd make you some breakfast before we went to work. I wouldn't want you to go to work on an empty stomach."

Morgan hadn't replied. She'd gotten up and gone over to the stove and stood there, with her back to her. And Elizabeth, startled at the abrupt movement, watched her and saw how her pants fit her just right and then knew they had to stop it right then. Immediately. It wouldn't work. It couldn't work. And she had to do something.

She went over to Morgan, trying to think of what she was going to say. But the woman didn't turn around when she approached and suddenly she was standing behind her, too close, and then it just seemed like a moment and she felt Morgan in her arms, her hands encircling Morgan's waist and pulling her towards her. She kissed her neck, slowly, and wanted to cry then because she knew she'd never be able to kiss her again.

But as Elizabeth lifted her lips off her neck, Morgan turned in her arms, and kissed her back. Full on the lips, and Elizabeth couldn't hear the voices in her head anymore; they were silenced by the sharp quiet of the electricity between them, the electricity streaming out of her like a river rapid and she kissed Morgan hungrily and then slowly, hard, searching inside, her hands pulling her closer, pulling her into her, as though she'd never kissed a woman before and she been waiting all this time, all her life.

As she reached up to lace her hands through Morgan's hair, Morgan broke away and walked back to the kitchen table, sat down and held her head in her hands. Elizabeth followed her, took a deep breath and said, "Listen. We are not going to do this. And we are not going to talk about it anymore. Okay? It just makes it worse."

And Morgan had nodded her head. And they had dinner. But it hadn't been easy. And she hadn't been able to eat. Or sleep. Or get much work done the next day. Or the next.

Finally, though, she'd gotten a grip on herself. And it had been easier since, but mostly easier when she didn't see Morgan. Once, she'd gone to a game of Morgan's and had had to leave. It had been too much to see her. Two or three times she'd taken her to lunch, but she'd stopped that, too; she had gotten no work done afterwards. And she couldn't afford that.

She couldn't afford any of it. And she knew it. So why had Sylvie laughed when she'd told her about Morgan? Who did she think *she* was? Nancy Reagan?

She got up from the table and started stripping the broccoli. What was happening with Morgan wasn't the same as with Terry. It wasn't. And it wasn't like any of the others Sylvie mentioned. Not that she was laughing by then. No, she had her personnel voice on. How dare she lecture her? How dare she?

She leaned over to get the carrots for slicing. When she did, she glanced up at the kitchen clock. How had it gotten to be five? She panicked for a moment then, and laid the knife down. Quickly, she decided to go change, to make sure she looked okay. Because tonight was the night she was going to tell Morgan that they had better not see each other, even as friends. She just couldn't do it anymore.

Forty-five minutes later, she stood over the dish drainer next to the kitchen sink, trying to remember if she'd told Morgan seven or seven-thirty. She picked up the dishes one by one to put them away. The curry bubbled the spicy sweet of garam marsala from the stove through the great room, but she couldn't smell it. She couldn't decide on the time. She decided she was obsessing.

God, what was the point of being so nervous? She was nervous. For God's sake, it was only a dinner date. She went to the stove to stir the curry and froze mid-stir when the buzzer for the outside door shattered the silence.

Oh God, she thought. She must have told her six. Her breath came out in a long sigh and she rushed to the intercom.

"Morgan?" she called into the machine.

"It's me," came back the static reply.

She buzzed her in, smoothed down her shirt, and headed for the door. She left it open, and went back to the stove. Morgan knew the way up. She didn't want her thinking she was too anxious about this. She stirred the sauce for a moment, and when she turned, Morgan stood in the doorway with a slow grin that spread through the air between them as she held out a bouquet of daffodils.

"Welcome," Elizabeth said as crisply as she could and walked over to greet the woman. Morgan didn't take a step. She was standing there, still as a photograph, smiling, holding out the flowers and wearing a T-shirt, clean jeans and her jean jacket, collar turned up against her bright cheeks.

Oh God, Elizabeth groaned inside, walking towards her, looking at her, the long lashes, the wide mouth, how often she'd thought of that mouth and how it felt, soft and then pressed on her own.

She closed her eyes, swallowed, and then found herself smiling back, and taking the flowers.

"Come in. I'm glad you're here. It's very nice to see you." Morgan stood in front of her, waiting. Finally, Elizabeth realized she had to move and she stepped out of the doorway. When she did, Morgan smiled and came in.

"It's nice to be here again. Jesus Christ, have I had a rotten day," Morgan said as she walked towards the kitchen.

"Well, it's good you're here then. What happened that was rotten? Did everything turn out all right?" Elizabeth closed the door and followed Morgan in. She stopped at the kitchen table, afraid to get too close to the counter where Morgan was standing.

Morgan nodded. "Now it is."

They stood there for a moment. And Elizabeth knew they both looked at each other longer than necessary. She began to feel short of breath again, as though Morgan, instead of leaning against the kitchen counter, was leaning against her. She swallowed, held on, and then she began to smile, really smile. It was going to be okay. She knew what she was going to do. It wasn't a question anymore.

And as she thought that, the memory of Morgan's wet supple lips and soft taut cheeks swept through her, and her desire became like a sharp awl on soft leather. She turned then and walked to the sink to put the flowers in water.

"What's for supper?" asked Morgan. "It smells great in here."

"Old family recipe for curry. I think you'll like it. Well, anyway, I made it with you in mind. You look like you could use a drink. I've got some very cold, very dry white wine in the refrigerator. Tell me about your day," she said, feeling once more she was chattering like an idiot.

But Morgan just smiled and began to take her jacket off.

"I'm feeling better just to be here. I don't know what I'd have done if you hadn't invited me for tonight; just sat around and felt sorry for myself, I guess," she said.

"Here, let me take your coat. Are you hungry?" she asked, as Morgan handed her the jacket and Elizabeth remembered when she had first seen that jacket, and how she'd wanted then to take her in her arms and bury her face in her hair. Morgan walked to the stove and lifted up the lid to the curry.

She turned around and grinned. "Smells really good," she said and then, her nose in the air, "and do I smell hot bread too?"

When Elizabeth nodded, Morgan rubbed her hands together and smiled again.

"How about some wine?" Elizabeth suggested again. "I noticed you've never had any at lunch, but on the off chance you just don't drink while you're working, I've got some chilled."

"No thanks. Actually I don't drink. I'd love some ice water, if you've got ice. Jesus Christ, I've been hot today," she said smiling. "It was *hot* today. Did you get out?"

Elizabeth nodded and worried, went to put some ice in a goblet. God, I hope she isn't one of those, but before she could phrase the thought, Morgan spoke again.

"That's two great dinners you've made for me now. How am I going to pay you back?"

Elizabeth started to set the table and tried not to look at her. She felt the pounding start again and wondered if her hands were shaking.

Morgan was standing near the table. "Listen, I want to thank you for asking me tonight. I don't know if I told you, but Georgia went to visit her family this weekend. Her mother had a stroke and she had to go see her."

Elizabeth suddenly saw her father's face, crumpled like a paper napkin, and then shook her head.

"Well, I hope she's okay. I've been through that. It's not fun."

"Oh, I think she'll be all right. Her mother's going to be okay. Her family's crazy though. She'll be nuts when she comes home."

Elizabeth watched her very carefully, and put Morgan's ice water down on the mat in front of her. Morgan took a drink before she looked at Elizabeth, but Elizabeth had seen, already, when she was talking, the love come into her face when she talked about Georgia. And she also saw how tired the other woman looked. Something was not right here, and she didn't think it was Georgia.

"Well, you'll have to take care of her when she gets home. Families can definitely make you crazy. But what's making you crazy right now? What happened today that made it such a rotten day?" she asked and before she could stop herself, she reached over to take Morgan's hand in hers.

Morgan was silent and drew her free thumb up and down the side of the goblet. She looked as though she might either throw the glass across the room or burst into tears.

"What is it, Morgan? What happened," she said as softly as she could, as though she were talking to one of her smallest patients.

"Oh, nothing really, I suppose," Morgan said, withdrawing her hand and taking another sip of water.

"Nothing?" she asked, and sat down.

"Well, I had an accidental meeting today with the woman who fired me from my job at the shelter last year. I literally ran into her. It wasn't pleasant. She hadn't changed a bit. Did I ever tell you about how I got fired? How they fired me and they weren't even paying me?"

She watched Morgan's mouth twist. What was this? A shelter? What was she doing at a shelter? And why was she so hurt?

She got up and held out her hands. "Come sit on the sofa and tell me all about this. How could anyone fire you?" she asked, as she walked to the couch.

Morgan stood and carried her glass to the couch, sat at the far end and looked out the window. This time, Elizabeth was sure she would cry.

"Do you want to talk? Or not? You don't have to," she said gently.

"Oh, I guess. I volunteered for five years at the Sunshine Shelter. I did the kids' sports programs on Saturdays. You know, teach the girls to swing a bat, teach the boys not to hit, but to wrestle with each other."

She stopped, and Elizabeth watched her try to compose her face.

"And then, about a year ago, they asked me to leave. Said they had a professional. Didn't need me anymore."

Elizabeth watched her; still Morgan didn't cry. And didn't talk. Finally, Elizabeth said, "Well, did they get someone with recreation therapy training?"

She thought Morgan would explode. She leapt up from the couch and stood at the window and shook her hands in the air.

"They *didn't* need a professional! I knew more than any kid just out of college can know. I designed the goddamn program. I knew what those kids needed," she shouted and then was suddenly silent. Abruptly, she came and sat back down.

"The professional crap is just a cover. They asked me not to come back because I'm a lesbian. And they were purging all the lesbians."

"You didn't tell them, did you?" Elizabeth asked, aghast.

"Of course. Everyone knows I'm a lesbian. I've been out for years," she answered and Elizabeth realized then Morgan was as surprised at her shock as she had been by her answer. She realized she'd made a terrible mistake. And so had Morgan, she thought. What the hell was she doing, telling people she was a lesbian and wanting to run a program for children?

Then she realized the other woman was crying. Shielding her eyes, but crying all the same.

In a moment, she had moved down to Morgan's end of the couch.

"I know how it can hurt," she said softly. She sat stroking Morgan's hair. "I know."

Morgan turned then, and Elizabeth caught her, put her arms around her and let her weep. Her whole body shook, and Elizabeth continued to stroke her hair and pat her on the back.

After awhile, Morgan pushed away and sat facing the windows again, and when she spoke, her voice was angry.

"I could have done a better job."

"I'm sure you could have," Elizabeth answered.

"I hate that fucking bitch!"

She had to laugh then, Morgan looked so much like the angry child she must have been.

"Yes," she said, tousling her hair, "I hate her too."

She got up. "Why don't you explain about this bitch over Bebe's curry? I'm starving."

She took Morgan's hand to help her up. Morgan pressed against her as she got up and muttered, "Thanks."

Then, in a louder voice, she said, "Um, food. I'm starving too. No lunch."

They walked to the kitchen together.

"Who's Bebe?" Morgan asked as Elizabeth put raita on the table.

"My nurse, my, ah, well, the woman who raised me. She was from Jamaica. She was the greatest cook in the world, and she would have loved you," she said, adding in her head, 'as I do.' She shook her head instead and went back to the stove.

"Bebe?"

"Yes."

"Do you still see her?"

"She died when I was fifteen, but she went away after I started in boarding school when I was twelve. I've always regretted I wasn't nicer to her at the end. I miss her very much."

She realized her own voice was shaking and she turned back to the stove.

"I bet you do," Morgan said softly. "I bet you do. When I was little, my mother used to farm me out to my Nanna's a lot. My father's mother. I loved her like nobody's business. She used to say I was a little hellion and she didn't know why she loved me. But she did. And I miss her too."

Elizabeth turned away from the stove and looked at Morgan. Her face, pale from her earlier anger, was luminescent. Elizabeth wondered if she knew how beautiful she looked when she spoke of love and if she would ever look at her that way. Her heart caught in her throat and she turned back to the stove.

She ladled the curry into the white china tureen and tried to find her voice. Louder than she meant to, she said, "Well, then, tonight we eat in honor of both Bebe and Nanna. One favor, though. Before you start about the shelter, you have to tell me how you like the curry." She brought the curry to the table and served.

"Now tell me about this bitch from your shelter," she said and managed a grin.

She wanted to say, 'Tell me how you like this? Tell me if you've thought about kissing me. Tell me if you thought my lips were as soft as I thought yours were,' but she didn't. She just got the salads out of the refrigerator and pulled the bread from the oven.

She put the other food on the table without speaking, taking care not to come close and not to touch the other woman.

"This is terrific," Morgan said, her face looking happy finally.

Elizabeth smiled back. "Well, enjoy it. It will make Bebe happy. And now that I think about it, let's not talk about the shelter at dinner. Bebe doesn't allow sad talk at dinner."

Morgan nodded and they sat there in silence, eating slowly, though Elizabeth barely touched a bite, jumping up to get fresh pepper, more butter, fixing more ice water, this or that. Finally, Morgan grabbed her by the arm as she went flying by, and pulled. Elizabeth jerked back, her small breasts almost flush with Morgan's cheek. Morgan looked up and grinned, never taking her arm away.

"Will you sit down, 'Lizabeth?" she laughed. "My Jesus, you're making me nervous." Elizabeth went back to her seat, sat down, and looked straight at Morgan, her hands in her lap. Morgan kept eating her curry.

"What do they call you?" Morgan asked, after a moment, putting her spoon on her plate and wiping her lips briefly with her napkin. She opened the cloth-covered breadbasket and tore off a piece of bread.

"Everybody can't call you Elizabeth all the time," she said, grinning. And Elizabeth thought then that she would lose it. Should she tell her the truth? She looked down at her hands and didn't answer for a minute.

"Did I say something wrong?" Morgan asked softly.

"No, it's just that, well, nobody but a child has asked me that for a long time. My patients, most of them, call me Dr. Liz. They called me Liz in med school and college. And before that, my parents called me Beth," she said, trying to keep her voice light.

After a moment she said, "But Bebe used to call me 'Wolfie'," her voice dropping almost to a whisper.

"Wolfie?" said Morgan back, her voice a whisper too.

"Wolfie. I don't know why we're whispering," Elizabeth said, talking normally and a little clipped. "Bebe was the only one. Said I looked like my father's little wolfhound. At one point, my father raised Russian wolfhounds for track racing. It's silly. I don't know why I told you that."

Morgan reached over and took her hand. "Don't be embarrassed, Elizabeth. We all have names like that. I can see it anyway. You do look beautiful and rare," she said, rubbing Elizabeth's hand.

"Like a dog?" Elizabeth laughed and Morgan joined in.

"No, like something gorgeous and good to look at."

"Really?" she asked, taking her hand back.

"Really, Wolfie," Morgan said.

Elizabeth thought then that she would just lean over and kiss her. She sat still, her hands in her lap, her eyes down.

And then Morgan spoke again. "What's going on? Where are you?"

Elizabeth answered her quietly, her face turned away, her eyes on the window, past the city view.

"It's so confusing to me. I don't know what to do with all this energy," she said finally.

Morgan took her other hand. "What's going on, kiddo? You look completely panicked."

"I am. You know, I asked you over here tonight to tell you I can't see you anymore. And I don't want to. But my God, Morgan, the sexual energy between us is going to kill me. I mean I've been hurting, I mean physically hurting, past throbbing, for a week now.

I can't concentrate on anything. I could barely read the patients' charts last week.

"And tonight is not making it any easier. I'm a complete wreck." She wouldn't look back at the table. In the silence that followed, she could hear Morgan moving her chair closer, and then she felt her hand on her neck, stroking her hair.

"I know. Me too."

Elizabeth looked up to see her six inches away. She leaned into her and kissed her, not a brush on the lips, but hard, then soft and long, sweet and long.

And then she pulled back. "Morgan. We weren't going to do this." And if they were, Morgan was going to have to participate, not just kiss back, she thought to herself. She wasn't going to seduce anyone. She wasn't. It was no good. It never worked that way.

"No," Morgan said briefly. "No, we weren't, I mean, aren't." She moved her chair back. Sat up straight. Took a sip of water.

There was a moment of awkward silence between them until Elizabeth, not even remotely interested in eating, picked up her fork, took a deep breath and started again, saying, "So, you have the advantage on me. What do they call you?"

Morgan played with the stem of her glass. "Well, my whole name is Morgan Mary Margaret McCormack. So you have your choice."

Elizabeth raised her eyebrows. Morgan laughed and the sound seemed to release them from the kiss.

"Mary's my saint name. Good 'eh? Well, Georgia calls me Em, for all the initial 'm's. So does Elliott. My family calls me Maggie Two. My Nanna, the one I told you about, was Maggie One."

"Maggie. Nice name. And it's not a dog's name," she said wryly. They both laughed and they finished dinner without another incident, but it was in the air and Elizabeth knew they both knew it.

After dinner she urged Morgan to leave the dishes in the sink and to come sit with her on the couch and watch the sun go down. Richmond had arranged the couch so it sat facing the west windows and the sun wasn't as bright as always, but they turned off all the lights and sat there in silence, watching the sky glow in the dusk.

After awhile, Elizabeth turned to Morgan and waited until the other woman looked back at her.

"Coffee? Tea?" she asked.

"No, nothing really," Morgan answered and Elizabeth could hear again the tears in her voice.

"What is it?" she asked.

"Oh, Mother of God, it's probably all this talk about my family and Nanna after the shelter meeting today. I don't know. Damnit," Morgan said in a whisper.

"Morgan, honey, take it easy. We can find you some other job with kids. Look, my kids need all the volunteers they can get. I know it's hard getting treated like that. But there's lots of kids who need you. I could really put you to use, I'll tell you," and she laid her arm over the back of the couch and turned to face her, watching her in the light from the windows.

"That's really nice, Elizabeth, but I, well, I want to work with battered kids."

"You think these kids aren't battered? For God's sake, Morgan, you should see their little bodies. And there's almost nothing we can do for so many of them. And what we can do just hurts them more. It's horrifying. The cancers, on a child, you... oh God. Even now, I, well, I'm used to it, but I... I..."

She stood up then and walked toward the windows, turning her back on Morgan, wanting to leave the room, to get away, to do anything to get away. She stood in the shadows by the corner window, her body tight as steel, except for the tears rolling down her face. And she wept for Jimmy Page as she couldn't do at the time, and for a moment, forgot about Morgan, forgot everything except her helpless grief when she had tried that one last time to get a bone marrow from Jimmy's back when she knew he'd be dead in a matter of days.

But as she stood there, she suddenly felt Morgan beside her and felt her hand pushing her hair off her hot forehead, turning her, facing her, holding her, long fingers wiping her tears from her eyes.

And somehow, even through her tears, she felt desire rise up like a storm and she knew she couldn't stop this time. She began kissing Morgan's shoulder and then her hair, burying her face in it, and then brushing her cheeks against Morgan's, kissing her eyes and then, then, she found Morgan's mouth and could feel the other woman kissing her back.

She heard her voice whispering, "I love you," and she was completely wet, her cunt pounding and filling her entire body from her knees to her throat, and then she heard herself say, "Come to bed with me, Morgan."

Morgan pulled back. And Elizabeth wiped the rest of the tears from her face and reached for Morgan's hands. She thought her heart would explode to see Morgan watching her, trembling, her lips slightly open and wet.

Elizabeth held the other woman's hands in both of hers and whispered, "Look. It's never going to get easier. I know you aren't going to leave Georgia. But I can't stand this. I can't. What else are we going to do? The energy doesn't seem to be getting any weaker, it seems to be getting stronger. If we do it once, we'll be able to get it out of our systems and be able to go on being friends."

She looked straight into Morgan's eyes and waited for an answer. Morgan looked back, sharp, wild, watching her and then, in a moment, nodded. Elizabeth held her and ran her fingers through Morgan's hair and knew she could not get enough of her.

She felt their energy surge into every part of her body, and she said again, "Come with me to bed," and pulled up on Morgan's hands, and led her to the loft and to her bed.

She sat Morgan down on the navy silk comforter and searched her face. Morgan looked back, eye held to eye, and slowly Elizabeth bent down and kissed her, long, slow and gentle. It was not as she had imagined nor was it like it had been before. She was so gentle, so light, God, she tasted so good. Elizabeth caught Morgan's face with her hands and licked her lips, opening her own under Morgan's tongue. And then there was Morgan at last, slipping her arms around Elizabeth, pulling her to the bed, pressing her face into Elizabeth's breast, brushing her lips against Elizabeth's nipples, quickly rising under her blouse.

And what Elizabeth wanted to remember for always, was how soft they were, each of them together, how soft their lips and how she could feel even her breath straining against her body, how differently Morgan tasted from any other woman she had ever been with, how different and how sweet.

She sat up when she could stand it no longer and stood, pulling Morgan with her. They stripped awkwardly in front of each other then, Morgan shyly turning away, asking where to put her clothes, taking her camisole off in one easy motion. Elizabeth looked at her and her breath caught in her throat. She turned, pulled back the covers and laid Morgan down on the lace sheets.

She felt Morgan's tongue in her mouth and soon felt her hands, reaching up to her, stroking her clitoris, softly, so softly and with each stroke, she thought she might cascade through the air. Long strokes and then short, circular and then between two fingers, sliding down into so much wetness they could have swum away.

She would close her eyes, swallow, and each time she opened them again, Morgan would still be there, bending over her, making love to her. She tried to find a place to hold on, Morgan's shoulders, her hair, those smoothly-muscled arms, but each time, Morgan would slip away and she would arch her back from the pleasure Morgan sucked from her body.

She watched Morgan make love to her in the skylight over the bed, watched her easy motions, sure and strong. And then she shut her eyes and felt hands reaching to her, pulling her in once again and she moved with them, under them, drowning in them. She didn't tell Morgan what she wanted, she just seemed to know, not too hard, but here, oh God, she shuddered then and slipped in the surf, wave after wave crashing into her.

After she came, Morgan wrapped around her and kissed her eyes. Moments later, when she hungrily asked Morgan what she wanted, Morgan said she wanted sweetness. And when Elizabeth took her cunt in her mouth, she stopped in the middle and asked if it was sweet enough for her, Morgan groaned in reply and soon clenched the sheets, rigid and rippling in answer. Eventually, they slept, tangled in each other's arms.

Once, in the middle of the night, Elizabeth found herself awake and knew without asking that Morgan was awake too, and had been awake. The woman was holding herself very still on the other side of the bed. She reached over then and drew Morgan to her, whispered, "I love you," felt Morgan relax into her after a bit and then she too went back to sleep.

CHAPTER NINE

BERNICE BOBS HER HAIR

Well, there y'all are. Finally, I'm here. Hey Nance, Deb. Y'all are a sight for sore eyes, let me tell you. Clear a place for me on the bench there, won't you? Let me get off these tired old feet.

Oh, sure, I'm fine. Just wore out, that's all. I'm glad y'all waited for me; I swan, I didn't think they'd ever finish tonight. No, wasn't such a bad game, just not much fun, you know?

Well, they both wanted to win real bad. My Lord, I hate it when we get mean with each other, don't you? Puts a bad taste in my mouth. And a hard day at work too.

Don't take it to heart, girls. Don't pay me no nevermind. Y'all keep right on talking. I just want to sit here with y'all for a minute. I feel like a flattened fly. Oh, Roo please, not tonight.

I'm sorry. I know it makes you sick; I don't mean to do it. I guess I'm a tad grouched tonight. How long y'all been here? Did y'all eat already? What's good?

Okay. Order me one of those. And a pitcher of tea. Oh, that's right, Janie. I know you can't get that out here; I just forget sometimes. How about, let's see. Yeah, good idea, Roo. A bubble water. I don't care which one. Let me go wash my face, see if I can't get me a better attitude in the Ladies Room.

There, that feels a little better. So, how are you, girls? Is everybody okay? Hey, what's wrong? Y'all? Deb? What's happening, Deb? Something's wrong, ain't it? Deb? What is it?

Oh, my Lord. I'm so sorry, honey. Last week? At a game? Oh Deb. Add insult to injury to do it there, sweet Jesus. Sure, it hurts. I know it does. Is that what y'all been talking about? Well, that just about tears it. We are one sad bunch tonight, ain't we?

But girls, now wait a minute here. Ain't this just about where we come in when I started with my story? What do you mean, Deb? Well, it ain't helping because we ain't got to the good part yet.

Now Nance, more sex may cheer you up, but that's not what

I'm talking about. And not what Deb means neither. I know what she means. Something to make her heart stop hurting, am I right, Deb? Well, honey, I don't know if it'll cheer you up tonight. You know, you got to want to be cheered, no matter what the story. You don't look like you feel much like getting cheered tonight and I don't blame you, honey.

But now that you mention it, maybe it's not a bad idea to finish the story tonight. I believe I could use a little of that story myself. I could do with a little good news for a change. But I don't want to go on with it, if y'all don't want. What do you say, Deb?

No, it couldn't hurt. You right about that. But you know what, honey? It might help. That surprise you, Deb, that it might help? I know you don't believe it. But if it did, would you be ready for that part?

All right, then. Thank you, ma'am, yes, it's mine. These others already cleaned their plates. Now that looks good, don't it. No, Nance, you may not have my salad. I ain't finished with it. Back girl, or you liked to get stabbed with my deadly fork here.

Y'all mind if I talk with my mouth full? I swear I won't spit. Thanks. Now, let's see. Where were we? Oh right, Janie. Did they tell you last week's part? Good. Good thing somebody around here knows what's going on. The storyteller's supposed to, but look at me. Lot of good I am when I can't even remember where we left off.

So. That last time in the story when y'all saw old Elizabeth was Sunday morning. I tell you, that was the longest weekend. But the thing is, even though it all came tumbling together that weekend, it took awhile for us to get there. It surely did shake out that weekend though, my Lord.

Of course, I didn't know until it was over. All I knew was George had finally went home and come back. I had no earthly idea what Morgan had done while Georgia was gone. And I do think, to this day, that Morgan had very bad, I mean, *very bad* timing. Not that any time would have been good, would it, Deb? I know, honey. But try to listen up now.

Better yet, come over here, you. Come sit with me while I tell you this little story, okay? Sit here with me and hold on, girl. The wheel turns, you just remember that part, the wheel does turn. Okay now. Got enough room? Your own story may not end this way, but you got to know you ain't alone. All right, baby.

You know girls, we do think we all know the end of a story like this. That's why Deb's crying now. But lesbians have been known not to do as they're expected. So let me tell y'all what actually happened. When I first heard what y'all have heard, I thought to myself, well, if it was me, they'd have to drag the river for the other two, I swear to God. But I'm getting ahead of myself again.

Roo, get her another cup of coffee, will you? You think you can listen, Deb, or you want to go home? No? Okay, cuddle in then.

Well, when I first heard something had happened, it was from a phone call. George called, like I knew she would, sooner or later. Of course I didn't quite expect the call to come at 3 a.m., but as soon as I remembered who I was, I was ready. It was Monday morning, the other side of that same weekend, and me and Annie was sound asleep, of course; we both had to work that day. And I think the ringing woke Annie up, but I took the phone in the other room to talk and she got back to sleep directly.

Not me. I didn't get back to bed for awhile.

No, Nance, she didn't tell me nothing right away. Poor sweet crazy George. All she said was, she was calling from a booth on a highway somewheres, didn't even know where she was, and she wanted to come by to talk.

Well, when I heard that, I started to ask her if she knew what time it was, but then I didn't. When I thought about it, I figured it didn't matter none, really, except to embarrass her about calling me at that time, so I just shut up and told her to come on. Yep, right then. It didn't matter to me *what* she wanted to talk about, you understand? You can't ask folks in that place to wait or ask what's on the menu, you know what I mean? I mean, a person can always sleep the next night, or next week if it come to that. If a body needs you so bad as to call before morning milking, well, it's time to get up.

So I sat up waiting for her. Put my robe on, washed my face, had a bowl of cereal. After about twenty minutes of waiting, I hear this tap-tap at the front door. I reckon she finally figured out what time it was and was trying not to make too much noise. I thought the tapping was kind of cute, but she sure didn't look none too cute when I opened the door. She looked like she was wired for sound and falling into the grave, all at once.

Well, you know I took her in. Or tried to. She was smoking cigarettes, one right after another, so we sat out on the back deck to talk. At first I thought she wasn't making much sense, on account of how early it was, but then I realized the hour of day or night didn't have nothing to do with it.

She'd had a hard weekend, she said. Then she said, hard, but good. She told me a little about her momma, about how she looked, about Cam and her daddy. She didn't really get into it, you know, it was more about the house and such. And how her momma looked. And she was telling me more than she was saying, you know what I mean. She was *almost* coherent about that part. The other, well, I don't know. I couldn't quite get the gist of it for awhile. And, I'll tell you the truth, girls; there was a lot there, all wrapped up in the same kind of packages, and a lot of it looked the same for the first little bit.

But then we got to the part that was unwrapped. I think she said she'd gotten in early Sunday night. Or something. Anyway, Em wasn't there at the airport for her. And not at home. And not at work. So George took a cab home, using some of little Cam's late birthday present money. And it sounded like she'd waited awhile at home, waiting to see if Em was coming home, or if she was in trouble or just what was going on. It sounded like she waited quite awhile and from what I could get, it sounded like the house was already dark when she got there. Anyway, she waited there in the dark.

Seems when Em did get home, she told Georgia where she'd been—not that afternoon, and not why she didn't pick her up—but where she'd been the night before, just blurted it out. Then she said she'd gone off to think things out that afternoon and that the Jeep had broke down and she couldn't get home. Said she was sorry. For all of it. Said she didn't mean it. Said it was an accident. Said it didn't mean a thing.

I know, Deb. It's what they all say. Well, I don't know if George believed any of it after the first part either. I mean, I don't know that she heard any but the first part. And soon as she said it, I had to hear it, too, but, Lord, I did not want to. It did seem like she had enough on her plate and I went and held her then. It was all I could do.

She was just able to tell the story, in between hiccups and crying. I mean, the poor thing, just sat out there pale and wan in the middle of the night, her eyes darker than the sky. I mean, she looked like she did when she used to drink, and she wasn't making much more sense.

Except it all made sense. To me, I mean, Deb. I mean, I could see it coming, soon as I forced myself to look at it. And it wasn't the worst thing that could have ever happened to them. No, I mean it. Now hold on, honey. Just try to listen tonight. You don't have to make sense out of none of it, okay?

Well, I tell you, George wasn't having none of it either. I kept trying to get her to say how she was feeling but all she would do was say she had to try to think, had to figure out what she was going to *do* about it. For awhile I tried to talk with her, but then, it seemed crazy to do anything but listen and nod until she'd wound herself down. So I just sat there and listened and held her hand.

What else could I do? This one was too big for me to even try to fix. Yes ma'am Roo, you bet. I hung it up before I started. Sweet Jesus, I know what she was going through. I been left before, you might remember. And more than once. Oh, I knew. And I knew there wasn't a thing in the world I could do, until she decided she wanted to leave too, I mean leave off giving over everything, all her power, you know? So I just sat there and held her hand. Then the cold got to her and she asked if we could go inside. And once inside, she looked so little, so little, and I felt my heart leaking sadness like a cracked cup.

I asked her then did she think she could sleep a spell and would she like me to make up the couch? Well, no, she didn't. When I left her about four-thirty, she was asleep. Sitting up in my recliner. I wrapped Aunt Verlie's afghan around her and crept back to bed.

Next thing I know, Annie's shaking me, saying, "What is Georgie doing in the TV room?"

I roused myself. "Sleeping, I expect. Why? She not asleep?"

Annie just grinned at me and shook her head, kissed me on the lips, and I knew it was okay. Then she whispered, "She all right?"

I shook my head and heaved myself over the side of our bed. We sleep on a waterbed, on account of Annie's back and, I tell you, it's a trick to get out of it.

"She ain't now, but she's going to be. Annie," I said, "I reckon I won't be making it in to work today. You think you could call them for me?"

She nodded and then cocked her ear to the doorway. "I think she's getting up, 'Niecie."

I was almost dressed by then. "Well," I said, "I'm going to go sit with her and see if we can't help her through this one."

She nodded again and I got dressed quick, kissing her goodbye when I left, as she was sitting on the edge of the bed frame, stretching on her hose.

I walked into the kitchen, and there was Georgia filling the pot with tap water. "Make enough for all three of us, George," I said, sitting down at the table. "You know where the coffee is, don't you?"

She nodded and went about getting the coffee, cleaning up after she spilled. When she had the coffee in the filter, pushed into the machine and the water poured into the top, she came over and sat across the table from me. She passed her hands under her glasses, rubbed her eyes and then ruffled through the tangles in her hair. All of a sudden, she squinted, looking sharp at me and said, "Bernice, how come you don't have your uniform on?"

"Ain't going to work today and neither are you. What time old Williams get in? Your nurse needs to call to say the doctor said you had to stay home."

"What are you talking about?" she asked, her face starting to light up. "You'll never get away with this, Bernice. What if he wants to call the doctor to check?"

"That's okay. I'll tell him I'm the nurse for Dr. Smith. He's at City this month; Williams'll never find him. And then I'll tell him that you'll bring a note from me when you return to work. I just happen to have some of the hospital stationery here. We can get Annie to type it up. And I'm going to tell him I told you to go straight to bed and not answer the phone and that I got you on Percodan and pheno and you couldn't hear the phone anyway."

Georgia started to smile. "And what you gonna tell him I got, Bernice?" she asked. "Cancer?"

"I was thinking highly infectious mycostatic vaginal condition gone systemic. That ought to shut him up, don't you think?"

She was grinning by then. "I doubt he'll ask you about that." But her smile began to fade. "I ought to go to work today, Bernice. He nearly fired me for leaving this weekend. It's been bad. Really. It's been the worst. I ought to go in and make sure things are okay. I may not even have a job if I don't."

"Now, wouldn't that just be a shame if you didn't have that job, if you didn't have that old boy to beat up on you. Wouldn't that be a shame."

"Bernice... " she started back, but by then, I was ready to let fly. She thought she was going to work in the condition she was in? Over my dead body.

"I don't care one single sweet breath of Jesus what you think you *ought* to do today, missy. You ain't doing nothing you *ought* to do today, you hear me? I'm telling you, you can't go to work today. You're as sick as a dog. Heartsick counts just as much as any other kind of sick. Heartsick counts. You're going for a home cure, baby, and you with the nurse."

The coffee had made enough for Annie's cup, so I got up and poured, trying to get another cup under the filter so coffee didn't drip and steam on the pot warmer. George sat at the table and sniffled; didn't say a word. Annie came in, grabbed her traveling cupful, kissed me again, kissed George on the top of her head and ran out the door. That girl's always late.

"Let me ask you this, my friend," I said. "Do you *want* to go to work today? Don't you think it's about time you started doing what *you* want to do, not what somebody else thinks you *ought* to do?"

She didn't answer. I brought the rest of the coffee to the table. She don't normally drink black coffee, usually only with cream, which we didn't have any of, since Annie don't do dairy, and I could see the coffee was a little of a shock to her system. I offered her an ice cube, which is what I put in my coffee. Cools it off and waters it down all at once. But she just shook her head.

She wouldn't look at me. I wasn't actually real sure what we'd do that day. But I knew for sure I couldn't let her go off like she was. I was sitting there, trying to decide on what we might do for this old home cure I was making up in a hurry, when she started talking.

"Bernice, I think if she wants to sleep with this woman, I ought to let her. She didn't say she'd leave me. I think I'm making a bigger deal over this than it was. It was just one night. She said it didn't mean anything. Well, I can accept that. I mean, we been together all this time."

She was looking at me, her little face all screwed up like a child explaining to their daddy why they stole a cigarette. I could hardly believe my ears. But she went on.

"And probably she's a little bored with me. And I doubt I'm any match for this other one, this Elizabeth. She's a doctor, did I tell you that? And what with this weight I've put on. Well... anyway, look it. I mean, I think it can't matter that much, really. Bernice. Don't you think?"

When she said that, I just looked at her. She looked away and started stirring her coffee, which, as I said, had nothing in it to stir.

I couldn't decide then if I wanted to put my arms around her and wipe her tears off her or kick her butt. What the devil was she doing? I couldn't get it. So I asked her to wait awhile, not to make any decisions right away, not right that very moment, but to spend the day with me, like old times. Just be with me for awhile. Not doing nothing. We could ride around in Lucille. How about that? We could talk about the situation, see how it was shaping itself.

That last part just popped out. I didn't have no idea what we'd do. But she nodded numbly and put her coffee cup in the sink. I don't believe she actually drank more than a sip of it. She gathered up her cigs and started fishing her keys out, making for the door. She was moving like a ghost.

I knew I had to do something right that moment. I wasn't sure what, but I knew it didn't matter what we did, if she stayed in that place. Only I didn't want to do like before, you know, and have us get into fighting ourselves. I didn't want to get in the way. But on the other hand, she *had* come over. And then, when I thought of that, I hit on the answer.

Why not go ahead and do my day like I would have anyway, excepting the work part? I mean, if she was needing to get a grip, she could share a little of mine. Maybe the best I could do was show her how I got my own support, you know? Worth a try, I thought. No time to start making changes like the present.

"Whoa," I called to her then as she was walking down the hall. "Hold on a minute there, girl. I ain't quite ready to go yet. Are you?"

"What, Bernice? I thought you said we were going out."

"We are. First, I have to get ready. I don't just go out without no protection. You want to come get some, too?"

She started shaking her head and the least little smile crept up on her face.

"Bernice, is this some of your witchy stuff again?"

"You know it is," I said, grinning at her. She just shook her head again, and started walking back my way. I got my arm around her and she looked up at me like I was crazy, but I didn't care. We witchy people know we are crazy, but crazy like a fox, you understand.

"So you want to do some with me?" I asked.

"Don't suppose it could hurt, could it," she said, like she was fixing to take castor oil.

"All right, come on then, girl," I said, propelling her into the bathroom.

I stopped her in front of the basin and turned the water on. "First is, you got to make yourself ready. You washed your face or brushed your teeth? I thought not. Do it now," I said, trying to sound like Shirley. She shook her head again, took her glasses off and started to wash. I could see her washing her hands over and over in the warm water and I remembered then how much she liked to play in the shower. She might be a natural at this, I thought.

"You want a whole shower?" I asked, gesturing behind me. "I can leave if you want."

Her eyes went dark again and I didn't know what I'd said, but she just shook her head and went on washing. When she'd scrubbed her teeth good, I made her stand there, facing the mirror, and I brushed out the tangles in her hair. She leaned forward onto the basin and held herself up with locked arms. I pulled and brushed and tried not to tear out any snags. She acted like she liked it and that put another idea into my head, but just then there was something else to do.

When I finished, I ran my hands through her curls, made them stand up pretty-like, and then I pulled on her shoulders to get her to stand up and look in the mirror. I'm a good bit taller than her and I stuck my head over top of hers and said, "Okay, this is how I do my little witchery every morning. I'm going to say some stuff for me and if you want, you can do some also for you. Just say the same as me if you can't figure out how to do it."

She nodded, looking at me in the mirror, her eyes big and scared again.

"Look at yourself in the mirror now," I said.

She nodded and didn't make a sound.

"And you have to say the words like you mean them, even if you don't just yet, or it won't take, okay?"

"Okay," she whispered.

I took a deep breath, closed my eyes for a minute, centered, grounded, and knew then what I had to say.

"Okay, here we go. I'm a child of the universe," I said and took a deep breath. That one always makes me feel right in the world.

George watched me and then said it slowly, as though she was hearing each word for the first time in her life. Right away, I could see her tears starting, but I just went right on with my stuff. First year I said those words, they made me cry every morning too. All I could do was hope the tears would make her feel good at the end.

"I'm a child of the universe," I said again. She nodded at the repetition. "And as such I got the rights of all children. I got the right to be alive," I said, taking a deep breath and looking out the bathroom window at all the green growing things, like I did every morning, feeling part of it all.

Then I heard George. She whispered, but she said the words. I started again, and her eyes followed mine in the mirror.

"I got the right to be alive. I got the right to have my own space in the world and the right to be happy."

I watched her close then and it took her awhile to get that one out.

Then I continued. "I got the power to make it through this day. I can get what I need and trust that the universe works to take care of the rest."

Her voice caught in her throat and she looked at me in the mirror. I repeated it for her. She looked at me for a long moment, and then she finally croaked it out. When she said it, I kissed the top of her head and said, "One more. I'll pay attention today, and I will not abandon myself."

She watched me, tears rolling down her face.

I held her tighter and said, "Georgia. Say it."

I repeated it for her. She finally said it.

"Good girl," I said, not acting like I understood that she had just promised me, and herself, that she wasn't going to drink through this one. She knew; I knew. That was enough. I picked up the wet washcloth she had used and handed it to her. "Now wash up again. We're going out and God don't like ugly."

She laughed a little through her tears then and I smiled back at her and left her to do whatever private things she might need to do.

I went back to the den, sat down in my chair and tossed Aunt Verlie's afghan on the couch. It had been the saddest affirmations I'd made in awhile and I felt tears coming in my own eyes. And then I noticed the morning sun playing in the window, and I watched out in the yard, saw the day lilies Annie had planted for me and, like always, felt my heart get full again.

I just sat there, feeling better by the minute and then, I got up and dialed the phone. I called Williams. Piece of cake. A lot easier than Georgia herself. Oh, he huffed and puffed some, but when I told him she had highly infectious Candidas Albercanius that had gone systemic and he was susceptible if he even touched the same doorknob, he backed off.

"I'm sure you've noticed a change in her behavior lately," I said smoothly. "It's the disease," I said.

And then, I really hated him for this, he asked when she'd be back. Not was she dying, not was she going to be all right, not was she in pain. Men like that oughtn't to be allowed around women, I don't think. Anyway, I got very cool and nurselike, even though I wanted to let off my beeper siren in his ear. I just said she'd have a note when she did return.

Well, see that she does, he harrumphed. I had to get off then. I couldn't let him hear me laughing at him. Those young boys, trying to act like their grandfathers, they're always such a hoot. I was still smiling when George walked into the den.

"Well, come on, girl," I said, getting up and hugging her. "How about some breakfast? When was the last time you ate?"

"Saturday night," she said as we went out. I just shook my head. But I was really surprised when she handed me the truck keys.

"I don't think I can drive right now, Bernice," she said.

This was worse than I thought. But I just took the keys and smiled. "Sure," I said. "Maybe you can drive this afternoon."

She nodded, her head down. I unlocked my side, got in and unlocked her side. She got in, but I'm telling you, except at the mirror, eye contact that morning was minimal to none. Soon as she sat, I started the engine up and then turned to her.

"Okay. I'll drive. But you got to work the radio."

She smiled a little at that.

"And I don't want to hear no news this morning. You can play any kind of music you like, but no Patsy or Don, okay? We had about as much of that bad news as we can stand, don't you think?"

Then she smiled, sad, but real. She started the radio up, still with that sad, half-smile on her face. I looked at her and worried, but figured the radio would at least start opening her heart, and mine too.

I swung the truck out on the highway, trying to decide where to go to miss the traffic, but soon's we were out there on the highway, it sure felt like back home to me and I knew if it did to me, it must have to her.

I took one look at her and decided for the bridge and the City. If things weren't bad enough, we didn't need no reminiscence about home. I figured a traffic jam was about as far away from home as we were going to get that morning. Well, I thought, I had said to myself I was going to just do the best I could in the moment, didn't I? I turned the truck into the lane for the City.

She surely woke up then. "Where you going, Bernice? We'll be stuck for hours this way."

"I know it," I said. "Give us a chance to talk," I said, smiling my most winning smile. She took one look at me and looked out the window in disgust.

"Now, that's no way to look at your best friend," I said. She snickered. "Besides. I got my reasons for going to the City."

"I bet you do," she said, like she was almost getting mad at me. Well, that wouldn't of been so bad. One thing I did know was she was going to have to do it sometime that day, and it was okay if some of it started coming at me at first. I could take care myself, long as I knew it wasn't really about me. But she didn't make it to the angry. She sighed. I decided I might's well go ahead and push it.

"Okay, girl," I said. "Let's do it. It ain't three in the morning no more. I figure you can talk now. So tell me, what is it with you? What is going on? You got a job you hate, and with reason; a family you can't help loving and hating, with reason; and a bad mess with the woman you love, for no good reason I can see. When you going to take things in hand here?"

She changed the radio station with a swift punch and looked out her window. Finally, she said, "Bernice, lay off. Will you give me a break this once?"

"Nope," I pounced. "Not this morning. Look, we got this whole traffic jam waiting for to pay their tolls. Let's do it, girl."

"Bernice," she started angry and then trailed off.

"Okay. Okay," I said, trying to make my voice mean. "Now, I want to know what happened to you. I remember you back home, holding your head up against all those folks. What happened to you, Georgia, that you don't lion no more?"

"Bernice, I don't know what you're talking about," she said, her voice real shaky. I looked out the window at the traffic. Well, that was it. The cab got real quiet and I could see I'd pushed dangerous close to that fighting place again.

Let it go, I heard my own self say. Let it go before you get yourself in worse trouble. When you going to learn this? Back down, girl. You ain't got the right of way here. I shook my head at myself. Boy, I just get into it without a hitch. At least I saw it then. Better late than never. I looked over at her. She looked worse than a whipped horse.

"Oh, darling," I said. "Well, that's okay. You don't have to know any more than you know. You'll know when it's time," I said. "But we don't have to talk about it now. I'm sorry I pushed." I decided to try to get back to my original plan.

"Listen," I said, reaching over to comb her hair with my free hand. "Listen. How'd you like to get your hair cut today? I'll spring for it. Get it washed, cut and dried, what do you say? Just like with Shirley, except no Shirley." I kept combing her hair as I talked.

She leaned into it like a puppy. "Okay," she said and after awhile, she pulled my hand down against her wet cheek and held it there. I only took it back because I needed to shift when our line finally moved.

When the traffic slowed again, I said, "I thought maybe we'd just have a day of fun things, what do you think?" I said. "We just do what we want. Playing hooky. How's that sound?"

"Good," she nodded, still looking away from me.

"Only one rule," I said.

"Oh, Bernice," she said, rolling her eyes around at me.

"Hold on, now," I said. "The rule is, you got to just enjoy the moment."

"I don't know if I can," she said with that old-stubborn-Georgia sound in her voice.

"I know it," I said, smiling, because the stubborn was a good sign.

"Will you try?" I asked.

"Yeah," she said, turning to look at me. "What choice do I have? I'm being held captive in a traffic jam on the Bay bridge in my own truck."

"That's right, girl. One crazy redneck's got you hostage. And I ain't letting go."

She just sighed then and turned to look out the window. Made my heart hurt to see her cut up so bad, but couldn't be helped. I was still trying to remind myself about all that stuff I had learned about not interfering. Not doing it for her. Oh, I hated it. I hated to see my darling like that. But I didn't say much else until I pulled up at the diner, except to remind her about the radio.

When I got us there, it wasn't real crowded. The place is, oh, y'all will know this part; I took her to the place where we met last week, you know, the grits and biscuits place. Well, when we got there, I could see just from looking at her that she was torn in two. But would she say that? Not for a cold day in hell. No ma'am. No, she had it all worked out again.

She started in again with that business about how she probably deserved it, or at least that Em deserved to do it, when I was parking. Well, I thought, better she start in on that there than in the diner. Because I got mad. Seriously. I finished parking and cut the engine off and turned around to her, not getting out of the truck. I tried to keep my voice down.

"In all this figuring you done, did you ever figure that this might make you mad? That you might feel hurt? And that what you ought to do, since you so into oughts, is go ahead and say so?" I asked. Silence on the other end of the seat.

Then in a real low and angry voice she said, "What good would that do? Is it going to take the hurt away?"

My Lord. That girl.

"I mean," she said, "I mean she's going to do what she wants to do anyway, isn't she? I don't own her, you know. And isn't it the same as before? What right do I have to stand in her way if she wants to go?"

Well, I listened to this and, I'm telling you, it made my blood boil. Now, I tell you something. I love Georgia. Always have; always will. You'll never find a more generous, kind and magical girl. She can make the sky light up with magic, you know what I mean? Some folks can just do that by the way they look at you and how much fun you are having.

But here's the thing. She doesn't think people can possibly love her. I know; I mean, it's the same for me in a lot of ways, that's how I know. But when she gets it in her head that she don't deserve to be loved, she acts like a chicken with her head cut off. Like the heart damage took a transfer to brain damage, you know what I mean? It makes me *wild*.

"Of course you have the right to stand up against what's hurting you, you idiot!" I admit, I was shouting at her. "How come you support every beaten-up group in the world and you can't support your own self? You're giving yourself away here, girl. I don't think you've had a feeling in the last two months," I yelled.

"And not only that, but you surely ain't been on the planet. This ain't the same as other times in your life, you know that? At least, it don't have to be, unless you want to make it that way. You're grown now. You can decide how *you* want this thing to be. You got a say here, got a chit you ain't using. So how you going to spend it?

"Tell me this. What are you and Em doing here? I thought y'all were in this forever, right? That means nothing got to end, you understand? Look, y'all could change together, ever thought of that? You want it to last? You want her? You fight for her. And fight for yourself. Feel this thing, girl. It's your life. You think somebody else going to live it for you?"

She looked at me full on, her eyes red and swollen and wet. She looked like she was fixing to pull a Mighty Martha on me, ready to cut me to size, but then she slumped back and stared out the truck window without saying a word.

We sat there. Maybe a dozen people passed by before she spoke. Finally, she turned back to me, her mouth wobbly, her face drained, her eyes like a well with no bottom.

"What am I going to do, Bernice?" she said. She took a trembly breath at the end and I reached for her hand. I knew she'd gotten somewhere, some little bit of something, even if I didn't know what.

"I'm not sure. I can't know. But you will. You're going to talk about it, even if it's yelling, and that's just what we're doing. And maybe you'll know in your mind, but I tend to doubt it. More likely you'll know it by feeling, but you'll know, if you keep your heart open and you want to know," I said, and squeezed her hand.

"But you have got to stop with the Mighty Martha and this sniffling business, okay? I don't mind the tears, you know that. I just can't stand it when somebody's beating up on you and you jump over on their side and start doing it to yourself. It fairly makes me want to cry myself. Here. Blow. Now, let's go get some breakfast."

She took the hanky I offered and wiped her face. She leaned her head back on the truck seat, took a deep breath, and got out of the car. On the way in, she said, "Okay."

Just 'okay.' Nothing else. Well, I figure, okay too. I wished then I knew what the devil was going on. If you think it's easy for me to trust the universe, think again friend. I was worrying myself just about to death.

But she went on in and so I followed. While the sausage was cooking and the biscuits getting put on the plate with the grits, I tried to figure out the next part of the plan. I tried to think back to how I would do it, if it was just me. So I decided to see if she wanted to take a drive after, see if she could feel the sun on the day, and then go for the haircut. But first have that ride, something pretty for her. Something to make her feel good, if she was trying to say such sad stuff.

Have to make a warm place in your heart for sad stuff, if you mean to get it out. That's what I think. Or it won't come. And there's got to be some love for to make that warm place, and that's what I was trying to get for us. Sometimes, you can't just talk. You got to make a place where the talk can be heard, you know? Hard to hear a thing without love and warm. You know what I mean?

And one of the worst times for loving or feeling that warm spot is if your girl steps out on you. You feel like a dog shut out the house during a ice storm. You feel all mangy and ugly and like to freeze to death on top of everything. Like you're the ugliest thing in the world. Like nobody's ever going to love you. Like nobody cares. I mean, I cared about Georgie, but you know what I mean; it didn't count the same way and I knew it. And anyway, nevermind the recent events, Georgia never did feel too great about her looks. I figured we'd have to hit that one straight on.

But before the plates got to the table, she was at it again.

"Bernice, do you think, you know, if I'd been more patient with her stuff around her father, you know, if I hadn't, ah, gotten mad about how we didn't seem to be making love ever again in our lives, do you think, that, ah..."

"Will you stop it? Will you just stop? My Lord. Georgie," I said, and realized I was losing it again when I almost had my finger raised to shake at her. She stopped looking at me and I could tell we was about two seconds from more tears. I took a sip of coffee before I started again.

"Georgie," I said, "look at me, will you? Now listen," I said, taking her hands across the table, glad as always this diner was queer.

"Listen. In the first place, it ain't what I think. What I think don't make no nevermind. It's between you and Em. And between y'all and your own selves, you understand?

"And anyway, didn't you tell me y'all had talked and talked about that incest stuff? Didn't you tell me y'all had devised certain plans and ways to work on it? Didn't you tell me y'all been working on this for a couple years? Even if you was supposed to be patient, don't you think two years is patient enough? I mean, you got to remember *you* ain't the only person involved here, Georgia. Em's a grown woman. She can do what she wants and can make her own mistakes, and it looks like she's making some here. Cain't you see it might not be all your fault?"

She began to play with the salt shaker, trying to stand it on end. I just about lost it again. I took another sip of coffee, took a deep breath, and tried one more time.

"Come on, George. You know and I know, and I'll bet my good silver dollar, that Em knows good and well, it's easier to have sex with somebody you don't hardly know. My Lord, you know almost every lesbian couple has great sex for the first two weeks. We can't help it. Don't know each other well enough to do serious hurt. So we tell each other it's the best sex we ever had in our lives. We'd better. I mean, the first time's always the best, right?

"Well, I'll tell you what. A lot of times, the earth had better move that first time, because we don't want to look at what else is there, you understand? I mean, for sure there can't be no relationship there. You know that. It's great sex, but why? Because God wanted it that way? Because the new one was made for you in heaven? Now you tell me, do you believe that? If you do, I got some swampland in Florida just waiting for you.

"Tell me one thing. You want to trade what you got with Em for that pack of foolishness? Looks like Em found out a little bit about how foolish that was for herself.

"She said she made a mistake. You know, a woman can only run so far before she sees she's running from herself. The question for you is, darling, whether or not you want to figure out how to get what *you* want at home. Your part of the relationship is to figure what *you* want."

I took a long breath—had about run myself out—but Georgia just kept her head down. Bruce brought our breakfasts, setting everything down just so, like he does, and ignoring the fact that it looked like we was both in tears. "Enjoy," he said as he floated off, just like always. He's like Old Faithful, you know? Bumped me back to the real world. I did know what I was talking about here. I didn't have to yell.

"Georgia," I said. "Now look. The woman's got troubles of her own, and they got nothing to do with you. She's got trouble all the time at work. She's got no time for nothing. And now you tell me, y'all ain't been intimate. So you figure this, George, if you want to figure. Now's the time. She's running from something in *her*, don't you see that? Some heartache, I'll bet dollars to donuts. If sleeping with some idiot's all she's going to do before she wakes up, count yourself lucky. Maybe this will get her awake.

"But we can't worry about her. We got to worry about you. And anyway, you's all you got control of. So now you think. What you want to do?"

She was looking at the food Bruce had put in front of her like it was pig slop. I could see this path was only going in a circle. I sipped some more coffee and doubled back. It might take me all day, I said to myself, but I was going to get this right, this business about being a good friend. I looked at my plate. It looked pretty good to me. So I withdrew the question, like Della Street would have, if she'd ever got the chance.

"Tell you what, don't answer that right now. You just feel around the edges of it. You eat now. Then we talk, okay? Just eat now," I said and let go of her hand. She picked up her fork three times before she got food on it and got it to her mouth.

"Good, ain't it," I said, grinning and happy as always with grits and biscuits.

She looked at me, pushed her glasses up on her nose, and smiled. I guess she decided I had stopped with the cross-examination, so she relaxed. I was glad then and knew I was doing right. Then she took a big bite out of her biscuit and waved the biscuit, toothmarks and all, in my face.

"Bernice, how you find places like this? You found this place when we first got here, you remember that? You always find these great places. How about finding me a place to work like this?" she said and you could tell she was kind of dreaming and changing the subject but that was okay with me. It was a place to start, and this time, it was her place.

"Okay. We can do that. You want a place like this, with the juke box in the back, right? Long counter down the side? That might be what you want? When do you want it? You'd be great at it."

"God, Bernice, that'd be wonderful. But," she sighed, "I can't do anything like that now."

"Why not?"

She took another big bite of biscuit, and put jam on her sec ond bite before she answered. "Too old to start. Not enough money to get it going. You don't know of a place, do you?"

"I ain't started looking yet and neither have you. How come you ain't out there looking, that's what I want to know."

"Looking to work in a diner?"

"No, you fool. Get you a decent job."

"I got a decent... " she started. But before I could get my interrupt going out of my mouth, she said, "Bernice, I am too looking. I mean, I'm thinking about it. I mean, I was thinking this weekend maybe I should try for this library job Ricky thinks I could get. I've been thinking about libraries, you know? Cool, quiet stacks of books. No people, or at least not any one who thinks he owns you. Just books. With stories in them. You know? Cool. Quiet. Books. What a relief.

"Anyway, I don't know. I don't know if I could even get this job Ricky talked about. I don't know if I have the right training for it. I mean, shelving books doesn't seem so hard, but, there's got to be more to it than that, and I don't know enough yet. I don't think I could. It'd be great though, wouldn't it?"

"Do me a favor," I said, mopping up my egg with the last of my biscuit. "You go ask Ricky if she thinks you could. You ask her how much she knew when she started her library job. Ask her what you need to do. And let me ask *you* one thing, girl. You want to work for Williams, or some cousin of his, all your life? You want this other job? Well, go get it. Shoot, you'd think you was stapled to all his paper yourself."

She wouldn't look at me. She pushed her plate away, only half-eaten and said, after sipping her coffee, "But I don't know, Bernice. I don't think I can leave my job just like that."

I could hardly believe my ears. I stared at her to see if they was signs of madness ringing around her eyes, but no, she just looked little again. I called Bruce for the check before I answered her and got her out of there. Once back in the car, I had about got ahold of myself and thought maybe I could answer her without yelling.

"What you mean 'like that?' What's his office got to do with you?"

"Oh Bernice, you know, I don't know... "

I was quiet for a minute, trying to recall why I shouldn't just kick her butt. I took a long breath and turned around to look at her. Finally, I caught it. I heard what she was really saying, you know?

I asked her, "Baby, just what is it you don't know?"

"What do you mean?"

"Georgia, you keep saying you don't know. What is it you don't know?"

"I don't know," she said, turning away from me. "I don't know anything."

My Lord. Time for a different path out of this field. I reached over and squeezed her hand. She didn't squeeze back. I fired the truck up.

"How about a drive to the beach?" I asked.

She didn't turn around. "Whatever you want, Bernice," she said.

"Georgie. It ain't what I want. It's what you want."

"Jesus, Bernice. Any thing. Do anything."

I just sat there and didn't make a move towards the four-on-the-floor. I just sat there and looked at her.

Finally, she turned around and looked at me, wiping the tears off her face as she did.

"Can't we go for a ride, Bernice? Get the hell out of here?"

"Sure we can, Georgie girl. You tell me. Where you want to go?"

"Bernice," she screamed. "Just get us out of here!"

I didn't move.

"The highway. The Coast Highway," she muttered at last.

I got the truck out of there quick as a thieving raccoon. Well, that was one request for herself. One down. Two thousand to go. We was almost to Devil's Slide before she said anything.

"Bernice, how many times you think we done this?" she said, her voice low.

I grinned at her and started to feel better. "Oh, maybe a hundred. Maybe more. Over the years."

And then she sparked it. I knew she would, sooner or later. I didn't know what, or when, but I knew it when I saw it. My Lord, there wasn't a happier woman alive in the world in that moment besides me.

"Yeah. More than a hundred. And how come we're still doing it? How come it still hurts? What're we doing wrong that it keeps hurting?"

The thing about Georgie girl is that she's a survivor, you know what I mean? I mean, she never thinks she will, but some little bit of her is determined like you would not believe.

"Why, George," I said, turning to look at her for a minute. "Georgie. What do you mean, keeps hurting? Don't you know you're supposed to be hurting now? It hurts to watch your momma being sick, I don't care if she is getting better some. It hurts like the devil when somebody does you wrong, like Em done."

"I'm not sure what you're meaning, George. But I think we're not doing anything wrong that it keeps hurting. You go through life; sometimes it hurts; you go through that and get to the other side. That's life. It won't kill you, this hurting, you know. And the thing is, hurting ain't all life does. They's other stuff what happens too, if you keep your eyes open. Look here. Are we not sitting here together, playing hooky? And ain't we been friends forever? Ain't we going to be friends forever? It ain't all that bad. You just got to learn to hold it all at once and go on through to the other side."

She looked at me, a strange look, like she was seeing me, but seeing something just past my left shoulder, too. She took my hand and we drove on, quiet as church mice.

In a bit, she said, real quiet, so low I had to turn the radio off, "I do know it, Bernice Sophia. I do know it. I thought there was something like that this weekend. I don't know how to explain it, but I thought about that. I thought about how it is all at once, not one simple thing being all of it, canceling everything else out. Something's wrong when we look at things just part and part. I saw that."

She took a very ragged breath and when I looked over, sure enough, the tears were rolling again.

I squeezed her hand. "Is that so bad?" I asked, nice as I could.

"It's not that it's bad, Bernice. It's that it's hurtful. Somehow, when you can't hate somebody, it leaves room to let the hurt rush in, like a wave rolling in, and I just don't think I can stop feeling it anymore. I think about my mom, and all I can see is the bridge game we tried to have on Saturday night, one of us holding her cards, along with our own, and playing hers when she nodded.

"And nobody cheated. We all played her hand, regardless of what we ourselves were holding. And we all took turns at it.

Whoever was dummy. I can't describe it to you. How could we do that, Cameron drunk, little Cam trying not to cry, me watching them all, and have it work? My family has never not taken advantage of each other. And there we sat, all of us playing for her. It was a real game; I mean, it worked.

"And you know what else? It was fun. It was lunatic. But it was fun. I don't understand my family. Every time I think I get them nailed down, they move. I don't understand them. And it hurts more this way. It hurts to look at them like that. I don't know how to act around them. I don't know what to do with all the hurt. It feels like I been hurting about this forever."

She stopped talking finally, and she wiped her eyes.

"But not going on forever, you know that part, right, girl? This is the part where it starts to not hurt so much, after awhile," I said when it looked like she wasn't going to keep talking. "This is the part where you really start to begin to understand what's been going on, because you got more of the pieces now. Right?"

"I guess," she said, her face turned to the window.

"So tell me, baby, tell me what it feels like, now, okay?"

"I don't know, Bernice. It feels like everything's lost again, you know what I mean? I mean, it's all there, but it's out of place somehow and now I have to figure out how to put it back together."

She started to cry, for real this time, not just the tears, but the tearing in her throat, too. I held tight to her hand, trying to watch her while keeping the truck on the road. She didn't look at me, but she didn't let go of my hand, neither.

She choked for a minute, turning her head away as she cried. I just waited. It's the time I hate most, but I had to let her have it. If I loved her at all, I had to let her have it. In a little while, she started to talk again.

"And then I get back here, I mean, I'm crying, partly, you know. Well, I get back here and Em's slept with another woman. I mean, what is going on? Bernice? What the hell is going on here? What am I supposed to do now? Leave? Am I supposed to walk out? What options do I have here? Goddamnit it all to hell, what was she doing?"

She took her hand back and, in her rage, her voice became a shout. "I leave to try to make some peace, to try to find out what is going on at home. I get some figured out; I feel hurt, but okay. Not so angry. Better. I come home and there's no home. No home here, either. No one to get me at the airport. An apartment with no lights on. Looks like no one lives there.

"And then she comes, finally, this one who's supposed to be my home, she comes home and tells me that while I've been trying to get my head straight about my family, she's gone and slept with somebody else."

I waited. She sniffled and took off her glasses and leaned her head back on the seat. I took one quick look and saw she was still crying. I waited longer.

"And I don't know," she said, after awhile. "Hell, it's not just about a home. It's my whole life. Bernice, I just don't know how to do this. I just don't know how."

She lost me then. I didn't have no idea what she was talking about. I looked at her; most of the tears were gone. She'd done something, threaded her way back around to be confused. I just didn't know what she'd done. She had been getting clearer, but then. Well, all I knew to do was to go back to the beginning.

"So let's start at the beginning, okay? What do you *want* to do?"

"Bernice, it's not that easy. Listen. I learned some thing at home. I learned something about my father. He wanted to be a farmer. Can you believe that?"

Well, to tell you the truth, on account of my own old man, the thought made my skin crawl a little. I mean my old man was a farmer until he lost the farm, and partly I knew he lost it because he couldn't get the yields, and partly because he lost his heart when momma died. But I knew he had been refusing to put into the ground some of those very chemicals Georgia's daddy made so much money off. It wasn't real easy for me to hear her, but I had to trust she didn't know how words like that would hurt me. And plus I didn't really think she was talking about her daddy.

"That so," I finally said, deciding not to take it personal. "What's that mean to you, girl?"

"Well, look at him. I mean, I don't know. Something in me, well, I know I have to leave that job with Williams, that's all. I understand it. I can see it. I am going to go. You just hide and watch," she said, grinning a little at our old joke. But the grin faded off her face.

"Yeah," she said. "That's what I figured this weekend. Get my act together, trying to do something, finally, for myself. And *look* at this. What the *hell* is she doing? I can't change jobs in the midst of all this, and she knows it. I don't even know if I have a home to come home to, and if I have to take a pay cut or get a new apartment, damnit Bernice, I can't do it all at once.

"Bernice. What the hell is she doing to me?" she spat out, her voice urgent and furious.

"Well," I said, slowly, "I don't know. Did you tell her all this?"

Her face fell and she put her glasses back on and turned away. To the window she said, "No. I don't know. I got all confused when she told me. And I felt like I didn't know where I was, even though I was sitting there, in my own apartment. I felt like, Bernice, it was like I was trying to explain to you before. It's like everything's changing. And I got no place to be anymore."

I didn't know what to say. I didn't know how to put it together for her. And finally, in the nick of time, I heard myself and knew that was the answer. I wasn't supposed to put it together for her. For all my talk about her lion, and what she ought to do, standing up for herself and all, well, it was easy for me to say. Not so easy for her to do, finding her own way home, not mine. And not so easy for me to keep my big trap shut, acting like I knew it all. I could see for sure then that I didn't know a thing she needed. God Almighty, some of us is slow with what we have to learn. But at least I got it before I made another mess.

I took her hand again. And I heard her crying. All I could say was, "You can be here with me for a bit until you find your own place." I heard her sniff and she squeezed my hand, but that was all the reply I got. I watched the road then, trying to give her some privacy for her tears. The truck slid through a curve down in the eucalyptus grove. We were getting near the ocean. That was good. It always calmed us both down.

"Georgia," I said after a bit, "Georgia, open up the window, my Lord, you are going to smoke me out of here." She had begun with the chainsmoking after the sniffles. I couldn't stand it. It wasn't what I meant to say, but she started grinning and rolled the window down.

Then I had an idea. I looked over at her and her face was pale. Well, it was all I could think of to do. "Georgia, look just for a minute, okay? Now what if this was all happening to somebody else. What advice would you give them?"

"I'd tell them that it was really all about their momma."

She grinned her sly grin at me and I laughed out loud. That girl. But then I thought, well? And I asked, "Really, Georgie?"

But she didn't answer me. She was quiet for awhile and we broke through the eucalyptus grove to the ocean. She gasped, like she usually does when we crest that hill and the whole Pacific Ocean stretches out in front of the truck like you're a tired fool and the ocean's a clean-made, warm bed.

"I don't know."

"What don't you know, girl? What is it you trying so hard not to know? Tell me what it feels like, what it would feel like if you did know."

She sighed long and deep and I knew I'd hit something. When Georgia hurts, she thinks she's got to think her way out. It ain't true; she don't have to think. She's got to feel, you know what I mean? And she hadn't been feeling much, because if she did, she'd know what she had to do.

"It feels like I'm lost again. It feels like it did when I was little and alone and Cameron was supposed to come and he didn't. Bernice, it feels like..."

She trailed off and then began again. "You know, I remember this feeling, Bernice. I remember thinking to myself when we got out here that I had finally found where I was supposed to be. And I loved it, you remember," she nodded at me.

"But it wasn't the first time I'd felt that. When I fell in love with you, I felt it for awhile."

She paused and I felt the pain streak through my heart one more time. Then she said, real soft, "I hope it doesn't still hurt you for me to say so. You've meant more to me all these years than almost anyone. I'm trying to tell you about this certain feeling, you understand?"

I nodded numbly and watched her, circling with my finger for her to keep rolling. Roll on past that moment, that's for sure. Even though we'd talked about it years before, it still hurt, and I just wanted her to keep talking.

And she did, thank God.

"You know, Bernice, when I drank, there was this time, there was always this place I was trying to get to. You understand? It was somewhere between the second and third drink, somewhere about two and a half. And it lasted for only a little while, but it was when I felt safe and that the world was safe and that I could come home, you understand?"

She gasped at the end then. "Oh, my God," she said and buried her face in her hands. I just waited. What else could I do, except look for a place to park so we could really talk. I didn't know what she had seen when she was talking, but I knew she had a lot more to say. Finally, we came to a turnaround and I pulled in. Almost as soon as I set the emergency brake, she started again.

"I mean, Bernice. I look around and I can't see anything. I can't see where I'm supposed to be or what I'm supposed to do. Am I supposed to be in that office? I'll choke to death. And at home, with Em, I feel like I gave away pieces of myself over and over again and I kept saying, 'Sure I see, sure I understand,' only now, my God, I just can't anymore, you know?"

I nodded. And took her hand again.

And all she said for the longest time was, "I thought I was home, Bernice. I really did."

I didn't say a word, but I didn't let go her hand neither.

And then, she turned to me, her face like a child's, desperate and asking. She looked at me and finally she said, "I got to make it myself, don't I? Is that what you've been saying? It's not someplace you go to, is it? I mean, not at first. You got to make it first, right? And it's not a place..."

She stumbled then and the big tears began to slide out from under her glasses, and I held to her hand tight as I could.

"And it's not a person, either, is it?

"Is it, Bernice?" she demanded. I just shook my head.

"I don't think so honey. I don't know, but I don't think so."

She nodded, finally something satisfied, took a deep breath, took her hand back, took her glasses and wiped her face. She went back to watching the waves. "I think this is right. I got to make it myself because nobody else can do it. I see that now. And love isn't enough to keep me and Em together, is it? I got to work at that too, right?"

She looked at me through new tears and I nodded. "I'm glad you learnt something after we broke up," I said, smiling at her, tears on my face too. She smiled back only it was real sad in her eyes and then she turned away.

We sat there through three more cigarettes. By and by, sometime after she put the third one out, she said, "Bernice, I love you."

I reached over and hugged her and her face was wet with tears. There are times when I love my girl, times when I think I see some of what the point of this whole thing is real clear. And I love her for showing me. You know? Friends can be like that. I am blessed, truly.

So knowing that I think that, you may think what I said then was silly, but to me, it was all about love, anyway.

"How about a haircut, then," I said. She smiled.

"Want to drive back?" I asked. She shook her head again, and so I cut on the engine and drove on back. When I looked at her sideways, she looked completely worn out, like she had been run over. Well, she was having to gather up all her own pieces, but she was making it. It wasn't over, but it was ending and myself, I felt so much better. I knew then she was out of the woods and if I hadn't been so tired, I might have cheered. Still, there was more to go. Help her make it real, I thought.

When we got to Karen, the haircutter, Georgia looked a little steadier. But I did notice when Karen washed her hair, Georgia cried a bit. And I did notice when she hopped in the chair, she couldn't sit still to save her soul, I mean, it would be hard not to notice that. But she actually looked in the mirror once or twice before we left the shop and I thought that was good.

I remembered then about the library I'd been thinking about earlier that morning, and since it was only just a couple blocks away, I told her we had another expedition to make and that she was to follow me. I led her down there and then stopped her in front of the lobby. Since it was Monday, and they had stopped opening Mondays on account of not enough money, we couldn't go in. But we could still see.

"What are we looking for, Bernice?" Georgia asked at first.

"Look in there. You see that statue?" I asked her. Inside the lobby of this particular library, the one down in the Castro, is a granite statue of the body of a woman. She's all polished up and smooth gray stone. And she's big, bigger than me, but not like a ritual statue or nothing. She's like a woman, broad hips, swelling breasts. She don't look like no adolescent boy. She's like a woman. She looks like Georgia. I loved that statue since the first time I laid eyes on it, but I wasn't sure Georgia had ever seen it.

"I see it. What about it?" she said, a little anxious like she was supposed to be getting something and she wasn't.

"You like her?"

"Yeah. She's beautiful. She's really beautiful."

"You notice anything familiar about her?"

"Like what? Come on, Bernice."

"She looks like you, Georgie. Her body is just like yours."

She looked at me and then back at the statue. And then she began to smile. My girl is not slow, I'll tell you that.

"You understand now they make art out of bodies like yours?"

"Well, at least one. Look at that. You really think I look like that?"

"Stop fishing. Don't you?"

"Well, there's certain similarities."

She turned to me and grinned and flung her arms around me.

"I do love you, Bernice."

"All right now, Georgie, no more p.d.a.'s. How about some food? I'm hungry now. How about you?"

It was about three. I was real hungry by then, seeing as how we'd eaten breakfast about nine or ten and nothing since, but anyway, I wanted to take her one more place, the diner where Chris makes her own potato chips right before your very eyes.

"I am starving," she said, linking arms with me. Some days, I tell you, it's good to be alive. I started us walking down to Chris' then, about five blocks away and I figured the exercise would do us good.

The place we were going is called Chris' Hamburgers and I wanted Georgia to see it. I didn't really think we'd get to talk; there's just a row of stools at the counter and a couple of tables in back. But see, Chris, this Filipina woman, owns and runs this place. And she does it mostly by herself, the cooking and whatnot. But the thing is, she makes her own potato chips, right there. I mean, she slices her own chips off her own spuds right there, as you watch. And she watches you; she don't watch the knife. Just whomp, whomp, whomp, and in a minute the spud is laying spread out in front of her, all sliced in the same paper-thin width. You never seen nothing like it in your life.

I wanted Georgia to see it. And so we sashayed down there, arm-in-arm, not talking about nothing for the first time that day. We got stools right away, I think because it was a weird afternoon time. Usually there's a line. And we ordered and Chris gave us lumpia while we waited for the burgers. And then she commenced with the whomp-whomp and I could see Georgie's eyes getting real big. And she looked at me and then looked back at Chris and then back at me with this big old grin on her face.

It was great. Maybe the best part of the day, except at the beach, or maybe the statue, I don't know. Anyway, we ate our lumpia and burgers and chips and Georgie didn't stop grinning the whole time. But when we got back out on the street, she looked at me sideways and said, "You didn't just bring me there for the chips, did you?"

"Well, she *is* a woman who owns her own place. And she is doing what she pleases. And she is happy, you can see it when she looks at you when she's making the chips."

I didn't say anything else, and Georgie grinned her sly grin and looked the other way. And then, as we went back to the truck, she took out her cigs again. "I need to go home, Bernice," she said, walking around to the curb. "Sooner or later, I guess Em and I are going to have to thrash this one out. If she really wants to go, well, I can't stop her. But I aim to make real sure she wants to go, and she's not just confused. Because I'm not anymore." She chucked the cigs in the trash can and came back around.

I hugged her and said, "You look more like a lion every minute, you know that, girl?" She just grinned at me and I leaned down and whispered in her ear, "I love you, Georgie."

And then I handed her the truck keys. I made sure I had enough chump change for the train home and I hugged her one more time. She was crying again, but I rubbed the tears away with my shirt sleeve.

"Georgie darling, you've only got a broken heart. And it seems bigger because it's about you and your girl and your home. But the honeymoon's over, that's all. Folks don't die from this. And they don't die from getting mad. They only die from giving up. And if they don't get mad when they *are* mad, that's a way of giving up. You understand that now? Try to hold on to today. You decide what you want and then go get it. But you call me, girl. You call me."

I kissed her and went down into the train station. I didn't look back when I walked away. When I got on the train, I leaned my head back and could almost sleep I was so wore out. But, you know, I knew she'd be all right. I did wish I'd been there that night when Em got home, just to see what was going to happen, you know, but I wasn't so worried no more. George would do just fine, I knew that. She's a good girl. Course, even as I had been standing there preaching reconciliation and all that, I had been thinking Em was a little lowlife, but as I walked down to the BART, I begun to think to myself, Lord knows, we all got reasons for our troubles, don't we? I felt like I could forgive a bit too, because me and George had done so good that day, I mean, real good. And I knew, like I had been knowing for a long time, that me and Georgie will outlast them all, Shiloh or no, can't stop us. She and Em would make it, too, I was sure of it, though God only knew how it would happen. Annie had said all along that she knew they'd make it. She just wanted them to get on with it so she didn't keep getting woke up with early morning phone calls.

But the phone calls didn't make no nevermind to me, you know. I mean, really, what are friends for? What are friends for if not to listen to you when you want to talk about your family, you know what I mean? I mean, my Lord, it ain't easy for none of us, but when somebody decides to move, to get on with it, to break through that cocoon and get on with life, why, I think that's cause for whooping and cheering, myself.

CHAPTER TEN

OUR DAILY BREAD

The electric teakettle was screaming full-throat by the time Morgan heard it. She was sitting with her stocking feet up on her desk, staring out the window, watching the afternoon light slip down the building across the street. When she finally heard the kettle, she pushed herself up, padded over to the other side of the office and unplugged the cord.

She stood there with the plug in her hand, trying to remember why she'd turned the kettle on, watching the steam slowly taper out the spout. The damn thing was like everything else in her life. It only had two speeds. On and off. When you turned it off, it was off; that's all. The whistle faded away with the steam. She stood there.

She was tired. And her feet ached. Mother of God, one weekend of no sleep, you come back to work and everything aches. She arched her back to crack it and then remembered the tea she had wanted. Some of Elliott's China black. As strong as she could make it, and hot. She was freezing.

Where the hell *was* Elliott? It was way past five now and he should have been here by four-thirty at the latest. She stood on one foot and dipped the tea ball in and out of her cup, watching the swirls of tea begin to drift through the water.

Abruptly, she yanked the tea ball out and stalked back to her desk, not paying attention to the sloshing tea dripping from her cup. She sat back down in her chair, muttering. Jesus, teaching. Teaching, she shook her head. And now there was also waiting. Two months of frantic work on the new contract application, right up to the last minute, for Chrissake. And now, they got to wait. For evaluations, recommendations, letters, meetings, forms, none of which they would know about. And finally, a decision.

Well, anyway, now she had some time. She unknotted her hands and picked up her tea. Now she had some of that time she had been screaming for last weekend. But now, it wasn't like she had any place she was in a hurry to get to.

Of course, she could go home.

Right, she thought, slurping the tea so as not to burn herself, but she did anyway. She put her feet back up on the desk. She wondered, not for the first time that day, if Georgia would be home for dinner. But she didn't move to call home. She didn't move except to recross her arms, push the chair back, and stare out the window.

She stayed that way until Janice poked her head in and said she was leaving. Morgan nodded to her, said goodnight and asked her to lock the door behind her. It wasn't long after that she heard Elliott's key. But she didn't turn around when he came in.

"Morgan?" he called out. "What are you doing here this late? It's past six. How did everything go?" he asked as he walked toward her, clothes disheveled, tie askew. He heaved his briefcase up on his desk and came around to take the seat by her desk. She didn't speak.

"*Nu?*" He leaned on his knees and looked at her. She looked back at him.

"*Nu*. No *nu*. Nothing new. Well, I did turn the application in this morning. I guess that's new. But Elliott, don't you ever get bored with this job?"

"Nothing about my life is very boring anymore, little one," he said, his eyes red and tired. He slumped back in the chair, extending his legs and crossing them in front of him, so that he looked like one long board.

She took her feet off the desk and leaned forward to play with the pencil Elizabeth had given her.

He asked again, "What's up?" She didn't answer. He took off his tie before he asked, "Class go okay? Are you okay?"

"Class was fine. It's all women this time, so I can teach from a conceptual point of view that starts and ends with the whole system instead of bit by byte by rote. Why is it women like that better than men, Elliott?"

"Em. How many times have we discussed that? Men and women are different; so what else is new. What's up?" He stopped folding his tie and laid it on her desk.

"I'm tired, Elliott. I'm so tired of this shit."

"When things change in your life, or even when things change for people in your life, you get tired a lot, Em. You've seen me these last couple of months. I don't know why. But you get tired. How's Georgia? She home yet? How's her mother? And how did it go finishing up our application? I'm sorry I didn't call, but I got hung up at the hospital. How come you didn't call Sunday to let me know how it was going? Are you okay?"

She didn't answer or look at him, just kept her eyes on her pencil. After awhile, she said, "This getting tired business, does it make you do stupid things too?"

He rubbed his hands over his face. "All the time," he said.

She twisted the pencil around and took it apart. She didn't say anything out loud but inside her head she kept thinking, as she had all day when the noise of the class stopped, when for no reason everyone in class was silent all of a sudden, the way groups of people sometimes are; she kept drifting away like she had when she looked out the window and lost her place and couldn't remember where she was for a moment, or who were the women sitting in front of her, or what they wanted. She thought again for the thousandth time that day: Jesus Christ, what have you done now?

He waited and when she didn't say anything more, he said, "Did you do something stupid, *shayna maydele?*" and his voice was gruff and low.

She put the pencil back together and threw it in the trash.

"Hey," he said. "That's your new pencil. Is it broken?"

"Broken," she agreed and put her hand on his arm when he moved forward to get it out of the trash can.

"Maybe I can fix it for you."

"You can't. Elliott, you remember that woman about two months ago who wanted a woman to teach her?"

He nodded, and she could feel his eyes intent on her face.

"I slept with her over the weekend."

He stared at her for a long moment. Then he said, "I think maybe you better tell me about it."

"I slept with her."

"You're in love with her?"

"No, I just slept with her."

He whistled, short and low. Finally he said, "Well, that's right. Stupid things. You'll be doing some very stupid things."

They were both silent. Slowly, he kicked his shoes off and went to plug in the kettle.

"Have you had supper yet?" he asked, his back turned to her while he got his cup ready. "You want I should order takeout and we talk about this thing?"

"I have to go home some time. See if Georgia's there. She left last night about ten."

"And she didn't come home?"

"No," she said, talking to the window.

He whistled again.

"Morgan, never in the entire time I've known you and Georgia... well, you did it, didn't you?" he asked, gruffly.

She took her feet off the desk. "What do you mean?"

"You think you made a big enough mess so that you don't have to think about your life? Playing softball twenty-four hours a day didn't do it? Do you think this will keep you from thinking about what hurts? Georgia and her mom? Or me? How much does this have to do with me and Joe, anyway?"

"Elliott, this has nothing to do with any of that."

"What odds do you want?"

"Stop it, Elliott. Georgia and I have been having trouble for some time now. I never see her anymore. It's always her job or her family or something."

"Or it's your work and your softball. Or you're home but watching TV. Or she's home but not with you. You've told me all about it, here and there. I thought you'd work it out or I would have talked to you about it before now. But now." He studied the teakettle.

"Okay," he said. "Well, better late than never, I guess." He turned to face her. "What you really mean to say is that she isn't there when you want her anymore."

"Elliott, whose side are you on?" she asked stiffly.

"Yours, little one. Yours. You want to tell me what happened?"

"I want *you* to tell *me*, you with your infinite faggot wisdom about nonmonagamy, what I'm supposed to do now."

"Oh, I'm the expert on that, am I now?"

"Elliott, please." She got up and placed her cup next to his so she could have a second cup. She looked up at him and felt suddenly exhausted.

"I just fucked up, Elliott. That's all. I just fucked up. I don't want to leave Georgia, I just wanted a little, you know, Jesus Christ, I don't know what I was doing."

"Do you now?" he asked, pouring the water.

She looked at him. "Do I now?"

"Yes. Do you know what you are doing now. Do you know what you want? That's your first lesson in nonmonogamy. You have to be clear about what you want," he said as he walked them both back to Morgan's desk. "What do you want to do now?"

She looked at him, looked up at his tired face and was suddenly angry with his shrink tone of voice. When she answered, her voice was bitter. "I want to not be here. I want it to be two weeks ago. I want Joe not to be sick; I want you to be healthy."

He didn't answer. They were both quiet, except for blowing on their tea. Then she said, more softly, "How is he, anyway?"

"He went back on the ward Saturday. Our favorite hotel, forget the Hyatt, we prefer good old 5B," he said, rubbing his eyes. "That's why I'm late. I was down there this afternoon, and I'm going back again as soon as I get cleaned up here."

She reached over and took his hand. "I'm sorry, Elliott. I know my mess is nothing compared to Joe. Forget about it. It's not a big deal." His hand felt cold and tired, and he didn't squeeze back.

After awhile, he looked up, and his eyes were red. "You're wrong. What's happening with you is a big deal. It's not death, but it's a mess. And it matters. You matter. And Georgia matters. You might want to think what you would do if Georgia was the one who was sick. Morgan, we're not on this earth for long. You can't just... You know, you and Georgia have come through a lot together. You remember that time you broke your ankle at a game? And she took care of you and nearly got fired over it?"

She nodded. Sure she remembered. It had happened early on; they'd been together maybe a year. The break had hurt like hell and in the pain she'd needed Georgia's hand to help her stay there, and not float back to the old beaten pain from before. She had needed her then; it was true. And Georgia had been there for her no matter what it cost her. And that was only the first time.

"You remember that?" Elliot was saying. "I knew then that she was good for you and was so glad you found her. You know, it's funny. I still don't know her very well, really, but it doesn't matter. I can see all over your face, maybe even when you can't, that the two of you need each other, like Joe and I need each other. And that you love each other. I've seen it all along. Lot of people look all their lives for that. Em. Listen to me.

"I heard about her going to all those softball games, and I watched you pay the rent. What do you want here, Em? You want to start over? You think this kind of thing grows on trees? That you can just go to Macy's and get a red sweater instead of the green one you have? You think things will be easy with this new one? That maybe she doesn't need as much as Georgia right now? That maybe she can give you more than Georgia right now?

"You know, Em, sometimes when people need you, you can make messes because you don't think you can do it. You don't think you have any more to give. Or you don't think you can give them what they want, and probably you can't. But you can always give them one thing. You can love them. It's not enough, but it's all you've got. Be there for her, Em. You need it; she needs it. Let her in. Sit with her when she hurts. Sit with her when you hurt. You can't make it better for her. She can't make it better for you. But you can sit together. And that's what it's all about."

Morgan looked at him and felt trapped, felt her anger start to rise, but this was Elliott and she wanted to talk to him. It seemed like all he could ever talk about these days was Joe, but maybe she could get him off it for once. She tried.

"Look, Elliott. I know you've learned a lot from being with Joe during this time. But this is a little different. I know I should be, well, I do feel like a louse about Georgia. But Elliott, it was so different with Elizabeth at first. I felt new. I felt wanted. I felt... I felt hot, Elliott. I can't tell you how good it felt to me after all this time and I..."

He cut her off. "Oh stop. You think this faggot doesn't know from sex and lust? You think I haven't heard that same crap from my dying friends? Stop it, Em. You're just scared. Hell, we're all scared. Think about what you're doing, little one. Don't make a bigger mess than you have to. Have you even talked to her today?"

Morgan looked out the window then and shook her head.

"You may not have all the choices anymore, you know that? You guys weren't nonmonogamous. That's lesson number two. You have to set it up beforehand. Otherwise, what you've done is known as cheating and is grounds for divorce. Is she going to leave you?"

"I don't know."

"Don't you think you better get home and find out? Or do you want to tell me what happened over the weekend so you can know what you are doing now?"

"I don't know what you're talking about, Elliott. What's to tell? I had a normal weekend. Well, anyway, usual. I coached in the morning, tried to scout an East Bay game after I coached. Then

I went home, listened to the A's game, took a shower, went for a latte, read the paper. Then I went to Elizabeth's for dinner. Sunday I went home, came to work, finished the contract application and then went off to think. The Jeep broke down over in Oakland, so I couldn't get back to get Georgia at the airport. When I got home, I told her everything. All hell broke loose. I think you can probably guess the details."

"So it was usual; nothing out of the ordinary?"

"If you want to call it that."

"So how did it feel?"

"Elliott, what is all this talk about feeling? For Chrissake, I didn't have any feelings. I don't know about Georgia. I have to wait until she tells me what she wants. I've already gone ahead and done things. My feelings don't matter now."

"Bullshit."

She turned to him and stared. She didn't care then who he was. This was fucked. Why was he pushing her so hard?

"What do you mean, bullshit? You weren't there. Don't tell me what you don't know," she said, her voice furious and her eyes threatening. She turned her head away.

"I'm not telling you what I don't know," he said. He waited for a moment and then went on. "But I know you had feelings. I know it. You'd have to be dead not to. You may not be acknowledging them, but you have them."

They were silent. She bent down and started to put her shoes on, wondering why she had ever waited to see him. And then she felt what she was going to say start to come out of her mouth. And she knew she should stop, but she didn't.

"What is all this 'feeling' shit? Is this what they teach you down in your little California touchy-feely grief group at the hospice?"

The words hung in the air between them like a wall of fire, scorching, acrid.

He let his breath out slowly before he answered. "You know, the entire time I've known you, you've almost never asked for help. And you never did it until it was the very last chance you had.

"So. What are you going to do? Are you going to fight with everyone you love before you admit to yourself that you hurt, that you're frightened?"

"Go to hell, Elliott."

"You go home, little one. Figure out what you want. Don't lose her if you have to. Don't make a *shanda*. Go home. I'll be here in the morning."

"You don't stop do you, you son of a bitch," she said, her voice low. She got her stuff, grabbed her coat and left.

Morgan rode the N-Judah home and didn't notice the fog slipping over the Seventeenth Street hill. She didn't see it until they came out of the tunnel at Carl and Cole and by then the Haight was wrapped in gray. She walked home, cold. The house was dark.

She trudged up to the second floor, opened the door, the lock cranky in the mist, and listened in the dark on the landing for a moment. No lights, not even in the kitchen. No sounds. She went in, dropped her briefcase in the hall and went to hang up her coat. As she opened the closet door, she heard someone in the kitchen turning pages of a newspaper.

"Georgia?" she called.

"Um."

She *was* in the kitchen. Well, Morgan thought, at least she was home. She walked down to the kitchen and turned the overhead light on.

"Didn't your mother ever tell you you'd ruin your eyes that way?"

Georgia looked up at her and blinked. She slipped her fingers under her glasses and rubbed her eyes before she answered.

"My eyes are already ruined, and my mother can't talk anymore," she said, adjusting her glasses, and then, looking back at the newspaper spread flat on the table, she turned the page.

Morgan sat down across from her. Georgia kept reading the paper. When she turned the next page, Morgan put her hand in between the pages to stop her.

Georgia looked up.

"I'm glad you're home," Morgan said. "I think we need to talk."

"Oh? You have something to say? You have more news? I'm surprised you're home. Or have you just been working late again? Don't you have a game tonight?" Georgia asked, ripping the page to turn it.

"Georgie. Look, we need to talk. I'm skipping practice tonight. I, well, Jesus this is so stupid. Yes, I was working late. I, look, I'm not in love with her, I just made a mistake."

"Have you told her that?"

They stared at each other. Georgia's voice was moderated and bored-sounding. She sounded like her mother. Morgan had heard that tone of voice before, not often, but she'd heard it.

"Georgia," she started again. "We need to talk about us."

"Really? Is that why you hurried home tonight? A little late, isn't it? I was willing to talk about this. I came home at four. Isn't that when your class ends? Where were *you*? I have been here, waiting. Like I always do. Well, I'm done waiting."

It was out in the open now. No hiding. She wasn't just sarcastic; she was mean. Morgan hadn't wanted it to go like this, but she could feel the anger rising back in her. When the house had been dark, she'd been afraid and thought maybe Elliott was right. Well, she'd tried, goddamnit.

"Oh? And you've been around to talk before, right?"

"Don't you blame this one on me. I've been around plenty."

Morgan heard Elliott again, but she couldn't stop.

"Oh, plenty. Every night. In your room with the door closed. Or working overtime. Or sitting at the table like a fucking ghost."

She leaned over the paper and put her face as close to Georgia as she dared. "Don't you ever get bored with those old pictures in your room? Do you remember you live here with me now? That maybe I need a little attention sometimes too?"

Georgia looked back at her so hard, she thought she might slap her, and quickly she sat back down. But when Georgia didn't answer, in the silence, her anger swelled again and she suddenly slammed her hand on the table and shouted.

"Oh, but no. If it isn't your family, it's your fucking job. This great job that makes you hate yourself. But you stay there, you keep yourself in a sucky job you hate. And come home, when you do come home, and piss your rotten feelings on me. You know, sometimes, I wish you still drank. Then you could blame your shitty life on that.

"Jesus, you don't even talk to me anymore. First you stop coming to the games, then you stop talking. It's been like Siberia around here. You don't tell me what's going on. You just end up talking to your idiot Southern friend on the telephone. You know you talk to her more than me?

"What the fuck ever happened to me? Remember me? I'm supposed to be your lover. I know your mother's sick. I've been wanting to help. I've been waiting for *you*, you bitch, not the other way around. I wait up for you, but you don't come home. Remember me? You even remember what I look like?"

Georgia abruptly pushed back her chair and Morgan jumped back, quick, out of the reach of her hands.

But Georgia just looked at her and said, "I don't have to take this anymore." She paused and Morgan watched her sharply, startled.

Georgia began to walk away from the table and then turned and said, "You don't like me, leave. You can leave anytime, as you have already found out and demonstrated. But I'm not going to put up with this anymore. You don't like being with an alcoholic? Leave. You don't like that my mother's dying? Well, neither do I. You don't like my father? Or how I deal with him? Leave. You don't like my friends? Too bad. You might notice you don't have any, except some faggot. But hey, that's okay. We know what you want.

"Sure, we know what Em wants. An easy ride. It's been tough on her, so we have to make it easy for her. Nobody ever loved her, so we have to love her more. Go to her damn fool ball games. Cook for her. Make a home for her. But what about my home, that's what I want to know. Who's making *my* home? What about me? Me need something? Oh no, never.

"You think it's hard to live with me, then get out. I'll bet your new girlfriend wants to take care of you and has money, too, lots of it. Bet she's not a secretary. Bet she takes you to great restaurants. But we both know what you are. You have merely demonstrated your price.

"Tired of me? Wore me out? Want somebody else to take care of you? Good, go find another fool.

"But you leave me alone, do you understand?"

By the time she said that she was back to the table, leaning over the newspaper and Morgan had scraped her chair back, away from her. Georgia's eyes, crying though she was, looked hard and shuttered. Morgan suddenly wished Georgia had just gone ahead and hit her.

Georgia drew back. "Perhaps you'd find it more pleasant to go to your new girlfriend, have a couple of drinks and, as you so quaintly used to put it, go fuck your brains out. You've been keeping it from me for long enough. You think I didn't know you'd go out and get somebody eventually? You think I didn't expect this? Go fuck your brains out, and see if it makes you happy.

"But understand this. Go wear them all out. Like you wore me out. Sure, I remember those days when we were first together, and you couldn't get enough. You even made me in the shower, you remember that? Well, you remember me good. Because you won't find anybody better than me, you understand that? You won't.

"I've been good to you. And now, now that I need a little something, a little support, why, you go right ahead and leave. Destroy us, but you won't destroy me, you understand that? You're just like my father, you know that? Just like him. No, you don't drink. You don't have to. But I know one thing. I'm not the sick one here. I'm not the one who isn't talking about what's happening. I'm not the one who's left home."

She stopped for a moment and drew a deep breath through her clenched teeth. Morgan sat there, her head down, with nothing to say.

"I'm going to my stupid Southern friend's house for the night. My stupid Southern friend who doesn't treat me like dirt. I don't know when I'll be back. When *I* want, we'll talk about dividing the house. And until then, I don't want to hear a word out of you."

There was silence for a moment and then Georgia stalked out, walking down the hall to their room. Morgan could hear coat hangers bouncing off the closet rack and could hear her frantic packing. She could also hear her crying. She sat there, slumped over the table. She sat there until she heard Georgia banging down the steps, and then she found her feet and her voice.

"Georgia. Georgie, wait. Wait!" She tore down the hall, screaming. She got to the railing and saw Georgia was waiting, her hand on the doorknob.

"Georgia. Wait."

"For what?" Georgia put her bag down. Morgan slumped down on the carpet and spoke through the railings.

"I don't want you to leave. Georgia, I need you right now."

Georgia picked up her bag and started to open the door.

"Well, that's too bad. I've had it with what you need."

"Georgie, wait. We can talk about what you need, too. Don't go. Please don't go. I have to talk to you. Please come back up here and talk to me."

"Say whatever you have to say. I can hear it from here," Georgia said and shut the door.

"Look, I'm sorry I said things that upset you. I'm sorry. Can't you come up here and we'll talk about it?"

"You have something to say you can't say from there? If it's so important, you talk to me from there."

"Georgia. Okay. I will say it from here. Look, I'm sorry. Don't go. I don't want to break up with you. I don't. Can't you come up here?"

"No, I can't do what you want. Right now, I'm going to do what I want. I'm sure you understand that. Maybe right now, I want to break up with you."

Jesus Christ, what the hell was happening here? She couldn't let her go. She couldn't. Morgan leaned against the railing posts, urgent, terrified. Go slow now. Go slow. She took a deep breath and spoke.

"*Do* you want to break up?"

"I don't know." Georgia answered quick and hard.

"Can we agree to talk about it?"

"I don't know."

"Can we talk about it for a minute?"

"Don't you have a date tonight?"

"Georgia, stop. I had a practice tonight. I'm skipping it. I'm trying my best here. I made a mistake. Don't make it worse than it was."

"It would be hard to do that."

She didn't answer that. She wouldn't answer that. Goddamnit. She wasn't the only one at fault here. What the hell did Georgia want? For her to crawl? Well, by God, she could forget that. Not for her, not for anybody. She wouldn't.

She heard Georgia sniffling. Well, that was enough. Enough. Georgia's mother was better, for Chrissake. What the hell was this all about? 'Hard to make things worse.' Bullshit. Hell, she didn't have to watch somebody dying. She could just float in and out for goddamn weekends. Well, tough shit for her.

She felt her anger sweep through her, flaring, like sulphur on a match, and she sat there, her hands gripping the railing shafts as though she could wrench them out of their sockets and hurl them like spears at Georgia's heart.

Fucking cold, heartless bitch. She closed her eyes and took a deep breath when she heard Georgia's voice again, cool, like a slap on her face.

"You say you waited up for me. When, I'd like to ask? I'd like to ask just what you think you've done for me in the last month. I'd like you to remind me of all the ways you've taken care of me, since you claim to care so much. Just what have you done, Florence Nightingale?"

Morgan didn't trust herself to answer, and slipped her head between her rigid arms.

"Oh, you have taken care of your friend Elliott. And your business. And your *two* softball teams.

"But, might I ask, could you even manage to meet me at the airport?" she asked, her voice precise, full of cold anger.

That did it. That was it. Morgan stood up and leaned over the railing. "No, I did not," she screamed. "I did not because the Jeep broke down because I haven't taken her in to be fixed because *we* didn't have the money."

She began to walk towards the stairs. "And we didn't have the money because you can't figure out what to do with your life and get a decent job. A decent job. No, Georgia's trying to find herself. Fine. Me, I don't mind. Hell, I like working my butt off. I like it. I like working all the time because somebody in my *real* family is dying. And I have to deal with it everyday, not just on some weekend visit. No, I don't go home and have a lovely fantasy about how my family loves each other. I have to sit here and work. If your family is so loving, how come you need a mother so much?"

"I don't need a mother," Georgia said, pronouncing each word slowly. "And if I did, it surely wouldn't be *you*." With each word, her voice had gotten quieter and more cold.

"Don't be too damn sure," Morgan spat out, her words wild in her mouth again. "You need somebody. You don't ever know what to do. You won't stand up for yourself at work. You can't even tell them off, not once. And not just work. You can't tell your parents off either. You just let them walk all over you, and then there's nothing left for me, or anyone else. So then you invent this fantasy about how it's okay.

"But it's a fantasy. And you make it up because you can't get mad. All you can do is sit in that room of yours and cry. And I'm sick of it. I left home because there was no one *at* home!" she shouted.

Georgia stood then and began to shriek, her words furious, her voice young and full of tears.

"Don't try to blame your cheating on me. I can't stand it. Get it off me. Get it off me! All you ever do is get mad and blame somebody else for what you've done. You're sick of me! I'm sick of you. I'm sick of your crazy anger all the time, destroying every-thing. I've seen it the whole time I've been with you. First one thing, then another. This whole year it's been the shelter. Eating you alive. And you want me to be like that?

"You want me to yell at my mother and she can't even talk back? You want me to yell at my father? For what? For what? I can't do it. I can't be like that. I can't be what you want me to be. And I won't. I won't, I swear to God. You want me to be mad at somebody? All right then. I'm furious at you. I hate you. I hate you, goddamnit, I hate your soul," she screamed, her voice a wailing cry.

Morgan listened in the silence as Georgia's voice fell away, listened to her cry, and she groaned inside, her anger melting away to fear, her hands opening from fists. Oh, God. Oh, Jesus Christ, what have you done now, she thought, and she began to weep as she listened to Georgia sobbing in the well of darkness at the end of the stairs. And all she knew was that she had to hold her, try to find her, try to hold that terrible grief.

She began to slide down the stairs then, crying too, saying, "George. Honey. I'm sorry. Don't hate me. I didn't mean it that way. I didn't mean for you to take it that way."

She got halfway down before Georgia said, "Don't come near me."

She sat down right where she was on the stairs. "Georgia, listen. Okay. You were right. You should be mad at me. I was wrong this weekend. I was wrong and I'm sorry. I don't know what I was doing. All I'm trying to say is that there was other stuff going on too. And other stuff going on now. With you. It doesn't mean I didn't do wrong. I did. But I still love you, Georgie."

She could see Georgia then in the dark, not clearly, but she could see the other woman leaning against the wall, her glasses off in one hand, her other hand covering her eyes. And when she saw her, she suddenly remembered waking in the middle of the night at Elizabeth's and wondering who she was in bed with and why wasn't she round like Georgia. And she remembered calling for her in the dark.

She took a long breath. "Georgia, listen. You have a right to be mad. But it wasn't that I was more attracted to her than you. I was confused. I don't know why I did it."

"Don't feed me that crap."

"It's true."

Georgia slumped to the ground. Morgan bumped down a few more steps.

"Why are you telling me this? I don't want to hear about it. I really don't. Why did you tell me at all? Why did you do it?"

"I don't know. I mean, it's like I told you last night. Because I had to. I didn't want to lie about anything anymore. And when you started in on what happened to you at home, I felt like I just couldn't hear one more story of you getting beat up by your father and calling it love. I mean, I know he doesn't actually hit you, but I got confused. I just couldn't stand it, and so I told you. But should I have lied?"

There was silence.

Then Morgan said, "I take back what I said about you and alcohol. I'm sorry. But I don't take back what I said about getting mad. I want you to stick up for yourself.

"George, your family is nuts. You come back from there and you act nuts. You act so far away, like a man almost, like I can't touch you, like you aren't there. Okay, it's true that I get mad a lot. And I know you think it doesn't do any good. But what you do isn't any good either.

"And it scares me. It scared me before you left. It felt like you weren't here anymore. You went very far away and I got scared. It's like you were drinking. And I need you now, Georgie. You need me, but I need you too. I don't know. This isn't working, is it?"

And she cried then, alone and with no sound, but suddenly she felt Georgia's hand on her knee and she held it tight. After awhile, Georgia started to talk.

"I don't know," she said, and Morgan had to try to remember what question she was answering. She wiped her eyes off and tried to listen, tried desperately, afraid she was floating into the old pain again, afraid her tears would form a river and float her back away, with only Georgia's voice to hang on to, the only anchor to the present. And so she listened, holding on to Georgia's hand, listened to Georgia's voice, her old familiar voice.

"I don't know if we weren't working. I thought we were okay, mostly. I mean, oh Em, I do love you. I don't want to break up. But maybe we have to change some things. I need some things, Em.

"You know, you start out by saying my family's nuts. Of course they are. Isn't yours? Isn't everybody's? But do you help me? Do you help me know how to deal? How do you think I feel? Every single minute I try to figure out what happened to me there. I try to figure out why I miss the country so much and why my father pushes every button I have, why even Bud makes it impossible for me to speak.

"I get there and I can't talk anymore. Do you have any idea how that feels? Do you know what it's like to be driven crazy and have your throat cave in at the same time?

"You say I don't stand up for myself, but do you know how it feels to not be able to talk? Or to know that it won't make any difference? You know, when Bernice and I came out in Carolina, we were against the law. You wouldn't understand that, coming out in the women's movement. You wouldn't know. But I remember it like it was yesterday. I'll never get over it. We were hunted down out of our house, do you understand? And sure, I could get mad at that, but what difference would it make? We still couldn't go home. There was no home to go to.

"And then we came out here and I thought, well, this is it. This is it. And it was all clear to me, like almost nothing ever is. And I thought, it's so safe here, so many lesbians, so many lesbians."

She stopped for a minute and Morgan could hear her sobbing. She slipped down another step and was able to touch the top of Georgia's head.

"I thought I was home. But I wasn't. And now, there's no more movement, we're all scattered and all hell's breaking loose all over the world. And my family's dying and Joe is dying. And you've gone away, more and more since the shelter, more and more games, and then I couldn't find me anymore. Everything's changing and I'm frightened.

"But you. You want me to get mad. How do you think it feels to say, okay, where I live isn't Carolina, but it's something? That my family's nuts and I can't go home, but there isn't anywhere else to go, because my girlfriend has decided the home we made together isn't good enough. Now she wants something new. So what am I supposed to do now? Okay. I got mad. But does it change anything? Em. My God. Why did you do it?"

She couldn't finish, she was crying so much. Morgan slipped down the last steps and put her arm around her. At first Georgia stiffened, but then she leaned her head into Morgan's shoulder and sobbed. After awhile, she pulled back.

"Bernice told me a long time ago I should just make my home in San Francisco and forget Carolina. And I was trying to do that with you, don't you see? I came home as much as I could. I *needed* to be in my room. I needed it. I can't explain it, but I didn't leave you. I was trying to be here. I was trying to be here and be happy with you. But I hurt. I hurt all over and I don't know how to make it stop."

"There was a time I made you happy."

"Yes, there was. And you still do, don't you see that? But those times of making love even while we were taking a shower together stopped happening, you remember that? There was a slight problem about *your* family.

"Besides, those times would have stopped anyway. That's how it is in lesbian relationships. You know that. The wild sex lasts about two years max. We were lucky it lasted as long as it did.

"But I wanted to stay with you forever. And that's part of the reason I stopped coming to the games. I felt like if I didn't get something for me, some place that I understood about myself, I would starve and leave. And then the trouble with my mother and the crazy business about home started. I couldn't help it. I didn't know what to do.

"I knew you were having trouble. But you didn't ask me for help. No, you went out and played softball, or stayed at work and came home a zombie. And there was nothing there for me. Not what I needed. That's why I was in my room; I was trying to do for myself. Maybe not good, but the best I could do, don't you see?

"It wasn't about you. It was about me. And the part that was us, well, when you pulled away from me in bed, I got scared. At first I thought you were going to leave. But you said no. It was temporary. So we talked about it. I was patient. I listened to you, to your memories. And I didn't mind that. I mean, what's two years in a lifetime together?

"But now there's this. Em, you explain this to me. I want an answer. After five years I think I deserve an answer."

The angry words hung in the air. Morgan took her arms from around Georgia and propped them up on her knees, her head in her hands.

"I don't have one. Not a good one. I don't know. I made a mistake. I don't know what I was thinking," she said and really, as she said it, she couldn't remember what it was she thought Elizabeth would give her, except a place to get away.

"It felt like a place to get away," she said after awhile.

"Was it so bad here?"

"It was so bad inside me. I didn't want to leave you. I wanted to leave me."

Morgan felt Georgia's arms go around her, and she knew then what she had said was true.

"I don't know why, besides that. I mean, George, I've been having a hard time, too. You know that. I had a hard day on Saturday. I saw Stockton."

She felt Georgia draw back and look at her.

"Oh, it wasn't just Stockton. It was a weird little interchange, but it wasn't just that. I just couldn't get in gear."

She suddenly felt so tired she could hardly speak. Georgia was saying something and she strained to listen.

"And so what happened, Em?"

"Nothing happened. I just had some memories." And then, suddenly, she felt the anger rising up in her again and she was afraid, afraid she would blow it completely but she was already speaking.

"I had some memories, that's all. And I was tired. You know that? I was fucking tired. I needed a rest, Georgia. I needed a rest. And I needed somebody who cared about what was happening to me, somebody who was *there*, who was listening, who wanted me. Like you used to want me."

Georgia pulled away and Morgan felt stunned at her own words.

And then, she felt herself start to cry. "Wait. Stop. Let me try again. I don't mean to be bad to you, George. But I'm lonely. I'm so lonely. And I'm worried about Elliott. And I'm worried about the business. And there's no place for me to go, either. You talk about home and all that stuff, but what is there for me? I don't have the shelter, I don't have work, and lately, I don't have you."

"You had me. I made you a home for five long years. And who made me a home? Nobody." Georgia's words were bitter.

"Wait. Please. Georgia. You asked me to tell you what happened. I'm trying to tell you. I was freaked out. I needed some relief. I..."

Georgia cut her off. "Did you find it?" she asked, her voice tight as wire.

"No," Morgan said and the word hung between them. "And I'm sorry I had to hurt you with it," she said in the echoing air. "I guess I have to learn by doing. Don't leave me now. I don't want anyone but you."

"To do what?" Georgia asked and her voice was softer, but still angry.

"I don't know. But I know I love you. And I want to be with you. I don't know what else."

Her voice faltered and her left hand crept out, looking for Georgia's; her right stayed put, held to shield her eyes as she cried. She cried and it all came back to her. When she felt Georgia's hand tuck into hers, she held on. For awhile, she didn't hear anything except the sound of her own tears. She felt Georgia come closer and put her arm around her. And then, it wasn't that she wanted to cry, she just wanted to sleep. She just wanted to sleep for a long time, in the circle of those arms.

"Did you sleep last night?" she asked finally.

"Not much."

"Will you stay here and sleep with me tonight? I can't sleep without you and I'm so tired."

"I will even though I probably shouldn't," Georgia said after awhile. "Actually, I can't sleep very well without you, either. But I'm going to learn if you make me."

Morgan looked up and saw Georgia looking at her, fiercely, like a child, but strong too, some core, some something in the dark. She reached out her hand to hold Georgia's leg.

"No," she said, shaking her head. "I'm not going to make you. We have to learn some other way to do this."

She got up then and helped Georgia to her feet and took her bag.

"We'll talk more tomorrow, okay? I'm sorry, Georgia. I don't know what I was doing. I was wrong. I'm sorry I hurt you. Truly."

"Okay," Georgia said and sighed. "Let's talk some tomorrow. You're right. This isn't working. And I want it to." She took her free hand. "I do want it to. I want to be with you, you crazy fool.

I guess there's a lot to talk about. And I guess I do feel a little better. Maybe getting angry has some future in it."

Morgan nodded, pulled their hands up to kiss Georgia's. "Maybe. If you don't get crazed behind it like me. But I'm glad you feel a little better. I want you to feel better. I want us both to feel better. Are you hungry?" she asked.

"I guess."

"You want to go for burgers?"

Georgia said yes, and they left the packed bag on the landing and went out. They didn't talk much, just tried to stay away from sensitive places, tried to find some way to be together. When they slept that night, they didn't sleep wrapped in each other, but Morgan was comforted when, just as she was about to sleep, she felt Georgia searching for her hand. They slept holding hands. The next morning as she drank her tea, she thought: it wasn't everything but it was a start.

When she got to the office, Janice gave her a message that Elizabeth had called. She tossed it in the trash. She didn't know what she was going to do about that, but she wasn't going to call. Things were complicated enough already and this time, they really were. She wasn't just playing with fire anymore, she was in it. Things with Elizabeth seemed smooth and easy, like she could just walk out, and that wasn't true, she couldn't, she wouldn't just walk out. She didn't want to. She wanted Georgia. She wanted herself. She wanted to try to be here, not always slipping away into what was familiar, what was furious. Not so easy, but better maybe.

Elliott came in and broke up her thoughts. He didn't speak right away, but she had laid out his tea, ready for him, and left water in the pot.

He got his tea and came and sat at the chair by her desk.

"*Nu?*" she said.

"Still speaking to me?" he grinned and ran his hands over his unshaven face. He had the smell of a man who hadn't bathed in awhile.

"Have you been at the hospital all night?" she asked.

He nodded. "Guess I'll have to use that fancy electric razor you and your girlfriend got me. How are you and Georgia?" he asked, after a pause.

"We fought most of last night."

"Where did you sleep?"

"Elliott, that's a little private," she said, embarrassed.

"You and me, private? Not for a long while, little one," he said back.

"We slept together at home."

"Good girl. I knew you'd do good," he said and sighed. "Look, I've got to go get ready. I'm glad you fought. That's the first step," he said and squeezed her shoulder on the way over to his desk.

"Is there something I can do for you, Elliott?" she asked, turning her chair around to face him.

He just shook his head and she wished again she could hug him like she could hug Georgia when there were no words.

She swung her chair back around to get ready for work and looked at her calendar. Oh Christ. Goddamnit. Dinner with Lisa. Could that be tonight? Jesus, Mary and Joseph. And too late to call to change it. On break, she called the office and Janice told her George had called. So at lunch, she called her back, feeling completely out of control again, wild at the telephone tag. No answer.

But finally, when she called back one more time at the end of lunch, they connected. And then George said she needed to have dinner with Ricky. Morgan couldn't get a good reading on what was going on, but at least Georgia laughed when she told her about Lisa. And made her promise to make it a quick dinner. Morgan told her it wouldn't be much longer than working late. But damnit. They should have been together, talking.

She found the place Lisa had suggested, near the library. She looked around, hoping she would be already seated but no, Lisa was even later than she was.

She sat at a table in the back, one of the few vacant, feeling anxious. She should have broken the date, too late or no. And so should have George. It wasn't a good sign, she thought, twisting her spoon over and over.

Jesus, it was stupid to be here. Lisa could have waited, it seemed like, nevermind how eager she was to talk. Lisa, God in Heaven. Always so impatient. Which was great for an infielder but Morgan wondered how Lisa was as a counselor, small, always jumping, always on the move. Cute, though. She was cute in the way Georgia was sometimes. Little, but where Georgia was slow and measured, Lisa was quick and impatient. She smiled and wondered how they would get along.

If she decided to get into this thing Lisa had in mind, she might be seeing a lot of her. And she thought then, taking a sip of coffee and scanning the doorway, she ought to bring her home to meet Georgia right away. Jesus, what a fool she had been.

There she was. Morgan started to stand so she could see her, and then Lisa waved and hurried over.

"Sorry I'm late," she said, sliding into the chair opposite Morgan. "I'm always late when I teach. But you're going to love it, Morgan. You're just perfect." She grinned impishly over the menu which she had opened while she was talking. Morgan just shook her head at the energy and smiled back.

"What are you having? Have you ordered yet?" Lisa asked all in one breath.

Morgan laughed. "Slow down, you aren't that late, though I can't stay for long. No, I haven't ordered yet. What's good?"

"The fish. The fish here is great."

"Order for both of us then, why don't you."

"Trout? You like trout?"

"Ah, no, not that. How about the soups? The carrot looks interesting. Is it good?"

"It is. Terrific," Lisa said, putting the menu to one side and patting it. "Okay, now listen."

"I'm all ears."

"Well, when I heard you got asked to leave the shelter a year ago, I felt bad because I knew what you were going through, because of my own thing, you remember."

Morgan nodded.

"And so then I started doing this stuff at the library, well, they don't have very many women teachers and I've been wanting to get more women in and so when you mentioned it on Saturday, I just remembered I knew you could teach and all that and I just thought you'd be a natural, really, and what you don't know, I can help you with. I wanted to talk to you about it right away because a new group of teachers is being trained next week and I wanted you in on it, oh God, listen to me running off at the mouth. I haven't even explained what it is, or asked how you are or anything."

"How are you?"

Morgan waved her hand as though she were waving the question away. "It's okay, I'm okay. I had a kind of hard weekend, but I'm okay. I ran into Stockton."

"You did?" Lisa stopped stock still.

Morgan laughed at her open mouth.

"Yeah. I did."

"What happened?"

"Nothing. I watched her in action against some guy. Much nicer than in action against us, believe me. I almost liked her again. But then I came to my senses. Anyway. Let's talk about this."

"Great," Lisa said, and Morgan nodded, and then the waiter came to take their order.

As soon as he left, Lisa's face lit up again and she asked, "Shall I continue?"

Morgan smiled and nodded, thinking, Jesus, she talks a mile a minute. How did I miss this on the field? Then she remembered Lisa shouting to opposing batters from shortstop.

Lisa went on, "Well, the thing is, it's teaching people how to read. And you can request, you know, all women classes. And I remembered you talking one night about your classes and how you teach the men different from the women and how it's so much easier to teach the women if you go at it from a different direction, well, I just thought you might be interested."

Morgan nodded and Lisa rushed on.

"Listen, I know what will really convince you. You'll really love this. You know what the statistics are for women who can't read?"

Morgan shook her head, interested now, well, reading, teaching women to read books, not just computer books; that might actually be exciting.

"Well, for the population in general, it's something like thirty percent are functionally illiterate and... "

"What does that mean, functionally illiterate?" Morgan asked, leaning towards her, not at all interested in her soup which the waiter was just bringing.

"It means, you know, that they can sign their names and stuff, but they can't, for example, read a newspaper. It's like they can sign checks, but they can't read a job form. But listen, here's the really interesting part."

Morgan pushed her soup away and leaned her arms on the table. Lisa got herself a spoonful of soup but kept talking while she balanced the spoon in midair.

"You know what the statistics are for battered women?"

Morgan shook her head.

"It's like eighty percent are functionally illiterate." She grinned at Morgan. "You know what that means? They can't read. That's why they can't get jobs. They can't read. So they can't leave. Makes sense, no?"

Morgan pushed away from the table and leaned back in her chair, staring at her soup.

Lisa went on. "Don't you see? You could still be doing the work. We can get around those jerks who asked us to leave the shelters. This could really help. Maybe even more than what we did at the shelters. And the government won't have to know a thing about us; the shelters won't know it's us. The program is administered through the public library. We could really do something, you know?"

But Morgan didn't hear her. She was watching her mother sign her name to a check her father made out and left for her. She was watching her explain to the clerk that she didn't have a driver's license. She was watching her mother's hands shake every time she put the amount in on a check. She was listening to her mother ask her to read the road signs that she couldn't see when they went on a new bus. She was watching her mother fold the newspaper and say, "No good news today."

And then suddenly, she was back, Lisa was shaking her arm and saying, "Morgan? Morgan?" and she knew she was crying and that she couldn't stop.

"Lisa," she gasped, "I can't, I have to go. I'm sorry. I've been having a bad time. Listen, I'll call you, okay? Don't worry, I'll be fine," she said, standing, somehow making it out of the restaurant, feeling that if she could just see, if she could just see enough to get to her car and get home, she would be okay. She drove, sobbing, and even as she parked and ran across the street she couldn't stop. And she ran up the stairs and threw herself across the bed and cried until she fell asleep.

She woke up when she felt Georgia tug at her. She rolled over and clung to her and started crying again when she tried to tell her what had happened. She could feel Georgia rubbing her hair and her back just like Nanna, and then she cried even more, until there was nothing left. She sat up a little, then wrapped her arms around Georgia, and said, "Georgie, I'm so glad you're home."

"Can you tell me? What is it, Em?" Georgia asked, rubbing her back while Morgan tucked her face into the crook of Georgia's neck.

She still couldn't talk. What were the words for this sadness, this pain? It wasn't anger, but oh Jesus, it hurt. After awhile, trying to get her breath back, she said, "I was at supper with Lisa and she started saying all this stuff about women, battered women who can't read and so can't get away, you know, and all of a sudden I realized that probably my mother couldn't read and I know it's silly to cry about that now, but suddenly, I couldn't help myself. Oh Georgie, goddamnit, I've been mad at her for so long. It doesn't make up for it; I still hate her, but oh God..."

Georgia kissed her cheek and rubbed her back. When Morgan could hear her murmuring "It's okay, baby, it's okay," she cried into Georgia's shoulder.

After a long while, Morgan drew her head back. "Georgie, Jesus, look at me, I drooled all over your sweater; I'm sorry." And Georgia wiped off her face with her sleeve and shook her head. She looked sad herself.

Morgan searched her face and drew a deep breath. "What about you, George? What happened with you tonight? Are you all right?"

"Well, I'm quitting. Ricky says she's got a friend who's got an opening for an assistant and she set up an interview. It was good, really. I guess."

She shook her head and her eyes looked dull to Morgan. Georgia looked down at the floor, so she took her chin and raised her eyes up.

"So, shouldn't you be excited?"

"I guess. I'm mostly frightened. But if Ricky says she knows the job and that I can do it, I guess I should try. But that's not it, I mean, that's not why I'm sad. I've been thinking about us. And thinking about what you just said. And you know, Morgan, you know what's true? It's all true. We hate what they did and we love them all the same. And there doesn't seem to be much that changes it, and it makes me sad.

"Why does it have to be so complicated? Do you think that's how it's going to be with us? That we end up hating and loving each other at the same time?"

"I don't hate you, Georgia," Morgan said slowly. "You mean more to me than anything."

Georgia just looked at her. Morgan wiped off her cheeks and leaned over to get a tissue from the box on Georgia's side of the bed. Georgia took her hand and said, "I know you love me. I do. I just wish you meant more to yourself than anything. Because I can't do it all. I can't make a home for both of us. I have to have some for me."

Morgan looked at her, trying to understand what she was meaning, listening to the words carefully, and then she nodded. Georgia hugged her. They lay together for a moment and Morgan said, "I think I know what you mean. We have to change some things in this relationship. We do.

"But I'm really glad about this job thing. Maybe that's part of the change. I want you to go for it. Georgie, you can do anything if you just decide you want to. I'm glad you're leaving that asshole. I hope these new people deserve you. What kind of job is it?"

Georgia sighed. "At a library. And Ricky says they have tuition benefits. So I could go back to school if I wanted. I think I do want to try for it."

"Good. At least it's one good thing to come your way. I know it's been awful for you."

"It's been bad," Georgia agreed in a small voice. "But maybe you're right. Maybe it will be better. But right now, I'm just exhausted."

"Me too. You want to go to bed?"

Georgia nodded. Morgan swung her legs over the side of the bed next to Georgia and sat there for a minute before getting up.

"Do you think it's always going to hurt this much?" she asked. Georgia got up, stood in front of her, and pressed Morgan's head to her breasts, combing her hair with her fingers.

"I don't know. Bernice says it doesn't hurt so much after awhile. Or maybe so often. That's what it's like with drinking, anyway. But I don't know if it stops hurting forever. It sure hasn't stopped hurting me about wanting to go home," she said in a low voice.

"We can make a home here, Georgia," Morgan mumbled into her shirt.

"I think it's something I have to do by myself."

Morgan looked up to see Georgia staring out the window.

"I love you, Georgia," she said.

"I love you too, Em. I just wish I knew what that meant about how we can live our lives. I don't feel like I know much of anything anymore," she said, and Morgan pressed against her breasts again for a moment, listening to her heart.

She pushed away then and looked at her and said slowly, pulling on Georgia's hands to make her listen, "I did want to say that I understand about your mother. It's all true. I know it hurts."

Georgia nodded and said, "Thanks." She smiled a small, sad smile and then said, "Now, let's get ready for bed," and pulled Morgan up off the bed. They walked to the bathroom holding hands and when they slept, they slept spooned together. Every time Morgan rolled over, she found Georgia there, and she tucked herself into Georgia's softness and steadied, tried to breathe into her own pain. It was only Georgia's body that felt solid, like it was the only thing she could hold on to, like it was the only thing that hadn't broken, that wouldn't break.

Chapter Eleven

Fire In The Night

Elizabeth, her damp body covered by a floor-length white terrycloth robe, bent over at the waist and shook her head. From that position, she toweled her hair off one more time and shook it out again. She swung back up and combed the tangled strands with her hands, her fingers feeling their way, her eyes unfocused. Only the pain in her stomach jolted her out of the warm, safe ritual of bathing.

The mirror in her bathroom was fogged and the air steamy. She opened the door, took a step out and peered at the clock on the far wall of the kitchen. She had an hour. She leaned against the hall wall outside the bathroom for a moment, breathing in the cold air, and then walked out to the refrigerator and poured herself a glass of wine.

She took a sip. As she did, she felt the electric wire in her stomach start to jolt and snap, as it had all week. First it was excitement, the possibility, the fullness of Morgan in her mouth, and the two of them, the memory, the delight of Saturday night. By Thursday, the electricity was a burn of panic, searing into cold pain. It kicked her hard as she tried to balance forward, working on the new assays, looking at the future. It rose up in her throat when she tried to balance back, adding up the sequence with Morgan, searching for her failure. It spasmed, twisting tight when she tried to sit still, tried to forget.

As soon as she felt the pain this time, she set her wine down and ran up the steps to the loft to put on some music. Without looking, she snapped in the first tape she found. She waited for a moment and then started back downstairs.

Shortly, Patti LaBelle's gorgeous voice swept out through the air near her and she grabbed on to it as though it were solid. She picked up her wine and walked over to the window. The bass line on the music swelled like a growl.

She tried to listen as she stood and sipped her wine. After a moment, she realized it wasn't working. The wine heaved up in her stomach. All right. Settle down. Don't pay any attention to these old voices, she said to herself. Only makes it worse. She told herself all she had to do was just jump tracks. Start new. She tapped her fingers against the windowpane in time to the music, and watched the sun letting go into the night. She forced herself to dance a little in the fading sunlight.

First she danced with her hands in her pockets, imagining a waltz, and then she danced with the tie sash on her robe. Finally, she stopped and took another sip of wine. Well, she really didn't have time to dance anyway. She looked back at the kitchen clock. She might as well go get dressed. She trudged up the stairs to the loft, her feet feeling heavy, the steps steep.

No energy. But she hadn't been sleeping too much. This stomach business was probably some kind of flu. She felt a little feverish, even now. Certainly, it wasn't all from Morgan. She wasn't *that* disappointed. And she had better things to do than worry about some tramp. Actually, she had a better something to do immediately.

She stood in front of the wardrobe. All right, Bebe, what was proper to wear to a scientific meeting with your collaborator on a Saturday night? She didn't feel much like getting dressed, even less like going out.

She shook her head at a stack of sweaters. Why was she doing this? When Agnes had called three hours ago to say she had some unexpected results and could Elizabeth come to the lab to see, Elizabeth had been surprised, and then angry.

What did Agnes think? She wasn't doing anything on a Saturday night? And even if she wasn't, it was no time for a meeting. And what was Agnes doing working on a Saturday? Good Lord, did she work *all* the time? Didn't she have better things to do?

Like what, Bebe asked. Like be with people, she replied, pulling out a pair of clean, but very faded jeans. I will not dress for this woman. I don't even know why I agreed to go. She slipped into the jeans, tugging them over her hips. She buttoned them and did deep knee bends and thigh lunges to stretch them out. They clung to her, but she knew they'd be looser and more comfortable later. And that's what mattered. She could care less what old Agnes thought about how she looked.

She stood then in front of her dresser, naked except for the jeans, and looking down at her breasts and the goosepimples on her arms, realized it was cold. Damn San Francisco weather. Honestly.

She slipped on a chemise and then her white angora cowl neck. At least she'd keep warm. And with her tweed coat, she'd look just right, she figured. Casual, like she was not working. Which she was not.

This was as bad as being on call at the hospital, which she hadn't had to do for the last five years. That was for junior staff, thank God. And so, what was she doing now, going to discuss research on a Saturday night? Insane. She sat on the bed to put on white crew socks and her Adidas. And then she sat still, took a sip of wine and looked out the window. Well, at least it *would* give her something to do. She had just been hanging around, waiting. Waiting until she felt better.

Waiting for nothing. Waiting for a woman who was never going to call her. Waiting like a lovesick adolescent. Like an idiot. Well, there was nothing she could do about it, she thought, as her stomach spasmed again. So big deal about Morgan. Who needed her? She had more than enough work to do. That was always the best way. Her father had taught her that, and it was true. Work it off. And she *had* worked hard all week, struggling to make order of the crushing new schedule Richardson had forced her into. The schedule had been exhausting. Useful, though, that exhaustion. Got you to sleep.

Anyway, Morgan was no big deal. Soon, it wouldn't even hurt. And it had only been a couple of nights that had been real bad. Actually, the worst was Thursday night when she'd gone to dinner with Sylvie. She'd thought, after all the drinks they'd had, after the trouble she'd had dragging herself up the stairs, she'd fall right to sleep. And she had slept. For about two hours. After that, she'd spent the rest of the night up, rattled, chasing ghosts.

Well, so what? As a doctor, she knew well enough that everybody had a bad night, every once in awhile. Probably, she'd been working too hard. So she took Friday off. Tried to get herself back in balance. That was the key, keeping everything in balance.

Besides, she deserved a day off. She spent the day reading a C. B. Greenfield mystery and playing music. And not thinking. She'd done her best to not think. Well, there wasn't anything to think about. These things happened. She just got caught at a bad time, that's all. She got caught in a common cheating scene. Happened to women all the time and only time would cure it. That's all.

Got caught and was going crazy, she said to herself Saturday evening as she sipped her wine, watching the evening come on. Only one night, she protested. And was drinking too much, she answered as she put the wine down.

She brushed her dried hair brusquely. What *was* this woman doing working at six on a Saturday night, she thought one more time, as she finished brushing and looked at her face. She began to put a touch of color on her eyes. Damn hangover. Alcohol was wreaking havoc with her skin, too. She looked pale and drained. Blotchy. But it might as easily be the flu. She shouldn't be going out. Why was she going out? And then, her mouth set in a straight line, she thought, probably Agnes doesn't have anything better to do. Probably some old lonely spinster with nothing better to do.

She had to laugh then, in spite of herself. She stood up and leaned over, brushing her hair towards the floor. Agnes? A spinster? Whatever she was, she wasn't an old maid. Too good looking for that. And she didn't for a minute look like she had never had sex. Or had a bit of trouble finding a man, or a woman, for that matter. Tall, gray hair going to white in front, she was reserved with that Midwest quiet Sylvie had. That quiet that might mean calm, deep calm inside. Or it might mean an uproar that they had decided not to share with you. Which might have to do with the uproar. Or it might have to do with what they thought of you. And you could never tell, much. Except to be sure something was happening. Something was planned. Usually everything was under control. And very unlike this evening's call.

At least she called. More than some people did lately. Pain shot through her, up her throat. She got a grip on the edge of the dressing table, put the brush down and said to the mirror, out loud, "I will not allow this anymore. Just get over it. The woman was no good for you; you knew it and allowed her to seduce you anyway. Even Sylvie saw it coming," and she couldn't keep from grimacing, but she quickly shook it away.

"She was nothing. This flu is psychosomatic. I want you to stop it."

She took a deep breath, kept looking at herself in the mirror, and then took a sip of wine. "Okay? Okay. Now get ready. You've got work to do." She finished with her hair, put her lipstick on, and took her robe and wine glass back downstairs, tapping her way in time to the music.

By the time she got in the car, she'd decided it was a good time for a meeting, and it was great to have some good results. It was nice Agnes had called, after all. She drove out onto the highway and had no delays on the bridge to Oakland.

The hospital lobby looked deserted as she approached the building, full-lit, but silent. She looked up to the eighth floor. Agnes' lab blared lights out into the twilight, yellow and luminous, surrounded by windows almost invisible and sheer in the dusk. Nobody else on the eighth floor had their lights on. Agnes must be the only one in her department working.

Well, that was familiar. She shook her head, smiled and went in, her tennis shoes soft in the hall, but she felt loud, exposed in the silence. She waited briefly for the elevator. When she got in, the door closed noisily in front of her and after punching for eight, she shrank to the back, made small in the emptiness.

The eight lit up on the overhead display, and the elevator stopped and opened. She stepped out into the window-walled hall and saw the sun setting over the city. She smiled into the sunset. Well, it was possible, if things worked with Agnes, things could change. They could change. She was due for something. She was due.

She walked down to Agnes' office and, opening the door without knocking, walked in. Agnes was sitting with her feet up on the desk, legs in old khakis, crossed, relaxed, as she leisurely looked at the black and whites from the electron microscope. She lowered one slightly and looked at Elizabeth over the top. She lowered it a little more and let Elizabeth see her smile.

"Come in, Dr. Bathory. Come in," she said, softly. "I think you'll like this. I hated rousting you on such a lovely evening," she took her feet off the desk, stood up, stretched and looked out the window, "but I think you'll find it worth your while."

Elizabeth smiled back. She really was a very handsome woman, she thought, accepting the print Agnes was holding out.

"Beautiful night, isn't it?" Agnes asked, her smile still no more than slight. "Care for a drink?"

She held up a bottle of Haig and Haig pinch. Elizabeth smiled back.

"Well, that would be pleasant," Elizabeth said, pleased that if she had to drink scotch, at least it was good scotch.

"Are they that good?" she asked.

"See for yourself," Agnes said, gesturing towards the photos and holding out a graduated cylinder with ten milliliters of straight scotch.

Elizabeth took the cylinder with one hand and with the other picked up the photo Agnes had just been looking at.

"See it? It's down in the left corner." Agnes stood by her right shoulder, pointing.

Elizabeth turned the photo upside down and stared at the photo. There it was. What they had been looking for. There were the pinched cells, rounded in a cluster. They'd found the sick little bastards. And with the pattern. She looked back up at Agnes and smiled.

Grinned and looked back at the picture. All right, where were the others? Where were the dead cells from the drugs? The dye? There. Middle left. And the movement was clearly towards the cluster.

Agnes chuckled when she saw Elizabeth put down her cylinder, lay the photo on the desk and trace the pattern with her finger.

When Elizabeth heard her, she turned around. Agnes was smiling, tapping her fingers over her lips as though she were hiding even the smile.

"I've just been down here, waiting until you could free yourself. I wanted you to see it right away. You know what this means?"

"That we've finally found the right dosage mix to retard the spread of disease," she said thoughtfully.

"And that we're a shoo-in for the NSF grant," Agnes said, smiling and lifting up her beaker.

Elizabeth lifted her cylinder.

"Well, I must say," she began, "I'm very impressed with your work, Dr. Johnson." She clinked her glass to Agnes'.

"And I with yours, my young colleague," Agnes said, her voice low and her eyes looking directly into Elizabeth's open and happy face.

Elizabeth brought her glass back, took a sip, and frowned for a moment. She turned to the window to keep her face from being seen.

So. Agnes was gay. She should have known. And what was this? A little Saturday night chance encounter? She shook her head and turned back around. Well, she'd had worse propositions. And lately, too. She smiled. Dinner couldn't hurt, could it?

"I don't want to keep you," she heard Agnes saying. "And I've been here entirely too long." She watched Agnes finish off her drink and begin to pick up the photos.

"I hope I didn't make you change your plans too much. You did say you were on your way over here anyway, didn't you?"

Startled, Elizabeth remembered that she had. Damn.

Agnes was still talking. "I'm so glad you could stop by for this little celebratory drink." She looked up from sorting the photos. "And I hope you're feeling better. John said he thought it was just a flu. You do look a little under the weather, my dear. How are you?"

Elizabeth took another sip and sat down in the chair next to Agnes' desk. "I'm better. I haven't been getting much sleep."

"You'll have to take care of your health. We can't have you becoming ill. Not now, not when we have so much exciting work ahead of us. We should get this written up and submitted as soon as we can. If you have any thoughts about which journal, let me know. Maybe you shouldn't stay out too late tonight, but you know best, I'm sure," Agnes said, handing her a set of prints. "I made an extra set for you to examine in your office. Shall we get together there Tuesday and discuss this?"

Elizabeth took the prints and tried to recover herself. "Certainly. Come at nine. Thanks very much for these and for your concern about my health. I'll be fine," she said and took the last sip of her drink as Agnes began putting journals and papers in her briefcase.

"And thanks for the drink," she said, inclining her head in a nod to Agnes.

"The pleasure was mine, I'm sure, Dr. Bathory," Agnes said, dipping her head back, and again, that slight smile. "I hope we can make this a regular occurrence." She smiled a bit wider, but then laughed a real laugh, one of the first Elizabeth had heard from her.

"Only next time, I'll try not to drag you away from your Saturday plans. I must have you over to the house sometime," she said, again looking directly at Elizabeth.

"I'd like that," Elizabeth said, her voice low. "I'd like that very much." And she realized as she said it, that she would like it. It would be nice to go to someone else's house for a change, to get away, see where Agnes lived, how she lived, what she was like when she could laugh from her whole body as she just had.

Agnes said, "Well, there's someone there I'd like you to meet."

If Elizabeth could have, she would have put her hands over her ears.

Agnes went on, smiling. "I think she'd like you very much."

Elizabeth looked up and forced herself to smile. "I'd be happy to meet your friends, Agnes."

She got up then, clutching the photos and saying goodbye as quickly as she could, leaving before Agnes could close up. On the way down in the elevator, she felt the scotch burning and tried to shake her head free.

"This is enough," she said out loud to the empty elevator. And then she thought silently, I'm going home. And stay there until I have to get up for the department meeting on Monday afternoon. Forget the rest of this. I shouldn't have come out at all. Her stomach lurched again, and she thought to herself, get home. You really are getting sick. Don't think. Just get home.

The drive back was short. The walk up to her flat was quick. And at last she was back. The house was warm and welcoming around her. She had forgotten to leave any lights on, so the room was unlit but not dark; she also hadn't pulled the blinds and the night swept into the room, the lights of the city sliding in with the moon, slipping in and making the silent furniture glow like light on a mist.

She walked in and threw the photos on the floor. She went right to the tall baker's cabinet and pulled out the vodka. Filled a double rocks glass and went to the windows. She didn't turn on a light.

She looked out, but didn't see the city. She sipped her drink and then the tears began. She took a breath and tried to swallow the cry there, and bring down the swelling with the smooth liquid. And then she said to herself, her rage a shout, "You're acting like a fool."

Settle down, Bebe said from the couch.

She whirled. The room was silent and silver-gray in the night. She took another deep breath and walked to the couch, sat down with a sigh. All right, Bebe, she answered silently. All right.

She knew it was probably just the aftereffects of Morgan not bothering to call, even to say forget it. She knew that. But lately, and maybe even before Morgan, she had been lying awake at night and wondering, wondering just how long she was going to have to do this, to live this way. And she would wonder then just what it had all been for.

But maybe it was just late night negativity, she thought as she pulled her hair back off her face. It would be okay in a little while. She was just fine. She'd make her way. It was mostly that she'd lost her head over that woman. Stupid thing to do. It wasn't the first time, but it was still a stupid thing to do. Well, screw Morgan and her stupid girlfriend. She would be okay. She brushed her hair back in rhythmic strokes. There would be others; there would be someone for her.

So it was just fine about Morgan Mary Margaret McCormack. Who needed her? Was she going to sit around, depressed, for some softball coach? With these new dosage results, she was on her way.

She started to laugh, a barking short laugh. Anyway, Morgan would call. She'd be back. She'd call. The ones that cheated, that's how they worked. When they had time. Morgan had wanted it, after all; she'd wanted it bad.

But when little Miss Morgan did call, well, it would be too bad. There wouldn't ever be anything besides that one imploring phone call. You can't treat Elizabeth Bathory like a cheap trick and get away with it. She took a long swallow of her drink. Yes, indeed. She'd just wait for that phone call. It would come. It would come. She smiled into the darkened room. And then realized there was no reason for her to sit there in the dark. What about dinner? Maybe she should call somebody for dinner.

She checked her watch, the round dial luminous. Eight o'clock. No, probably anyone she would want to call would be already having dinner or, at least would have dinner plans. She wondered what Morgan and Georgia were doing for dinner. Probably going out for a great meal together during which they would only talk about their boring work and she didn't care anyway. She didn't move to turn on the light, moved only to take another sip of her drink.

Well, fine. She'd just have an evening in. Have a little liquid dinner. How about some music then, Dr. Bathory? Fine. Thank you. She put her drink down and slipped upstairs, her feet finding their way in the shadows. She turned on the tensor light by the tape deck, and after a moment's perusal of tapes, she picked out the old Scheherazade and slipped it into the tape deck. She turned the volume way up and pushed the switch so that all eight speakers, including the four downstairs, were fed the sound.

The Scheherazade began, and for a moment she contemplated getting into bed with all her clothes on. Immediately, she knew she shouldn't have played that tape. No, it was all wrong. It wouldn't comfort her tonight. But she didn't take it off the machine. God, would she never stop hearing the old words? Honestly, it was just an old ballet. Why couldn't she stop remembering how it sounded when she was a child? Why wasn't Morgan here tonight? Didn't she deserve at least a phone call? At least a word that she was okay?

Damnit. She ran her fingers up through her hair and grasped her curls. She looked around after a moment for her vodka and realized she hadn't brought it up with her.

As she walked back downstairs, back into the night-lit room, she stumbled and thought, oh the hell with them all. The Scheherazade played on. Morgan, her father, her mother, they could all go to hell. Suddenly, the old nursery words, made-up words to the Scheherazade record she'd listened to as a child, words to make the symphony real to a child younger than five, floated back into her ears, the love songs, how the lovers had wanted each other, how dreadful it had been, the violins weeping the tears.

She saw herself again in an old familiar memory, shut in her room with her mother shut in the sick room, no noise, couldn't disturb her mother. Under no circumstances. And she, too, was undisturbed, with her record player on the floor, volume low, listening quietly for hours. Bebe said it was the only way to keep her quiet. Bebe would sit there with her sometimes and that made it okay.

But not forever, she remembered sharply. She sat down on the sofa and held herself, the memory coming sure and strong, without her bidding and without her control.

There was that final time. That November. Bebe had sat with her, darning somebody else's socks. She was reading, crabby at being cooped up, irritated that field hockey practice had been canceled due to the threat of rain. They worked together silently. When Bebe tried to talk, she told her angrily that she had to finish her book before her father came home.

And then, the phone broke through the cold afternoon silence hanging above the music. Bebe lifted herself heavily out of her chair, answered it, and a moment later, slipped back into Elizabeth's room with her old coat on and said she had to go out for awhile. Something about her father. And she left her there with a kiss and her book and a stack of records, even though Elizabeth only played the Scheherazade over and over. Over and over. And the night came on. And it got cold. And finally, she stopped playing the record and got up to watch for Bebe. To watch from the window. And she waited. And waited. In the dark. Just like tonight.

As she sat staring into the darkness, tears pushed out of her eyes and she did nothing to stop them; she barely felt them at first, and then didn't feel them at all. She was watching, her hands clenched on her thighs, and she leaned forward, watching the memory. Watching out the window. Watching out in the cold, rainy November night for Bebe. Remembering she had fallen asleep finally by the window and awakened to hear the front door closing. She rushed to the hall, but it was only her father, his dripping hat in his hand, his tie askew.

She cried out, "Bebe!" as she raced to the hall, full of demanding, and anger, wanting to know where she had been and why she had left her there alone.

But it was only her father, and she stopped abruptly when she saw him.

"Where's Bebe?" she asked anxiously. "Is she with you?"

"Hi, Princess," he answered. "Don't you have a kiss for your tired Poppa?"

She went to him and obediently kissed his cheek. He threw his dripping coat over the coat rack and opened the sliding doors to his study.

"Come and talk to your old man," he said, turning to her and beckoning.

She went in. He made himself a drink.

Finally, she said, "Dad. Have you seen Bebe?"

He poured his martini, straining the single ice cube in the mixer with his fingers. He took a sip, bared his teeth in pleasure and then sat down in his leather chair. The chair and he sighed at the same time.

"Sit down, honey," he said, gesturing at the other wing back chair opposite him. "I've got something wonderful to tell you."

She sat, her back stiff, her thighs resting only on the edge of the chair.

"Beth," he started, and then took another sip. "Bethie, I'm sure you know it's the last day of November. And in a week or two you have your exams and then it's holiday vacation, right?"

She nodded.

"Well, honey. I'm not supposed to be telling you this now; your mother made me promise to save it for Christmas, but since you're asking, your mother and I have enrolled you in Miss Maude's over in Cambridge for next term!"

She sat there, stunned, unable to talk.

"No smile? Aren't you excited, darling?" he asked as he chewed the olive, then took another sip of his martini. "You remember last month, when we were talking here, and you were so mad at Bebe for not letting you stay after school? Well, I talked to your mother about it that night and we both agreed it *was* time for you to go to Miss Maude's. Your mother loved it there and thinks it's time for you to get a real education. I know you'll love it. All the girls your age do. Time you started learning to dance instead of learning those aggresive field hockey blocks." He winked at her.

She stared at him. Finally, she croaked out, "But Bebe, Dad. Where's Bebe?"

"Why, it's the end of the month, honey. And next month you have vacation. I didn't see any reason to keep her on if you're going to be with me for most of the month. You remember. In December, we're going to start getting you ready for medical school. How did your reading go? Did you finish?"

He drained his glass.

"Yes sir," she answered, her head spinning, wondering, trying to remember if she had ever said she was angry with Bebe. Bebe gone? And because she had asked for her to go?

He stood up. "Good. Let's talk about it. Come on down with me to the kitchen while I get something to eat."

She stood then, too, like a springboard, and he went over and hugged her.

"Now don't tell your mother I told you," he said, tipping her chin back. She looked at him without focusing. "Let it be our secret. Isn't it a wonderful present, Princess?"

She pulled away. "Yes, Daddy. It's a wonderful present." She began to walk to the door, desperately trying to think.

"Listen, Dad," she said as she turned to him at the door. "I did finish the anatomy chapters. But there's an educational television show I've been assigned to watch for school. Can we have our lesson tomorrow?"

He smiled at her. "Sure, honey. Too much excitement in one night, already. But tomorrow, be ready for the examination!" He held up his hands in mock horror and smiled, then turned and started to walk down the hall. "Did Cook leave me anything for supper?"

"I think so," she said, rooted to the spot where she stood by the door.

"Great," he said and vanished down the hall.

She had stood in the foyer looking at the door for the longest time. She couldn't even remember what had happened then. What *had* happened then? She looked around and saw her own house and she pounded her fists into her lean legs as she sat there.

What had happened? Why had she ever told him she was angry with Bebe? Why? What had happened? She sat still, as immobile as she had been in the foyer. Minx came up, stared at her, then leapt into her lap for comfort. She shoved him off angrily, then, repenting, drew him close and buried her face in his neck.

What was going on now? Why was she remembering this old thing anyway? How many times was she going to have to remember this? How many years? What was the half-life of pain?

She stiffened then, heard herself say out loud, "Stop it. Just stop it. Stop this self-indulgence. It's over. It's been over. How many times are you going to do this to yourself? Every time somebody leaves you are you going to muck around in this old mess? You're just being self-indulgent, as usual, just like mother used to say. Honestly. Everybody has something. You just bring yours up to make you feel sorry for yourself. Chin up now. You can do it."

She heard the words, sagged as though she'd been struck and then, shivering, took a deep breath, turned the lamp on and stood up.

"Okay, enough of this, don't you think, Minx?" she asked, her voice stern and too loud. He leapt down off the couch and followed her into the kitchen. She sang to him from the Scheherazade, "Down, down, down in a deep dark cavern." She opened the refrigerator. "One more step and then I'll have him, then I'll have him," she sang to the music, the violins frightening and loud even now. She picked him up and danced in a small circle with him.

"Only they got me, didn't they?" she asked the struggling Minx as she let him go and bent to pick up his dirty dishes.

"Yes they did," she turned to nod at him, wishing she'd turned the music up. "All of them. Didn't they, boy?" she asked, looking down at him.

"This new one, who lied and left me hanging, is just like all the rest. Only thinking of herself. And what she needs. What she wants. Fucking lesbian couples. This is exactly what they do. One of them gets interested because she's bored. She isn't really interested in you. Remember Terry? Oh hell, Minxy, they're a dime a dozen."

She washed his dishes and dried them. "What they like to do, boy, is get you to fall in love with them, and then, suddenly they get scared, all that ties-that-bind crap and they run back to each other." She slammed a new can of cat food down on the table.

"Fucking used, I can't believe it." She put his food down, weaving around his outstretched paws. She rocked back on her heels to stroke him as he ate, wiping her eyes with her other hand.

"God, be glad you aren't a lesbian," she said, wishing she weren't, for the moment. She paused, thinking, if she wasn't, she'd be straight and that seemed even worse. Out loud, she said, "Well, I don't care. I've got lots to do."

She suddenly realized how very quiet the room was. And then the music started again. She leaned against the kitchen table. God, how long was this going to go on? Forever? Why did she see Morgan's eyes everywhere, feel her hands where they hadn't been, and where they had, feel her mouth over and over, her feather-soft lips brushing against her own, and now nothing?

The lunches, the presents, the ever-moving closer, that wonderful night, and now nothing? That one night? Just one night? How could that have been enough for Morgan? How could it have been enough? She was still starving for her, and at the thought, she felt her stomach twisting again, coming up through her and ramming into her throat. For a moment, all she could do was hang on to the table and keep her mouth clenched shut.

Finally, she picked up her vodka and walked to the window, taking small sips as she went, swallowing the lump left in her throat. At the window, she pressed the whole of her free hand against the glass. She stared out, her hand hot against the cold pane. Well, she thought grimly, it looked like it was going to be one of those nights you just tried to get through. She took a deep breath. Okay. It happened.

She got the latest Sara Paretsky mystery from the bookcase and, propping it up against the glass and chrome salt and pepper shakers, started to read at the kitchen table. She read, sipping her drink, until her back started to hurt, and then she turned the open book over, holding her place, stretched, and got up to go to the bathroom. There, she got ready for bed, slipping into a black silk pajama top she kept on a peg in the bathroom and enjoying the

the ritual of cleaning her face with astringent. She looked at her eyes. Well, they had circles, but at least she wasn't crying them red. And no more vodka. She brushed her teeth. No more tonight.

She went up to the loft, turned the looping tape off, and settled herself into bed to read. When she finished the book, about one in the morning, she got up, went down to the bathroom, brushed her teeth again, came back up, let Minx out the window by the bed, and turned the light out. She pulled the comforter up around her neck. She closed her eyes and tried to relax her breathing, waiting for sleep. She waited. And gradually, all semblance of sleep vanished.

An hour and a half later, she sat up and looked out the window by her bed. She hadn't slept a bit. She lay there, rigid, trying to call up new images, to imagine a new time. She looked out into the night and saw from the bedside window the city lights sparkling around her.

She thought, panicked then, maybe she should try again to sleep. To dream of the face of a new woman. She brushed aside the thought of Morgan and tried to make her mind blank so other dreams could come in. As she turned to lay on her side, she began to hold on to the other pillow, pulling it down against her chest.

It was only these damn late night thoughts that kept her like this, she thought fiercely, rolling over to the other side. Eventually, she knew fantasies about new women would work, but still she lay there, huddled against the cold, with her eyes open, watching the lights, small and yellow against the fog, trying to convince herself it didn't matter, she didn't hurt, and things were great, really. She thought again, she should try to sleep. Probably she could now.

But when she drew her gaze back into the confines of her room, as she began to close her eyes, she felt a little afraid, and so she quickly looked back out so the feeling would not have a chance to grow.

She panicked then. She heard in her mind, her own voice, loud, pleading, I don't want things to be like this. I've got to take care of this. I can't do this anymore. I can't. I can't. The sound tore at her ears until, after she forced herself to breathe, she heard Bebe. Bebe. She said, Bebe, I can't do this. And Bebe said, okay honey, it's okay. We can make it be right. It won't always be like this.

And then she began to cry. To cry in earnest. To scream, crying. She wept into the pillow she was holding and then she pounded it, cursing, and weeping and finally, she slept. She slept, the pillow clutched to her chest.

CHAPTER TWELVE

COMING HOME

When the truck pulled over the Twin Peaks crest and they rode down the hill on upper Market, the whole of bright night San Francisco lay before them.

"It always makes me happy to see that," Georgia said.

"It is pretty," Ricky agreed.

"I mean, it makes me feel, I don't know. It's not just that it's pretty. Whenever I come this way, I feel like San Francisco lies in the palm of my hand. Like that Sylvia cartoon about cat language, when she interviews the cat doctor and he reports cats only say two things, you know? They say, 'When is dinner?' and 'All of this is mine.' Well, I go by here and I think, hey, all of this is mine."

Ricky laughed. "So, are you going to put that in your video segment? Sounds like a winner to me."

"I don't know. I hadn't thought about it. Maybe. Sure. Why not? I think so. It would be a good frame to start with. I mean, it would be good footage, even as a bridge to something else.

"But let me ask you something, Ricky. Do you think it's going to work, all of us bringing in some segments and *then* deciding from those pieces what we want to do as a group? Do you think if we couldn't decide beforehand, we'll be able to decide later?"

"Well, I don't know. Sometimes seeing someone's idea, instead of just hearing about it, makes a difference. One thing I do know, girl. I am sick of sitting in those meetings. Doing these individual things, we won't be any worse off than we are now. At least we're going to do something. Could be the individual segments will help us focus. We'll have to see.

"But at least we got the camera this weekend. You could come out and shoot this picture you like so much and show it with your interview next week if you want."

"I could. I could do it after I interview Bernice tomorrow night. When I'll sleep is another matter. Will we ever finish these meetings before eleven?"

"Why? You got somewhere you need to get to late Wednesday night?"

"Not especially. It's just that every Thursday morning I come into work and can't keep my eyes open and Clarissa says, 'Go work with the microfiche, sleepy fool. I can't let you out amongst the public looking like you got raised from the dead.'"

"Could be worse, girl," Ricky said, laughter hanging in her voice. "You could still be working for Williams and not making videos at all."

"Right. Only I wouldn't still be working with Williams. I'd be dead by this time, I swear to God. Murder-suicide. You and Clarissa saved my life, you know that, Ricky?"

"No. You saved your own life, child. But from this time last year to now, it has been a year full, that's for sure."

Georgia was quiet for a moment. "Yeah, I guess it has," she said after awhile. "Hard to believe it's been a year. I can hardly remember most of it. But I remember quitting, that's one thing I do remember. Once I gave Williams notice, he worked me like convict labor up until the last hour."

"You expected different?"

"I expected some kind of acknowledgement that I had worked there for him and was leaving. But there was nothing. If you hadn't taken me to lunch that day, I would have been totally crazy."

"You were totally crazy. But you pulled it out. You look like you doing fine now. Anyway, you were good at the meeting tonight, getting us back on the point. If Marcy doesn't start pulling her own weight, I don't know what I'm going to do to that girl. And Janice. I don't care if she's having a love affair with the Pope, I don't want to hear it anymore. We are supposed to be making this video, not just talking about making it."

"I know it," Georgia said. "But once we start shooting, it'll be better. Smart of you, cookie, to get the camera for us this first weekend.

"You got that right. I am *smart* and don't you forget it." They both laughed. Georgia stopped the truck at the light on the top of the Seventeenth Street hill. Ricky craned her neck around, looking out the window.

"Pretty night. Stars out tonight."

Georgia twisted around to see too.

"Not like back home, though. Back home, you could see them all. I used to lie out in the back yard with Bernice and count them."

"When you drank?"

"Yeah." The light changed and Georgia swung over to the street Ricky lived on. "Yeah, pretty sick, isn't it? I used to lie there and it was nice until I got to thinking about the stars burning out, exploding, and then I got to wondering when our star would and I'd get crazy behind it."

"That's what drinking'll do to you."

"Yeah. But you know, since I've been here, I read somewhere they say the universe isn't going to burn out, I mean, not exactly. It's just going to keep expanding and expanding until it begins to draw back and then it'll inch back, compressing and compressing. But anyway, I figure I'll get enough time to finish what I need to do."

"The video, anyway," Ricky said.

"Yeah. The video for sure."

Georgia pulled up in front of the Edwardian where Ricky lived with her nine-year-old, Aisha, and her girlfriend, Denise.

"How's the kid?" Georgia asked, setting the hand brake and putting the truck in neutral.

"Wild. She thinks she's Prince."

"Not Appolonia? That's a step in the right direction."

"You may think so but her teachers don't. And it looks like her light's still on, even though I told her she had to be asleep by the time I came home. I bet she conned Denise into letting her read before she went to bed."

"I'd wait up for you, too."

"You and her are two of a kind. Trouble." She leaned over and kissed Georgia on the cheek.

"She coming on Sunday? She understand she's invited too?"

"Sure she does. If she wants to come, she'll come. Probably she will. She loves the Parade. What time do you want us?"

"Well, I thought we'd sit down about ten."

"You want help in the kitchen?"

"That'd be good. Probably Em will disappear with Aisha into the joysticks."

"Okay. We'll come about nine."

"Good. Hey, how's Denise making out in that computer course?"

"She's doing good. She'll probably bend Morgan's ear all morning. Maybe we should just let the three of them eat by the computer and then the rest of us can talk normal at the table."

Georgia laughed at her. Ricky wound her window up and patted around for the door handle.

"Listen, why don't you keep the camera until Sunday, if you're going to shoot that Twin Peaks scene and your friend tomorrow night," she said. "I don't need it until the Parade. I may need some help there. You into it?"

"Sure. And if I have questions setting up tomorrow night, can I call?"

"You know you can."

Ricky opened the door and started to get out of the truck and Georgia leaned over and laid a hand on her friend's arm.

"You know, about this past year. Thanks for everything."

Ricky reached back in and touched her cheek. "See you Sunday," she said and went up the stairs.

Georgia waited until Ricky was inside and then put the truck in gear, her head swirling with ideas for the video segments. Bernice would be perfect. And the Parade. What a great idea! She turned on to her own street and started looking for a parking place. Her favorite illegal spot was open. She slid the truck in front of the driveway of the boarded-up garage and gathered the camera and her stuff.

Her first camera work tomorrow! And that old Bernice; when she talked to her a month ago about maybe doing an interview, Bernice's natural mugging ham came right on out. She'd be a great interview.

It was going to be like doing the oral histories she'd done one semester at school. Only better. A personal history of queers in San Francisco. If Bernice couldn't talk about that, she didn't know who could. She grinned as she walked up to the house.

She looked to the second floor, searching for signs of life in their flat, but no. Em was probably still working with Elliott on that new program. Only the outside light on and she'd turned that on before she left. Well, she thought, Morgan would be home soon.

She went up the stairs, left the outside light on and went in, dropping her sack by the door and looking for a place to lay the camera where it would be safe. She held the camera like it was a baby.

But as she walked into the living room, Morgan called from the kitchen.

"Hi, honey. How was your meeting?"

"Hi, Em, just a sec," Georgia called out, laid the camera down in the middle of the couch, arranged the pillows around it so no one would sit on it and walked back to the kitchen. Em and Elliott were sitting at the kitchen table, takeout wrappers strewn about and the remains of hamburgers and fries littering the table.

She went to Em and kissed her. "Hi, honey. Hey, Elliott. Nice to see you again. I'm glad to see you got her home before midnight. Did y'all work late again?"

"We did. But we finished. Now she doesn't have to work this weekend, and I can come to the brunch. Aren't you proud of us?"

"I am," she said, laughing, picking up a fry and the end of Morgan's shake. "But y'all didn't save me any."

Elliott offered her the heel of his hamburger. "I didn't know you hadn't eaten. You want I should go get more? It's easy," he offered, his hands apologetic.

"No, I was just teasing. How are you two?" she asked, and sat down next to Morgan.

"Wasted," Morgan said. Elliott nodded and began to gather up the remains of dinner.

"But we did get the new program together. And it will be really good for us. We've met the cost criteria and overcome all the objections to the contract application they turned down last year. I know we'll get it this year," Morgan said, turning to Elliott.

He nodded again, throwing the trash away. "But you know what, Em," he said, standing in the middle of the kitchen, brushing his hands off. "You know, I think it might have been better that we didn't get that contract. We learned a lot more this year."

Morgan stopped wiping off the table and turned to look at him, hard, and then finished wiping. "Well," she said slowly, taking the sponge back to the sink and standing next to him, "Not getting it did keep us busy all year. Maybe that was a blessing."

"Maybe so," he said, putting his arm around her shoulder and hugging her. Georgia felt her heart tighten for both of them. He looked better now, she thought, better than he did nine months ago, that's for sure. She watched Em disentangle herself awkwardly.

"Well, anyway, we finished this new program. And it is better," Morgan said, lightly touching Elliott's arm as she moved away. "I'll get your jacket and let you go home."

He stood there in the middle of the room, suddenly looking haggard. Georgia stood up and smiled at him. "You take good care now," she said and they both began to walk down the hall. "I want you in good shape for the brunch. Ricky and Bernice and I are cooking, and I want you hungry and awake."

He shook himself and laughed. "I wouldn't miss it for the world. But can I bring a friend?"

"Of course you can," she said quickly. "In fact, you'd better. If you don't, you'll be the only man here."

"Good," he said, slipping on the coat that Morgan held out. "I like to even the odds a little bit. I think you'll like this guy, anyway. Joe and I used to play softball with him. And he and I have been working together a lot down at the hospice. His name is David. I think he'll like you two, too. Anyway, it would be nice for everybody to meet."

Georgia exchanged glances with Morgan. "You know he's welcome here if he's a friend of yours."

"Okay. I'll see you all then on Sunday." He touched Morgan on the arm. "You get some rest, too, *shayna maydele*. Don't come in on time tomorrow."

Morgan nodded and then he was gone. She leaned against the door as she shut it behind him, and Georgia looked at her, moved forward and took her in her arms.

"How are you, honey?" she whispered.

Morgan hugged her back and said, "Oh God, I am so tired. We worked straight through today. Twelve hours."

She slumped against Georgia and tucked her head in between Georgia's shoulder and her neck. "I'm going to fall asleep on you right here, if we don't move," she said after a moment.

Georgia continued to rub her back. "Maybe we should get in bed then," she said, slipping her arm under Morgan's shoulder.

"Good idea. How are you? How was the meeting?" Morgan asked as they walked towards the bedroom.

Georgia sat on the end of the bed and started to take her shoes off. "Good. Pretty good. We decided that we couldn't decide what to do, so we're all going to shoot a little segment and then bring them in, and then we'll decide what to do together. Ricky, the cool cucumber," she chuckled, "got the camera for us first. I'm going to interview Bernice tomorrow night."

"Does she know that?" Morgan sat on the edge of the bed and started to unlace her shoes. Georgia kicked her loafers off and then sat at the end and began to unbutton her shirt.

"No, but she's coming for supper and I'm sure she'll do it. She's such a storyteller. She loves that kind of stuff. And then, Ricky will shoot the Parade on Sunday. It's going to be a great weekend!"

Morgan stripped off her shirt and camisole. "Don't forget you're having dinner with me on Saturday. Just us."

Georgia leaned back on the bed, reaching her hands up over her head for Morgan and pulling her down. She kissed Morgan's back, gave her a long hug and then sat up again. She stood to take her pants and shirt off and then walked naked over to the closet for her nightshirt.

"Where are you taking me for supper?" she asked, suddenly shy.

"My secret," Morgan said, turning and grinning. "Some place special. You'll see."

Georgia slipped on her nightshirt and stood, waiting for Morgan to get hers on before they went to the bathroom. She leaned against the bed and watched Morgan.

"You know, tonight on the way home Ricky was reminding me how much had changed since last year."

"Oh?" Morgan said, pulling her nightshirt over her head. Her head emerged. "I guess it has. I'm glad it has." She came up to Georgia and took her hand. "I love you, Georgie," she said and then they walked to the back of the house, shutting off the lights, brushing teeth, getting ready for bed.

Soon, after they had nestled in bed, Georgia heard Morgan's slow steady breathing and knew that she had fallen asleep almost as soon as her head had hit the pillow. She propped her own head up, watched the streetlight streaming in under the window shade, and listened to Morgan's breathing. She wasn't going to sleep with her mind churning like this. But at least she didn't have to be awake for her job anymore.

Not now. She had at first. She remembered Clarissa giving her reams of instructions, all detailed, like a government job. So much to do. The person who had the job before her had left no order. No system. Just a set of regulations, those unbelievable regs. It was crazy.

And she was crazy. Ricky had been right tonight. Her heart tightened against her and Morgan rolled away when she sat up. She sat still for a minute, listening for a disruption in Morgan's breathing, but it didn't come. Slowly she slipped out of bed, gathered up her robe and went back to her room, sat in her mother's old rocking chair in the dark, and folded her robe around her. She watched out the side window, watching the fog swirl in the night.

That time last year. Wandering around downtown at lunch in a daze, wondering how to get through, how to live through the pain that pierced her side like a spear, invisible life bubbling out of her like a hole in her lungs. She felt her fear of the pain again and didn't want to think about that time. She didn't want to see it again, how she had been so angry she had refused lunches with Morgan, how she had held on to Clarissa's regs like boards floating in the ocean, how she had sat in a public park in the sunshine and tried to eat her lunch while the tears rolled down her face under her sunglasses, and how no one noticed or said a word.

Had there really been months of that? Getting up, going to work, her relationship with Em a brush of lips on a cheek almost out the door. Coming home, staring out this very window. Enraged at the woman sleeping in the bed next to her who still, to this day, worked late. Enraged and betrayed and frightened. So frightened. There had been no place to hang on, no place to be, and she had floated in the pain, lost and delirious, for months.

Her fingers laced themselves in her lap, and she looked around the room, dim and glowing only from the city lights, in the dark side of the moon. But she caught her breath when she began to recognize things, her things, from home and from here. Well, she did have a place to be.

She looked at the room, remembering the weekend she and Bernice had painted it, and remembering them laughing together while they did it. That had happened right after last year's Parade. Well, maybe the pain hadn't gone on for months. That part couldn't be true. Actually, she realized, what happened was, the pain got shorter and shorter. It wasn't like it didn't come anymore. It just didn't last as long.

But how? How *had* things started to change? It had been a year. Almost exactly a year. Because last year, she and Em hadn't gone to the Parade at all. They had meant to go together and then have her hook up with Bernice, because Morgan had to go to work that afternoon. But it didn't turn out that way. Joe had gotten sick again, and Morgan had to work the whole day. And then, it didn't seem like much fun to go by herself, without Morgan, even though Bernice was going to be there, and well, in the end, she just hadn't gone at all. She'd sat at home. Sitting in this very rocking chair.

And furious. They'd had another blowout when Morgan came home, another three day wonder of hatred and bitterness. She hadn't walked out but...wait. She stared out the window at the night sky, at the light fog swirl through the trees. Wait. Wasn't that the night she had sworn she was going to get for herself, that if Em couldn't come to be with her during the most important holiday of the year, well, by God, she'd still have the holiday? Morgan had said she would not give up her life. Well, she had yelled back, she wasn't going to give up hers either. She remembered, her face feeling as icy as it had been then. That night. Was it then? Or another night?

What had happened? How did it go? She forced herself to remember past the numbing new job, past her anger, past her terror of Morgan leaving again, her terror of another phone call from her folks. How had those months passed?

She fished a hanky out of her robe and blew her nose. Well, there had been Bernice in those hard weeks, and if she hadn't been there, Georgia thought, she wouldn't have made it. She and Em wouldn't have made it, either. She shifted in the chair, wide awake in the memory.

If it hadn't been for Bernice, and the time they spent together, doing nothing, just driving in the truck, well, things would have been very different. But gradually, gradually, she had put one foot in front of the other and things got better. One step was painting her room. One step was joining the video collective and getting to be real friends with Ricky. One step was her new job. And one step was about Em, or no, about them. She smiled and got up to get a glass of water.

She went to the kitchen, making her way in the dark. She filled a glass up at the sink, took a long drink and then sat at the kitchen table.

She folded her hands around her glass and sipped as she remembered how she and Em had eaten at this table, fought at this table. And how they had sat around this table the night Joe had died, and she had finally understood—not why or how—but just that somehow Em's heart was breaking too. She saw then how frightened Morgan was, how she drank the warm milk Georgia had made her like it was brandy. And Georgia knew then that Em was fighting the brandy hurt that never seems to stop, that never seems to let go, as though you must put a fire down there too, a fire to put the fire out, so that you can live.

She had gotten up from the table and gone to Em, wrapped her arms around her, gathered her, Em like a frightened bird fluttering against her, and they had ended up on the floor, sitting in the darkness like she was now, sitting with the night light bathing them, as she rocked her, rocked her with her arms around her, her breast to Em's back, while Em cried for Joe, for Elliott, for all the things she couldn't say.

And something broke that night. Because the next morning, Em began to join her on her walks before work. At first, they didn't say a word. But then, the day after Joe's funeral, Em began to talk about her mother in a way she never had before. And then she talked about Elliott and how afraid she was.

Georgia listened. The words spilled out of Em as though a volcano were erupting, and she was frightened by the torrent, frightened but relieved, too. And glad. And closer, she thought as she got up for a little more water. She had felt closer.

She sat back down with a rueful smile. Because eventually Em had said, one day when they were about three blocks from the house—it was bitter cold and foggy—Em had finally said, "I need you to talk to me."

"What do you mean?" Georgia remembered herself asking. "What do you mean?" Feeling terrified. "There's nothing to say." Terrified that the months of furious, melted pain, hardly healed over, were about to be ripped open. Terrified to say a word.

She remembered Em had just waited, and she grew impatient with Em's patience. And angry. And she said then, "Okay. I was wrong about some things. I did take out some stuff on you. What do you want me to say? Or is it that you've talked to me and you figure it's my turn? What about the months, the years, you didn't talk to me?"

Morgan looked away, and Georgia didn't notice she was crying until she kept sniffling. "Okay," Morgan said after a bit.

"Okay, you're right. I didn't talk for a long time. I want to talk now. Will you talk to me? I'm worried about you," she said, wiping her face with the back of her hand.

Georgia took Em's wet hand and pulled it in her jacket pocket and the fear went somewhere, not between them, but drained somewhere, and she remembered this woman was her friend who loved her. She stopped walking and looked at Em.

"I'm sorry," she said. "I am sorry. I don't know what gets into me these days. I don't know where I am. And I get angry about nothing these days. I just get set off and I can't seem to stop it."

"Talk to me," Em pleaded, her hand pulling on Georgia's in the coat pocket.

"Okay," Georgia said finally, reluctantly. She remembered feeling in that moment that she hadn't known what she would say, or where she would start.

She looked out the kitchen window and took another sip of water. But there had been so much to say. So much. About her own mother. Her father. About how it was that a person died as they had lived, and if that life was in denial, it stayed in denial. How much she had wanted the stroke to make some last chance for her mother. For her. For some peace there. For some help. For some real connection beyond their lives that made a difference. That would heal the pain. The stone that would land, finally, at the bottom of the well, and she would be home at last.

She sat up, fingering the words of the old wound. But there was no blood now. Just sadness. And it hadn't killed her to talk about it. Though she thought it was going to, at the time. She wiped her eyes. But actually, she thought, after she had talked, somehow she could hear better.

Wrong well, she heard Bernice's voice talking in her head. She smiled through her tears. You just went to the wrong well. Got to get your water somewhere else. Remember, you can't get pizza at a Chinese restaurant. You want pizza, you got to go where it is. You want really good food, you got to fix it at home.

She started to laugh. She was going to have to get Bernice to say that stuff on tape. Really. She laughed as she took her glasses off and wiped her face. She stuck her feet out in front of her, leaned back and closed her eyes. Well, she had taken Bernice's advice, step by step. And she remembered then another time, that time last year when she knew Em and she were going to be different, but were taking steps that were leading to the same home.

It was as though they had been swimming under water and suddenly broken through to some other world, except it was their own somehow; some place new, but as though it had been waiting. They had gone away, gone up to Elliott and Joe's cabin on the Russian River, some months after Joe had died. The place needed to be set up for the rainy winter and Elliott couldn't quite bear to go yet, so Em had volunteered them.

And Georgia didn't mind. Things had been better between the two of them since they had started walking together, not back the way it was, but maybe, she thought then, maybe it wouldn't ever be the way it had been between them. Maybe time didn't go in a line or a circle, but sometimes perpendicular. She didn't know.

But she did know that weekend was when she had begun to understand how much she had missed Em in those months before. Well, she hadn't exactly let herself know it was even there before. She had only begun to let herself feel it as pain, not anger, after Morgan had begun to walk with her, when she knew she was coming back, and she realized one morning that the heart place between her breasts was aching with loss, and desire.

And she knew as she recognized the feeling, she had to go home and sit until she felt her way through it. So she sat in her room every morning until it was time to go to work. She'd just be in her room. By herself.

And she would lie on the sofa and look out the window. Wondering and crying and frightened of wanting Em again, afraid of falling back into the old ways. Wondering what it meant, to want someone. What it meant about belonging and where she could belong, if she didn't belong to Em, didn't fit in Carolina, couldn't stay near her parents. She wondered where she belonged until one morning she said to herself, well, maybe home was not just where you hung your hat; not just some place where, if you had to go, they had to take you in. Maybe, it wasn't just a place that you made like Bernice said. Maybe home was where you belonged. And maybe where she belonged was with herself.

She smiled, her eyes closed, remembering. That one day was worth all the rest. But was it that weekend in the country when she first realized they were both coming home? She didn't know. All she knew was that at some point they were back together. And they hadn't found their way together. They had come home separately and then found each other again. Love is the balm, not the way to Gilead, she thought. And then she wished that somebody had told her earlier, as a child, that she had to find her own way home, but she smiled into the darkness, maybe she wouldn't have listened anyway. Maybe she had to find it out herself.

But something, she thought with a slight frown, something *had* happened on that weekend. And not just that they made love, either. It was something else. Or something more. Or maybe it was all tied up together, and the string was part of the parcel, not something to be thrown away. She almost laughed. As if she would have thrown that string or any part of that weekend away.

Elliott's need for the cabin to be taken care of and his own pain, so big she could put her whole hand through his heart, had given them a place to heal. She had not thought at the beginning that would happen.

They'd come up Friday night late, not talking much. It was clear and cold as Em drove them up on winding Route 116, a clear and cold winter night, and at one point Em had shivered, turned the heat up, and said, "Jesus Christ, we've gotten here too late. It's already winter and fifty below."

Georgia felt Em's hand on her leg. She looked at her then and said, "Maybe only thirty," and they smiled at each other in the weak green light from the dashboard. They didn't talk much. And in the silence, Georgia felt the ache starting in her pelvis, an ache that filled her whole body, radiating out from deep inside her cunt, filling up her heart and hands and taking her breath away.

Morgan held her hand for the longest time and didn't say anything. When she gave Georgia a little squeeze before she took her hand away, Georgia thought to herself, as she had so many times in the last few years, oh, how she still wanted her. She wanted her like she had wanted water when she had a fever in the night; she wanted her sudden, sharp, aching.

She wanted her like she had when they were first together, but she was afraid. Even though things had changed, this hadn't. She hadn't faced her own desire, and neither had Morgan. And she knew it and was afraid.

They went on in silence, the car slow on a road full of unfamiliar turns. The trip took longer than they'd planned and it was about 11:30 when they parked the car. They entered the dark and damp cabin and hardly spoke as they went about making the bed, unpacking as though they had been doing it for a long time, instead of it being the first vacation they'd had in years. But without words, Georgia took care of the food; Morgan made a fire. They got into bed together then, exhausted, like animals knowing nothing but tiredness.

The next day they slept late, and when they woke, they lay in bed, companionably, without talking, side-by-side for a long time.

Finally, Georgia got up and looked for things to make tea, got the bread and cheese and winter oranges from the little table, and they ate in silence. But Morgan hugged her and touched her as she dressed, cupping her hands on her ass for a moment before Georgia put her pants on, and she flamed inside and was silent. Morgan said she had to split some wood. Georgia said she would clean up.

She stood at the kitchen window and watched Morgan, watched as she washed the dishes, watched as she dried them, watched as she put some water on for tea. She watched her and she wanted her. Let herself trust her and want her. Felt it flood through her and was glad it was back, and she felt clear, as clear as the air off the ocean.

And all that time, in the silence, she could hear Morgan splitting the wood in her own steady rhythm. Standing there at the sink, washing the odd set of plates and cups that Elliott and Joe had apparently collected for the cabin over the years, she thought about what they had learned during this time, and what Bernice had said about being present and not running away; she thought about whether or not Morgan would ever want her again, whether they would ever make love like they had at the beginning.

She thought about that, and she listened to Morgan out there, and watched her. Morgan had started out with a sweatshirt on, but now she was down to her navy camisole, the afternoon sun brilliant on her beautiful red hair. She moved in and out of the light drifting between the redwoods as she raised a round of wood to the block, moved back then to swing full out, muscles silhouetted out of her softness, swinging down into the light, her navy corduroy pants and camisole so stark on her white winter skin.

Georgia watched her. Camisole lace on muscle and her lean body circling like a willow branch, taut in the wind, arching with her swing. Over and over, the same motions. Swing, step, raise, scatter, the long arc of the ax glinting in the air to resting in the block, the sound of wood splitting into two even halves. It seemed like she watched her for a long time, watching the muscles in those arms that had rocked her and filled her so many times, the muscles in those arms that let her keep rocking her for as long as she wanted.

Morgan caught her staring and waved, grinned, facing her, her small nipples hard against the cold, her breasts, firm, round, just a little more than her cupped hand. Georgia kept watching as the split pile grew, and Morgan finally stopped to stack the splits into ricks. Georgia turned away then, built the fire up and watched as the sun slid through the trees at an angle, making even the webs in the barren tickbush glisten.

She sat down finally, awkwardly, on the straight chair, stirring her tea and wondering what to say. She had to say something. Finally. She had to say some word, some motion, some kiss of meaning. But she didn't know if she knew how anymore.

Shortly, Morgan came in, stamping her old Oregon farm boots, and began to wash up in cold water, bending at the sink. She was solid and sweaty and Georgia watched her and didn't say a word. For several long moments, there was silence in the cabin.

And then Morgan turned to her, leaning her back against the counter, wiping her hands with a towel. And grinning. The flame in Georgia's cunt leapt into her mouth and still she wondered what to say.

Morgan grinned. "Well, look what we got here—the life of Riley. You ever work, honey?"

Georgia looked at her, hardly believing her banter, wanting badly for it to be the start of something, but after all, after all they'd been through, not wanting to start it herself.

Morgan took a step closer and then closer and then she stood over her.

"How'd you sleep last night?" she asked, standing still, so close, so taut, the towel wrapped in her hands.

"Good," Georgia said, watching her closely now, watching her eyes for some sign. Morgan just stared back.

"Me too. I'm not so tired any more. Are you?"

She stood about a foot away, hand on her hip. The grin came back.

"No," Georgia said and the word came out clipped. She watched her.

"Maybe you should start earning your keep around here, then," she said slowly, moving back towards her in very small steps, accentuating each word. She dropped one end of the towel she'd been holding and brought her hand up to cup Georgia's chin and brought her open mouth down on her lips, hard.

And slow. She kissed her deep and slow, and then backed off, her lips lightly, so lightly, brushing Georgia's. She stood back, pulled Georgia up, wrapped her arms around her and drew her in.

Okay then, Georgia thought slowly. She'd started. But I can't, she thought, frightened, we can't do it this way. Something's wrong here. It's the wrong road, she thought, frantic, we've got to turn around.

"I don't earn anything, girl," Georgia said, slowly, trying to keep herself from jerking away. She rubbed her hands down Morgan's arms. "You know that." And then she felt Morgan stiffen and she remembered all of it, just in time.

She let her go, pushed her away gently and stood apart, facing her. "You want to do it like this? Are you sure you want *me* like this?" she asked, not frightened anymore, clear, staring at her steadily, wanting her but not willing to go the old way.

Morgan held her look for a minute, then went around the table and sat, her head in her hands, the towel cast away on the table.

"Jesus," she said briefly. And then there was silence again. Finally she looked up at her. "I do want you, do you know? I've never stopped wanting you, oh Georgia, it's just that..." she said stubbornly, her eyes reddening. "It's just that I got confused and wanted...

"I wanted to skip, to leap... Jesus, Georgie, don't you remember how it was in the first days? Georgie, I wanted to fly again."

"Me, too," Georgia said slowly, sitting down at the table with her. "Me, too."

"I'm afraid. I'm afraid to do it another way. I get afraid to think about it. When I do, I remember," Morgan said and was silent.

"Your dad again?" Georgia asked.

Morgan nodded. Then she said, her voice winding up high, "Why is he always here?"

"Because he was before. Because we haven't made our own memories strong enough. Because we haven't been conscious long enough," Georgia said, moving hands towards her, reaching for her hands.

How many times had they talked their way through this, talk, talk and then stopped? And Georgia felt afraid again, too. But somewhere, she thought to herself, this time, in the silence of the redwoods, after all that time of sitting with desire shining out of her like light, this time, she wanted to try to push forward into themselves, to break on through.

She started again. She didn't know if Morgan was ready, but she had to try.

"We can do it a new way. If you really want me, we can try. We can do it. We can try, girl," she said, her ache back down to a small fire burning low, scared, and wanting her, but wanting her whole.

Morgan didn't answer. Finally she reached her hand across the table to meet Georgia's.

"Help me remember how to start," she whispered.

"Remember me. Remember it's me, Em. Look at me. Look at me," she said low, keeping hold of her hand as she got up and went around the table to her. She stood and pulled Morgan to her.

"Feel me. I have breasts. I'm a woman who is small and round. I have this special place here, this scar from when I fell when I was drunk. Remember me? I'm the woman you know," she said, touching her cheek to Morgan's. "Feel? Remember me?"

"Yes," Morgan murmured. "Yes."

She held her close, pressed into her, sharing the fire that was burning so high now, the power of the two of them, as if Morgan could feel the fire through her very skin, through her heart, if she held her close enough.

"We'll stop and start again, if we need to. We'll just go as far as you want," she said into her ear, her hands now in her hair, pulling her head back gently so she could see her face and know her.

"Georgie. My Georgie. I remember you. Oh God, I remember you," she said, finding her lips again. Georgia took her hand and led her to the bed.

She sat her down. "Are you sure it's me you want and not Elizabeth?" she asked, sure her voice was sounding more strained that she would have liked. Morgan sighed heavily, then grabbed her hands and pulled her down on the bed with her.

"It wasn't Elizabeth I ever wanted," she said slowly, as if to hammer the words home. "I just wanted to feel again—feel anything—and I lost myself and you with her, do you know? Oh, Georgie. I missed you.

"And I want you—you—to be with me now," she ended, nestling into her shoulders. Georgia held her and then pushed her away.

She stripped slowly, following Morgan's eyes, cupping her breasts with her own hands, bending, reaching, undressing for her.

And then she went to the bed and undressed Morgan. Morgan watched her, her eyes following Georgia's, and Georgia could see her paying attention, fighting off the memories, coming back into the present. Soon, she reached up for Georgia's breasts and laughed, putting her face in between them.

"Oh you," she said, her teeth scraping against Georgia's nipples. "I stood out there and split that wood, so easy, and I felt the muscles in my arms and knew I wanted you. I knew, could feel you again, oh honey," she said.

"You don't have to put words on it, you know," Georgia said, afraid the words would go back into the old way, the taunting, leering old way.

Morgan stopped and sat up. "Yes, yes I do," she said slowly, not touching her. And then she started again, her hands moving in circles on Georgia's belly. "Yes, I do, I have to find new words, words to stomp out the old.

"Talk to me," she said, her hands sliding down to stroke Georgia's inner thighs, making the long startling circles around her legs and over her abdomen, circling the fire, as though she could bring the fire into burning rings, tightening. Georgia held her, and smiled.

"Em," she said. "Look at us. Remember that. Remember I love you through all time. Can you see us? We are a feast."

She reached her hand to Morgan's mouth and touched her lips. She began to kiss her all over, slowly down her arms, to her hands, over to the softness of her belly, back to her face, her lips then brushing hers, her hands moving on her breasts, sliding across her nipples, then cupping underneath, then back to the nipple. She moved her legs between hers and started to rock.

"Look at us. You see how beautiful we are, breast to breast?" She whispered into her ear, rubbing her lips on the outside.

She kissed her lips then, licking and opening them and slipping her tongue in to meet Morgan's. And then she pulled back again.

"Actually, you don't have to see anything," she said. "You don't have to see a thing. Here," she said, taking Morgan's hands. "Here, feel this," she said, guiding Morgan's hands to her breast and shifting slightly. She slipped on top of her, her hip bones riding between her legs, her hands moving from her breasts to the small of her back and arching her up into her.

"Oh, Georgie," Morgan murmured. "How I missed you."

She reached under Georgia and turned her over. Georgia felt her lowering herself onto her back and could feel her drawing circles on her skin with her nipples. Morgan slid two fingers down her spine, one stopping in the cleft in her ass and the other slipping in the wetness of her cunt. "Oh Georgia, I do love you," she said, and Georgia heard her whisper it again as she filled her.

Morgan reached around under her and began to stroke her clitoris with her other hand and Georgia sucked her in, aching for her and greedy, as Morgan rocked her. She knew if she could have seen them then, could have seen the two of them from across the room, the muscles in Morgan's back and her arms would have stood out like they had when she was chopping wood that afternoon, and she would have been full underneath her, stretching too. And when she felt herself stretch she knew she wanted more than she could hold, even as Morgan was inside her, reaching up further and further and then when she gasped, Morgan followed that rhythm, her rhythm.

She felt Morgan there and didn't want to come, ever. She wanted her to stay there, inside her, rocking her like that forever. She felt stretched to meet her, as though her insides ballooned around Morgan's hands, as though her insides had melted into total sensation, and she heard Morgan cry that she loved her, and she felt her rock as she rocked her.

There was nothing to her body but Morgan's hands and her own pleasure, the edge of flight. Then suddenly, she felt the way begin and she nursed it, didn't rise up into it, but let it take its own sweet time into the rhythm and she heard Morgan say she loved her one more time before she sped away, falling over that edge into the space and clear light of the winter afternoon. She floated away and into the flight of time good love makes, away and around, into another place altogether, the lightness of love. And then after awhile, she felt Morgan's head resting on the small of her back, that she had pulled her hands out of her and was pulling herself up to cover her.

Georgia turned to smile at her and Morgan wiped her face off with the edge of the pillowcase, smiling in turn at the tears Georgia always cried when, by forcing her to pay such close attention to the joy of her body, Morgan could send her into the very heart of air.

"Rest now," Morgan said, as she had before, in those years before, when they had loved each other often this way, and Georgia caught her hands and drew them down to her waist. She tucked her head into the small place in Morgan's neck where the smell of her lived and listened to her breath steady itself, and hers too.

And then Georgia began to match breathing with her. And her hands crept down to Morgan's cunt and found the wetness there to match her own and she asked her, with their new plan, she asked her if she was ready, if she did want that, if she was there, right in the moment.

"Oh God, take me quick, Georgie," she gasped. "I almost came when I was making you come. I'm so ready for you," she said, her mouth on Georgia's ear. And then, more slowly she said, "It's you, I know it's you now."

Georgia didn't say anything back with words for a minute. But after lifting Morgan up to stretch over her hips, to stretch her muscles and her skin, Georgia cradled her and stroked her, entering her almost immediately and then she talked to her, and told her secrets, how she loved her, how she had always loved her and how she always would.

She stroked her slow and then in circles, rubbing her clitoris in between two fingers with one hand, the other hand deep inside her and curled up towards her on that rough spot that made her gasp. She listened to her, listened to her breathing change, listened to her listening to her.

"Strong, fine woman. You whole woman," she crooned to her. "Em, oh Em, I love you. Feel me here." She moved her hand in deeper inside her, "Feel me here. I love you, honey."

Morgan's voice didn't answer her but her body did. Her breathing was like a heart pattern, full of steady jagged peaks, building up, slowing down. When her breathing got slow, Georgia changed her rhythm or her position, watching Morgan carefully, trying to make sure she did everything she could to make her pay attention to herself.

Georgia listened, worried, but passed into some new place now, and carried with her there the old love and desire, like a secret small sack of magic around her neck, resting over her heart. And she knew then that she had always wanted Morgan, even before she knew her, even when she was a dream from high school and she hadn't found her yet. Now that she had, she wasn't going to let her go. Not now. Not ever. She began to sweat lightly, and with each movement she whispered to her, so Morgan could hear her voice and know she was there, still there, loving her, and wanting.

She tried to match her hands with the movement of her hips and then Morgan caught the two of them, too. Her breathing caught in a steady pattern and her hands sought out Georgia's hair, her arms pulling, holding. And Georgia knew she had started and she began to suck her breast to give the final gust to push her up and out into the air. And Morgan cried out, a sound from deep inside her and went rigid in her arms for a moment as she came, and suddenly relaxed into her arms, gasping and crying. Georgia moved out from underneath her, but not from inside of her, trying to stay at least a little inside her and still cover her as she cried. Morgan clung to her as she had been clinging to the hem of her nightshirt, all those nights before.

After awhile, Morgan spoke, the words coming out as though she tore each one from her heart. "I stayed here the whole time, Georgie. I started to slip away once or twice, but I pulled myself back."

And then she cried for a long time and Georgia held her and smiled, though she cried a little, too. For her as well, it had only been her in the bed, and she knew it. And she knew then that they would make it. She didn't think it would be easy, and it hadn't been. But it had been worth it. All of it.

Georgia suddenly opened her eyes, looked around, saw her kitchen, saw where she was and smiled. She stretched herself out of her memory in the heart of the night, rubbed her eyes and felt her shoulders relax. She went back to bed, sneaking in softly. She pulled the covers up and thought, even now, she didn't know when the end would be, even now in bed together six months later, she still didn't know if they had come to the end.

But she knew they were on the right road home, each a different road. It might take awhile. But that was okay. She closed her eyes and snuggled into the sleeping Morgan, fit herself like a spoon against Morgan's back. And just before she slept, she thought again, that was okay. They had time, after all. It didn't matter if it took time. They had plenty of that. If you were counting years, not hours, she thought sleepily, and then she slept.

When she woke Sunday morning, it was early, and she stretched, languid, like a cat, opening her eyes to the sun as though its presence were her due. Then she was awake, and realized it was sunny and Gay Pride Day. She turned over and saw Morgan was lying on her side, her hands reaching for her, her eyes open, her mouth smiling and whispering, "Happy Gay Pride Day, you gorgeous lesbian, you."

Georgia folded herself into Morgan's arms and smiled as she kissed her neck. Morgan was whispering, "Do you have a date for the parade today?" and she nodded.

"Yes," she said, sitting up, turning to face Morgan. "Oh yes. I'm going with my girlfriend."

"Your girlfriend?" said Morgan.

"Oh yes. My most beautiful girl in the whole world." She started to get up and as she did, she gathered her robe up under her chin and then stood at the end of the bed, her robe like a cape. "Perhaps you know her. She's quite famous for her beauty in these parts. Entire softball teams have swooned over her beauty."

Morgan threw her pillow at her. She ducked and continued. "Also, she's brilliant. Perhaps you know her work. She and her partner, the very brilliant and flamboyant Elliott Samuels, have created an entire new universe for computers. They are genii together. Quite famous."

Morgan was shrieking from under the covers. Georgia went over and goosed her and Morgan shrieked again.

"I'm not coming out until you stop," Morgan said, her voice muffled against the covers.

Very carefully Georgia pulled back the covers from the bottom of the bed, unhinging them and then flipping them off, so Morgan was exposed, huddled in the middle of the bed.

They were both quiet for a moment and then Morgan leapt up, screaming, "I am the ghost of Gay Pride Past. Mess with my covers at your own peril." She lunged again at Georgia and roared. Georgia fell back, laughing, losing her balance and ending up on the floor.

Quickly then, Morgan was on her, laughing, holding her, whispering in her ear, and then they were kissing, long and slow and soft. When they stopped for a moment, Georgia pulled back and looked at Morgan, a smile on her lips, and she felt her heart singing in the morning sun, singing in the light that streamed in under the shade.

"Is this what happens when you wake up the ghost of Gay Pride Past?" she asked softly. "This ghost, does she immediately become a sex fiend? Tell me how I did this, so I can do it again."

Morgan bit her cheek and Georgia screamed. "The ghost of Gay Pride Past is a vampire!" she shouted, quickly jumping up, laughing. Morgan lay sprawled on the floor, laughing too, her legs askew, her beautiful mauve cunt smiling in the light.

She saw where Georgia was looking and quickly covered up with her nightgown, saying, "You letch, you."

"Hardly a letch to admire you. Just your lover," Georgia said, offering her hand to help Morgan up. "Just your lover admiring what she hopes will always be there for her to see and admire."

Morgan caught her hand and pulled herself into Georgia's embrace. They held to each other for a long moment and then Georgia said, "Honey. It's eight. Everybody's coming at nine. And we've got to look presentable. You have to save this for tonight Will you?"

Morgan answered with her hip in Georgia's crotch. "Are you going to make this hard for me?" Georgia groaned.

"I just don't want you to forget what you've got at home when you go out there and see all those lovely lesbians at the Parade."

"I don't forget. Last night will help me not forget," Georgia whispered in her ear. "And don't you, either."

"I don't. I swear. I think I learned that lesson."

Georgia broke away and patted her on the butt. "Thank God you're a quick learner. You want the first shower?"

An hour later, Georgia was combing her hair in the hall mirror when the doorbell rang. She went to the door and Ricky and Aisha and Denise were standing there, looking like they'd all just had showers too. She ushered them in, shouted to Morgan to hurry in the shower, grinned at Denise as Aisha tugged her into the living room, and nodded okay for Aisha to turn the computer on.

She and Ricky went back to the kitchen and sat for a moment, drinking a little of the fresh juice Ricky had brought and lining up brunch. Morgan scooted out of the shower and raced up to her room to get her clothes on and they both laughed at her. The bell rang again. This time it was Bernice and Annie. But before they could even get back to the kitchen, the bell sounded one more time, and Georgia shook her head and grinned, as she turned back to get it.

Elliott and his friend David stood on the open stairway, decked out in Hawaiian shirts, shorts and sunhats. Behind them, Lisa walked up the stairs. Georgia waved them all in and smiled as Elliott ducked to hug her hello. Friend David offered half of a full, fresh watermelon and she smiled at his good manners. She led them and Lisa in and by that time Morgan emerged, looking radiant and lovely in her softball T-shirt and clean jeans.

Well, Georgia thought, palming her ass as she went by, well, a little night entertainment can certainly do wonders for a woman's skin, can't it. She wondered if she glowed in the same way and caught Bernice looking at her smiling and nodding. "Real nice to see you two looking so happy," she murmured as Georgia came to sit by her and Ricky.

"We going to get to making some food for these critters?" Bernice asked, grinning at them all, but turning to Georgia.

"You going to have to get them out of here so we can get down to work, Georgia," Ricky said, beginning to shoo Elliott and David and Morgan out of the room.

"Get Annie out of here too," Bernice said, laughing.

The three of them put the brunch together, laughing, pushing each other around, Bernice and Ricky opening the wrong drawers, Georgia laughing at them both. Once the eggs were on, Bernice went up to the front to gather the others, and in the quiet of the kitchen, Georgia looked out over the stove into the beautiful day.

"Should I open the back door?" Ricky asked, pulling her blouse up off her breasts and fanning herself.

"You better or we'll all faint," Georgia said softly, her eyes still looking out the window. Ricky opened the door, looked at Georgia and walked over to stand next to her.

"You here with us today?" Ricky said, her voice low and loving.

Bernice came in then and the three of them looked at each other. Georgia looked back to the window and then said, "Yeah. I'm here. I'm here. You know, for a very long while, I felt like I'd been kicked out of the party, that the others were having a party and I'd been disinvited. And the 'they' was, at different times, my own family, or other lesbians, or straight people or sometimes even my friends and loved ones. But you know, today, standing here, cooking my world-famous cheese and eggs, I just realized, I am the party. I am the goddamn party. They can't kick me out. I am the party.'

She paused, looking back and forth at her two friends, and grinning.

"You know?"

Bernice grinned and hugged her. Ricky, standing on the other side, looked amused and said, "Quit crying in those world-famous eggs or you'll ruin them," and gave Georgia a push with her hip.

Georgia kept grinning. "I am the goddamn party."

Ricky said, "You right, now get the cornbread out of the oven."

By the time they were eating the watermelon, everybody seemed to have known each other for years. Georgia looked across the table at Morgan, and watched the watermelon dripping down her chin and grinned.

Morgan grinned back, trying to wipe her chin off, and then smiled apologetically. "I'm your girl," she said in answer to Georgia's shaking head. "You know I make messes."

Georgia just smiled at her and looked around the table. And then at the kitchen clock. "Good grief, y'all, it's ten thirty."

Everybody looked up, except Elliott who turned languidly around. "So true. Best we amble on," he said in his Tallulah voice. But by then Ricky and Bernice were already clearing the table, Morgan had gotten up with Aisha to find them both shirts to wear that didn't have watermelon down the front, and David had started washing the dishes. Georgia followed Morgan into the bedroom to gather up her hat and an extra shirt to wear over her Carolina tank shirt, in case they marched on the shady side.

"See if this one won't do," Morgan said to Aisha and then, "Change in the bathroom, if you'll feel more comfortable there." Aisha took the shirt and headed towards the bathroom.

"God, don't ever make me nine again," Georgia said.

Morgan came over and put her arms around Georgia, a sad smile on her face.

"What is it, Em?" George asked, feeling more than knowing that something was not as right as she thought.

Morgan stood before her with her head down. Then she looked at Georgia and said, "Bad news, honey. Elliott found a bug in the program this morning. We've got to go in and fix it. But at least I told him I wouldn't go until after the Parade."

Georgia broke away from her embrace. "Em, what the hell was he doing working on it this morning, of all mornings?" she whispered and then turned her back to her.

"Better this morning than tomorrow morning," Morgan said, her voice apologetic. "But did you hear me say I told him I wouldn't go until after the Parade?" She tried again to put her arms around Georgia.

Georgia stood still, stiff for a moment, and then held Morgan's arms around her. She held her tightly. "Well, thanks for that."

Morgan whispered, "I was doing it for me and for us, too, do you know that?"

Georgia nodded, her eyes wet for a moment. Morgan took her chin in her hands and made her look at her.

"Is it never going to be easy?" Georgia asked.

Morgan shook her head. "No," she whispered. "But it's going to be fun. And full of love, I swear. You've got all those people standing out there in the hall loving you, too. And me, with my whole heart. You want to go to a Parade with your girl today?"

Georgia took a deep breath and smiled, a little sadly, but smiled nonetheless. And then she kissed her. "Yes, I do," she said. "And I can stay at the Parade after you go."

"Anyway," she brightened. "I've got to help Ricky. That will be fun. I guess. But I'll miss you."

"I'll be home before you get home, I promise," Morgan said, holding her tight for one more minute.

"Well," Georgia said, taking a deep breath and wrapping an arm around Morgan's waist as she moved them towards the hall. "Well, I won't hold my breath for that," she said, flipping the outside light on and looking for her keys.

Morgan caught her for one last long hug before they went out to join the others. "You mad?" she asked, her voice small, but hopeful.

Georgia hugged her back. "Mad that you have to go do something you have to go do? Mad that Monday follows Sunday? I'm disappointed. And I'm a little mad. Or was. Oh, honey. I guess maybe we *have* changed.

"I'm just sad. And, possibly, I can be talked out of it. By the time we get to the Parade, I'll probably be glad just to be together, lesbians on our day, and me helping make Ricky's first video. Come on, girl. You want to go to a parade?"

They kissed one more time and then went out. As they locked the door, Bernice shouted up to them, "Fine day for a parade, ain't it?" Georgia, who was bending over the key, heard the lock fall into place and turned to Morgan and grinned.

"Yeah," she shouted back. "It's a great day for a parade." She took Morgan's hand, and they walked down to join the others. They all walked over to the streetcar then, laughing, shouting, pulling at each other, on their day, in the middle of that beautiful sunny Sunday.